MAGIC

by

Edmond Humm

"The disposition of noble dogs is to be gentle with people they know and the opposite with those they don't know... How, then, can the dog be anything other than a lover of learning since it defines what's its own and what's alien?" ~Plato

Prolog

Location: National Institute for Genetic Engineering and Biotechnology facility located near the Iranian city of Bakhtaran

A noise wakes the animal from its fitful dream. It is the sound of the card reader as it energizes the solenoid that retracts the hardened steel bolt from the metal door marked Xi7. The animal sniffs once, and its highly sensitive olfactory nerves send a signal racing to its brain. Dr. Abdul Ali Emadi stands with the door open. There is another human nearby, female. The animal's acute hearing picks up the humans' conversation, and its highly developed brain understands the words spoken in Farsi.

The female says, "Good evening, Dr. Emadi."

The animal hears the female footfalls as she walks down the hallway. After a short pause, Dr. Abdul Ali Emadi says, "Do you have a minute, Yara? There is something I would like to show you."

The animal hears her stop and say, "Yes, Doctor?"

"It's in here. Inside the laboratory."

The animal hates Dr. Emadi; the purveyor of more pain than any animal should have to endure. Hatred is not an emotion inbred in the animal. It is foreign to him. He has learned it from the humans. Experience has taught the animal to accept the painful experiments without attacking with its long sharp teeth. It was not an easy lesson, but the animal is highly intelligent. He will wait, not for revenge, but to escape.

The animal opens its large, deep brown eyes and follows the two scientists as they walk between the double rows of identical cages, stopping occasionally as Dr. Abdul Ali Emadi explains the various experiments. He stops in front of cage 21, and unlatches the cage door. He reaches in and shines a small light into the animal's large eyes. The animal quivers slightly, but holds its ground.

The female asks, "Is he dangerous?"

Dr. Abdul Ali Emadi shrugs and says, "Perhaps, but I do not frighten easily."

The female laughs coyly and says, "I do not think you would be frightened of anything, Doctor."

The animal senses Dr. Abdul Ali Emadi's emotions. The man is aroused by the female and mumbles, "There are some specimens I would like to show you. This way."

The animal watches him lead the female to the specimen locker at the rear of the lab. They both go in and close the door.

The animal listens and sniffs the air. His cage has been left unlocked. He presses his nose on the cage door and it opens. He waits a moment before jumping to the white tile floor. He looks around and nudges his cage door closed and then quickly hides behind a large box of supplies near the entrance.

Ten minutes later, Dr. Abdul Ali Emadi and the female come out of the specimen locker, both red faced and short of breath. The female hurries to the entrance and pushes through the door. Dr. Abdul Ali Emadi rushes after her. He stops with the door open and calls to her, "Yara, you must come back."

When she doesn't reply and keeps walking away, he hurries after her and doesn't see the big but stealthy animal slip through the door behind him and move silently down the hall away from Dr. Abdul Ali Emadi and to freedom.

CHAPTER 1

I first saw First Lieutenant Ryan Quinn on a desolate stretch of open desert not far from the city of Al Kufah, Iraq. I didn't know his name then. He was leaning against a Marine vehicle called a Humvee. There were five other Humvees and a big tank spread out over a fifty meter perimeter. The Marine crew moved around slowly outside their vehicles; drinking water, eating, cleaning their weapons and grumbling about the taste of the water; their food, the powder like sand in their weapons, and the incessant sun—the same sun that burned down and sucked the moisture from my tongue, which hung down from my mouth like a worn out red tie.

Ryan had taken off his helmet and utility jacket and was drinking from a large, gallon water bottle. He finished drinking and poured some of that precious water over his head. I was fifty meters away but could smell the delicious water. My mouth began to water and my vision blurred. The desert does that to dogs. It's the heat, and I believe humans were affected as well. I watched the waves of heat reflect off the top of the tank. The Marines and their Humvees began to shimmer as heat escaped from the baked sand. I slowly rose and started to walk closer to the Marines, watching for signs of aggression. A week ago, I was kicked by a policeman in Al Kufah, and I was still leery of humans. My ribs were sore, maybe broken, but the smell of water was strong. Stronger than my fear. By nature, I am a trusting dog, one who likes humans. Actually, I like about everything, except maybe the laboratory back in Iran and the heat of the desert.

The Marines didn't seem to notice me at first, then I heard one say, "What's that?" and point my way.

Another Marine looked toward me and said, "It's a short camel."

I think he was joking, but I kept walking slowly to the source of the water: the back of a Humvee with crates of bottled water stacked on the tailgate.

When I got near, Lieutenant Ryan looked my way and said to another Marine, "Sergeant, watch that dog. It might be rabid."

I wasn't rabid, but I knew I didn't look good. My long golden coat was matted and dirty, and I had a slight limp because my ribs were sore and the pads of my feet were tender. I had been walking for two months, with only short breaks to forage for food and find water.

Now more Marines were watching me. They stopped their talking and it became quiet except for the wind and a radio squawking from one of the Humvees. Some of the Marines brought their rifles around, not aimed at me directly, but I could see their eyes. If I acted like I was going to bite, my short life would be over in a heartbeat.

I stopped behind the Humvee with the bottled water and looked up.

A Marine standing nearby said, "Lieutenant, the dog looks like he needs a drink."

Lieutenant Ryan slipped his utility jacket back on as he slowly walked up to me. He showed no fear. I can sense fear, smell it if given time. He did look me over carefully and then took out a combat knife from a sheath on his belt. The hair on my back stiffened, but I remained still and watched him closely. He reached up and pulled one of the big plastic bottles out of a crate, and with one slash of his knife, cut the top off. Some of the water splashed out and I almost jumped for it, but caught myself in time. He squatted down, looked into my eyes, and sat the water bottle down in front of me.

He stood up and said, "Go ahead, fella. Drink."

Drink I did. I understood why he cut the top off of the bottle; the neck would have been too small for me to drink from. He cut it down far enough so that my snout would fit in and my tongue could lap up the life saving elixir.

The Marines left me another bottle of water, also opened and fed me from their rations. When they left, I knew I would see them again. I sense these things.

***

A month later, south of the city of Mosul, Iraq, I watched Lieutenant Ryan from behind the wheel of a Humvee. Taller than the other men, he stood out. His scent was familiar: friendly, compassionate, American; I remembered it. He was in charge, and the others followed his lead.

I heard one Marine say, "Lieutenant, we need ammo for the Ma Deuce." I think that was the big machinegun mounted on top of the truck. When he finally walked off from the others, I trotted up behind him and nudged him with my nose.

"Hey!" He spun around and said, "What the hell are you doing, mutt?"

It's what dogs do, Lieutenant. Like a handshake. Of course I can't speak, so I put my head down and looked at his feet. After a few seconds, I felt him pat my head. I knew he would. He couldn't help himself. I can sense such things. I also know when a human is going to kick me or run, maybe even eat me. Children are much harder to figure out. Some want to pet me, others grab my ears and some run screaming to their mommies.

When he stopped petting me, I sat and begged with one paw.

"Okay, fella."

He opened a MRE (Meal Ready to Eat), and after a few minutes, threw me a beef patty, which I caught with my mouth and gulped it down. Delicious. I wagged my tail and begged again.

He gave me a knowing look and said, "Didn't I see you before? Near the—"

An explosion sent sand and dirt into the sky and ended our little chat.

***

The explosion sent a column of dirt into the air, but it was too far from the convoy of Humvees to do any damage. First Lieutenant Ryan Quinn yelled to his men, "Move out!"

The Marines quickly climbed back into their vehicles as Sergeant Ramirez ran up to Lieutenant Quinn and asked, "What do you think, Lieutenant, IED?"

"No, sounded more like a mortar round. I think I heard it leave the tube. My guess is it came from behind those trees." He pointed to a stand of eucalyptus trees about three-hundred meters off the road. "We don't have the time or firepower to hunt them down. I'll switch vehicles with you and take the lead. You bring up the rear."

Lieutenant Quinn started toward the lead Humvee as Sergeant Ramirez called out, "You gonna call in some heat on those assholes?"

"Plan on it. I want to get to Mosul before nightfall. Now move before they adjust and put one down our throats."

The large golden retriever that Lieutenant Quinn had been feeding stood with his front paws against the door of the Humvee. His large brown eyes stared into Lieutenant Quinn's eyes without blinking.

After a moment Quinn said, "Sorry, pal, no room. Now go home. Get."

The big dog obeyed and ran off toward the rear of the convoy, but not before stopping once and looking back at Lieutenant Quinn. His ears perked up as if listening for Quinn to call him, but Ryan Quinn had a job to do, and it didn't include caring for a stray.

Ryan Quinn had been in Iraq for five months on his current deployment and fourteen months on the one before that, plus three months in Afghanistan. He knew the single mortar round might be a trap. Marines, by training and disposition, were aggressive. It took a strong hand to keep them from rushing into a fight. Ryan's convoy was a small one: six Humvees and one seven-ton truck. He didn't have the firepower to engage a large enemy force or one well emplaced. His orders from the company commander were simple: "I want you to haul ass up to Mosul and get there before dark."

As soon as Ryan was in the right front seat of the lead Humvee, he did a quick radio check with the other vehicles and motioned for the driver to move out. He then contacted his commanding officer on the battalion radio communications net and gave him a situation report and the coordinates of the suspected insurgents.

Now they were someone else's problem. Ryan had been a new second lieutenant in an infantry company on his first tour in Iraq. Called to active duty from his Marine reserve unit, Ryan had to put his plans to finish college on hold.

The driver, PFC Richard Horton, seemed nervous and watched Lieutenant Quinn out of the corner of his eye. Ryan noticed and said, "Relax. If I tell you to stop, you don't even think about asking. Just hit the brakes."

"Do you mind if I ask a question, sir?"

Lieutenant Quinn kept his eyes moving, scanning the narrow concrete road. There was little traffic and only an occasional building near the road. Battalion S-3 said there was no activity in the area, but that didn't ease the tension. He had heard screwed up intelligence reports many times.

"Go ahead."

"Sir, I heard you were here before with a line company."

"Yeah. Now I got it made."

"Got it made?" the young Marine asked.

"Last time I was humping seventy pounds of gear, not including my weapon, ammo, water; and sleeping in a hole. Now I ride most of the time."

"I think I would rather walk."

Ryan had to smile to himself. The young Marine knew that most of the current casualties had come from IEDs—Improvised Explosive Devices.

"Where you from, Horton?"

"San Francisco, sir."

"Been there a couple times. Cold and damp, but I would trade it for this heat."

"I've got water and ice in a cooler in the back, sir."

"I'm fine now. The a/c seems to be working okay. The troops in the back of the seven-ton might need it before long."

They rode in silence for another hour, and it was sunset when PFC Horton asked, "Sir, you ever been in a firefight?"

Ryan nodded. "Too many. Pick up the pace. It's getting dark."

PFC Horton pushed down on the accelerator, and the big Humvee barreled along the pot-holed road. The men in the back of the stiff riding, seven-ton truck would be cursing the driver and Lieutenant Quinn.

"Where you from?" PFC Horton asked, and then added, "Sir."

"Florida. Near Daytona Beach. A little town called New Smyrna Beach."

The lights of a small pickup truck came toward them and Ryan reached for his radio and spoke to his convoy. "Road runners, road runner six. Increase intervals. Heads up. Vehicle approaching."

A few seconds later, the small pickup truck passed by. The turret gunner followed it with the fifty-caliber machinegun on top of the Humvee.

"You were saying you lived in a little town near the beach, sir. Do any surfing?"

"Some, whenever I could find time. Stop—"

The explosion blew the Humvee into the air and across the road, where it rolled twice before coming to a stop in a shallow irrigation ditch.

Sergeant Ramirez, riding in the rear Humvee, hadn't been under fire before, but his training took over. He organized the convoy into a defensive position and then rushed forward to see the damage first-hand. From the rear of the convoy, he hadn't seen the fireball that lifted the lead Humvee. He did hear the thunder clap and felt the concussion seconds later.

The Humvee lay burning in a ditch near the road. There had been four men in the Humvee with Lieutenant Quinn; now only one man lay in the road, his clothes smoldering. Two men from the closest Humvee were already bending over the man in the road. Lieutenant Quinn and the other Marines were nowhere to be seen.

When Sergeant Ramirez approached, one Marine turned and said, "It's Horton, Sarge."

PFC Horton began to moan and Sergeant Ramirez said, "Get some water on him. Anyone else?"

A lance corporal shook his head and motioned to the burning Humvee. "Couldn't get in."

Heat from the burning Humvee radiated off Sergeant Ramirez's face. He shielded it with his forearm and walked closer to the inferno. He stopped thirty feet from the Humvee and then came back to PFC Horton. The lance corporal had removed most of Horton's outer clothing.

Sergeant Ramirez looked down at PFC Horton and said, "If anybody is still in there, they're ..." He was going to say toast, but thought better of it.

"I'm going back to call in a medevac for Horton. How's he doing?"

"I'm no corpsman," the lance corporal said, "but he's breathing and I can't find any big wounds. Should we move him?"

"Not yet. He might have some broken bones or some other shit wrong with him. I'll be right back."

***

I had been riding in the back of a big truck with the Marines. I jumped up there after the lieutenant told me to go home. I didn't have a home, not then, and it was terrible. Americans are great. Lots of petting and more MREs to eat, but as I was getting comfortable on a Marine's bedroll, bang!

No, it was more like a lightning strike real close. The driver must have hit the brakes hard, because I flew all the way to the front of the truck and landed on a Marine. Sorry.

I knew what caused the noise. I had heard it before. It was one of those homemade bombs they call an IED. Of course, they come in all different sizes. I watched one being made one night in a town not far away.

Anyway, the Marines grabbed their weapons and looked for targets, but I jumped out onto the road to see what happened. It was almost dark, but I can see fairly well at night, better than humans. There was a fire up ahead. I trotted up there and started sniffing. It was obvious where the bomb had been planted. A big hole on the side of the road was easy to see, and the smell was distinctive. I sniffed further and could tell there were two men, not Americans, who had been there recently. Probably Iranians.

There was a man in the road who looked hurt. I could smell his burnt hair and flesh. Two Marines were with him; one gave him water. He was talking and I could smell his breath. He was scared and I didn't blame him. There was a truck, called a Humvee, burning next to the road. The wind brought me a whiff of more flesh burning. Hate that smell. Then I caught the scent of the Marine who was the leader. The one they called Lieutenant. I didn't want to get too close to the fire as my coat isn't fireproof, but the scent of the lieutenant was strong now. I followed it off the road and picked up his scent again after circling the burning Humvee.

We dogs have a great sense of smell. I heard we have a hundred thousand times better sense of smell than humans. We can also hear about four times better than humans can, but I didn't hear him walking, although he had walked, maybe staggered, away from the Humvee and into the desert. Maybe he was thrown out, or blown out.

I finally found him laying face down in the sand about two hundred meters from the burning Humvee. His clothes smelled of the smoke and his leg was bleeding, but not badly. I nudged his face, and he groaned but didn't move. I dug some of the sand away from his face and smelled his breath. He was alive and not seriously hurt, as far as I could tell. People who are hurt seriously have a smell I can recognize. I nudged him again but he didn't move, so I barked in his ear. That usually gets humans moving, but he just moaned. I dug a little more sand away from his face. Didn't want him breathing sand.

I looked around, but no Marines were coming from the road to help him. I started barking. Not once but about twenty times. Maybe they didn't hear me because of the helicopter that was landing on the road. After a few minutes, the helicopter flew away and I started barking again, but nobody came out. I would have to bring them to the lieutenant. I licked the lieutenant's face a couple of times and ran back to the road. The Humvee wasn't burning now, just smoking, and the Marines were trying to look inside. I ran up and started barking and jumping around. I wanted them to follow me, but no one seemed to understand.

"Shut up, mutt!" a big Marine yelled.

Another one said, "Get away. Y'all get burned."

I wasn't going to give up. That lieutenant was a good human; I can tell these things. I had seen him before, and I have been with a lot of humans who were not good and many who were somewhere in between. I have also been with some who were bad, evil, cruel and not even human. I didn't want one of the good ones to die out there. I started barking even harder and running toward the desert and then back, hoping a Marine would follow, but no luck. Finally, I ran back to the open truck thinking, maybe one of those Marines would understand. I jumped up into the back of the truck and started barking.

"It's okay, fella. Calm down. We'll take care of you," said one Marine.

That was nice, but I kept barking and jumped down, thinking maybe they would follow, but no. They kept telling me to stop barking. It didn't it occur to them that I wasn't barking to hear my own voice. I thought, maybe I should howl; however, they might have thought I was nuts and put me out of my misery.

I jumped up in the truck again, which was a big jump, and licked the hand of one Marine. He petted me and I grabbed his wrist, not too hard, and tried pulling him off the truck.

After a few tugs he said, "What you want? You want me to go with you?"

I put my tail into full high-speed wag and barked at him. I jumped off the truck and he climbed down. This Marine had dark skin, and they called him Corporal Lewis. He started to follow me, but I had to keep running back to him. He didn't want to leave the road, and then I remembered, humans can't see so well in the dark, and they can't smell worth a darn. Maybe that explains their little noses. I would have to go back and tug on his arm or pants.

"Hey, Lewis, get back on the truck," a sergeant ordered. "We're moving out. A reaction platoon is coming out. Sergeant Ramirez is staying here with two squads. You and three Humvees are supposed to haul ass to Mosul." He then added, "Hey, why don't you take that dog with you before he gets hurt out here?"

Oh, no. He was going to pick me up and put me in their truck.

CHAPTER 2

Lieutenant Quinn slowly rose on shaky legs, spat out sand, coughed and tried to orient himself. He staggered and pain ran up his right leg. He put his hand on his leg and felt warm blood oozing from a wound. He would put a compress bandage on it, but first he had to gather his men. How many casualties? he wondered.

He called out into the pitch-black night, "Road runners. On me." He called out again but nobody answered.

Strange, he couldn't hear his voice. A ringing noise in his ears seemed to block out all other sounds.

"Where the hell is everyone?" he yelled, but again he heard only the ringing in his ears.

"Okay," he said to himself, "the IED wiped out my hearing, but why can't I see anything? Not even a fire."

Lieutenant Quinn placed his hand in front of his eyes. "Damn," he said as he realized that he couldn't see. It was only temporary, he hoped. His knees gave out and he slowly dropped onto the sand. It wasn't the soft sand seen in desert movies but sand mixed with dirt. He rested for a few minutes before he tried to stand again. After two attempts, he stood on wobbly legs. He would find his men.

Lieutenant Quinn was well trained, but being both blind and deaf bewildered him. He had to find his men. Hardnosed instructors had pounded "Take care of your men" into his head. He had always been a natural leader. In Little League baseball and Pop Warner football, he led. In high school, he was the captain of the football team and president of his senior class. He found he had both the ability and inclination to take charge. Now, both blind and deaf, he felt vulnerable, confused and on the threshold of panic. He knew he needed to find his men and move the convoy away from a possible ambush.

He reached for the first-aid kit but found it was gone, as was much of the gear attached to his outer vest. His sidearm—a 9 mm Beretta—and helmet were gone. He also carried an M16 rifle, but it too was gone. He touched his face and gently probed. His eyelashes and close cropped hair were charred. His Kevlar vest was ripped and his utilities torn. He touched his right leg and found the wound again. It felt sticky but wasn't pumping blood.

He wasn't sure of the direction, but he started to walk. He decided he would walk a hundred paces, call out, and if his men couldn't hear him, he would walk back and then walk in another direction for a hundred paces.

He would find his men.

***

Corporal Lewis was a big man, almost as big as the lieutenant, so he had no problem lifting me and putting me in the back of the truck. I intended to jump back out once he let go, but it was not to be. He said to another Marine, "Grimes, use that tie-down strap for a collar. If the dog falls out and gets hurt, it's your ass."

Grimes, who was a PFC, made a quick loop in a strap, and in no time I was tied to a tie-down fixture in the bed of the truck. The truck took off with a lurch, and as much as I pulled and barked, I couldn't get loose. I did manage to cut off air to my lungs for a while and felt dizzy. I knew better than to pull against a collar, but I really wanted to get back to the lieutenant. If the locals found him, they might turn him over to the insurgents, which would mean a very painful death for the lieutenant.

The truck bounced and jerked around, but after awhile they must have found a better road. The ride smoothed out, and before long I could smell food cooking. Not American food but local food. After awhile longer I saw lights from buildings ahead and the truck slowed. I smelled Americans. In another five minutes the truck stopped. We were at a checkpoint near an airbase close to the big city of Mosul.

One of the Marines threw a blanket over me and told me to be quiet. I wondered if he thought I could understand human talk, which I can, but most dogs don't, as far as I know. It was apparent that dogs were not allowed on the airbase, which seems wrong to me, but I went along with the fun. Once they untied me, I would be gone.

It took a lot longer than I thought. They kept me under that blanket past another gate and finally took it off when we stopped in front of some temporary, metal-sided buildings. The Marines unloaded boxes of helicopter parts. Once the truck was unloaded, an officer came up and saw me tied to the truck. He acted angry, but I can smell anger, and he wasn't angry. He told Corporal Lewis he had ten minutes to get rid of the dog. Corporal Lewis didn't argue. He said, "Aye, aye, sir," but when the officer left he didn't let me go. He took me into a building —I am skittish in buildings—and led me into a room he called the head. He then poured water out of a faucet into a deep sink and told me to drink. He didn't have to tell me twice. I needed water. I rose up on my haunches, put my forepaws on the edge of the sink and drank until my belly was full.

He said, "If you are going to sleep here, you need a bath."

Bath? He had to be kidding. I hadn't had a bath since I escaped from the white laboratory where I was born. I like water, hate baths. No thank you.

The Marine walked over to a urinal on the wall and began to open his fly. He struggled using only one hand and dropped my leash. That was all I needed. I ran out of the head and raced to the door we came in. Fortunately, a Marine was coming in and opened the door. I ran between his legs and made for the gate.

"Hey! Stop that dog," he yelled.

Too late. I was on my way.

Now, the security at an American base is tight, but most of it is designed to keep people out, not dogs in. I followed my own scent and soon saw the lights at the gate. When I raced through, I heard a sentry shout, "Where the hell did that dog come from?"

The road away from the airbase at Mosul was easy to follow. The scent of the Marines and my unique scent made following it easy. Well, not easy, but once I hit the two lane road I picked up the pace to an energy conserving trot. I moved off the paved road and on to the softer dirt to save my pads.

I was not very good at judging time, haven't had to in the past, but I had an idea we had traveled for two hours or more. The Marines had been grumbling about missing chow, but later they talked about midrats, which, as far as I could tell, was a meal served near midnight.

I have learned that in addition to my amazing sense of smell, I can sense which direction to travel. I have no idea why or how, but I knew I was headed back to the lieutenant. If I could find water on the way, I would find him.

The road wasn't used much that time of night. A few trucks came by, but I was off the road. I could smell them. They were Iraqis.

I smelled water and followed that scent to a river. The riverbank was steep and I almost fell in, but I drank. Didn't want to overdo it. I still had a long way to go.

***

Lieutenant Quinn found that without sight he could not be sure he was walking in a straight line. He also knew from training that people tend to walk in circles unless they have visual references. Hours had gone by and he felt even more confused than when he began. He once tripped and fell, and when he arose, he wasn't sure of his direction. Another time he stumbled over a low fence. He felt it with his hands and guessed it to be made of stone or concrete. If the fence surrounded an Iraqi home, it might lead him to a village. He wondered, would the Iraqis be friendly or alert the local insurgents? He decided not to take a chance and backtracked away from the fence.

After three hours, Lieutenant Quinn sat down and rested. He realized that if he hadn't found his men by then, he wasn't going to find them. He must have walked in the wrong direction, or worse, his men had been ambushed and he hadn't heard the firefight.

A noise startled Lieutenant Quinn. Not that it was that loud but it was the first sound he had heard since the IED blew him out of the Humvee. He looked around and tried to follow the sound.

He began to yell again, "Hey, somebody. Over here."

He could hear his voice now, although his ears still rang with a high-pitched noise. He stopped abruptly when he realized he might be heard by insurgents or locals friendly to them. Becoming a prisoner of those bloodthirsty people was not a pleasant thought. He had seen picture of beheaded and butchered prisoners. Not a pretty sight.

He thought, if my hearing is coming back, maybe my sight will return. Ryan Quinn was by nature optimistic, but he also knew that the damage to his eyes might be more serious. He gently touched his eyelids and felt for signs of burned flesh. They stung slightly, but he couldn't find any blisters. The wound in his leg had stopped bleeding, as far as he could tell, but now it throbbed. His head also hurt and his stomach felt queasy. He needed water, but that would have to wait. The sun had been down for hours, and the temperature had dropped considerably, but the heat rose from the sand and the humidity seemed higher, if possible.

He decided to save his energy. He sat in the sand and began thinking about the escape and evasion course he had taken. His thoughts also drifted to his parents, who lived in Tampa Bay, Florida, on the West Coast, as they called it. His father had been a Marine. Correction, once a Marine always a Marine. Ryan had followed in his father's footsteps, and he knew his father was proud of him, but Dad did not encourage him to join the Marine Corps.

"Join a branch where you don't get your ass shot off. Maybe the Air Force or Navy," he had said.

Ryan knew that some Air Force and Navy personnel were in harm's way, but not as many as the Green Machine.

His mom wanted him to be a lawyer, and Ryan thought he might still take her advice, assuming he got out of his present predicament.

***

The eastern sky was beginning to brighten. The inky blackness was now a dark gray, and I could see the outline of houses ahead. I had picked up their scent a mile back. I must admit, I was getting tired. My pads were sore and I had to find water more often. Fortunately, the road ran parallel to a river. There were also irrigation ditches that carried water, although some of the water tasted foul.

I felt I was getting near. I could still follow the scent, but it was faint, and had it not been for the road, I might have lost the scent. A few trucks and cars began to use the road, but I was still safely off to the side.

Another dog must have picked up my scent. I heard him barking ahead in the direction of the houses. As I grew closer, I could tell it was a large dog and not happy about me parading through his territory.

I could have circled the homes, but I was not in the mood to waste time. I am not an aggressive dog. I would rather play than fight, but I can hold my own. My long hair makes it difficult for another dog to get a good hold on my throat, which is where most dogs attack. I have found that most dogs will run if I stand up to them, but not all. Some breeds are particularly dangerous, mainly those bred to fight or to bring down large animals. If I have to run, I will. I guess that is where my human intelligence comes in handy.

As I got closer, the dog went wild. I heard him snapping his teeth together and lunging against a rope or leash of some kind. A human voice was yelling at him to shut up. The voice was an Iraqi. The dog kept barking. I hoped the leash held because the dog sounded like he was nuts.

I conceded by crossing the road and passing the house a hundred meters away. I could hear the dog yelping in the distance. Maybe the human had taken a stick to him. I must admit, some dogs are not too smart and require more than tender conversation. My leash was flapping behind me and occasionally I stepped on it. It was a makeshift leash, made by the Marine in the truck. I used my front paws to loosen it and slipped it over my head. I should have done that earlier.

The sun was up when I came upon the burnt spot in the road. The smell of burnt rubber and other odors still hung in the air. The Humvee was gone, but after a few false starts, I picked up the lieutenant's scent again.

The lieutenant had walked away from where I left him. As I thought: he wasn't too badly hurt. His trail confused me a few times. He had walked back across his own tracks, and I couldn't get a strong feeling where he was going. After running back and forth for a long time, his tracks led off away from the road and river. The wrong way.

Then I was able to follow at a better pace, because he wandered across open fields and away from the flood plains near the river. He came close to a small village, but then moved away from it. His trail stopped once where he must have sat down. His scent was strong because he had been there a long time. When I followed it away from there, I picked up the scent of another human, an Iraqi male. The lieutenant was being followed.

CHAPTER 3

Lieutenant Ryan Quinn began to see the difference between light and dark. He knew it was day and could make out a dark shadow when he put his hand to his face. He also knew that, even though he couldn't see clearly, looking directly at the sun might injure his eyes. He pulled a scarf from his utility pocket and tied it around his head, covering his eyes.

Ryan's hearing was improving. He could now hear the buzzing of insects and the crunch of his boots on the ground. He was no longer walking in sand but on hard packed earth. He tripped occasionally on low ridges or furrows. Perhaps the ground had been a farm.

"Oogaf!" The words startled Ryan. He turned to face the direction of the man's voice. The word was Iraqi Arabic for stop.

Ryan stopped and said, "Hello."

An Iraqi man stood not five meters from Lieutenant Ryan Quinn. Ryan could not see the man or the AK-47 assault rifle in his hands. The man dressed in western clothing with baggy black trousers and a long sleeved, dirty white shirt. He was a small man compared to Lieutenant Quinn, and thin. He wore a long, black beard, and shaggy black hair cascaded from under his headscarf.

Ryan said in English, "I am an American. Is there a telephone I can use?"

The man answered in Iraqi Arabic, "Inta 'asiir!"

Ryan understood the words: "You are a prisoner."

Ryan stiffened. He couldn't see the man. He repeated, "I am an American."

The man circled Ryan, and observed the scarf over Ryan's eyes. Ryan heard his footfalls and turned to face the sound.

The man moved closer and watched Ryan closely. He kept the AK-47 pointed at Ryan and nervously touched the trigger with a shaking finger. He yelled in broken English, "Put hands up. On head."

Ryan sighed but raised his arms and placed his hands on his head.

The man moved closer, reached out with the barrel of the weapon, and jabbed it into Ryan's side. When Ryan jerked away, the man stumbled back, almost losing his footing, and jerked the trigger, sending a burst of automatic rifle fire into the air.

Ryan tensed, awaiting the impact of bullets into his body. He had no weapon and couldn't see to run or fight. He asked himself, is it going to end like this?

A dog barked, close by.

The man turned his rifle toward a large golden dog that stood ten meters away with its teeth bared and the hair on its back bristled up. The man shouted at the dog, but the dog only barked and growled menacingly.

The man took aim and fired at the dog that was now moving closer. The dog jumped to one side and then ran away. Dust flew up where the rounds hit near the dog, but none struck it. The man stopped, aimed and fired again, but the dog was moving from side to side, throwing up clouds of dust as it ran. The bullets raised their own clouds of dust, but dug harmlessly into the ground.

Ryan used that opportunity to run. He ran away from the sound of the AK-47 and the barking dog. He ran as hard as he could but expected the bullets that would end his life to hit him in the back. They finally came, but fortunately only one hit him. It hit him in the back knocking him to the ground, but did not penetrate his MTV (Modular Tactical Vest) body armor. The wind was knocked out of Ryan and his back throbbed, but he slowly pushed himself up and tried to run again. Then he knew the man was close. Too close.

Ryan heard the metallic sound of a magazine being ejected and a new one inserted into the automatic rifle. Ryan waited, but the man didn't fire. He yelled something in Arabic that Ryan didn't understand. He then said in broken English, "Get up. You walk."

So Ryan walked. He walked slowly, wondering about his fate and about the dog he had heard. Ten minutes later, Ryan heard the voice of another Iraqi. Two men were talking, but much too quickly for Ryan to follow with his limited Arabic.

Although Ryan couldn't see him, the second man was older and much larger, almost as large as Ryan. He wore traditional Iraqi clothing and carried a large, curved knife in his waistband. He grabbed Ryan from behind and placed the sharp blade under Ryan's chin. He said something into Ryan's ear, but the words were lost.

Ryan felt his knees weaken but braced himself. If this foul smelling bastard was going to kill him, so be it. Ryan wasn't going to beg for his life.

Ryan felt the sharp knife against his neck. Then the knife moved slowly across his neck, stinging as it cut across his throat. Blood flowed out of the shallow incision.

***

I followed the lieutenant and the Iraqi man, but now from a safe distance. Those bullets were too close. One cut through my coat and stung my back, but I wasn't hurt. If I could have gotten closer, I might have jumped him, but it would have been risky. I have long, sharp teeth and my jaws are strong, but a full-grown human is a formidable opponent.

I could see them walking toward the village, and then another man came out and joined the first man. I saw the sun reflect off of a long knife, and for a second I thought they butchered the lieutenant, but the lieutenant didn't fall to the ground. He kept walking with the two men behind him.

Once they entered the village, I was able to get closer. I hid behind a low, hard mud-packed wall and then jumped over it and followed them to a house. They took the lieutenant inside and I moved next to a window and listened. The house, like most in the village, was a one story, flat roofed, white, simple stucco structure.

The windows had wooden shutters but no window glass or screens like the better homes in Iran.

The men spoke in Arabic with a strong local dialect, so I may have missed a few words. They were going to tie the lieutenant up, and then they were going to summon a man whose name meant nothing to me. Apparently, that man would decide the lieutenant's fate. One man wanted to torture the lieutenant. He wanted revenge for the death of his cousin. The other man said they should wait.

I heard them move the lieutenant into another room. They yelled at a woman and told her to leave. I moved around the house and could smell the lieutenant. He was bleeding and the scent of his blood was strong, but I didn't hear him cry out. I moved next to a window and waited. The shutters were closed, but I could hear and smell the men inside. A narrow alley ran between the house and another similar house. An old pickup truck was parked in the alley.

I heard the lieutenant gasp for air. Apparently, one of the men had hit him in the stomach. I heard more sounds. They were hitting the lieutenant, but he didn't cry out or plead for mercy. He did grunt a few times when they hit him. Eventually they stopped and I heard one say that the lieutenant would not be able to get away. I thought they must have tied him up, or crippled him. I was losing my normal good nature. I wanted to bite those men and hard, but I would wait my turn. Given the opportunity, I wouldn't attack their necks first; I would go for the genitals.

After awhile I heard them coming out the front door. I moved around the corner of the house in case they came my way, which they did. They got into the pickup truck and drove away.

I ran around the house, stopping at each window. I couldn't hear anyone in the house. I guess the woman left as commanded by the men. I looked for an open window and found one open to a room they had used for cooking. I was able to stick my nose between the shutters and nudge them open. Getting in was another matter. I could reach the window easily enough as it was low, but pulling myself over the sill was hard work. Finally, I backed up a few paces and leaped through the window.

Finding the lieutenant was easy, since there were no interior doors in the house. The smell of his blood took me to a room without furniture. He was slumped against a wall with his head hanging down. Blood covered his neck and soaked the front of his undershirt. His vest was gone as were his boots and socks. He wore only his utility trousers and undershirt. His belt was wrapped around his neck and tied to a metal ring in the wall. If he fell, he would have hung himself. There was tape around his mouth and eyes. I sniffed him and could tell he had been injured but not fatally. The long cut under his chin had stopped bleeding. His hands were behind his back, and after I nudged him, he moved. I could see his hands were tied together by a rope and tape.

He sensed me, or maybe he could have smelled me, so I put my paws against his chest and licked his face. I think he said something, but the tape over his mouth kept the words in. I carefully pulled at the tape with my teeth and soon it came away from his mouth.

He asked me some questions that I couldn't answer, like, "where did you come from?" and ",did you follow me?" He moved his head down and I understood. He wanted me to pull the tape off his eyes, which proved to be difficult. The tape was wound around his head, but my teeth are sharp, and after gnawing on the tape, it gave, and I pulled it free.

His eyes were red as blood and he kept blinking. He also moved his head around trying to free his belt. He then turned his back and pushed his hands out to me. I understood; the rope and tape combination were tough, and I set out to gnaw through them. Once I tore the tape off, the rope was easier to cut through but not without pain. My mouth and gums were bleeding by the time the rope gave, and the lieutenant raised his hands and rubbed his wrists. He took a moment to pat my head, which helped more than he knew. My jaws were aching. Then he worked at releasing his belt from around his neck and from the metal ring in the wall.

He held his hands out feeling for the wall and didn't seem to be able to see well. I reached out and grabbed his hand, but not hard. I then pulled him through the doorway and out into the room with the wooden door. When we got to the door, he felt it with his hands and opened it as I hoped he would. I pulled at his hand again and he followed, but after saying, "I hope you know where you are taking me because I can't see worth a damn."

I had no idea where I was taking him, except away from the house where he was held. I felt that if we could find an American or friendly Iraqi, he would be safe. I can usually tell a lot about a human, but I need to get close, smell them and listen to them talk if possible.

The sounds of people in the village came from the direction of the sun; I led the lieutenant away from the sounds. We reached a low wall and I stopped to let the lieutenant climb over first. I jumped over and took his hand again. Once we had gone a ways he said, "I can see a bit now, fella. Take me to the road. Do you understand, road, cars, highway?"

Of course I understood, so I barked softly and headed to the road where his Humvee had been blown apart. I got another pat on the head and a bonus ear rub. Darn, that felt good.

He followed closely behind me and soon we were near the road again. Cars and trucks now whizzed by. I slowed and he tripped against me and said, "What's the matter, boy?

What was the matter? The matter was, after he got a ride back to the Marines, what was going to happen to me? I had grown fond of this human, and I thought he liked me too. I didn't want to lose him. It is hard to explain, but I wanted a home, a place where I could relax and play. I didn't want to hunt for food all the time, go hungry for days and not have a human to pet me. I guess I got spoiled living in the laboratory, not that I want to go back, but they did feed me, and occasionally one of the attendants would pet me. They also struck me with needles and hurt me with their experiments.

Well, there was not much I could do about it, so I led him closer to the road. Once we got within a few meters, I stopped in front of him and he seemed to understand. At first, he stood still. I guess he was trying to decide what to do. Cars whizzed by and even a few trucks. Then a big Army truck slowed and pulled to a stop on the shoulder of the road. A Humvee pulled in behind it and the right side door opened. An American soldier leaned out and shouted, "Hey, are you alright?"

Dumb question. The lieutenant's chest was covered with blood and he was standing by the side of the road unarmed and barefoot. Americans didn't do that.

"I'm First Lieutenant Quinn. I could use a hand." That was the first time I heard his name. Two Army men piled out of the Humvee, both carrying automatic rifles. They looked around, I think expecting an ambush.

"You've been wounded?"

"I'm okay. Can't see much. What happened to my convoy? We hit an IED last night. Have you heard anything?"

A female soldier got out of the Humvee. She ran over to Lieutenant Quinn, took his hand, led him to the Humvee, and said, "We'll get you to an aid station."

Lieutenant Quinn started to get in the Humvee, and I waited. Then he turned to me and said, "Come on, boy."

I didn't have to be asked twice. I leaped up and into the Humvee, which wasn't easy. The driver must not have liked dogs because he said, "Hey, we can't take a dog with us."

Lieutenant Quinn said, "Yes, you can. He's a war dog. Special Ops."

Reluctantly, the driver shrugged his shoulders and drove on to the road. The female soldier reached out as if she was going to pet me, but then drew her hand back and asked, "Special Ops? What's he do?"

It took Lieutenant Quinn a few seconds to answer, "It's Top Secret, but I can say he does magic."

She asked, "Magic? What kind?"

"You wouldn't believe me if I told you."

She seemed to accept that but asked, "Does he bite?"

"Only bad guys. You can pet him."

"What's his name? I have a golden retriever at home."

It took Lieutenant Quinn a few seconds to answer, "Magic. His name is Magic. Isn't it, fella?"

He patted my head, and I gave him a big lick. I never had a name before, just a number, and Magic was okay. In fact, darn good. It had a nice ring to it.

The ride to an Army medical unit didn't take long, and the Army soldiers gave us both water and food on the way. A medic worked on Lieutenant Quinn and then a doctor examined him. I did have to wait outside. After awhile a convoy of Marines came for him. The sergeant who was in Lieutenant Quinn's platoon was with them, also a captain who was his company commander. They all seemed glad to see him. He would get more medical care back at the big airbase near Mosul.

The story of how First Lieutenant Ryan Quinn got me shipped to the United States is complicated. For a long time I thought he wasn't going to get permission, but I never gave up hope. He told me I was going to be shipped to Saudi Arabia and then sent by an airplane to America, and that is exactly what happened. I think he had to pay for my flight.

CHAPTER 4

It is my opinion that I wouldn't be here today if it were not for a shortage of primates for medical experiments in Iran a few years ago.

I guess cutting into a big monkey's head is preferred to cutting into a human's. A highly biased view if I may say so. Nevertheless, when some Iranian scientist with a Frankenstein complex transplanted the left cerebral cortex from a recently departed human into my mother's brain box, she surprised him by not dying as most of his bizarre experiments had. She survived, but it wasn't a happy existence. She was blind, could not smell very well and wobbled when she walked. Dad, another big dog, did almost as well after he had a similar brain rebuild.

Now, I don't claim to be a scientist and understand exactly what they did to my parents, but before I was conceived, Mom's reproductive cells were removed and injected with a strand of human DNA. They may have done something to Dad's seed as well, but I couldn't find many records about him.

I don't know much about my brothers and sisters, as we were separated once we were weaned. There was a notebook that contained notes about similar experiments even before my parents came under the knife. Perhaps I am the results of a long line of weird cross breeding, DNA snipping, and other genetic engineering; however, I look like any other one-year-old golden retriever. I can't talk, and that has been a major problem for me personally, and I don't know if I am the only dog who is smarter than most humans.

How do I know that I am smarter than humans are, you ask? Well, do you know any human one-year-olds who can write a coherent sentence on a computer? There have been other hints that I am not your average eighty pound mutt. I can read and write in Farsi, English and Arabic. With paws instead of fingers and opposable thumbs, you might surmise that my hand/paw writing looks like my vet's scribbles, but given enough time, I can tap out a mean sentence or three. Not that I let humans see me do that; if they did I would end up in a cage with a bunch of scientist sticking needles in me and eventually doing an autopsy to see what made me tick.

It's been a long struggle to reach Florida from Iraq, but thanks to Ryan, my savior, I am now living in the lap of luxury. I love that guy. I get fed every day, have plenty of water, and when Ryan's girlfriend isn't visiting, I can come inside.

What I really love is watching television and using Ryan's computer. My English is much better now, and I've learned a lot about America, although I am still confused by some of the television shows. They have reality shows that aren't reality. At first, television confused me. I had seen outdoor movies on the Marine base in Iraq, but now I was seeing what appeared to be humans, but with bodies that were quite different. One called Bart Simpson didn't look like any human boy I had ever seen. His personality was also strange. Then I saw animals, even dogs, that talked and flew and did all sorts of strange things. I thought perhaps the Americans were way ahead of the Iranians with genetic mutations. Then I noticed a recurring word in the TV guide, *animated*. I thought that meant excitable and active, but there was another meaning. An online dictionary solved my problem. It said under animated, "... containing representations of animals or mechanical objects that appear to move as real ones do."

They weren't real. That was the answer, and it made me feel much safer in America.

Ryan doesn't know I have my own website and blog. I'm thinking about writing my life story and making a million dollars, maybe appearing on a late night talk show. Well, maybe not.

Now, don't think I am a couch potato. I run around our small yard every day chasing anything that will move. Once, Ryan took me to the beach while he surfed. I really like the water, but it makes Ryan nervous because of the sharks. He worries more about me than himself. Can you believe that? What a guy.

Ryan has a job as a watchman at Port Canaveral. His schedule works out so he can take classes at the University of Central Florida. Once he is finished, he is going to apply for the FBI.

Another thing I love is riding in Ryan's pickup truck with my head out the window. Humans don't have any idea how much we dogs use our sense of smell. Riding down the road is like an exciting adventure, with hundreds of characters that pass by, each with their own short story.

I love this place.

Now, there have been some problems, but not many. Ryan is a handsome man. He stands about six-feet two or three and weighs about two-hundred pounds, maybe a little more. No fat on his frame. He has let his black hair grow since he was in the Marine Corps, but it is still neat. His eyes are brown but so dark they look black, more so when he is angry, which isn't often. His voice is deep but not too deep. Now, you wouldn't think that being good looking would be a problem. I'm good looking, but modesty does not allow me to elaborate, but I digress.

Now, here is the problem. When Ryan got back home from Iraq, he was treated like a hero, which he is. This attracted a lot of pretty girls, of which there are a bunch in this area. He naturally dated a few—dozen—but finally grew tired of the big party. His old sweetheart from high school came into his life and Ryan dropped the other girls, but, for a while, they didn't drop him.

Ryan's old girlfriend, Megan, was a year behind him in high school, and when he went off to UCF on a scholarship, she stayed behind. The following year she went to stay with relatives in Los Angeles, California. She started college at UCLA, but because of financial problems she moved back to New Smyrna Beach, Florida.

When she saw his picture in the *Observer* newspaper, she checked around with his old buddies and found his telephone number. Now, she didn't simply telephone him and say, "Hey, how you been? Remember me?" No, she made sure one of his buddies told Ryan that she was in town. I got this all second hand and had to put the pieces together, but I think it is accurate. I am not sure why humans play such silly mating games, but on the other hand, I can see some logic in controlling those basic urges. More on that later.

Megan Alvarez is a beauty and not at a loss for admirers, or simply lusting men and boys. She is petite, about five-foot two or three and weighs—I am guessing—one-hundred fifteen pounds. She has her father's dark Latin hair and her mother's blue Irish eyes. Her build causes serious whiplash when she walks by, and her voice has little bells in it. I think I am in love. It is, I fear, unrequited love, because as friendly as I am, she only has eyes for Ryan, and, of course, I am a dog.

CHAPTER 5

Ryan stood in his small living room in New Smyrna Beach and talked to his father in Tampa, Florida. He was dressed in blue jeans and was barefoot. He held an old style, black telephone in one hand and his white tee shirt in the other.

"Okay, Dad. Give my love to Mom." He hung up the telephone and the doorbell rang. It rang again and Ryan called out, "Just a minute," as he slipped on his tee shirt.

He opened the door and Megan brushed past him and threw her purse on the sofa. She came directly from work and still wore a blue dress suit and high heels.

"I cannot believe it. They fired you?" Megan said as she plopped down on Ryan's worn green sofa, pulled off her jacket and slipped her feet out of her shoes.

Ryan, who was still standing by the door, said, "I couldn't believe it either, but it's true."

Megan patted a place next to her and said, "Come here."

Ryan hadn't told her much over the telephone except that he had been fired and the police had held him in jail without fully explaining the charges. He sat down next to Megan, who wrapped her arms around him and kissed him passionately. When Ryan began to actively respond, she pushed him back and breathed deeply before saying, "Tell me all about it. I still can't believe it. You? Fired from a night watchman's job? They should be honored to have you. I still cannot believe it. Tell me about—"

Ryan's kiss stopped Megan's tirade.

"Now, if you will shut that pretty little mouth for a minute, I will tell you."

Megan was both excitable and passionate about life, which included her love for Ryan. She tended to see life in black and white, with no shades in between.

He began, "I won't go into all the details but I heard, or rather Magic heard, something. I was looking in the back of a truck when these guys came out and one pulled a gun on me—"

"A gun?" Megan interrupted. "Were you hurt?"

"No, but if it hadn't been for Magic, I might have been. Anyway, I was able to knock the guy with the gun down and then held both of them at gunpoint until the police arrived."

"But you said the police arrested you?"

"At first they listened to me, and I told them what happened. But after they looked at one man's identification, they changed. They asked for my identification, and my weapon permit. Then they asked for my weapon, which I gave to one of them after unloading it. After that, they asked me to step over to their car. Once there, the older cop told me to turn around. I started to ask why, but he snapped handcuffs on me and shoved me forward. He patted me down and told me I was under arrest."

"Arrest!" Megan shouted.

"I know. I couldn't believe it, but the good news is that the charges were dropped."

"What charges?"

"As best I can understand, the two men said that I attacked them and held them against their will."

"Why would they believe them and not you?"

"I couldn't get the police to answer that, but my guess is that one of them pulls a lot of weight."

"I don't understand?"

"There were two men, one was a Middle Eastern man named Babak. He was dressed like a tourist, but the other was dressed in an expensive suit, looked confident, had a subtle New England accent. When they saw his ID, their faces changed and I heard a lot of, 'yes sir' and 'no sirs'."

"Some big shot, you think?"

"That would be my guess, but something wasn't right. The police refused to tell me his name. Said it was none of my business and I should be grateful he wasn't charging me."

"That is ridiculous. If they had a case against you, they would have filed charges. They're hiding something."

"I know, but what? Now that I don't work there, I won't have a chance to look around."

"You'll get your job back," Megan said, "My boss will see to it."

Megan worked for an attorney in New Smyrna Beach, and knew he thrived on suits of that nature.

Ryan said, "My boss is a man named Frank Kurns. He came to the police station, and as I was leaving he told me he had to let me go. I asked him why, but he never gave me a straight answer. Just kept saying 'I'm sorry' as if he didn't really want to fire me."

Scratching at the back door caught their attention. Ryan got up and said, "Magic's dinner time. He's reminding me."

Megan followed Ryan out of the small living room and into the kitchen, which was also small, but clean. The decor was 1970s and the appliances looked like they were the originals. A chrome kitchen table sat with two chairs—Ryan's dining room.

Ryan opened a large bag of dried dog food and poured it into a large bowl. Then he opened a can of dog food and mixed it into the dry food, added a little water and carried it through the back door. Megan was already outside and had found Magic's favorite ball, or maybe he had brought it to her. She threw the ball and Magic leaped after it and caught it in his mouth. He trotted back to her and dropped it at her feet. When she didn't pick it up immediately, he barked and ran in a circle once before stopping in front of her and nudged the tennis ball with his nose.

Megan reached down and rubbed Magic's head. "Good boy. I hear you kept Ryan from getting shot."

Magic nodded his big head, but then turned away as if embarrassed.

Megan turned to Ryan, who was filling Magic's water dish, and said, "Sometimes I think he really understands me."

"I get the same feelings. I don't know who owned him before, but they must have taught him well." Ryan put Magic's water dish down and then said, "Magic, eat."

They both watched Magic devour his food and Megan asked, "Where are we going for dinner?"

"Considering my current employment status, I thought we would eat in. How about —"

"How about we drop in at my house. Mom's cooking Dad's favorite tonight. Red Snapper."

"Honey, you know how I hate to bother your parents. Besides, your dad and brothers hate me."

Megan snuggled against Ryan's chest and ran her fingers through his hair. "But mom loves you and so do I."

Ryan took her hand and held it as he said, "That's wonderful, but eating with four sets of eyes staring at me as if I was about to rape their baby sister is not my idea of a fun date. And your dad, he's even worse."

"Don't pay any attention to my brothers, and Daddy hates everyone I have ever brought home."

Ryan looked down at her and said, "How many have you brought home?"

She smiled up at him demurely and said, "I lost count."

Eventually, Ryan made a large omelet and opened a bottle of unlabeled white Riesling wine that someone had given him. After dinner, Ryan wanted to walk to the beach, but Megan said she had to get home early.

After she left, Ryan called Magic and they both went to Ponce Inlet Park where dogs can run on the beach with their owners. Both Ryan and Magic exhausted themselves running in the soft sand. They finally crashed on the sand and watched the sun drop down over the inlet where the Atlantic Ocean flows into the Indian River. Magic laid his head on Ryan's stomach and snoozed. Ryan wrestled with the events of his firing. Later he fell asleep as the sun dropped below the horizon and a warm tropical breeze cooled his body.

***

From: golden1@cfl.rr.com To: RQuinn@cfl.rr.com
Subject: badnews for USA.

Hello Ryan,

You don't know my name and I want to keep it that way; however, I have information that is crucial to the defense of our country.

Located in a truck that you were investigating at Port Canaveral, is a prototype power pack for a new powered exoskeleton. It is destined to go to Iran, a country that supports terrorists and the torture of dogs and other animals. Its final destination may be Iraq.

I suggest that you take Magic your wonderful dog with you and investigate.

Sincerely yours,

Your freind

Ryan read the e-mail and started to delete it. Some nut was playing games, but how did they know about the truck he was investigating at Port Canaveral? Whoever it was also knew the name of his dog and misspelled the word *friend*. Probably some kid heard about it from his dad, maybe one of the cops. No, the police didn't know the name of Magic. Only Frank would know that, and he did have two sons in school.

Ryan dialed Frank Kurns's number from memory.

"Hello," Frank Burns said as he answered on the second ring.

"Frank, this is Ryan Quinn—"

"Listen, Ryan. I am sorry about all this but...well there is nothing I can do. If you need references I will be glad—"

Now Ryan cut him off.

"Yeah, sure, I can see it now. 'He is a good worker but I had to fire him,' but that's not why I called. Tell your son, whichever one it was, to knock off the phony e-mail. I don't appreciate it."

"E-mail? I don't know what you are talking about."

"I got an e-mail telling me about some terrorist crap. Only you know about what happened at the warehouse."

"No, Ryan. That's not true. Let's see. There was the police, the two men you caught, then the gate security and—"

"Only you knew the name of my dog. That narrows it down to you. Now, if you talked about it at home and one of your boys heard, I put two and two together."

"My boys are at camp. My church sponsors a camp each summer. They've been there for a week."

Ryan was visibly taken back. He didn't usually jump to conclusions, particularly wrong ones, and this was obviously a wrong conclusion.

After an uncomfortable few seconds, he said, "Oh, well ...I don't know what to say, but somebody knew a lot of details. I am sorry."

Ryan hung up without further explanation. Frank Kurns had been good to him until the firing. Ryan was miffed, but not angry with Frank. He knew there was more to his firing than he was told. Now, who the hell knew all the details?

Ryan reached down and patted Magic's head. "What do you think, boy?"

Magic laid his head on Ryan's lap and put both paws over his eyes.

***

That didn't go as I anticipated. I must remember to check my spelling or use spell-check. Ryan's a smart guy and it won't take him long to figure out I sent the e-mail, so I had to change strategies. There was another potential problem. He might recall that he told Megan the whole story, and she certainly knows my name. Perhaps the old saying "Love is blind" applies to the other senses as well. In any case, somebody has to stop that shipment. I could have sent a letter from Ryan's e-mail to the FBI, but that idea was packed with problems.

I have heard the expression from Megan, "If you want something done right, do it yourself."

Considering I hadn't found a way to get Ryan to look into the illegal shipment, I had to do it myself. Port Canaveral wasn't too far away, but riding in Ryan's pickup truck might have confused my sense of distance. I am just now getting use to feet, yards and miles. The metric system makes it so much easier to do the math, but I'll learn.

After thinking about this problem, I decided to use the Google map site. Ryan drove on the highway, and I was not certain I could follow that trail. So I did what millions of people and maybe a few animals do: I looked at a map on the internet.

I started out with our address and the destination of Port Canaveral. The route took me down Highway 95 and then across to Merritt Island and on to Port Canaveral. The distance was 66.1 miles and would take 1 hour and 11 minutes. There was no entry for dog speed, so I guess I would have to travel at sixty miles per hour, just kidding. I think I can travel at about four miles per hour for a long distance, but I decided not to take the automobile route. There is a tollbooth on one of causeways to Merritt Island, and I don't do money. I used the satellite view and discovered that I could work my way down A1A until it ends and then walk in the sand next to the ocean all the way to Port Canaveral. It sounded simple, but like most plans, it had a few pitfalls.

I estimated it would take me about sixteen hours to reach Port Canaveral. I wanted to arrive there as the sun set, but that would mean I would be walking much of the way in daylight. It would be hot, and I would need fresh water and some food. I can live without food for awhile, but I would need water. I finally decided to leave as soon as Ryan went to bed, which was usually around midnight. I would get to Port Canaveral when it was still light, so I planned to hide there until it got dark.

I anguished over part of my plan. I knew that Ryan would be very worried if I was missing for a day or two, but what could I do?

I prepared as best I could after Ryan went to bed. Ryan keeps bottles of water in the pantry, and there was a small Publix shopping bag left there by the last tenants. I was able to put my neck through the shopping bag's straps and put four bottles of water in the bag. I would bite the tops off as needed. The bag hung down but didn't touch the floor when I stood. I couldn't open the bag of doggy treats, so I settled for the three apples Ryan kept in a bowl on the kitchen table. I don't care for apples, but it beat starving.

Ryan allows me to sleep in the house but not on his bed, although I don't have flees now. I usually sleep on the floor at the foot of his bed. After a few nights, when I woke him to go out to my toilet, he made a small swinging door in the backdoor so I can come and go as I wish.

Fortunately, the fence around our backyard is wooden and not too high. I took a running leap and cleared it, but the darn shopping bag caught on the fence and I did a very embarrassing flip. The bag came loose and my water bottles and apples flew out. Nobody was around to see me, but I hate doing stupid things. It must be my human genes.

After I gathered my composure and supplies, I set out at a fast pace, not a run, but an energy conserving trot.

It seemed to take forever before I got to the beach. As I was going up the south causeway, in the pedestrian lane, a police car slowed and an officer called out to me. I think he wanted to read my collar to see who I belonged to. I didn't want them waking Ryan, so I ignored them and kept going until I was over the bridge and on the beach side. They must have had a call because they turned on their flashing lights and roared away.

Once at the beach, I picked a route that kept me out of the soft sand. The tide was out, so I was able to make good time on the hard packed wet sand. I passed a few surf fishermen, but they ignored me. The odors at the beach are unique. I was tempted to investigate some large turtles but kept at my task. I startled a possum who hissed at me, but I kept going. He was eating a fish.

I passed Bethune Beach and then the road that goes to the ancient site of Eldora. I wanted to see the old house they restored there but that would have to wait.

The time passed slowly and, I must confess, it got a little scary once I was away from civilization. Clouds covered the moon and stars and it got very dark. The white surf hissed as it ran up the incline of the beach. I could judge where to trot by hearing the waves, but once in awhile a big wave came in closer than I anticipated and soaked my paws. Land crabs scrabbled out of my way, but a few didn't make it. I hate that feeling. Some parts of the beach were very narrow and I was forced to wade in the surf until the beach widened. As the tide began to change and the surf moved up on the narrow beach, it became increasingly difficult to stay out of the water. I actually love the water, but this was not the time for play. There was one place where it looked like I would have to swim; it was that narrow and apparently that the ocean had flowed into the inlet on the other side. According to a beach sign, I was in the Canaveral National Seashore.

The sun was beginning to come up over the ocean, which is a beautiful sight, but it also signaled the start of a very hot and humid day. I stopped to bite off the top of my first water bottle and rest for a few minutes next to a barrier and sign that said I was on government property. There were a few other warnings, some downright threatening, like I could be shot, but I figured I was going to save American lives by stopping the illegal shipment, so I didn't think I would go to jail if caught. Shot maybe, but not jailed. I was on the John F. Kennedy Space Center.

I had forgotten to watch the news and see if a space launch was scheduled. I wasn't that far from the giant launch pads, but there was no activity. I kept going.

It got hotter and I had to stop and rest, drink more of my precious water, and eat an apple. It actually tasted good.

A big sign and fence alerted me to the fact that I was trespassing on the Cape Canaveral Air Force Station. It didn't stop me. I had trespassed on both Marine and Army bases in Iraq and lived through it.

My mind wandered. I was back in Iran following a road that led away from the cursed laboratory where my mom and dad died. I've often wondered if my siblings survived, but those thoughts always make me depressed, so I went to work on my plan to find the power pack and destroy it. Not knowing what it looked like could be a problem, but I did remember the scent of the men who were in the warehouse and the stenciled sign on the crate, *Atlantica Foods*.

Once I arrived at Port Canaveral, I realized I had made a strategic error. I was on the north side of the port. The warehouse I wanted was on the south side. The ocean inlet and the Indian River Lagoon stood in my way. There was a road that went over a movable bridge, but I would be vulnerable walking over it. I had to wait until dark. After a number of false starts where I had to backtrack because of high fences, I finally stopped within sight of the bridge and lay in the high grass at the side of a parkway. I was behind schedule but I needed to rest. I finished off my water and ate another apple. I must have dozed off when my senses woke me. Something was watching me. I also smelled a strong odor. It was unfamiliar and I opened my eyes slowly and looked around. It was almost dark. Then I heard movement. I sprang up in time to see the biggest damn lizard in the world. Later I learned it was an alligator. It rushed at me but I was able to leap out the way and then run like the wind.

Now, I have large teeth, but that brute had a set of ivories that made mine look like baby teeth. Now fully awake with my heart beating out of my chest, I ran over the bridge and to the Southside road. It didn't take long to find the warehouse. My plan was to wait under one of the trucks parked by the loading dock. Once anyone left one of the large doors open, I would dash through unseen, at least that was my plan. The reality was slightly different.

While the port is a very busy place most of the time, that night no one loaded or offloaded from the small warehouse. I had to improvise.

I walked around that warehouse five times before it hit me. There was a firebox at both ends of the warehouse. If I could break the glass and pull the handle, fire trucks would soon appear and maybe knock down a door or two searching for a fire. Not perfect, but considering the importance of stopping the shipment, it seemed like a reasonable plan. I tried to break the glass.

So much for that plan. The fireboxes are set at about eye level for a human. I could stand on my rear legs and put my nose on the glass or scratch at it with my claws—Ryan calls them nails—but I could not break the glass.

Not one to give up easily, I lifted my leg and marked my territory. Then I saw the wires that came down from the firebox and into a heavy conduit. Maybe I could short circuit the wires and hope that would send a signal to the fire department; then again, maybe it had to be an open circuit.

I began gnawing on the wires and in no time I was through the insulation. I knew that by the nasty shock it gave me. I may have yelped instinctively but it was worth it. I renewed my efforts on the other wire without the shock. The wires now hung down and I decided to wait to see if that would bring the fire department. When it didn't, I knew what I would have to do. I had to close the circuit by biting them together. It was going to hurt, but if I wasn't grounded, maybe it would work without frying my head. I was about to try when a breeze blew across the dock and the wires touched. An alarm went off above the warehouse eaves, and I ran off and hid under a truck.

As I waited for the fire truck, I began to think about a deeply disturbing issue. The wires touching at just the right time and a few other lucky breaks in my life caused me to wonder if there was a God and if this was divine intervention or just blind luck. Logic tells me there is something behind this universe and it was here before the big bang, but what troubles me more is this: do dogs have souls? I was still reflecting upon the issue of my mortality when a red pickup truck came flying around the corner and stopped with its tires squealing in front of the warehouse.

A man jumped out dressed in a fireman's uniform and shined a flashlight on the pole with the dangling wires.

CHAPTER 6

I guess it was the fire marshal who arrived; at least he looked like management. After looking at the wires hanging down from the fire alarm box, he used a portable radio and called someone. I could only hear his side of the conversation. He wanted the warehouse opened and checked out.

Not long after that, Ryan's former boss, Frank Kurns, arrived and unlocked one of the doors. They both went inside, and I made my move. The open door hadn't slammed shut, so I nudged it open with my nose and looked inside. It was an office, but I could hear the men talking close by. Another door led out into the warehouse.

My plan didn't include being locked inside the warehouse, but I was improvising and had to take the risk. I poked my head into the warehouse and saw both men with their backs to me. The fire marshal was shining a flashlight up on the sprinkler system outlets. I slipped into the warehouse and silently moved behind a pallet of boxes. I was hidden from view unless they searched the rows of boxes, which I figured was not what the fire marshal had in mind.

The men talked for a while longer and then turned off the lights and left. I heard the door close and the lock click as the deadbolt slid in place.

I ignored the possibility that I couldn't get out and started a systematic search for the *Atlantica Foods* box. I did that by putting my nose to the floor and sniffing. The odor of the fire marshal and Frank Kurns was strong, but after a few yards, I picked up the faint scent of the man whom I bit on the butt. It wasn't a pleasant odor but distinctive among the thousands of other odors in the warehouse. I followed it to the end of the warehouse and then backtracked. I had missed where he must have turned to walk between two rows of boxes. Then I found it. The man had handled one crate, and the scent of the other man was also on the crate. Luck was with me, and the crate, that probably measured four feet by four feet, was alone. No other boxes sat on it and it wasn't on top of other boxes.

I had hoped to be able to expose what those men were trying to do, but communicating complex issues with humans is not my strong suit. I decided to destroy the power pack if possible. But first I had to get to it. I probed with my nose and then pulled with my paws, but the crate was nailed shut. I shoved against it and found it wasn't too heavy. I put my head down and shoved harder. The crate moved a little and then started to slide across the floor. It was hard work and I was soon panting. I lost my little shopping bag when the alligator tried to eat me, and along with it, my last bottle of water and an apple. I needed a drink. The floor was concrete and my nails couldn't dig in for more traction, but eventually I pushed the crate across the aisle, down another aisle and ended with it in front of a large metal door. The door was wide enough for trucks and forklifts to enter.

I laid on the cool floor and waited until my heart stopped beating like a bass drum. It took a while, but I finally stood and looked at the door. It was the kind that rolled up on rails and an electric motor supplied the muscle. The only lights in the warehouse were small, red fire exit signs above small doors. Maybe I could have gotten out one of the small doors by jumping up against the door bar handle, but the crate was too big to clear the small doors. I had to open the big metal door. Then it dawned on me: There must be a switch that opened the big door, and I found it in the dim light. Next to the door, an electrical conduit led from the motor to a small electrical box. The box had two buttons. Simple enough. Open and close. The electrical box was about five feet from the floor, but by standing on my rear legs I could reach it. I listened for sounds from outside, and, hearing none, I pushed the open button. The motor whirred and the door started up.

I looked outside briefly and then started pushing the crate again.

You probably wonder what I was going to do with the crate. Push it home? No, I was going to drown it. The dock was only about a hundred feet away, and with luck, I could push it that far.

It took much longer than I thought. First I had to get the crate off the loading ramp, which I finally accomplished by pushing it off the ramp. I hoped it would break open but it didn't, so I kept pushing. The surface of the warehouse was smooth cement, but the asphalt road outside was rough and had cracks and ridges that kept catching the bottom of the crate. Eventually, I got it to the edge of the dock, but I had to rest for awhile before pushing it up and over a band of angle iron that ran along the length of the pier. The angle iron looked to be about six inches wide, but it rose up another few inches, which meant I had to push the crate up and over it before it would fall into the water.

This was where my plan began to fall apart. I could not get the crate up and over the angle iron, even though it was only a few inches thick. Try as I might, it would not budge. It was stuck behind the lip of that reinforcing metal angle iron. Finally, in desperation, I trotted back about thirty feet, took a deep breath, and ran as fast as I could. I took the impact on my front paws and it sent a jolt through my body that hurt. The crate flipped up on one end and then started to fall back on me, but I pushed again and it dropped over the edge and into the water. Unfortunately, so did I.

***

Ryan Quinn searched the neighborhood, calling out, "Magic. Here, boy," over and over. He was due at school by 9 a.m. but attending class was the furthest thing from his mind. He had to find Magic. It was so unlike Magic to leave. Ryan didn't think he needed a fence to keep him in; the fence was there to keep other dogs out.

Ryan telephoned Megan, hoping that somehow Magic had decided to visit her, not that he had ever taken Magic to her parents' house, but Magic had the uncanny ability to find his way.

Megan assured Ryan that Magic would return home. She thought he might have jumped the fence while pursuing a lady friend. Ryan thought about that and said, "I guess it is possible, but he had never chased after females before."

Megan answered, "Maybe he found that special one."

Ryan thought about her and how, after all the others, Megan was special. Certainly worth jumping a fence for.

"I suppose you're right, but he should be back by now."

"Maybe she is playing hard to get."

It took Ryan a few moments to phrase his reply. "Yes, like somebody I know."

Now Megan was silent. When she did speak, she said, "I'll come over and help you look for him. Give me a while to finish some typing. I am sure Ted won't mind."

Ted Louis was a local attorney and Megan's boss. He was also Ryan's friend and racquetball partner.

Ryan said, "If I'm not in the house, drive around the block. I shouldn't be far."

After driving around for ten minutes, Megan found Ryan. He was looking behind a house three streets over from his house on Live Oak Avenue. She tapped the horn on her Honda Civic and he looked around. He jogged out to her car and opened the passenger door.

"No luck." He glanced at his watch and said, "It's almost noon. I'm worried now. Maybe someone stole him. He is a beautiful dog."

"Get in. We'll drive over to the humane society. Maybe he was picked up."

Ryan got in and said, "I already phoned them. Besides, I put my phone number on his tag. They promised they would let me know if he is picked up."

Megan put the car in gear and drove slowly, looking for Magic. After thirty minutes of driving with Ryan calling out through the open window, Ryan said, "Go to my house. I've got an idea."

At home, Ryan went into the house, and after ten minutes he walked out to his pickup truck and mounted a large loud speaker on the roof. He then ran a wire from the amplifier in his truck to the speaker. He placed a music CD in the under-dash player and adjusted the volume. Satisfied, he went inside and used his computer to record a voice CD.

Megan left but promised to come back after work. She was still at work when Ryan telephoned her again.

"Megan, is Ted there?" Ryan asked without preamble.

"Yes, but why—"

"Just ask him to come to the phone. Okay?" Ryan said sharply.

Ryan's tone surprised Megan. He seldom raised his voice or used that tone with her.

Megan put Ryan on hold while she went into Ted Louis's office and asked him to pick up line two.

She stood in the doorway, listening to Ted talk to Ryan for a moment, until Ted looked at her. She went back to her desk, and after a few minutes Ted came out and said, "I'll be gone for a while." He then added, "To get your boyfriend out of jail."

Megan followed Ted to the parking lot, peppering him with questions. When he got to his car, he turned and answered, "Apparently, Ryan has been driving around town with a loud speaker on his truck calling for his dog. The police stopped him and told him he could not do that. Something about an ordinance against loud music, which I am not familiar with. Ryan insisted it wasn't music and wouldn't stop, so they pulled him over and charged him with being a public nuisance. He told them to go to hell, and, from what I understand, they may charge him with resisting arrest."

Megan got into Ted's car without being asked and said, "I'm going with you."

Ted smiled and said, "I gathered as much."

Two hours later, Ryan walked out of the New Smyrna Beach Police station with Ted Louis and Megan Alvarez. Ryan was still fuming but grateful that he hadn't been charged with a felony, which could have ruined his chances to join the FBI. He was given a ticket for a burned out brake light, and a stern warning about abusive language to a law enforcement officer. Ryan thanked Ted and asked what he owed him.

Ted shrugged and said, "Megan handles the billing for me."

Megan stayed with Ryan until midnight when she announced she had to go home. Ryan sat outside on the front porch until two in the morning waiting for Magic. When he did go to bed, he couldn't sleep. At three a.m. his telephone rang and Ryan leaped out of bed to answer it.

"Hello," Ryan said. "You found my dog?"

The familiar voice on the other end surprised Ryan. Frank Kurns said, "Yeah, how did you know?"

"Frank? What do you mean? Magic ran off and I thought someone was calling to tell me they found him."

After a short delay, Frank Kurns said, "Look, Ryan. I don't know what's going on, but the roving patrol saw a dog in the water, riding on top of a crate near one of the locks. They fished the dog out with a boat hook, but the crate sank before they could get to it. I've got your dog here, but he doesn't look too good."

Ryan rubbed his face and looked at the clock. "Put him on."

Frank Kurns thought he misunderstood Ryan and said, "Do what?"

"Put the phone next to Magic's ear."

Frank Kurns shook his head but said, "Okay, but you have some explaining to do."

Magic was lying on the floor of the gatehouse, exhausted. Frank held the telephone next to Magic's ear, and he heard Ryan say, "Magic, you alright, boy?"

Magic immediately stood and barked twice into the telephone. Frank Kurns brought the telephone up and said, "Satisfied. Now what do you want me to do with him. "

"Give him some water and food. I'll be there as fast as I can."

Ryan hung up and Frank said to Magic, "He says he'll be here as fast—What am I doing?"

The gate security guard, who was looking at Frank strangely, said, "Talking to a dog?"

"Shut up and get the dog some water."

***

Cynthia Morgan brought two glasses of chilled wine out to the covered veranda in her British West Indies style oceanfront home. She handed one to Preston Winn, who reclined on a chaise lounge, and stood next to him. Dressed in casual blue slacks and a white polo shirt, which showed the outline of his well-maintained muscles, Preston stared out at a large sailboat with the tops of its sails emblazoned by the setting sun.

"Well?" she asked.

He looked up and motioned for her to sit next to him. She adjusted the dressing gown she wore over her bikini and sat down. Cynthia Morgan was the widow of oil magnet Howard Morgan. She was also twenty years younger than her frequent houseguest, Preston Winn. Winn, at age fifty-one, had managed to build a creditable career in government agencies for twenty years. A lawyer by training, but now in the upper echelons of the Department of Homeland Security, he aspired to even loftier titles. Preston Winn came from a blue-collar family in Detroit, but never accepted his humble beginning. He managed to win a scholarship to Yale, where he quickly made friends with the very wealthy sons of prominent families. In his early years, Winn spent most of his income on memberships to the finest clubs and on expensive clothes. He leased large Mercedes Benz cars and only dated women from wealthy families.

When he married Susan Villery, the heiress of the Villery Investments Bank fortune, Winn thought he had arrived. They made a lovely couple on their honeymoon in Europe. She was tall and sophisticated, he handsome and athletic. Then she found him in the arms of the stunning Contessa Maria Avalon while visiting her villa in Spain. Susan flew home to daddy, whose lawyers went after Preston Winn like barracudas in a school of tuna fish. He was fortunate to get off easy and did not contest the quick annulment. Winn's second wife was not as rich, but not poor. She seemed to adore him and accepted his predisposition to stray.

He finally looked at Cynthia Morgan and said, "Please forgive me. My mind was on business as usual."

"Darling, can't you ever forget work? Relax. Now, drink up and we can go to dinner."

"You go ahead with your friends. I'm expecting an important phone call. I'll join you later at the club."

She stood, feigning disappointment with her pouting lips, and said, "Promise?"

Preston Winn saluted with the Boy Scout three-finger hand salute and said, "Scout's honor."

Preston was no Boy Scout. An hour later, his cell phone rang and Babak's familiar voice said, "You must come immediately."

Winn sat up, now fully alert. "Why, what's wrong?"

"The XSCMES is missing." Babak used the acronym for the prototype Experimental Self-Contained Miniaturized Energy Source.

"How can that be? Where are you?"

"At the warehouse."

Preston Winn rushed out of the house and found the keys in one of the three cars remaining in Cynthia Morgan's West Palm Beach garage. Appropriately, it was a new Porsche 911.

**

I had never seen Ryan so upset. At first he hugged me and I gave him a big kiss, but once he had me captive in his pickup truck, he lectured me repeatedly about running away. He didn't understand that I may have saved American lives, but I guess I can't blame him. It still hurt my feeling and I guess I showed it, because after awhile he reached over and patted my head and said, "You had me worried sick."

Once we got home, Ryan nailed my dog door shut and went into his bedroom. I came in looking for him to play ball, but he was fast asleep, so I curled up at the foot of his bed and took a long nap.

CHAPTER 7

Preston Winn drove up to the warehouse and climbed out of the Porsche. Babak stood on the loading dock and looked down at him.

Preston said, "Now, what do you mean, 'the XSCMES is missing'?"

"It is as I said. It is no longer in the warehouse."

Preston jumped up onto the loading dock and said, "How can that be? We have the keys. No one else can get in."

Babak, still dressed in his cheap floral shirt and now wearing blue Bermuda shorts, said, "Apparently, that is not true. One of the large doors was open. They can only be opened from the interior, so someone does have a key."

Preston hurried into the warehouse and began searching. Babak had turned on the overhead floodlights. Preston didn't trust Babak completely, but stealing the prototype didn't make sense. Preston had already received half of the promised six million dollars, and Babak would get his cut when the prototype arrived in Iran.

As Preston searched, Babak sat on a crate and watched. It was obvious that he had thoroughly searched for the crate before telephoning Preston.

It took an hour for Preston to satisfy himself that the precious cargo was missing. It had been his idea to ship the prototype in a crate marked *Atlantica Foods*. He knew that food shipments on boats were seldom if ever searched, whereas air shipments were routinely searched.

It had taken a year for Preston to arrange for the prototype to be shipped to his office at the Department of Homeland Security, ostensibly for testing. Only five prototypes existed; the Army had two, a private firm developing advanced exoskeletons was testing one, and a private firm that developed the power pack had the others. Preston had already covered his tracks by having a box filled with junk electronic parts sent back to the university, supposedly with the power pack in it, and then alerting them anonymously that a bomb was in the box. He then made sure that the potential bomb was destroyed by the DHS bomb squad.

Getting another prototype would be very difficult, but not impossible if he couldn't locate the missing one. The people who paid him would not accept an excuse and they could be very nasty, even to a high-ranking American bureaucrat.

Preston's position in the Department of Homeland Security gave him access files on the sources of funding for terrorist groups. Transcripts of prisoner interrogations gave him names, and, in many cases, locations and telephone numbers.

Preston's many visits to Saudi Arabia, Kuwait and the United Arab Emirates provided the opportunity to make the connections he sought. China was another potential buyer for the new technology. He had hired Babak Shirazi at the insistence of the buyers in Saudi Arabia, who were funding the illegal transaction.

He looked at Babak and said, "Of course, the security company has a key."

Without waiting for Babak, Preston jumped down from the loading dock and drove off in the Porsche. In less than a minute, he parked next to the gatehouse and went inside. The security guard, an aging retired policeman, saw him and came out of the gatehouse.

"Evening, sir. Can I help you?" It was no longer evening, but good morning didn't sound right. Preston didn't answer but presented his badge and ID. The guard read the ID and said, "Is there some problem, Mr. Winn?"

"Apparently. Warehouse 7B is missing some cargo and the door was found open. Do you know anything about that?"

The guard thought for a minute and said, "I don't know anything about missing cargo, but the roving patrol noticed the open door. I telephoned a Mr...." He went back into the gatehouse but returned with a clipboard. "A Mr. Babak Shirazi. He came through the gate about an hour ago."

"Yes, I know. Who is your supervisor?" Preston demanded.

"That would be Mr. Kurns."

"Tell him I want to see him."

The guard looked at his wristwatch and said, "It's almost one o'clock in the morning."

"I am aware of the time. Call him."

The guard shook his head but went into the gatehouse and telephoned Frank Kurns.

***

A knock at the front door woke Ryan. Magic barked once and ran into the front room. It's a small house and the front door opens into the front room. Magic sniffed the door and wagged his tail.

"Just a minute," Ryan said as he hobbled while trying to pull on a pair of blue jeans over his jockey shorts. He looked through the small sidelights and recognized Frank Kurns.

Ryan unlocked the door and Magic almost knocked Frank Kurns over and licked his face.

Ryan pulled Magic back by his collar and said, "Magic, down." Magic moved behind Ryan, who said, "Frank, what brings you here?"

"I'm not sure I should be here. You have a cup of coffee? I've been up most of the night."

Ryan was still miffed about being fired, but couldn't stay mad at the man who helped save Magic.

"Sure. It will take a few minutes. Come in the kitchen. I've got a few questions."

Frank pulled out a chair and sat at Ryan's kitchen table while Ryan began preparing coffee. Once the brewer was perking, Frank said, "Ryan, I shouldn't be telling you this. Maybe I could go to jail for it, but, damn, something doesn't sit right with me."

Now he had Ryan's attention. Ryan pulled back a chair and sat. "Why'd you fire me, Frank? I was doing my job."

Frank leaned forward and said, "I know that, and that's why I'm here."

When Frank hesitated, Ryan said, "Go on. I'm listening."

"Apparently, you are the subject of a federal investigation."

"A what?"

"This guy, the one you busted at the warehouse, is with the feds. Homeland Security. He was back again this morning. Seems somebody lifted a crate, but he wouldn't tell me what's in it. He got me out of bed to ask a million questions."

"That's why you fired me?"

"No, that was this morning. I fired you because, while we were in the police station, I get a call from the state licensing department. They told me that you were a security risk and would pull my licenses if you worked for me."

Ryan shook his head. "That is so much bull. I had a Top Secret security clearance in the Marine Corps, which meant I was investigated by the FBI."

"I know it. But what could I do? It was obvious that that guy pulled some strings. Why else would some state official know to phone me at the police station and after normal working hours? "

"So, I've got my job back?"

"I would like to, Ryan, but they'll shut me down. I've got a wife, two kids and a fat mortgage."

Ryan stood and went to the coffee pot. He poured two cups and came back to the table.

"Sugar, cream?"

"No, this is fine."

Frank brought the cup up and inhaled the aroma, but put it back down to cool.

"Ryan, this guy, Preston Winn, he asked if anyone suspicious was around. I almost told him about Magic and that crate he was on, but then he pissed me off with his threats about lying to a federal officer, so I shut up."

Magic, who had been lying on the kitchen floor, sat up. His ears perked up and he turned his head to one side. He then came over and laid his head on Frank's lap.

Ryan said, "You think that the crate Magic was on was the one that was missing?"

Magic banged his head on the underside of the kitchen table as he jerked up and looked at Ryan.

Both Ryan and Frank stared at Magic, who looked at one and then the other before trotting out of the room.

Frank Kurns watched Magic leave and said, "Ryan, that dog of yours is scary."

Ryan would not have used the word scary, but Magic certainly was different.

"Frank, dogs have extra senses. They know when something isn't right. Magic knew those guys were up to no good; why else would they pull a gun on me?"

"Did you ever think that there might be some government secrets in those boxes?"

"You're kidding. Our government protects its secrets. I've seen secret shipments with guards up the wazoo. I've been a currier and had to carry a weapon until I passed a briefcase with secret documents to their destination. The security around 7B is almost nonexistent. No offense, Frank, but anybody could break in there. Maybe not at the other warehouses, or the security areas, but 7B? It just does not make sense."

Frank sipped his coffee before saying, "I agree. I wanted you to know what was going on. I felt bad enough about having to let you go."

Ryan smiled and said, "A little guilt is a good thing."

"Where'd you hear that?"

"Just made it up."

Frank rose and said, "Good coffee, but I gotta get home and hit the sheets."

Ryan followed him to the door. "Let me know if that guy comes around again, okay?"

Frank was out on the walk before he turned and said, "I wasn't here, Ryan, promise."

"Right. By the way, who leased 7B?"

Frank waved as he drove away but didn't answer.

Frank drove off, and an unmarked state police car followed him.

***

I had to be more careful around humans or they might've suspected I can understand them. Actually, I am still working on understanding humans. I was reading as much as I coulc find about human psychology, but I really needed to take some university level courses. Even then, I wondered if the human mind is too complex to ever be completely understood. Speaking of human minds reminded me of Mr. Winn at the Department of Homeland Security.

It was obvious that this Mr. Winn was not a good guy. Of course, I knew that before, but what was worrying me was what he might do to Ryan. After Ryan left to talk to an old friend about a new job, I booted up his PC and found the Department of Homeland Security web site. Mr. Preston Winn was way up there. So much so that he might be able to direct the coast guard, immigration and border people, and just about anybody involved in homeland security. How he got involved with a power pack for powered exoskeletons was a mystery to me.

I was going to try once more to tell Ryan about the power pack. Maybe he would listen this time and not go off half-cocked, so I wrote an e-mail.

> Hello Ryan,
>
> The last time I wrote the following information you didn't reply. You don't know my name and I want to keep it that way; however, I have information that is crucial to the defense of our country.
>
> Located in a truck that you were investigating at Port Canaveral, is a prototype power pack for a new powered exoskeleton. It is destined to go to Iran, a country that supports terrorists and the torture of dogs and other animals. Its final destination is Iraq.
>
> I realize I misspelled the word friend but my intentions were as stated. I am a friend anyway you spell it. I suggest you contact the Army as they funded the development of a power source for the powered exoskeleton. I also suggest that you take your dog with you whenever possible. While he may not possess your keen insight and clear logic, he has, like many animals, the ability to see into men's souls.
>
> Your friend

I went back and deleted that bit about men's souls; it was too melodramatic; besides, I got it from an old movie about the Shadow. I left in the part about my not having Ryan's keen insight and logic; although it hurt, but he needed a little ego rub to get him going. I changed the last part to read, "...he has, like many animals, a sixth sense which can be useful."

***

Preston Winn left the DHS Investigative field office in Miami and headed for Cynthia Morgan's home in West Palm Beach, Florida. He still had her Porsche and enjoyed the powerful sports car. His meeting with the field office director served no useful purpose other than to legitimize his presence in Florida. Being in the Directorate for Science and Technology, which was the primary research and development arm of DHS, gave him access to private industry and universities, ostensibly to accomplish the DHS mission: The S&T Directorate, in partnership with the private sector, national laboratories, universities, and other government agencies (domestic and foreign), helps push the innovation envelope and drive development and the use of high technology in support of homeland security.

He planned to meet Babak Shirazi at Cynthia's house, although she told Preston that Babak made her feel uncomfortable.

"His eyes undress me," she said.

Preston assured her that Babak was harmless, although he wondered about the man himself. It had surprised Preston when Babak pulled a gun from under his loose fitting floral shirt and aimed it at the young security guard. That scene could have been handled with much more tact; however, once the gun was out, there was little Preston could do. What still puzzled Preston was how the security guard knew there was something in the truck. Perhaps it was only a guess, but it unnerved Preston. Everything had gone so smoothly until then.

Now the crate and the power pack were missing. Of course, there were others who could have realized the importance of the shipment. Having the security guard fired seemed like a good idea at the time; now Preston was not so sure. What was his name?

Quinn, yes, Ryan Quinn. The other fellow, Frank Kurns, he might also be involved. He owned the security agency and had gone to Quinn's house immediately after being questioned. Preston had them both under surveillance as a possible security risk with connections to terrorist cells. At least that was the story he gave to the field office who contacted the state police and the border patrol. They were to report Quinn and Burn's activities to Preston. While not the usual activity of a senior officer in the S&T Directorate, Preston was not about to be questioned by a mere state level official.

Preston turned on to the Highway 95 North on-ramp and pressed down on the accelerator. The Porsche responded by pressing him back in the leather seat. The 73 mile trip would take less than an hour, assuming traffic was light. It wasn't, but Preston maneuvered the agile machine through the traffic with a surgeon's skill. He imagined himself a formula one driver as he shifted gears and watched the tachometer move quickly past 6,000 rpm. The speedometer read 140 mph and was climbing. A car appeared in the distance and quickly grew in size.

Preston was about to pass it on the right when the car changed lanes. Preston stood on the brakes and the Porsche threw him against the seat belt and bled off the speed, but not soon enough.

The impact sounded like an explosion as the Porsche dug into the trunk of the Lincoln town car, sending both cars into a spin across three lanes of highway. The airbag brushed across Preston's face as it inflated with a pop and a shearing pain shot up his right leg. Another impact stopped the spinning cars as they hit the guardrail and came to a stop.

Preston didn't see the unconscious elderly couple being extracted from their car and placed in an ambulance. He did feel the paramedics and fire department men and women lift him out of the wreckage of the once sleek sports car.

In the ambulance, he looked down at his feet. His right foot pointed away from the left one at a strange angle. When he tried to move it, pain shot through his leg so severe he screamed and passed out.

***

Megan looked at the e-mail Ryan handed her. She read it twice before handing it back.

"Who do you think sent this?" she asked.

Ryan crumbled it up and threw it into a trashcan near his desk in the second bedroom of his home. He used the second bedroom as an office, but it had a bed that could be used for guests. He hadn't had any overnight guests, but his parents promised to visit, someday. Megan sat on the bed; Ryan sat in front of his computer. Magic laid at Megan's feet and watched her every move. She had her sandals off and used her foot to rub the back of his head. He reacted by laying his head on her lap and closing his eyes.

Ryan studied the e-mail on the screen and said, "I have been racking my brain. No idea. Nobody but Frank Kurns knows about the truck and Magic, except... you and me."

Megan reached down, rubbed Magic's ears, and said, "You are wrong."

"Wrong?"

"Yeah, Magic knows."

Magic's eyes snapped open and he jerked back from Megan.

"What's wrong, Magic?" she asked.

Magic looked from Megan to Ryan and then settled his head on Megan's lap again. Ryan frowned and said, "He's been acting jumpy since he ran off."

Megan hugged him and said, "You could have drowned."

Ryan went back to the e-mail and after a few minutes began to type a reply.

> Whoever you are, tell me your name. If you are my friend, you have no reason to hide your identity.
> Ryan.

"What are you doing?" Megan asked.

"Sending a reply. If this guy is on the up and up, he'll tell me his name."

"If he was on the up and up, he would have told you his name in the first place." She then added, "I don't trust him."

Magic moaned and closed his eyes again.

Ryan said, "Maybe not. If he or she is hiding their name, maybe they have a good reason."

"Like what?"

"I don't know. Maybe they..." Ryan stopped and looked back at Megan.

"What's the matter?" she asked.

After a long pause, Ryan said, "Don't take this wrong, but did you tell anyone about my arrest and about Magic?"

Megan moved Magic's head off her lap and stood before answering coolly, "Don't get this wrong, but do I look stupid?"

"Hey! It wouldn't be stupid to tell your brothers, or your parents. I was just asking."

"I've got to go, but no, I didn't tell anyone."

Megan headed for the front door and Ryan followed. Usually, they kissed before she left, but Megan was out the door, leaving Ryan standing next to the open screen door.

He called out to her as she got into her car, "See you tomorrow."

She didn't answer. Once she was out of sight, Ryan said to Magic, who stood watching, "I don't think I will ever understand women."

Magic wagged his tail.

CHAPTER 8

Babak Shirazi waited in the hall beside room 210 of the Palm Beach Hospital. He wore the same floral shirt he had worn for two days. His green trousers were new, but too short to cover his bare ankles and shower shoes. When Cynthia Morgan came out of Preston Winn's room, he leered at her and said, "I trust Mr. Winn is feeling better now that he has seen you."

Cynthia Morgan unconsciously pulled the lapels of her powder blue jacket closed, although she wore a blouse that adequately covered her cleavage.

"You can see him now, but the nurse said not to tire him."

Babak smirked and said, "I will do my best."

Babak walked into the single occupant hospital room. Preston lay in bed with one bandaged leg elevated by a pulley. He wore a hospital robe and scowled at Babak. "Find it yet?"

Babak shrugged and said, "Where would I look?"

"I think those rent-a-cops, Kurns and Quinn, either have it or know who does."

Babak fingered a small toy dog that sat at the end of Preston's bed.

"A present from your lovely lady friend?"

Preston ignored the comment and said, "I want you to interrogate those two. You know what I mean."

"My job, Mr. Winn, is to ensure the safe passage of the device. Not to, as you say, interrogate. You have the immigration and border patrol people at your disposal as well as other agencies, why not use them?"

"Are you out of your mind? One word about that damn power source and my ass is—"

A nursing assistant came cheerfully into the room. She ignored Babak, who stood back to let her reach Preston.

When Preston scowled, she said, "Sorry, but I have to record your vitals."

Preston motioned with his head at the monitor behind his bed. "Doesn't that machine take my blood pressure and monitor my heart."

Still smiling, she quickly copied his blood pressure, respiration and other details on a chart.

"Yes it does, but it doesn't transmit to the nurse's station anymore. I guess it's getting old."

"Wonderful. I'm in a secondhand hospital in a second rate state."

Miss Smiley lost the edge of her smile but managed to say, "Well then, I understand you are going to be transported to a hospital in Washington. I am sure you will like it there. Maybe they can fix your foot."

After she left, Babak said, "And how will you find the power pack in Washington?"

"I won't. You will find it here or you'll not be paid."

"Oh, yes. I am almost forgetting."

Babak produced a cell phone and speed dialed a number he had in storage. After a short delay, he spoke to someone in Arabic and handed the telephone to Preston.

Preston frowned but took the telephone and said tentatively, "Yes?"

After a few seconds he said, "Of course, but there is no need to threaten me. I too am a businessman. You will have your product, but unfortunately I have been in an accident and need a little time."

He listened again and his normal deep tan visibly lightened. He then said, "Yes, I understand. No, of course not. That won't be necessary."

He handed the telephone to Babak and rang for the nurse. When a nursing assistant appeared at the door he said, "I need something for this pain."

Babak looked up at the blood pressure display. It read: 169 systolic and 96 diastolic. His heart rate was 92 bpm.

Babak said as he walked out, "Calm down, my friend. We wouldn't want something to happen to you, do we?"

***

I didn't know how to answer Ryan's e-mail. It was simple enough, but I couldn't tell him my name, so I did what many humans do when confronted with a situation where the truth is not acceptable, like, "Does this dress make me look fat?" I lied. I had to do some research, but eventually I came up with a name.

> Ryan,
>
> You may never disclose my identity under punishment of federal law. My name won't mean anything to you, but my mission will. I am currently in the employ of the federal government. Specifically the CIA. I am investigating the alleged sale of military secrets to China and Iran.
>
> You may wonder why I asked you to contact the Army. I am not able to tell you my reason at this time, suffice to say, your inquiry may provide amplifying information with layered response.
>
> You may call me Mr. Kunastros.

Once I finished my e-mail, I looked it over and sent it. I was proud of my "...amplifying information with layered response." I stole it from a news site where they were questioning some general about a new military system. I had no idea what it meant. I am not sure the general did either, so I felt it was sufficiently obtuse. The Mr. Kunastros was my invention. It is Greek for Dog Star. Seemed to fit at the time.

Ryan is a man of habit, not bad habits like smoking or beating his dog, but routine habits. Once he is awake he opens the backdoor, and I run out to sniff my territory and to use my toilet. Ryan uses the bathroom and then puts on a pot of coffee to perk. He opens the front door and picks up the newspaper, which he sets on the kitchen table. Once the coffee is ready, he pours a cup and lets it cool while he reads the news. In the evening, Ryan will watch both FOX and CNN. According to him, it is the only way to see both sides of an issue. He may be right, but I like the gals on FOX better.

Once he finishes his coffee, he walks into the second bedroom and turns on his computer. It is an old one and takes forever to boot, so he pulls on a set of running shorts and tee shirt—he sleeps in his shorts—and goes back to the computer. He has two e-mail accounts, one for his friends and relatives and one where he gets tons of junk mail. He looks at his friends and relatives account, which is where I sent my e-mails.

Today, he broke with his routine. When Ryan got up, I waited for him to check his e-mail. He called me in from the back yard, held a leather leash in his hand, and said, "How about a nice long run today. You up to it Magic?"

I love the runs, but I wanted him to read his e-mail, which he usually does before his run. Today, no luck. He snapped on the leash and off we went.

We ran down Riverside Drive to the North Causeway. From there we ran toward the beach, up and over the bridge, and down Peninsula Avenue to the Ponce Inlet Park. We ran in the sand near the water where the sand is firm. When we started back, Ryan slowed the pace. I was happy about that because having a human outrun me would be a serious blow to my ego. Ryan stayed in shape in the Marine Corps and is still in great shape, although his leg injury slowed him down for a few months before he was released from active duty. He still has a small metal fragment in his thigh.

There is a water faucet at the park pavilion and Ryan let me drink my fill. He drank too and then we ran back, but this time we took the South Causeway home.

Now, instead of looking at his e-mail, Ryan dropped his running shorts and shoes on the bathroom floor, threw his wet tee shirt over the towel rack, and turned on the shower.

I was watching him, waiting for him to read my e-mail, but he misunderstood and said, "You want a shower, boy?"

No, I did not want a shower. Humans sweat when they exercise; must feel the need to wash it off. We dogs don't sweat like humans, we pant and the pads of our feet sweat. I walked out of the bathroom and went to the computer where I brought up my e-mail and began to type.

Hello Ryan,

I feel you should know that you are being followed. Today while you were running around the town of New Smyrna Beach, a car was following you and your wonderful dog. It was a big white car, obviously from a government motor pool, but what is more interesting, a second car was following the first car. It was a late model Toyota, probably a rental car.

You friend Mr. Kunastros

I hit send and closed my account just as Ryan came into the room with a towel around him. "What is so interesting on my computer?"

If only he knew.

***

Ryan was waiting by the front door when Megan arrived. She reached for the doorbell as he opened the door.

"What's so urgent that you couldn't tell me over the phone?" Megan asked as she walked past Ryan and into the house. She stopped off at her house on the way and changed clothes. She wore a simple white blouse and blue shorts.

Ryan handed her the two e-mails he had printed. She took them, glanced at Ryan for a moment, and sat on the worn sofa. When she was finished reading, she looked up at Ryan who had been standing by the door, watching for her reaction.

"Do you think it's true? I mean, about being followed?" she asked.

Ryan sat next to her and said, "I don't know what to think. Whoever wrote this must have watched me this morning."

Megan looked at the two e-mails again. After a few seconds she handed them back to Ryan and said, "I guess that clears my brothers. You would have recognized their old van."

Ryan stood and said, "Why don't we start over?"

Megan looked at him for a long five seconds before a smile crept across her pretty face. He pulled her up to him and kissed her. She kissed him back and, after a minute or so she pushed him back and said, "I think you should do what he asked."

Magic, who had been watching, barked once and ran into the second bedroom.

"See, even Magic agrees."

"Okay," Ryan said and laughed. "But I'm not convinced this guy is really a federal agent."

Ryan followed Magic to his computer and said, "Well, Magic, what should I say?"

Magic's ears perked up and he stared at Ryan for so long, Ryan had to turn away.

"Are you going to answer him?" Megan asked.

"Yeah, but first I've got an idea. Let's take a ride, and you watch and see if I am really being followed."

"Do you think that's wise? It could be dangerous."

"I wouldn't have suggested it if I thought it was dangerous."

Megan's eyebrows arched and she said, "Now who is the touchy one?"

"Okay, this has me a little on edge. I'll drive my pickup and you can follow back a bit in your car."

"Fine, I need to freshen up first."

Ryan said to Magic, "Wanna take a ride?" to which Magic ran around the room with his tail wagging and barked twice before waiting at the front door. Outside, Magic raced over to Ryan's pickup, which was parked in the driveway. Megan had parked her Honda Civic behind it.

"We have to wait for Megan. Settle down, boy."

When Megan came out, she said, "Want me to lock the door?"

"Yes, I've got the key. You drive around the block and then come up behind me. Keep back about a block. I'll drive down South Riverside and then come back on Highway One."

Megan got in her car, rolled down the window and leaned out. "This is exciting."

Ryan said, "I just want to know if I am being followed. If I am, call me on your cell phone but don't get too close to whoever it is. Understand?"

Megan threw him a crisp salute and answered, "Yes, sir."

Ryan waited until she backed out and headed down the street before he unlocked the pickup. Before he got in, Magic turned toward the street and growled at a passing silver Toyota.

Ryan watched, but it didn't slow.

"Someone's dog you didn't like?" he asked.

Magic barked and jumped into the pickup bed.

Ryan didn't usually let Magic ride in the pickup bed, fearing he might fall out, but today he relented. He would be driving slowly on residential streets.

Ryan drove out into the street, turned, went to Riverside Drive and headed south. Riverside Drive is only two lanes as it meanders along the Intra Coastal Waterway. In his rear view mirror, Ryan saw a car fall in behind him. He slowed and it turned off. There was a car further back. Ryan thought it might be Megan. He speed dialed her from his cell phone.

Once she answered, he said, "See anything yet?"

"There was a car behind you, but it turned off. Wait, another one just turned onto Riverside."

Ryan said, "Okay. I want you to take one of the side streets over to Highway One and wait for me to pass. See if that same car is behind me."

"Roger, my leader."

"Can the BS."

Ryan drove south until he came to Indian River Road, where he turned west and then back onto Highway One. He then drove north. If someone followed him back to his house, Megan would see them.

Magic paced back and forth in the pickup bed and Ryan watched him in his mirror. When they passed 4th street, a side street that intersected both Riverside Drive and Highway One, Magic barked excitedly.

A minute later Ryan's cell phone rang. "Bingo. A white Ford sedan is following you. It even has government plates. I couldn't make them out from here, but—"

Ryan looked at his cell phone. The battery was still charged enough. Maybe she accidentally hung up. He dialed her back but her phone was busy. He waited awhile longer and dialed again. This time it kept ringing and finally went on to her voice mail.

Magic was frantic in the back. He barked and barked until Ryan pulled over and stopped the truck. Magic jumped out and took off running at full speed down Highway One.

Ryan yelled, "Magic! Come back here," but Magic was almost out of sight.

Ryan looked once and made an illegal U-turn and pushed the old truck to its limits. A few blocks later, he saw Magic ahead of him, but still running at full speed. Ryan swerved around a truck and lost sight of Magic again. A few blocks later, Ryan saw Magic turn a corner. Ryan slammed on his brakes and managed to make a left turn onto 4th street.

Magic barked and ran around a car Ryan recognized at once. Megan's Honda sat with the driver's door open. The car was empty.

CHAPTER 9

Megan parked on 4th street and was talking to Ryan on her cell phone when her door was flung open, and a tall man with a long knife in his hand grabbed her phone. She grabbed for it and he hit her with her phone, opening a cut on her forehead.

He then reached down, unsnapped her seatbelt, and said, "You will walk to my car and get in. If you do not, I will cut your throat and leave you to die."

He held the long knife under her chin and pressed with enough force to elicit a cry from Megan. "Don't," she said, and added as she tried to lift her chin away from the sharp blade, "What do you want?"

"Get out of the car and walk or I kill you. You understand?"

Megan eased herself out of the Honda and saw a silver Toyota parked behind her. The man grabbed her arm and dug his fingers painfully into her bicep. Megan bit her lip, but didn't cry out in pain. He pulled her to his car, but didn't open the door. Instead, he took her to the back and opened the trunk. She pulled back, but he overpowered her and pushed her backwards into the trunk. He then slammed the trunk down, hitting her knees. He slammed it again harder and it closed.

Babak looked around to see if anyone saw him. He picked up Megan's cell phone, which he had dropped, and slipped it into the pocket of his floral shirt. He drove off and used her cell phone to call the man who was paying him. He then looked at her address page and dialed another number.

***

Ryan looked around frantically and tried Megan's cell phone again. It was busy. Maybe she had car trouble and left the Honda to get help, but why leave the door open? When Ryan looked inside her car, he saw the keys in the ignition. He got in and started the engine. It ran perfectly, no engine warning light. He put it into gear and moved it a few feet. It seemed to drive all right.

Magic was sniffing the ground outside and about twenty feet behind the car. He looked up at Ryan and barked.

"Where'd she go, fella?"

Magic looked around and then put his nose down and began to walk. Ryan followed on foot until they got to Highway One. While traffic was not heavy, it was still dangerous to walk in the middle of the road.

"Wait, Magic."

Magic stopped and looked back at Ryan as if to say, come on, we need to hurry.

Ryan signaled for him to jump back into the truck. "Come on, Magic. Show me where she went."

He opened the passenger's door and Magic jumped in. Ryan closed the door, but Magic immediately hung out the window so far that Ryan thought he might fall out.

Ryan eased the pickup into the traffic while Magic sniffed the air. In a few seconds, Magic looked back and barked. Ryan made a U-turn and drove slowly in the right lane. Cars came up behind him and impatiently passed, giving him irritated looks. He drove on slowly for a few blocks before Magic drew his head back in and barked. Ryan stopped and put on his flasher lights.

"What is it, boy?"

Magic looked at him uncertainly, then laid his head on the seat and whined. Ryan tried Megan's cell phone again. It was still busy.

She must be around her somewhere if she's using her phone, he thought. Then a chilling thought came to mind: Maybe someone else has her phone.

Ryan drove back to Megan's car and parked behind it. Magic jumped out when Ryan opened his door and began sniffing around Megan's car again. Ryan sat in the front seat of her Honda and took the keys out of the ignition. He looked down and noticed something under the front passenger seat. He pulled it out and recognized Megan's handbag, a black classic envelope clutch. He'd seen it hundreds of times. He opened it and found her wallet and driver's license. He then telephoned her parents. Megan would not have left her handbag in her unlocked car.

It took awhile to convince Mrs. Alvarez that Megan was missing under strange circumstances. Ryan wasn't sure she actually believed him, but she said she would contact her husband and the boys. Maybe they saw her and she went with them.

"That would explain it," she said.

His cell phone beeped before he left Megan's car and he heard a vaguely familiar voice say, "Ah, you must be Mr. Ryan Quinn?"

"Yes. Look, I'm busy right now."

"Do not hang up, Mr. Quinn, or you will not hear from your pretty girlfriend again."

Ryan glances at the caller ID and saw it was from Megan's cell phone.

"Where is she?" Ryan demanded.

"In due time, Mr. Quinn. In due time. Now listen carefully."

"Look, you creep. If you hurt one hair on her head, I will hunt—"

"No, Mr. Quinn, it is I who will hurt her if you do not shut your mouth and listen. I will not repeat myself."

Ryan felt the hairs on the back of his neck bristle and sweat pop out on his forehead. He also felt hopeless.

"Go ahead," Ryan managed to say through his dry throat.

"Now. You know the whereabouts of the crate you were looking for at the warehouse—"

"Look, I don't know a damn thing about—"

"If you interrupt me again, I will take pleasure cutting your girlfriend's body into small pieces. Do not deny your knowledge of the crate. Why else would you be looking in the truck? And now the crate is gone. Do not take me for the fool, Mr. Quinn. In exchange for the crate, I will let your girlfriend go free."

Ryan's mind was a whirling dervish of thoughts and ideas. It would be a death sentence to Megan if he continued to tell the truth. He didn't know where the crate had gone. After a few seconds he said, "Okay, but my partner has it now. I'm not sure where he hid it. I'll have to get back to you."

Babak didn't reply for a moment. When he did, he said, "I suggest you contact your partner at once. It is very warm in the trunk of my car. I do not know how long your girlfriend will endure. Oh, and if you contact the police, I will make her death most excruciatingly painful. Do not try to reach me at this phone. I will contact you very soon."

Ryan reacted quickly and said, "Look, this is no bullshit. I may not be able to reach him for a few days. He might be out on his boat again. He's a fisherman."

Again there was a delay before Babak said, "Pray he is in port. The Florida sun is very hot this time of year."

"I will get your crate, but I need a little time—" Ryan realized he was talking into a dead telephone.

Magic, who had been listening attentively, licked Ryan's face and barked loudly.

Ryan pushed Magic away and said, "Let's go home, boy. Maybe that... Kunastros guy can help."

Magic waged his tail and barked again.

It only took a few minutes before Ryan pulled into his driveway. He opened the front door and Magic ran in. As Ryan was about to close the door, a white Ford sedan drove by. It had spotlights on both sides and government license plates. Ryan rushed back to his truck, started it, and spun the tires as he backed out into the street. It took him two blocks to catch the white Ford. The man driving it was surprised when Ryan pulled out around him and them cut him off, forcing the Ford to the curb.

Ryan pulled his .45 caliber Glock from the glove box and stuck it in his waistband before rushing out of the truck. The startled driver of the Ford looked around as if trying to decide if he could get away.

Ryan banged his fists on the driver's window and yelled, "Open up!"

After a brief hesitation, the window came down and an angry faced Hispanic man in civilian clothes said, "What the hell do you think you're doing?"

"Why have you been following me?"

After a brief pause, the man produced his wallet. He opened it and showed both a badge and a government ID to Ryan.

"Now move your truck," the man said.

Ryan said, "Why is the Border Patrol following me?"

"Move your truck now, or I *will* arrest you."

Ryan backed away from the window and said, "Open your trunk."

"What?"

"I'll move my truck once you open your trunk."

"You are pushing your luck, mister."

The man opened the door of his car and stepped out. He adjusted the loose sports shirt he wore so Ryan could see he was carrying a pistol.

Ryan laid his hand casually on the grip of his weapon.

"You have a permit to carry that? The man asked.

"Yes, now open your trunk."

The man seemed to weigh Ryan's words, and perhaps his instructions about reporting Ryan's activates but not interfering, took hold. Reluctantly the man walked to the rear of his car and opened the trunk.

Ryan looked in the empty trunk and stepped back. "You think I am an illegal alien?"

The man slammed the trunk lid shut and got back into his car without answering. Ryan climbed into his truck, started it and backed up. As soon as he was clear, the man spun the wheels on the Ford and drove away. Ryan drove home still wondering why he was being followed.

Magic waited in the front room for Ryan, who had forgotten to close the front door. It was still open a few inches. Ryan was relieved to see that Magic hadn't run off.

Magic jumped around waiting until Ryan opened the front door and walked in. Magic ran to the computer, then out of the room, and barked at Ryan. Ryan followed him to the computer, booted it up and clicked on his e-mail logo. He saw a new message from golden1@cfl.rr.com. He opened it and read:

Ryan,

I know about Megan being kidnapped. Believe me, there was nothing I could do. Your dog Magic tried his best to follow her, but I guess there was too much traffic and other scents. The man who took her was the same man your dog, Magic, bit at Port Canaveral. I don't know his last name but your former boss, Frank Kurns, may know.

I do know approximately where the crate is located. Your dog Magic was riding on it when it sank near the dock in Port Canaveral. He can take you to that location. The man who pulled Magic out of the water should know and your former boss, Frank Kurns, may also know.

Your Friend

Mr. Kunastros

Ryan was still studying the e-mail, wondering how anyone could have known so quickly, when his cell phone rang. It was Mrs. Alvarez. She now sounded concerned and excited.

"Ryan, Eduardo called the police and the FBI. Have you heard from Megan?"

"No, Mrs. Alvarez..." he hesitated to tell her about the kidnapper, but finally said, "I'm sorry, Rose," using her given name, "but Megan has been kidnapped. The kidnapper phoned me."

"Oh, Mother of God..."

Ryan immediately regretted telling her over the phone. What was he thinking? Her only daughter kidnapped by a mad man. Of course, he didn't know all the details. He hoped the man wouldn't find out that the police and FBI were called, but Ryan thought it might be best if they were involved. He felt he was over his head.

Eventually, Mrs. Alvarez came back on the line. "Ryan," she said, "what does this kidnapper want? Maybe I shouldn't ask. There are so many sick people in this world today."

"It isn't what you might think, Rose. He wants something he thinks I have."

"What could that be?"

"It's a long and complicated story. And I will tell you, but every second counts."

"Then you know where she is?"

"No, but you must believe me. I will phone you the second I hear anything. I should go now, Rose."

"God bless you, Ryan. Find my little girl."

Ryan said, "I will, Rose," not knowing if he could save Megan in time. Ryan's throat tightened and he felt tears in his eyes, which he brushed away. He had to remain calm if he was going to find his loved one. It was not the time to think about the possible tragic outcome. He tried to shut out the thoughts of Megan suffocating in the trunk of that madman's car.

He telephoned Frank Kurns, talked for a minute and said, "You want to spell his name?"

Frank said, "Babak Shirazi," and began to spell phonetically. "That's b as in boy..."

After Ryan hung up, he said to Magic, "Let's go, boy. We've got to find that crate."

Magic put up his paw and Ryan gave him a high five.

Ryan's cell phone rang again before he got to Port Canaveral.

"Hello," Ryan answered.

"Are you Mr. Ryan Quinn?"

"Yes, but I am very busy now. Please—"

"Mr. Quinn, I am Special Agent Howard Lowell of the Federal Bureau of Investigation."

"Yes, sir," Ryan answered.

"Mr. Quinn, I would like to talk to you as soon as possible."

"Sure, go ahead. I'll tell you everything I know."

"We would like to see you in our office—"

"Fine," Ryan cut him off, "but right now I can't come to your office."

"Mr. Quinn, I must insist—"

"Look, insist all you want, but right now I may be able to save Megan's life, so listen to what I tell you. I'll come in as soon as I can."

"You don't understand Mr. Quinn. There may have been a kidnapping and you—"

"Not may be, there was. Megan Alvarez was kidnapped by a man named Babak Shirazi."

After a slight delay, Special Agent Howard Lowell asked if he could record their conversation. After Ryan agreed, he started to ask Ryan questions but Ryan said, "Listen to what I have to say, and then I will answer any questions you have. But don't screw around. Get someone looking for Babak now. Megan's in the trunk of his car."

Ryan went on to tell his story from the beginning. He did withhold some information. He didn't explain how he knew where the crate was located, and he didn't tell the FBI about Mr. Kunastros.

CHAPTER 10

Megan felt the car stop and heard the door open and close. The engine was still running. She expected the man who abducted her to open the trunk. She was ready for him. She had found the jack and lug nut wrench under the spare tire, which was painfully difficult to retrieve with her weight on the tire cover. She finally managed and held her only weapon behind her back. If the man opened the trunk and reached for her, she would swing it around and try to take his head off. She wrestled with many scenarios, but knew she might have to improvise at the last second. She worried that there would be more than one man when the trunk was opened, and that was a possibility. After thinking more about it, she recalled that the e-mail said there were two cars following Ryan. Maybe this was the second car. If that was so, then she was kidnapped because of Ryan, which made her slightly less fearful. Maybe the man wasn't a rapist or a murderer. She also realized she might have only one attempt for freedom. Failure was not an option.

Megan waited in the hot, claustrophobic confines of the car's trunk, growing hotter and thirstier by the minute. She heard the car door open again, and she tensed, getting ready to strike out at her abductor. Instead, the car moved again, but only a short way and then the engine shut off. The car door opened, but the trunk remained shut.

Minutes passed, and then an hour, maybe more. The heat was becoming unbearable. Megan loosened the simple blouse she wore from her shorts. Her sandals had come off in the trunk and she hadn't bothered to find them. She was soaked in perspiration. She tried to slow her heart rate by meditating, but she could not stay focused. The real threat kept invading her consciousness like a recurring song.

***

I was happy about being in Ryan's pickup truck, and that he finally believed my e-mails, but I was heartbroken about losing Megan. She is a sweetheart, and not being able to find her was driving me nuts. I do know my limitations, and as good as I am about reading and following scents, I could not follow her or that man's scent once they turned onto the larger street and picked up speed. The man was evil, I could sense that. I could hear him talking to Ryan, but what Ryan might not know was that the man was lying. He intended to let Megan die or kill her. I could tell by his voice. I could be wrong, but I didn't think so. He also wanted to kill Ryan once he had the crate, which contained the power pack they talked about. I doubted if the salt water did it any good. Now my job was to find the crate, and then to find the man named Babak Shirazi, who was probably Iranian, and rescue Megan.

***

Ryan was pulling into the Port Canaveral entrance when his cell phone rang again.

Babak spoke without preamble: "Do you have the crate?"

"Not yet. Hopefully within the hour."

After a few seconds of silence, Babak said, "I am a patient man, but those with whom I work are not. Your little girlfriend is surely ready to be plucked from the oven. Do not delay. You don't want her overdone."

Ryan yelled, "Get clear on this! If Megan is hurt or worse, you will never see that crate again, and I will personally hunt you down. You will curse your mother for bringing you into this world!" He then added, "Do you understand me?"

Ryan realized Babak had broken the connection.

Ryan drove through the gate at Port Canaveral and found Frank Kurns and Ali Mossberg looking over the side of the dock. A small crane, called a cherry picker, sat next to the dock with a cable hanging down to the water.

Ryan stopped and Magic jumped out. Frank Kurns saw Ryan and waved him over.

"We think this is where it sank. Of course, the tide could have moved it."

Ryan was already pulling off his shoes and tee shirt. Magic was looking over the dock at the water.

"How deep is it?" Ryan asked.

"It's plenty deep in the middle but next to the dock it is probably about twenty feet. They don't pull the big ships in here."

Ryan dropped his jeans on the dock, looked into the water and dove in. He didn't hear Frank Kurns call to him, "Be careful."

After a minute, Ryan surfaced and blew out. "Nothing yet. Do you know where I can get a scuba tank and rig?"

Ali answered: "I've got a friend at the dive shop. Not far from here. You qualified?"

Ryan answered: "Yeah. I'm certified but time is critical. I can't explain now but get the scuba gear. Someone's life depends on it."

Ali, a tall, thin native of Haiti, jogged off toward the parking lot and Frank asked, "Whose life?"

"Megan's. She's been kidnapped."

Before Frank could ask more questions, Ryan dove again. Magic looked into the water and barked.

Ryan surfaced and dove again and then again, each time taking slightly longer to breathe before submerging. Ryan was a good swimmer. He had taken the underwater course at Dam Neck, Virginia, as part of his special operations training and was certified for cave diving in Florida.

A white Ford sedan pulled up to the warehouse and a border patrol official in civilian clothes got out. He walked to Frank Kurns and showed his credentials before asking, "Have you seen Mr. Ryan Quinn lately?"

Frank waited for a minute and then nodded toward the water. "I believe that would be him now."

Ryan broke the surface of the water and blew out a thin spray. He was about to say something but stopped when he saw the same Hispanic man he had stopped near his home looking down at him.

"What are you doing?" the man asked.

Ryan took a deep breath and blew it out before saying, "Looking for something I dropped."

The border patrol official looked at Frank Kurns as if he knew what Ryan meant.

"What's he looking for?"

Frank said, "Stick around and we'll both find out."

The border patrol official went back to his car and left. A few minutes later, Ali Mossberg drove his car out on the dock and unloaded two sets of scuba regulators, masks, frames, goggles, swim fins, two high-powered submergible lights and two air bottles. When Ryan surfaced, he called out, "I have the gear and will dive with you."

Ryan swam to the dock and put his hand out. Ali took it and helped him out of the water.

"Fine, I could use some help. First I have to find my cell phone."

Ryan jogged over to his pickup and found his phone that was still connected to the battery charger. He unplugged it and took it back to the dockside.

"Frank, hold on to my phone. If it rings, stall and tell whoever it is I will be there in a minute. Then signal me."

"Signal you? How do I do that if you're underwater?"

"Use your imagination. I don't know. Throw something in."

Ryan's frustration showed. He would be nice later. He quickly pulled on the scuba rig and attached the bottle. He looked at Ali, who was checking his rig.

"Ali, I've been running a search grid west and east, working my way north. You stay on my right side. The bottom's murky as hell, so stay close."

Both men slipped into the water, adjusted their masks and dove beneath the surface. Magic hung over the side of the dock and watched the air bubbles pop at the surface. He sniffed the air and barked.

With the scuba gear, Ryan and Ali could stay below the surface and search for the sunken crate without coming up for air every minute or so, but Magic didn't like not seeing Ryan for such a long time. He pranced back and forth on the dock, occasionally barking at the air bubbles that traced the divers' progress.

Ten minutes passed and then twenty. The screech of tires behind him caused Frank Kurns to turn and look back. Two men were getting out of a green Ford Taurus. Both young and athletic, they walked directly to Frank and held out their FBI badges and IDs.

They introduced themselves and then asked Frank for his identification. Once they looked at his driver's license, they asked if Mr. Ryan Quinn was still under the water. Ryan obliged them by surfacing before Frank could answer.

"Is that him?" one special agent asked.

Frank called out to Ryan, "The FBI is looking for you."

As if anticipating that Ryan might submerge and escape, both agents drew their weapons and pointed them at Ryan.

One agent began yelling to Ryan, "Mr. Quinn. Please do not dive again—"

Ryan removed his scuba mask, goggles and said, "Relax. I'm coming out."

Frank leaned over and helped pull him out, while Magic's tail wagged at high speed.

Before the FBI could start questioning Ryan, he asked, "Did you find Megan?"

The agents looked at each other as if questioning the appropriateness of answering Ryan.

Finally, one said, "I anticipate Miss Alvarez will be found shortly. Now please come with us."

"Then you have Babak?'

When they didn't answer, Ryan said, "As long as you have Megan. I want to see her."

"That won't be possible at this time, now come with us."

"Okay but there is something down there you might be interested in." Ryan pointed at the water where Ali was now treading water.

The FBI agents turned and talked in hushed voices for a minute, and then one went back to their car.

Ryan walked to the cherry picker and examined the cable that hung down to the water.

"Frank, how much cable does this thing have?"

"Don't know. How much you need?"

"It's about forty feet out there and about thirty feet deep. I need a little more to wrap around it. Say ninety to a hundred should do it."

The FBI agent interrupted, motioned toward the water, and said, "Is this the object you told Special Agent Howard Lowell about?"

Ryan hesitated for a second before he said, "Yes."

An FBI agent said, "We have summoned a Coast Guard unit. They'll bring the object up. Now, Mr. Quinn, follow me."

Ryan's cell phone rang and Frank Kurns handed it to Ryan. Ryan took it and answered, "Yes?"

Babak said, "Apparently you did not believe me. Now that you have notified the FBI your girlfriend will die a very unpleasant death."

Ryan shouted, "You filthy son-of-a bitch!"

He tuned to the FBI agents and screamed, "You assholes just killed Megan!"

CHAPTER 11

What happened next was not pretty. I had never seen Ryan so angry, not like he was then. I thought he was going to attack the FBI agent, and so did the agent because he backed away and warned Ryan not to come closer. Frank Kurns wrapped his arms around Ryan, but Ryan threw him off as if he was a rag doll, and Frank is no lightweight. I finally intervened.

I rushed between the FBI agent and Ryan, barking as loud as I could. Ryan's eyes were glazed over, and I had to admit, I thought he might hit me, but he didn't. Instead, he looked down and finally put his hands to his face. I think he cried, but I couldn't hear him. His body shook and his chest heaved. He turned and walked away. The FBI agent looked relieved and didn't follow Ryan, who went over to the cherry picker and leaned his head against the body of the machine.

After a few minutes, the FBI agents walked back toward their car and talked for a few minutes. Ryan was still leaning against the cherry picker but his body no longer shook. I think he was getting himself under control.

One agent walked to him and spoke softly to Ryan. Of course I could hear him easily. He said, "I am sorry, Mr. Quinn, but we would like you to come with us. Do you think you can identify the car that was used in the abduction?"

Ryan looked at the FBI agent. His eyes were blood red but he said, "I'll do anything I can to find him. I might not be able to recognize the car, but I am sure my dog can."

The agent looked at me and then back at Ryan. I trotted over and nudged Ryan's hand.

"How can your dog recognize the car?"

Ryan reached down and patted my head before he said, "Because he chased after them. He must have smelled Megan and followed her scent. He knows her well."

The agent looked at me again before he said, "This is a little unusual, but we'll give it a try."

They had a brief argument about which vehicle we were going to ride in. I could tell the FBI agents didn't want me to ride in their car, which hurt my feelings, but they didn't want Ryan to drive the pickup. They wanted Ryan to get in the back of their car.

Ryan finally agreed, but by then a Coast Guard boat came down the channel and tied up at the dock. A chief petty officer, dressed in blue utilities, hopped off the boat and came over to the FBI agent. They talked for a minute and then Ali, who Frank Kurns had helped out of the water, came forward and told the chief where the crate was located.

Frank, Ali and the Coast Guard people stayed behind while Ryan and I went for a ride in the FBI car. I was not impressed. I expected to see elaborate electronic devices and maybe a heat-seeking missile attached to the underbelly, but other than a radio and a laptop computer setup, it looked like most American cars. I could tell they had been eating pizza earlier and drank coffee with cream.

They didn't even use a siren, which was another great disappointment. The ride didn't take long; apparently Babak had stopped at a small family-owned motel near Coco Beach. It was one of those places with small separate cabins and a parking place next to them for the cars. I have no idea how the news media knew so quickly, but three news trucks festooned with high antennas and satellite dishes sat in the driveway. Local police had already strung crime scene tape around a silver Toyota that sat next to a cabin. The door to the cabin was open and a uniformed policewoman stood in the doorway.

The FBI agents got out of the car and flashed their badges to a policeman who blocked the way to the Toyota. Four men with blue jackets, with the words FBI on them, came out of the motel and talked to the FBI agents who brought us to the motel. A sign over one cabin, that must have been the office, read, "Clam Diggers Motel, locally owned."

The FBI agents talked for a while and then one came back to the car. He introduced himself to Ryan as Special Agent Howard Lowell. He then said, "I am truly sorry, Mr. Quinn, that we didn't get here in time. I understand you think your dog," he paused to look at me and continued, "can identify the car that Miss Alvarez was riding in."

I barked once and looked up at Ryan.

Ryan nodded to me and said, "Yes. Is that the car over there?"

The agent turned and looked at the silver Toyota before saying, "Yes, but we can't let him contaminate the crime scene. Perhaps you can put on his leash and see what he does."

My leash was still in Ryan's Ford pickup, so that caused a small problem. Eventually a few of the FBI agents relinquished their belts, which became a makeshift leash, not that I needed one. I'm not dumb enough to mess up the crime scene. I've seen CSI.

We got out of the FBI car and Ryan led me to the Toyota. I could smell Megan from ten feet away. Babak's scent was also there.

Ryan stopped a few feet away and said to me, "Was Megan here, Magic? Tell me, boy."

I barked twice nice and loud.

"Open the trunk."

The FBI agent walked over, slipped on latex gloves, and popped the trunk release.

Ryan led me closer and I barked twice again. Her scent was very strong. Ryan's shoulders slumped and he said to the FBI agent, "She was here."

"Are you sure?"

Ryan nodded and asked, "Where is her body?"

"Body? There's no body. The car was empty, including the trunk."

Ryan dropped my leash and said, "What are you saying?"

Special Agent Howard Lowell was a tall man, almost Ryan's height but older. He touched Ryan's shoulder and said, "Babak used his credit card to pay for the room, and earlier he bought gasoline with the same card. As far as we can tell, he never used the room. We had the local police watch the motel until we arrived."

A newswoman called out, "Is it true a terrorist kidnapped a woman and held her here?"

Another FBI agent walked over and spoke with her, but I was too busy to hear what they said. Megan had not only been in the trunk of the car, she had walked away. I began to follow her trail and nobody noticed.

The Clam Diggers Motel sat near Highway A1A, which at that point was busy with local traffic. Behind the motel was nothing but palmetto plants and small local palm trees. Megan had been there recently. Her scent was strong. She had been perspiring but had stopped and was in distress. Humans and some other animals smell differently when they are hurt or dying. I wasn't sure which one applied, and I kept my nose to the ground.

A hundred yards into the deep palmetto grove, I found her. She lay on the ground, unconscious and face down. I licked the side of her face. She was breathing but shallow, and her heart was racing. She was hot and clammy. I licked the side of her face and barked in her ear. She didn't move. She had scratches from the palmettos, and her shorts and blouse were torn. I started barking as loud as I could.

After a long time, I heard Ryan whistle for me. I ran back and barked at the FBI agents. Ryan saw me and took off running. I swung around and let him chase me through the bushes. I was standing over Megan when he saw her. He knelt down and tried to revive her. He then lifted her in his arms and started jogging back to the motel. The FBI agents met him about half way and tried to take Megan from Ryan, but he shook them off and yelled, "Call an ambulance."

They wouldn't let me ride in the ambulance with Megan and Ryan, but Ryan made the FBI promise to take care of me. To their credit, they did take good care of me. I got two big hamburgers on the way back to New Smyrna Beach, where they went to see the

Alvarez family and give them the good news; however, Megan was not, as they say, out of the woods. In her case, she was literally out of the woods, but she was still badly dehydrated and maybe had heatstroke. I'm not a doctor but I've watched them on television, so I know a little bit. I also watched corpsmen work on wounded Marines in Iraq.

A television crew arrived about the same time as we did in the FBI car. Mrs. Alvarez, who I only knew by listening to Megan, stood on the front porch of their home. She looked a lot like Megan except for her blond hair. I could see her face; she was worried sick, maybe past sick. The FBI agents took her inside and left me in their car. After a few minutes, one of the news crew must have noticed me. This lady, who I had seen on television, came over while giving directions to the cameramen and started talking about me while the cameras rolled.

The bright lights made it hard from me to see out, but I could hear her go on about how I saved this woman from a known terrorist who had tortured her. I don't know where they came up with all that, but I tried to show my best side, which is my left profile. I had never been on television before.

The news lady knocked on the window of the car. Maybe she wanted me to bark, but I didn't. I did stand up on the back seat and wagged my tail. She seemed to like that and had the camera take more pictures while she talked about the FBI, sheriff department, and the local police. How they knew about the Alvarez family, I have no idea. They must have a better intelligence network than the federal government. Maybe they have a mole in the sheriff's or police department.

Eventually, the FBI agents came back to the car. I thought they were going to take me home, but they lead me out of the car. The news people converged on them like locusts. One of the agents stopped and said there would be a press conference later in the day. That didn't seem to satisfy the news people and they kept shoving microphones at the agents and at me. I barked for them and that got a lot of attention. Finally, we made it to the front door, which opened and a tall man with thick, black hair greeted me in Spanish, which I don't speak or read well, but I have heard enough to recognize the language. He smiled and reached down to pet me. I sniffed his hand and found he was a good man. He also washes with Dial soap.

The FBI man led me through the house. I could smell Megan. Her scent was strong. Mrs. Alvarez came over and hugged me. I licked her hand. I would have given her a kiss but she stood back up while four men began to pet me. They all smelled faintly like Megan. I learned later they were her brothers. Then tragedy struck. A cat came out of nowhere and saw me. It hissed at me and I started to chase it, but the FBI man grabbed my collar.

Now, understand, I have no grudge against cats. I don't know any personally, and I try to be fair and unbiased. But a million years of evolution is hard to overcome. Dogs chase cats and other small animals. I have seen pictures of dogs and cats together, and either they are retouched photos or the dogs were brainwashed—trained—to act like a cat is another dog, maybe a small dog or a puppy. I have seen a few cats sitting on top of my fence, but they always left when I barked at them. This cat acted like it belonged and wasn't going to leave, which is pretty much the truth. Mrs. Alvarez picked up the cat and said, "Be nice, Star, the doggie saved Megan."

Cats have names? Next they'll want the vote. Getting back to my story, I was put out in the backyard, which wasn't that bad. Ryan's backyard was a yard, dirt and a little grass. The Alvarez backyard was a garden, with trellises, a fountain, trees, hedges, flowers of all kinds, and outdoor furniture. There was a white fence all around and gazebo at the far end of the yard. After I sniffed around for awhile, I found a nice spot under an old oak tree and took ten.

***

Megan was taken to a hospital in Titusville, and then by helicopter to the Orlando Regional Medical Center. Ryan stayed with her in spite of the flight crew's objections. He waited outside the emergency room as a doctor and nurses examined Megan. He took that time to telephone Rose Alvarez and tell her Megan was alive and in the hospital. She said she knew, and that she would leave for Orlando as soon as possible. An hour later, she arrived with her husband and three of her sons. She ran to Ryan and hugged him tightly.

"How is she?" she asked.

"I don't know yet. Maybe you can find out. They keep telling me the doctor will be out soon."

Mr. Alvarez and his sons stood behind Mrs. Alvarez, but now Mr. Alvarez said, "Tell us what you know and why our little girl was kidnapped."

Ryan lead them to a string of plastic chairs where they all sat, except Mr. Alvarez who stood looking down at Ryan, who said, "I'll start from the beginning."

Mr. Alvarez said with ice in his voice, "That would be nice."

"I was working at Port Canaveral as a security guard—"

Mr. Alvarez interrupted and said, "Is that like a night watchman?"

"Yes. More or less. Anyway, Magic started carrying on, so I—"

"What do you mean 'carrying on'?" Mr. Alvarez asked.

Mrs. Alvarez looked up at her husband and said sharply, "Eduardo, for heaven's sake, let him talk."

Ryan did finish. He left out the part about the e-mails and the mysterious Mr. Kunastros, and how he knew he was being followed. Shortly after that, a nurse came out and asked if this was the Alvarez family.

Mr. Alvarez said, "Yes, except for this man." He pointed to Ryan.

The nurse said to Ryan, "You're the man who brought Miss Alvarez in?"

Ryan answered, "Yes. I am her fiancé."

Mr. Alvarez glared at Ryan who ignored him. The nurse said, "This way, please. Doctor Pernill will be with you in a few minutes."

The nurse led them to a waiting room with more plastic chairs, but it was private. Dr. Pernill was a short, balding man in his mid fifties with a pleasant face. He looked around and asked, "You are Miss Alvarez's parents?"

Rose Alvarez answered, "Yes. How is our Megan? Can we see her?"

"She is stable, but she has been through a lot. We finally stabilized her core body temperature—"

Mr. Alvarez broke in with, "What are you telling us? Was she burned?"

Doctor Pernill was temporarily taken back by the question but responded, "I thought you knew. Your daughter is suffering from severe hyperthermia, heatstroke. She has a few minor abrasions but no other injuries that we can determine. She has not regained consciousness, but we are hopeful she will respond soon."

"Can we see her?" Rose Alvarez asked.

"We are moving her to the CCU. Once they have her settled, the nurse will contact you."

He smiled and left the room before Ryan could formulate the questions that had been bothering him. How had Megan escaped? What happened to Babak? Of course, if Megan was not conscious, he had no way of knowing the answer.

CHAPTER 12

Babak Shirazi waited patiently for his ride. Providence was with him. The first police car that pulled into the motel parking lot alerted him. When two more police cars arrived, Babak simply walked away. He had been in the manager's office because the telephone in his cabin did not function. The manager, a rumpled elderly man, walked out to talk to the police. Babak went out the backdoor of the cabin used by the manager as an office. He didn't attempt to reach his car; the police were parked behind it. He walked down A1A for a hundred yards, waited for traffic to clear, and crossed the road. Two hundred yards more and he entered a CVS drugstore.

Inside, he found a vacant aisle, took out his cell phone and telephoned a contact he hadn't used in years. Babak used a code name, and then said, "I need a car," and gave the address. He then called Ryan and told him he was going to kill Megan. Of course, he did not intend to return to his car. He only called to punish Ryan Quinn who had caused him so much trouble. The girl may or may not have survived. It didn't matter to him. The leverage he had with Ryan Quinn was gone, but he would find another way to get a power pack, but not now. The United States was becoming too warm. He would return to the more hospitable land of Saudi Arabia and then on to the home of his birth: Iran.

When his ride arrived, he didn't recognize the driver, but that wasn't unusual. New recruits were easy enough to find. The driver took him to a safe house in Orlando where he changed clothes; selected a new ID, passport, and visa. He then telephoned Preston Winn; however, Preston didn't answer his cell phone. Babak would phone him again before his flight left for England. From there he would change identity again and fly to Saudi Arabia. He would report to his controller by telephone and then fly to Iran.

***

I stayed at the Alvarez home for a full week while Ryan stayed close to Megan. I overheard the humans talking and found that Megan was in a coma caused by hyperthermia. I wanted to look up the medical description on the internet, but I was not invited into the house after the first day. While the Alvarez family was nice to me, and one of the boys played ball with me almost every day, I had to endure the humiliation of sharing my food, water and toilet with a cat.

The cat, who the humans called Star, looked like a white version of a Siamese cat. She had a birthmark on her forehead that with a little imagination could be called a star. The cat was a female, although I could care less about her gender. The reason I had to share my food was one of convenience for the Alvarez family. They fed me cat food in large amounts, which smelled like fish. I am not fond of fish, but when you are hungry, well, I can compromise.

As I mentioned, the Alvarez yard is really a garden, but without an area where I could dig a hole and do my thing. I tried it once but succeeded in ruining a patch of their manicured lawn. It was then I was led to a box containing chemicals that resembled sand. I had seen the cat use the sandbox as they called it, so, not wishing to destroy their lawn, I submitted myself to another indignity.

By the time Ryan saved me, my patience was wearing thin. I am by nature an easygoing dog. I don't like to fight, or cause trouble, but that cat tried deliberately to provoke me. It would walk slowly past me, and then without provocation, jump on my tail and bite it.

As a houseguest, I didn't feel I could growl or chase the cat, so I ignored it as much as one can ignore something with little sharp teeth biting your tail. Once, I jumped up and barked at the cat, who hissed and took a swipe at my nose, missing it by a fraction of an inch. The human named Paul, the youngest son, said, "Magic, Star is trying to play with you. Don't hurt her."

Hurt her? I wondered what he would do if she bit his tail. As I said, I am easy going, so I decided to play with the cat. I found the ball that Paul had thrown to me and dropped it in front of the cat. She turned her back on me and walked away with her tail in the air, as if to say, "I am too good to play with a dog."

When Ryan finally came through their backdoor and into the garden, I must confess I was overcome with emotion. I leaped up, knocked him backwards, and covered his face with kisses. He seemed genuinely happy to see me too.

He took me home and fed me real dog food, but I could tell he was still worried about Megan. Later that night, after he fell asleep, I did a little research on the internet and found that he had good reason to be worried. Megan's high body temperature could have done irreparable damage to her organs. Her brain was the most vulnerable. In layman's terms, Megan could be a vegetable for the rest of her poor life.

Ryan had quite a few messages on his home telephone. I listened with him. He was very popular. Three television stations wanted to talk to him as well as the local newspaper and one from Daytona Beach. Among those who also wanted to talk to him were the FBI, the local police, U.S. Customs and Border Protection, Immigration and Customs Enforcement, and the U.S. Department of Homeland Security. There were two messages from Frank Kurns.

Ryan was indeed a popular man; however, he ignored them all, took a shower and went to bed, but not before unplugging the telephone and saying to me, "Magic, if someone rings the door bell, do not bark and do not wake me."

I barked once.

***

Preston Winn came out of orthopedic surgery early Monday morning. His wife visited with him briefly once the anesthesia had worn off. She then went shopping. By Wednesday, he was well enough to be interviewed by a physical therapist, who informed him that he would be fitted for an ankle-foot orthosis because of his peronal nerve damage. She told him it would improve his gait and stability. He told her to get the hell away from him, which she did. Later that day, a doctor he had never seen before told him the injury to his foot was extensive, and that he had a healing fracture that lacked normal anatomical integrity or anthropometric proportions.

Preston said, "Cut the crap, doctor, and tell me what is wrong."

"You are lucky to have a foot at all. What's left will not support your weight or allow you to walk normally. With help and physical therapy, you will learn to walk, but a device called an orthosis will be needed. In your case, one that is custom made to your anatomical... physical dimensions."

After Preston digested the distressing news, he said, "How long before I leave the hospital?"

"It depends on how that foot heals. I can't say with any certainty. We'll know better in a week or two."

"A week or two? People with heart attacks go home sooner than that."

The doctor ignored his outburst and said, "I'll drop by again tomorrow. Are you in any pain?"

"More than you can imagine."

The doctor frowned but said, "I'll prescribe something to help you sleep."

Preston didn't sleep. He used his private room telephone and called Babak, but the number was no longer in service. He then telephoned his office and instructed Susan Humphrey, his administrative assistant, to forward all calls for other directorates and agencies to his hospital room. He also told her to forward his e-mails to his private e-mail address.

Susan Humphrey asked how he was feeling, to which he replied, "I could use a back rub, but for now I want you to do me a favor."

Preston thought about Susan's back rubs and more. She had talented hands. Susan was a busty beauty with thick honey blond hair, a flawless face with sensuous lips, and large green eyes. He asked her to fly to West Palm Beach, Florida, where he had left his laptop computer and some personal items. He authorized a round trip first class ticket and per diem, plus expenses. He gave her

Cynthia Morgan's address and told her keep the trip and her actions confidential.

Susan Humphrey understood Preston's use of the word confidential. He hired her not only for her shapely body and affectionate manner, but she had been around Washington and understood some of the men and women in their prominent positions. Discretion was more important than her other skills, of which she had many.

A full week had passed before he received the call that he dreaded. The voice was familiar: it was Babak Shirazi's, who soon handed the telephone to another man. Preston did not know the man by name but had talked to him on three occasions.

"Mr. Winn, I trust you are recuperating from your unfortunate accident?"

"Yes. It will take some time before I am up and about. Thank you for asking."

"And your family, are they well?"

"Yes, thank you."

The polite talk went on for a few minutes before the man said, "Mr. Winn, I expect that either the device or the advance will be forthcoming."

Preston thought about lying and telling the man he had the power pack, but with Babak there the chance that his charade would succeed was zero.

He said, "As I am sure you know, there was an unforeseen incident, but given enough time I can assure you I will provide a suitable device."

"Ah yes, time. You will have sufficient time; however, I expect the funds, advanced in good faith, to be returned within the week. Including, of course, interest accrued from the date we sent you the funds."

"A week? You can't possibly think I can—"

"Seven days from today, Mr. Winn. I will send you the account number. I almost forgot; the interest rate is twenty percent. Do not be late."

Preston heard the telephone click. The man had hung up.

He laid back and pressed the call button. He would need pain medication. Somehow, he had to find that damn power pack. He had spent some of the three million, which he had for over a month, and now the interest would eat up the money he'd salted away for a trip to Las Vegas.

Sending the money back was the smart thing to do, but the thought of giving three million dollars back, plus interest, was so distasteful, Preston immediately began planning. There were other power packs, but getting one in a week was almost impossible. He needed someone he could trust to go to Port Canaveral and find the damn power pack. After a few minutes, he dialed Susan Humphrey and said, "Susan, this is Preston. I would like you to drop by my hospital room again."

"Yes sir. Shall I come over this evening?"

"Yes. The sooner the better."

After Preston hung up, he thought about how he would handle this. He finally decided the best chance of success was the motivation of money: greed. He would let her in on his scheme and promise her half of the money if she found the power pack. A few seconds later, he revised the offer to one fourth. No use throwing away money. Maybe she would do it for less.

***

Ryan waited outside Megan's hospital room while the nursing assistants gave her a bath, changed her bedding and checked her catheter. After about ten minutes, the nursing assistant came out and gave Ryan an exaggerated smile. "You can go in now."

It had become routine. Ryan brought his books with him each morning and studied while she lay there. Her vital signs were being transmitted to a monitor at the nursing station via a portable transmitter. The portable transmitter would be useful for an ambulatory patient, but Megan did not move. She breathed normally and, when Ryan massaged her shoulders and legs, he thought she might have smiled. Megan's mother, father and brothers visited every day, but not all at once. Ryan was usually the last one to leave in the evening and the first to arrive in the morning. He had neglected his classes, but had dropped by and talked to most of his professors and explained his problem. Graduation was near and finals were uncomfortably close. He had a thesis paper to turn in and a number of administrative details to complete. If he was going to be accepted by the FBI, he would need letters of recommendation, but he wasn't sure how much weight the letters would carry.

Ryan sat close to Megan by moving a chair next to her bed, and he often touched her hand as he read. Sometimes he read aloud when he came across an interesting article or piece from his textbooks.

He was reviewing a text on the competing ideologies in social and political conflicts that have given rise to terrorism. He mumbled his own ideas regarding the confusion that reigned in America about the various religious and ethnic sects in Iraq when he felt Megan's hand quiver and then tighten on his hand. He looked over, and to his amazement, she was looking at him.

"Nurse!" he shouted, found Megan's call button and pushed it repeatedly.

A nurse and her assistant ran in to the room and said, "What is it?"

"Look. She's awake."

Megan's eyes followed Ryan and she tried to speak, but nothing came out. A nurse examined her and said she would notify a doctor. Ryan leaned close and Megan whispered, "Could I have water?"

Ryan rushed over to the pitcher of water on her nightstand. He hesitated, wondering if she could swallow without choking.

"Let me check with the doctor first," he said.

Megan's eyes moved around the room and she said, "Where am I?"

Ryan sat on the edge of her bed and began telling her what he knew of her condition and of the events leading to Magic finding her in the field behind the motel.

Megan looked puzzled but said, "I don't remember any of that. I do recall being pushed into a car trunk, but nothing else."

A young doctor entered the room with a nurse and asked Ryan to wait outside while he examined Megan. Five minutes later he came out and told Ryan he could go back in.

"How is she, doctor?"

"She appears to be fully conscious and aware of her surroundings. I've ordered some tests and will ask Doctor Shah, our neurologist, to look in on her."

Ryan went back in and then used Megan's telephone to call her mother. In the meantime, a nurse let Megan sip water slowly through a straw. Once Ryan had Mrs. Alvarez on the telephone, he held it up to Megan and said, "It's your mom."

***

Susan Humphrey rang the doorbell at Frank Kurns' modest home in Merritt Island, Florida. When he answered the door, she presented her DHS credentials and told him she was investigating the loss of a package. He asked her in and introduced his wife, Ellen. Susan asked if there was some place they could talk in private, as this was a matter of national security. Ellen excused herself, saying she had to do the dishes, and Frank led Susan into a room he called his den. It was no more than a room with two overstuffed chairs, a small TV, and three walls covered with family photos and a few souvenirs of Frank's four years in the Navy.

Susan, dressed in a simple but expensive business suit, sat back in one of the chairs, crossed her legs, and slipped a small recorder out of her handbag.

"I will be recording our conversation, Mr. Kurns," she said matter-of-factly.

Frank nodded and said, "What's this about?"

"Tell me about the events concerning the loss of a packing crate from warehouse number 7B on July second. I understand you own the company that provides security for that warehouse."

Frank rubbed his face and said, "Yeah, I'm the owner, but you'd never know it from the hours I put in." Then he asked, "Do you know a man named Winn?"

"Why do you ask?"

"Just curious. He was here before the crate disappeared. Then after it disappeared he came back and asked a lot of questions. Told me I wasn't supposed to talk about the crate. I guess it's okay to talk to you, being in the same organization and all?"

Susan wasn't sure what Preston Winn had told him but went on. "Please tell me what you know about the missing crate."

Frank paused and then said, "Okay. I was wondering if anybody was going to ask about it. I've been calling Ryan Quinn to ask him what to do, but we keep playing phone tag."

Susan tried not to show her excitement but said, "Then you have the crate?"

"Yeah. After the Coast Guard brought up that empty crate, Ali and me decided to look a little more. That dog of Ryan's acted like there was something down there, so the next day we dove. Actually, Ali dove, I never learned to use the scuba gear."

Leaning forward, Susan asked, "Then you have the crate?"

"Yeah. We put it back in warehouse 7B, but I haven't been able to reach the owner."

Susan stood and said, "Who else knows about this?"

Frank rubbed his face again before he said, "Let me see. Ali of course. I guess that's all except for me. Like I said, I never got through to Ryan."

Susan said, "I think you should take me to it, now."

"Okay, let me tell the little missus where I'm going."

Susan reached out and grabbed Frank's arm as he started out of the den and said, "Mr. Kurns, this is a very sensitive national security matter. Do not tell anyone, including your wife, about the crate."

"My lips are sealed."

"This Ali..."

Frank filled in with, "Ali Mossberg."

"Can you reach him?"

"Sure thing. In fact, he's at the port now. Came in at five."

"We'll take my car," Susan said as she put the recorder in her handbag and followed Frank out of the den.

The ride to Port Canaveral took ten minutes. It would have been quicker but work traffic clogged the roads. Frank directed her to the warehouse after stopping at the gate to contact Ali, and told him to meet them at 7B. He also picked up a key for the 7B office.

Frank was unlocking the office door when Ali arrived in a pickup truck.

"What's going on?" Ali said before noticing a woman standing by a car, using a cell phone.

Frank nodded toward Susan and said, "She's from the Department of Homeland Security. It's about that thing we found."

"Oh. Maybe she knows what it is."

"Maybe. I hope you didn't blab to anyone about it."

"I told the guys at the dive shop, before we dove."

"Anyone else?"

"No, mon. You said keep quiet; Ali, he keep quiet."

Susan had finished her call and walked up the stairs to the loading dock. She held out her credentials to Ali and said, "Mr. Mossberg, I am conducting an investigation into a crate stolen from this warehouse. Mr. Kurns tells me you found the crate. Is that correct?"

"Yeah, it's still in there." He motioned to the warehouse.

Susan put her credentials back in her handbag and followed Frank Kurns into the warehouse. Frank turned on the lights as they entered the warehouse and walked to a crate that sat in the center aisle. He put his hand on it and said, "Here it is."

Susan looked at a crate approximately four feet by four feet with faded markings on the outside, *Atlantica Foods*. Dried mud caked on the top.

Ali came up behind them and asked, "What is that thing?"

Susan looked at him for a moment before saying, "It is none of your concern."

Ali put his big hands up and said, "No problem."

Susan looked at the crate for a few seconds and then pushed it. It moved, but very little.

"How much does it weigh?" she asked.

Frank answered, "I don't know. Maybe two hundred, two-fifty."

Ali said, "You mean the crate or the thing?"

Susan turned and looked at Ali and then back at Frank before asking, "Have you been inside this crate?"

Frank sighed and said, "We did look but we put it back."

Susan said, "What did you see?"

Frank answered, "Not much. A lot of food; some cans, but mostly boxes of rice. And of course that thing that was wrapped up in bubble wrap."

Susan considered Frank's comments for a moment before she said, "Open it up. I want to see it."

Ali, anticipating her order, walked over to a corner and brought back a hammer and pry bar. He quickly loosened one end and let the food flow out on the floor. He reached in, pulled out a cardboard box, and opened the top. He shook out the contents on the floor, and a bundle of plastic bubble wrap rolled out along with the can goods.

"Be careful with that," Susan said. "It's very expensive."

Ali finished unwrapping a small package. It looked like a child's backpack and had the markings XSCMES on a hard plastic plate. Ali held it out to Susan and said, "Heavy for its size. Maybe twenty-five pounds; could be more."

Susan took it and noticed it felt slightly warm. She held it up to her ear and heard a faint whining sound, like wheels turning. It had two power receptacles and three switches.

"What's it do?" Frank asked.

Susan had to suppress her smile and thought, *it makes me rich, that's what it does.* She was a smart woman and had negotiated a full million dollars from Preston Winn once she knew what this little device could do. There had to be more buyers for these devices, and Susan intended to explore her chances for even more money. A million was great, but Susan already had her sights on more, much more. She placed the power pack on top of the empty crate and said, "Gentlemen, do you know what this is?"

Frank answered, "No, that's why I asked. It looks like a thick laptop computer."

She put on her most serious face and placed her hands on both Frank Kurns and Ali Mossberg's shoulders before saying in a conspiratorial tone, "This thing... device could mean the difference between life and death to thousands, no, millions of people. If news of this were to reach certain people, well, I shudder to think of the consequence."

Ali said, "No shit?"

Susan almost replied, no shit, but stayed in character and replied, "I am deadly serious. Neither of you must ever mentions this device to anyone, ever."

Frank asked, "What if the FBI asks?"

Susan frowned and said, "This is a matter of national security. The Department of Homeland Security will tell the FBI what they need to know."

"But what if they ask? Do I tell them to see you?"

This was not going as well as she had hoped. After a few minutes she said, "Let me make it clear. You may disavow any knowledge of this device and be protected by the law. You have my word."

Frank said, "Okay, but I thought the FBI worked with you DHS people."

"I can't discuss this case further except to say, if you tell anyone about finding this device, you will be prosecuted to the full extent of the law. Am I clear?"

Both Ali and Frank shrugged and Frank answered, "Clear."

Susan stared at Ali until he said, "Sure, you're clear like crystal. Ali don't talk about it or go to jail."

Susan lifted the small but heavy device and walked out of the warehouse. She paused in the doorway, looked back and said, "Destroy that crate."

As she drove off, Frank said, "Damn, there goes my ride."

CHAPTER 13

The days that followed Megan's release from the hospital were idyllic. Ryan decided to pull the nails out of my dog door; however, not before he scared the pee out of me. I heard him talking on the telephone with Megan. He was going to have a microchip inserted into me. The thought of some Orwellian device that controlled my mind had me shaking. I knew Ryan loved me, but why would he want to treat me like a science experiment? I'd been one long enough in Iran; I didn't think it was allowed in America.

On the day he took me to the vet's, I tried everything I could to stay at home. I stayed out in the backyard acting like I was using my toilet. When that didn't work, I went into the house and hid under Ryan's bed, but he found me. When we got to the vet's, I dug my paws into the sidewalk outside and refused to budge. While I am a big dog, Ryan is bigger, so he picked me up and carried me into the vet's waiting room. Inside there were six humans and as many animals: three dogs, two cats, and a large parrot. One of the dogs, a little Chihuahua who sat on the large lap of a middle-aged lady, snarled at me. Unbelievable. I could eat it and not even get heartburn, and it had the gall to snarl at me. Some dogs are nuts. The cats ignored me but the parrot gave me a funny look. I guess I couldn't blame it, I did look silly in Ryan's arms.

Ryan put me down and I stayed next to him, hoping he would change his mind, but he didn't. Eventually a lady came out and said, "You must be Magic."

I assumed she was talking to me, so to be polite I barked once. Wow, did that get that little Chihuahua going.

The lady led me into a room with a big metal table and I began to shake. I couldn't help it. My teeth were rattling and my whole body quivered. I had been strapped down on tables like that before. The last time some crazy man stuck electrodes into my head and stomach. After hooking me up to some machine, he began to torture me. First, he gave me little shocks, but later they grew stronger; so much so that my whole body went ridged and my muscles twitched beyond my control. The following day it started all over, but then the same madman used a hot probe and burned my nose, ears and butt. Then it got worse and I must have lost consciousness.

Ryan, who followed me in, bent down and petted my head. I looked up and wanted to ask, "Why are you doing this to me? You love me."

Then he said, "Steady, boy. This won't hurt. Now if you get out, they can use a scanner to see where you belong."

I felt a little better. The lady rubbed some medicine on my shoulder, and a man came in. He introduced himself to Ryan and to me, then the lady handed him what looked like a hypodermic needle. He gave me a shot in the skin near my shoulder and said, "Now, that didn't hurt, did it?"

I barked once and the little Chihuahua in the waiting room went crazy again.

What a relief. I knew Ryan wouldn't let anyone hurt me, but still my puppyhood memories kept coming back. When we got home, Ryan pulled out the nails to my door from the kitchen to the backyard. Boy, it felt good to run in and out whenever I pleased.

Ryan spent a few days talking to the FBI and other agencies. Unfortunately, he didn't tell me much about it, but his telephone calls to Megan gave me some idea. The FBI was still looking for Megan's kidnapper and suspected terrorist. I think Ryan may have taken copies of my e-mails to the FBI. I didn't know what I'd do if they traced them back to me. There were a lot of unanswered questions, like who was Mr. Kunastros and who did he work for, but I let the FBI worked on that while I enjoyed having Ryan back to play with me.

A few weeks after Megan came home from the hospital, Ryan started bringing her to his house during the day. We got to be very good friends. I didn't try to sniff her and Ryan let me come in while she was there. We watched TV together and went to the beach and to the river. Sometimes we took long walks in the evening when it wasn't too hot. Ryan bought a two-place kayak and took Megan on short trips down the Intra Coastal Waterway to Mosquito Lagoon. He took me on short rides near our house and I had a great time. Two porpoises swam close to Ryan's little boat and looked at me. They looked intelligent. I barked and they blew mist out of their blowholes and did a few flips. I got the feeling they were saying, "Try doing this, dog."

Ryan graduated with a 3.9 GPA from the University of Central Florida; however, I couldn't go to the graduation. I did attend the party at Ryan's house that night. Ryan doesn't drink very often, but he did imbibe that night. His friend, Ted Lewis, gave a toast and a few old school chums came by; also a few old girlfriends came by and that caused a little tension. Megan acted as if it didn't bother her when one of the gals gave Ryan a big hug and then a kiss, but I could feel the vibrations across the room.

Ryan's parents were at the graduation, but then they drove back home to Tampa that night. They dropped by and met me first, and I liked them both. They are kind and caring humans who have aged well. His mother took Ryan into the kitchen and asked when he was going to marry Megan. He said, "As soon as I can get a good job and save some money." Ryan's dad took him out on the porch, pushed some money into his hand, and asked when he was going to marry that girl. He got the same answer.

Ryan applied for the FBI but his NCIC—National Crime Information Center—record turned up a problem. Apparently, he was still under investigation by the Department of Homeland Security, but try as he might, Ryan could not get the record cleared. Megan finally suggested that he have Ted Lewis take the case and try to get a federal judge to force the DHS to respond to Ryan's inquires.

Ryan talked to Ted, but like most things involving the law, it took time. During that wait, Ryan took a job at a local steakhouse serving tables. I know it doesn't make sense, a college graduate, a former Marine officer, the captain of his high school football team, waiting tables.

As he explained to Megan, "It's only temporary until my record is cleared and I begin my career with the FBI. Besides, I am making more money now than I did as a night watchman."

With Ryan gone during the evenings, I started watching more television. I really enjoy Jeopardy. Some of the contestants are smarter than I am, or at least they have knowledge that I do not have at this time. Which brings me to the next reason that it was a very good time for me. I enrolled in an online university and am studying computer science and philosophy. It took some tricky manipulations, and I won't bore you with all the details, but I opened a bank account with an online bank that advertised no social security number needed. I borrowed twenty-five dollars from Ryan's online bank account, which I later gave back, and he will probably never notice the credit and debt to his bank account. He leaves his password and user ID on a scratch pad by the computer, which is not smart.

I had been writing a column on animal care for one of the few online magazines or eZines that pays. I have a how-to book on dog training in the works and a few other ideas. The money was not great but it paid for my college courses.

It took three months for Ted Lewis to get anywhere with a very busy federal judge, but when it looked like something was going to happen, it did, but not what we expected. Some men tried to kill Ryan.

***

Susan Humphrey sat on the corner of Preston Winn's expensive antique desk. Preston didn't like her new persona, but there was little he could do with his new partner. He had to admit, she could get things done. She seemed to know everyone's secretary and administrative assistants by their first names, and not just in the DHS. She knew people at Justice, State, Defense and even at the White House. One day he found her talking to someone at the super secret NSA.

She wore a short skirt and showed long, well-shaped legs as she crossed them. A demonstration of the new powered exoskeleton by the civilian contractor had gone better than expected, and Susan was already outlining her plan to steal one and have it duplicated in China. She also had a line on the new power pack.

She moved closer and Preston could smell the expensive perfume he had given her for her birthday. She spoke softly into his ear, "Sweetheart, stop worrying. I can lose that power pack in a ton of paperwork. No one will be able to follow it, no one. Trust me."

He reached up and patted her face. He didn't trust her but said, "Of course I trust you, believe me, but the thought of your beautiful body behind bars makes me nervous."

She moved off his desk and paced the spacious office before saying, "It should, but it won't happen if you listen to me."

Preston pushed his chair out from his desk and spun it around to look out the wide window behind him. After reflecting on Susan's plan to eliminate any witnesses, he said, "These people, the ones who will do this thing... you can trust them?"

"Trust them? Sure, like I trust all hired hitmen, but they are professionals. He'll simply disappear."

"What if he doesn't?"

"For heaven sakes, Preston, for a sophisticated man sometimes you can be so... " She searched for the right word but came out with "...thick."

Preston did not like her tone but would wait until the time was right, then he would get rid of her. Now he said, "How do you know they won't snitch if they get caught?"

She had been over this but she said again slowly, "They will not know where the order came from, or why. They have been promised to go into the witness protection program. They think it's part of the deal. Some hush hush CIA thing. I've covered my tracks and it cost me a few favors."

Preston smiled. Blame it on the CIA; sounded like a popular Washington game.

Susan went back to Preston's desk and picked up his telephone. She looked at him and said, "Do we do it or not? It's your ass too."

Preston nodded and Susan dialed a number from memory. She then waited until someone answered and said, "It's on."

She hung up and said, "Now what do we do about those other two, Kurns and Mossberg?"

Preston thought for a minute and said, "They haven't been a problem. Only Quinn and his damn lawyer have been making waves. Besides, if both Kurns and Mossberg... disappear, it's going to draw too much attention to me. The local police know my name."

"Yes, that wasn't your shining hour."

Preston didn't want to be reminded. He stood and pulled Susan to him. "Let's take a long lunch."

***

Two men watched Ryan's house for a week. They ate dinner at the steakhouse where he worked and twice followed him to a woman's house. On Monday, Ryan's day off, they watched him take the same woman for a ride in a kayak. They went back to his home, knocked on the door, and a large dog came to the door and started to bark. They left.

On Tuesday they received a telephone call telling them to proceed with their assignment.

These were large men, tall as Ryan but thicker, and older but not soft. They knew each other well; they had been in business together since their early twenties. Their skin was not darkly tanned and they didn't sound like native Floridians. Their accents were northeastern and their dress fashionable. They bought shorts and sport shirts at a local store; however, they kept their dark dress shoes and black socks.

They bought a 19-foot fishing boat after reading the *Penny Saver* paper. The man who sold it to them offered to give them a demonstration ride as they looked like green easterners, but they declined, saying they had lots of experience with small boats, which was marginally true.

A rusty boat trailer came with the boat, along with a Mercury outboard motor, fuel tank, two oars, and one life jacket. The man, who called himself Jake, paid in cash and said he would take care of the registration the next day. The other man, who called himself Lew, hooked up the trailer to the new trailer hitch on their rented Cadillac SUV.

The men took the boat to the Edgewater Park boat ramp and tried out their new purchase. Satisfied with its performance, they pulled it out of the water and drove to their motel.

They continued to follow Ryan the rest of the week. On Thursday, Ryan left early for a run with the dog that was usually at his side. The men knocked on Ryan's front door and then went around back, through the gate. They saw the kayak sitting upside down on wooden blocks. The man called Jake examined the fiberglass kayak and quickly attached a very small tracking transmitter under the transom. The man called Lew took a small GPS device out of his pocket and looked at the display. He gave the man called Jake a thumbs up and they both left.

The following Monday morning, the GPS device emitted a beep and both men dressed quickly. Jake checked the magazine in his .22 caliber pistol. He attached a silencer and put it in the new fishing vest he bought at Kmart. Lew checked the magazine in his 9 mm pistol, and put it in the holster under his new fishing vest, also purchased at Kmart. Both men went out and loaded the fishing boat with four concrete blocks and twenty feet of chain they purchased at an ACE hardware store. They worked together with the smooth movements of a well-oiled machine. At the last moment, Lew went back into the motel room and brought out a cooler filled with water, ice and two beers.

Lew drove and Jake watched the GPS. He didn't look at his partner as he said, "He's gonna pick up the babe. Damn shame." They had learned that her name was Megan and knew her address.

Lew answered, "Yeah, good looking broad. Wish we had more time for her."

Jake smiled and watched the GPS again. "He's stopping at her house. May as well get this tub in the water before he gets there."

Lew didn't answer but drove directly to the Edgewater boat ramp and began backing the trailer into the water. Ten minutes later, Jake started the engine and backed away from the ramp. Lew parked the SUV and walked back to the seawall where Jake waited. He carefully stepped down into the boat while Jake held it steady. They motored slowly out from the seawall and waited. A few minutes later, Ryan arrived with the kayak in the back of his pickup truck. He parked it and then carried the kayak to the sandy beach on the opposite side of the park, where bathers waded in the shallow water. Megan followed him and Magic brought up the rear.

Ryan slid the kayak into the shallow water and Megan handed him an oar. She kept one for herself and stepped into the shallow water after throwing her flip-flops up on the sand.

"Watch my shoes, Magic."

Magic barked once and began sniffing around. Ryan pushed the kayak out farther and yelled back to Magic, "We won't be long. Don't go away."

Magic barked and started digging furiously in the sand. A sand crab dug in even deeper.

The two men in the fishing boat watched Ryan and Megan paddle out from the park and head north against the current. There were hundreds of small islands between the Intra Coastal Waterway and the peninsula that divides the mainland from the Atlantic Ocean. In a shallow draft boat, exploring the islands can be an adventure; however, getting lost is one of the major hazards as one island looks much like the others. Ryan grew up fishing with his father in those waters and knew them well, but still exercised caution so as not to become lost in the maze of islands.

The two men could follow him with their GPS device, but if the water was too shallow, they would run aground. They watched and waited. If Ryan paddled out of the main channel, he would be hidden by the islands, which is what they wanted. If he stayed in water deeper than the 18-inch draft of their boat, they would move in and quickly kill Ryan and Megan. They would put both bodies into their boat, release Ryan's kayak, then take the bodies north to

Ponce Inlet, and out into the ocean. Once out of sight of other boats, they would weigh the bodies down with chains tied to concrete blocks and dump the bodies overboard.

Ryan didn't cooperate. He paddled in the channel for fifteen minutes and then returned, which only took ten minutes with the current behind him. Once back at the park, Megan climbed out and Magic climbed in. She took one paddle with her and went back to Ryan's pickup truck to open a cooler with water and soft drinks.

Ryan took Magic across the channel, let him run loose on a small island for a few minutes, and then returned to get Megan with the cooler of water and soda. Then they all sat on the bank of the small island and watched the other boaters sail by.

The men watched them but did nothing more. Ryan, Megan and the dog were in plain sight of the people sitting on the park benches. They would have to wait until the time was right. After almost an hour, Jake said, "Let's go back, I gott'a use the john. Besides, they ain't going nowhere."

Lew maneuvered the boat close to the loading ramp and Jake stepped off into shallow water, soaking his expensive Italian leather shoes. He came back ten minutes later and said, "I got a better idea. What say we bug that heap of his and catch him alone? I'm getting tired of this shit."

Lew didn't argue. His aftershave attracted the mosquitoes and they buzzed around his head. He swatted at them ineffectively and said, "Go get the caddy and back the trailer up."

The two men got their boat back on the trailer and then walked slowly past Ryan's pickup. Lew watched while Jake bent down and attached a very small tracking device under the lip of the rear right fender. Then they went back to their SUV, opened their cooler and took out the two beers, which they drank before throwing the cans out the window. They were professionals and never drank on the job. On the way back to their motel, they stopped at a liquor store and bought a case of beer.

***

We had a great time with Ryan's kayak. Maybe he will buy a three-place one someday and we can all ride together. I found a big turtle who didn't want to play, and watched fish swimming in the shallow water. Later, I found an old Indian arrowhead and took it back to Megan. She gave me a big hug and said, "Thank you, Magic. I will treasure this always." She is such a honey. She then said, "I know a place where you can run and play."

Ryan asked her where that was and she said, "One of my brother's favorite spots. Divine Springs. It's in the Ocala National Park. We can camp out and kayak, or hike the trails, or you can scuba dive in the springs."

Ryan seemed like he was interested and said, "I have tomorrow off."

"Okay," Megan said, "I'll have Momma pack us some food and you can pick me up bright and early. Oh, and bring something for Magic."

Ryan shuttled us back to the park on the other side of the Intra Coastal Waterway channel, or Indian River, as it is called. When we got to the truck, I was about to jump in the back, but waited for Ryan to lower the tailgate, when I noticed a new scent. I sniffed around and found something under the rear fender. It was small, about the size of a coin but thicker. I rubbed it with my nose and was about to bite it when Ryan dropped the tailgate and said, "Up you go."

I jumped in but didn't feel right. As far as I could tell, two men had been touching Ryan's truck. One smelled of aftershave. I didn't like their scent. Something was wrong.

The next morning, before the sun was up, Ryan was up and packing the truck with his scuba equipment and Kayak. He filled a backpack with BugOff, a snakebite kit, compass, sunscreen, a small .22 caliber pistol with snake shot, protein bars, doggy snacks— beef flavor—socks, hunting knife, a dog whistle, which he had never used, and a few things I didn't recognize.

Ryan drove to Megan's house, but she wasn't ready, so he had a cup of coffee with Rose Alvarez. I stayed in the pickup. Ryan asked me if I wanted to go in, but I didn't bark or jump out of the truck bed. That cat was probably still there.

After about thirty minutes, I remembered that thing under Ryan's fender. I figured it was a good time to investigate. I jumped down from the pickup and began sniffing. It was still there. I nudged it couple of times but it didn't move. It was then I heard Ryan yell, "Get back in that truck. You know better."

I jumped back in, which is much harder than jumping down. A minute later, Megan came out. Ryan followed with a large cooler and bottled water.

The ride to Divine Springs was longer than I thought it would be, but I enjoyed the ride. The different smells were like a slide show with new and exciting scents every few seconds. By the time we turned off of the paved road and entered a dirt road to Divine Springs, I was having sensory overload. The Ocala National Forest area is huge, mile after mile of wilderness. A dog could get lost in there and never be found. Maybe not me, but your average dog.

Ryan drove down the bumpy dirt road that twisted and turned like a snake between groves of old oak, pine and palm trees. We were only a few miles off the main road, but it might as well have been a thousand. The forest seemed to swallow us up. I smelt things I had never smelled before. Some were a little frightening.

Eventually we came to a sign that told us to stay to the right. Another sign said, "This way to Devine Springs."

Divine Springs was much smaller than I imagined. An area of about three acres had been cleared. Ryan parked the truck and went into a little store with a sign that said, "Pay here." Megan stayed with me.

When Ryan came back, he said, "The lady said we can drive to the springs or to the river."

Megan said, "Let's go to the springs. You can dive. Magic and I will take the kayak up the stream that leads from it to the river."

So off we went down another dirt road, this one narrow and winding. Ten minutes later, we came to a clearing.

Megan announced, "We're here. Why don't you pull the truck over there," she pointed, "out of the sun in those trees?"

Ryan parked in the grove of trees and under the limbs of a giant oak. It was a great spot, plenty of shade and secluded. I jumped down to stretch my legs. Ryan unloaded the pickup and carried the kayak over to the springs, which was about three hundred feet across and shaped like a pear. Water from the underground spring ran into a stream, which disappeared through a grove of palms and tall pines.

While Ryan and Megan took everything over to the spring, I decided to look around, but first I wanted to check out that thing under the fender. I nudged it a couple of times but it still held, so I pulled it off with my teeth. Then I saw the strangest dog I have ever seen. It had on a mask and walked toward the truck.

When the strange dog saw me, it bared its teeth. I barked and accidentally swallowed the darn device. I hoped it wouldn't give me gas.

Later I looked up the strange dog on the internet and found it was called a raccoon. We didn't have those in Iran. The raccoon was smaller than I am, but he had sharp teeth and I wasn't looking for trouble, so I ignored his rudeness.

Ryan called me. I ran up and saw him dressed in swimming trunks and wearing a cylinder on his back. He was also wearing funny looking shoes called swim fins.

He said, "Magic, you go with Megan and don't let anything happen to her."

Like I would let anything hurt her. Megan was safe with me. Ryan pulled on a diver's mask, stuck a small mouthpiece into his mouth, waved and slipped under the water. A second later he surfaced and yelled, "Wow, that is cold!"

Megan laughed and said, "You've never been to a spring before?"

Ryan didn't answer but dove, and soon bubbles came to the surface.

Megan stood there looking down for a long time. I could see Ryan below the surface. The water was clear as crystal. Finally, she said, "Come on, Magic. Let's take a ride."

Megan let me get in the front seat of the kayak, which made sense because I have better eyes, ears and sense of smell. She paddled, which would have been impractical for me.

CHAPTER 14

Lew drove the Cadillac SUV while Jake watched the handheld GPS display with the tracking receiver. "What are these people? They get up before the damn sun is up. It's not natural."

Jake agreed but didn't answer. He was still pissed off and didn't talk until he had at least one cup of coffee. Today he had none. They rushed out of the motel after the receiver beeped telling them that the pickup truck was moving. The transmitter had a limited range and they didn't want to miss again. They wanted to get back to Philly and their friends and family.

The big caddy rode smoothly over the first dirt road they turned on, but the second one bounced them around, almost throwing the boat off the trailer.

"How far away?" Lew asked.

"Mile and a half. Looks like they stopped."

"Tell me when we're about a half mile back. Don't want to run into them sudden like."

"Right," Jake said and laid the tracker down on the center console while he checked the magazine in his weapon. Satisfied it was fully loaded, he shoved it back in the loose pocket of the fishing vest he wore.

In a few minutes he said, "Slow down, we're almost there."

"Sign back there said Divine Springs. Must be where they're goin'"

"Yeah, but they're moving again. Step on it."

Lew slowed when they came to a clearing with a few small buildings, more like shacks. A sign told them to "Pay here," but Jake said, "They went that way," and pointed to a small one-lane dirt road that led to the west.

Lew drove on as a woman came out of the small building and yelled something at them, which they couldn't hear and ignored. They weren't going to slow down and miss Ryan Quinn again.

After awhile Jake said, "Looks like they're stopping again. Slow down."

Lew drove slowly until they were only two-tenths of a mile away from Ryan, according to the tracking device. Then Jake said, "Son-of-a-bitch. They're moving again. Move."

The big Cadillac SUV barreled into the clearing next to the spring and slid to a stop. Lew and Jake both looked around for another road that would follow the slow moving blip on their tracking device. Finally Jake said, "They must have found a way through those trees over there." He pointed to a grove of scrub pines and maneuvered the big machine toward them. A narrow path opened up and Lew carefully drove between two pines and followed the path, scraping the sides of the Cadillac.

"Why the hell would they go through here?" Lew asked.

"Beats the shit outta me. These hicks are nuts anyway. Maybe he's growing some pot out here. Don't want nobody to know."

"Yeah, that makes sense." Lew then added, "Which way are they going?"

Jake studied the display and said, "Hard to tell. Try turning left."

Lew found space between trees and crept along, occasionally dragging the bottom of the SUV on shrubs and mounds of dirt. After a few minutes he said, "Are we getting closer?"

"Na, maybe we should go back. They gotta come back to the road."

Lew stopped the big SUV and looked back. He put it in reverse and moved a few feet before he ran the trailer into a tree he had missed in the rear view mirror.

After cursing loudly, he slammed the SUV into forward and spun the tires. He tried again and the tires dug a trench in the soft sandy soil.

"Now what?" Jake asked.

"Now we are stuck, asshole. Get out and see if you can push."

Jake bristled. He didn't take that disrespect from anyone, but now was not the time to waste Lew.

Jake got out and stepped into soft water-soaked sand. He cursed but walked to the back of the caddy and saw that both rear tires had sunk almost to middle of the rim. He walked forward and lost one shoe as the wet sand pulled it off. He stopped to retrieve it but lost his balance and stepped into the wet sand with his bare foot. He took a few seconds to control his anger and then he yelled to Lew, "I'll try pushing and you pull ahead in low."

"Okay. Tell me when you're ready."

Jake went back, placed his hands on the rear of the caddy and yelled, "Go ahead."

Lew slowly pushed the throttle, but spun the tires again without moving the heavy machine. Jake looked down at the mud and sand that covered his legs and chest. He walked forward, opened the driver's door and looked at Lew, who burst out laughing, which was not the thing to do.

Jake pulled out his pistol, a Beretta 9 mm semi-automatic, and stuck it in Lew's face, before he said coldly, "Get outta the car." When Lew hesitated he grabbed him by the shirtfront and pulled, but Lew was wearing his seat belt and only moved a few inches. Infuriated, Jake reached down and pounded on the belt release. It finally gave, but now Lew held his own pistol to Jake's face and said quietly, "Let it go."

Jake waited long enough to redeem his pride and slowly lowered his pistol. Lew kept his pistol pointed a few seconds longer before he lowered it to his lap. Both men breathed heavily and looked away. They had been friends since boyhood, but this damn swamp and the stuck caddy was driving them both mad.

When their breathing was back to normal, or close to it, Jake said, "Look, these jerks are moving so slow we can catch them on foot. Leave the damn truck here."

Lew climbed out of the SUV and looked around. "Which way are they going?"

"Looks like that way." He pointed north.

Both men began walking in the soft water-soaked sand, occasionally stopping to check the receiver GPS. Thirty minutes later, soaked in perspiration, with bugs swarming around then, Jake said, "Hey, this thing says the battery is low. We better get back to the caddy and plug it into the charger."

Lew shook his head and said, "What next? Are we closer?"

Jake looked at the display again and said, "Yeah, I think so."

"What the hell does, 'I think so,' mean? Are we?"

"They've been moving in a circle or something like it. Here, you look at the damn thing."

Jake thrust the GPS receiver into Lew's hand, which was filthy with sweat and mud.

Lew said, "How could they drive that damn truck in circles in this place? Maybe they got out and walked. No, maybe they took that kayak down a river."

Jake said, "Listen, numb nuts. If they did that, you'd have two of those little blips on the screen. Not one."

Lew realized that with a transmitter on both the kayak and the truck, Jake was right. There would be two blips, but he didn't like Jake's tone of voice, and he really didn't like being called "numb nuts."

Lew stopped and looked at the display. "Let's go back to the caddy. I'm tired of this shit. The feds can kiss my ass. I ain't gonna testify. And I don't give a rat's ass what you do."

They turned around and walked about a hundred feet before Jake said, "Is this the way we came?"

Lew looked around and said, "Yeah, I think so. Sure. Well, maybe?"

***

The stream Megan took me down was amazing. I saw animals that were hard to describe. Alligators sunbathed on the banks and tall herons walked on incredibly thin legs in the shallow water near the bank. Ospreys dove down to snatch fish out of the water and once I saw a black bear drinking the fresh spring water. He looked up once, but other than that, ignored us. When Megan saw him she whispered to me, "Magic, quiet. Don't bark."

I didn't want to start trouble with that guy even though he looked peaceful. When we got back, Megan said she was tired.

Ryan was sitting on a park table eating a sandwich. She dug into the cooler and pulled out a cold soda and some chips.

After I made myself embarrassingly obvious by laying my head on her lap and looking up with my best puppy eyes imitation, she said, "Momma sent something just for you."

I barked and acted happy, which was easy, because I was. Ryan and Megan are the best things that could ever happen to me. I would die for them. Thirty minutes later I almost did.

Megan unwrapped a huge roast beef bone and told me not to make a mess, which I did, but how else can you eat a big juicy bone covered with tasty meat and fat? Rose Alvarez sure knows how to make a dog's day.

A little sand on it didn't ruin the taste, and before long, I had the bone clean. I then went off, dug a hole and buried it. Don't ask me why. I have no idea. It was purely impulse.

After they finished eating, Megan said she wanted to sun bathe. When she slipped off her shorts and blouse, I was surprised to see she was wearing a blue bathing suit. There wasn't much to it, but it wasn't one of those string bikinis I've seen at the beach. Ryan said he had a novel by Jeremy Robinson he wanted to read, so I trotted off to explore. Another family had arrived while we were eating but they stayed on the other side of the clearing. They had two small children that looked like they would keep the adults busy chasing them. I like children, but I'm careful. They can hurt you while laughing.

I followed a trail for awhile and then picked up a faint but familiar scent. I followed it for another ten minutes, and it grew stronger. Finally, I saw a large blue SUV with a boat and trailer. How it got that far in the woods I didn't know, but once I got close, I realized it was empty. I sniffed it and at once recognized the scent. It was the same one on the little device I swallowed and on Ryan's truck back at the park in Edgewater. I wanted to go back and find Ryan, but how was I going to explain what I had found?

Instead, I followed the scent of two men away from the big SUV. It was an easy trail to follow. Their body odor was strong and one wore an aftershave with mint in it. About a half mile later,

I heard their voices. They were arguing and cursing each other. I thought they might fight, but as I moved closer, I saw that they were sitting against the trunk of a rotten palm tree. They looked a mess. I laid still and listened.

One of them said, "Why you think the feds want Quinn taken out?"

"How should I know? If I ever get out of here, I am going to cut that Quinn guy's guts out. Maybe his pretty little girlfriend too."

"After me. I think I'll let her watch."

That did it; I rushed toward them. No one was going to hurt my humans. I wanted to separate the men, because two against one is dangerous for me. I ran at full speed and managed to catch one off guard. I hit him from the side and managed to rip the side of his face, but I missed his throat.

I spun quickly and attacked again, but this time he saw me coming and kicked out as I was almost on him. His foot hit me in the snout and I fell back. It brought tears to my eyes, but I jumped up and started at him again. This time I dodged his foot and sank my teeth between his legs. He screamed as I pulled away and I saw the other man out of the corner of my eye. He was on his feet now and kicked me in the side, knocking me away from the first man. It knocked the wind out of me, but I was able to get back to my feet before he could kick again. This time I decided to back away and think how I could separate them, but thinking too long in a dogfight, or human fight, is not a good idea. The man, who was standing, drew a big pistol out of his vest and shot me. I felt the impact that threw me back into the sand. He was aiming again, and I jerked to one side. The sand next to me exploded and the sound was deafening. I rolled away from him and scrambled to my feet. He was aiming again and I turned and ran as fast as I could, which wasn't too fast as my shoulder was numb and my right front leg refused to work properly. However, luck was with me, or a greater power, and I managed to get a tree between us. I thought he might shoot the tree down because he kept firing. When he stopped for a moment, I took off again. I made my way back toward the spring, taking a short cut I knew instinctively was there.

I heard Ryan blowing his new dog whistle and heard his voice calling me before I got to the clearing. Both he and Megan came running to me and I tried to jump up in Ryan's arms, but I just fell down and passed out.

***

Ryan knelt next to Magic and examined him closely. Magic was unconscious and bleeding. Ryan picked him up in his arms and ran back to his truck. He laid Magic carefully on the front seat and said to Megan, who was out of breath from the run, "In my backpack is a first aid kit. Get it."

She found the first aid kit in the back of the truck and quickly handed it to Ryan.

"He's lost a lot of blood. Give me that compress bandage and some tape."

Megan handed him the sterile compress bandage and the roll of tape and asked, "What happened? He's covered with blood!"

"Looks like he's been shot. I see an entrance wound. We have to get him to a doctor and stop the bleeding."

"Think it was the shooting we heard in the distance?"

"Could be." Ryan moved Magic's thick fur out of the way and probed with his fingers. "Okay. I see where it came out."

He placed the bandage over the entrance wound and ran tape around Magic's neck and down between his front legs. He then placed another bandage over the ragged exit wound and wrapped more tape over Magic's withers and under his chest.

"I'll ride in the back with him," Ryan said. "You drive."

"No, you drive, I'll hold him on my lap in the front."

Ryan didn't argue, and he didn't bother to load his kayak or scuba gear. He took off with Magic on Megan's lap. She still wore her bathing suit, which was now getting soaked with blood.

Ryan only slowed at the Divine Springs entrance to yell out to the lady standing in the shade of a porch. "Where's the closest vet? My dogs been shot."

"He's been shot? Where?" she asked.

"Back there. Now, where's the vet?"

"Oh, that would be in Silver Springs."

"Thanks, "Ryan said, and hit the accelerator pedal. The old truck fishtailed and a plume of dust rose behind it as it careened down the dirt road. When he turned onto the paved road, he said to Megan, "In the glove compartment is a cell phone. Use it to find the vet's in Silver Springs. Then tell them we are bringing in a wounded dog. Get the driving directions."

Megan did as she was told, and soon they skidded to a stop in front of Silver Springs Animal Hospital. Ryan rushed in with Magic as Megan wiped off Magic's blood with a towel and pulled on her shorts and blouse. By the time she got into the waiting room, Ryan and Magic were in an examination room. Magic was still unconscious.

Megan sat down on a plastic chair and waited. She feared that Magic wasn't going to make it. She loved the big affectionate pooch, but worried about what Ryan would do if he lost Magic. He had told her about Magic saving his life in Iraq, but only after she kept after him. Ryan seldom spoke about his two tours in Iraq and his short deployment to Afghanistan, except to tell her about some of the friends he had made.

Megan was deep in thought when a woman came out and said, "It may take a while; Doctor Spenser is going to operate on Magic. Would you like to come in and see him now?"

"Yes, of course. Is he all right?"

The woman, dressed in a blue smock and gray slacks, didn't answer Megan but led her into an inner office and then into an examination room. Ryan stood next to a metal table. Magic lay on the table as if asleep.

She made eye contact with Ryan, who was gently petting Magic. The bandages had been removed and Magic's fur had been shaved on his right shoulder and part of his chest. The entrance wound, on his chest, looked like a swollen red pimple the size of a dime. The exit wound on his shoulder was larger and jagged. It still oozed blood.

Ryan said, "They are about to give him plasma and then operate to repair the torn muscles. They looked at his x-rays a few minutes ago."

Megan touched Magic's head. He didn't move. She asked, "How is he?"

Ryan seemed to have trouble speaking but finally said, "I don't know."

***

Preston Winn tapped his finger nervously on his antique desk while he waited for Susan Humphrey to get off the telephone with her connection to the Justice Department. When she finally put the telephone down, he said, "Well?"

She looked out the window behind his desk before saying, "Nobody's heard from them in over two weeks. Nothing. It's like they vanished off the earth."

Preston swung his chair around and faced her. "Well, they sure as hell didn't get rid of the troublesome Mr. Quinn. Our legal department wants me to tell them what he wants to know. They don't want some judge nosing around in our business any more than I do."

Susan kept looking out of the window but said, "If you hadn't used your muscle to get him investigated, we wouldn't have this problem. Can't you just call off your dogs and leave him be? Maybe that's all he wants."

"He wants his damn NCIC record and any other record cleaned. It's out of my hands now."

Now she turned to face him. "Use that Ivy League trained brain of yours and do something."

"It would have been easier if he disappeared. Now I have to convince a number of people that he was never a problem. It's like stopping a snowball that's rolling down a mountain. It keeps getting bigger and bigger."

Susan Humphrey didn't try to hide her disgust. She said, "We've got a multi-million dollar payday if we get those new exoskeletons and another power pack. That snowball better melt damn quick or your ass is grass."

She then walked out even though Preston shouted, "I didn't tell you to leave!"

***

Ryan sat across from attorney Ted Lewis. "Not good news," Ted said. "The DHS has filed and now we have to wait for the judge to rule on it."

Ryan, clearly irritated, said, "What the hell do they want? I haven't done a damn thing. They can't do that, can they?"

Ted sighed and put his feet up on his desk. "Look, I know it is a pain, but in the end you'll be cleared. They're dragging their feet, and I don't know why."

"Well, that's what I'm paying you for. To find out."

Ted smiled and said, "Matter of fact, you are not paying me. I'm doing this pro bono because I am a great guy, and I want to keep Megan working for me. By the way, when are you going to marry her?"

Ryan shook his head. This lawyer business was driving him crazy. He wanted to get on with his life, join the FBI, marry Megan, have a child—that was Megan's idea—and rip the heart out of the person who shot his beloved Magic.

Ryan stood and offered his hand to Ted. "Thanks, Ted. I know you are doing your best, but to quote my old battalion commander, 'Sometimes, son, your best is not good enough'."

Ted shrugged. Ryan had a way of getting to the heart of a matter. Ted knew he was a small-town lawyer and he was up against some very big guns. Still, he felt confident. Maybe there was something he could do to speed up the process. Of course, if Ryan married Megan and moved to God knew where, he would be losing a great paralegal and a real piece of eye candy.

Ted shook Ryan's hand and said, "Stay in touch. And, Ryan."

"Yeah?"

"Marry Megan before she gets away."

Ryan hesitated before saying, "Get my record cleared, Ted. I'll take care of Megan."

Ted watched his friend walk out of the office, stopping in the front office to bend over and give Megan a quick buss on the cheek before saying, "Watch out for that dirty old man in there." He motioned toward Ted's office door, where Ted now stood grinning.

Ryan left Ted's office and drove to the Marion County Sheriff's district office in Silver Springs. It was the Forest District where Ryan reported Magic being shot, and although he doubted they would send a deputy out searching, he was surprised when he received a telephone asking if he could come in and answer a few questions.

Ryan said he would do anything to help catch the person who shot Magic, and made an appointment to meet a Deputy Sheriff Clive Williams.

Ryan took a seat in front of Deputy Sheriff Clive Williams, who Ryan guessed to be in his late forties, but was fit and not the false stereotype of fat southern sheriffs; however, he did have a distinct southern accent.

They had already met in an outer office, so the deputy started by reading Ryan's initial complaint.

"So, Mr. Quinn, what makes you sure your dog was shot by a pistol, or as you said, a handgun?"

"Because it sounded like a handgun. A semi-automatic. Whoever fired, fired quickly. Maybe emptied a whole magazine."

"Did the vet take bullets out of your dog?"

"No, it was just one and it passed through the skin on his chest, then through the muscles of his shoulder and out."

"So I guess you can't be sure it was not a rifle. Maybe some deer hunter?"

"I know the sound of a handgun and a rifle when I hear one. It was a handgun."

"I see." The deputy opened a file on his desk and handed a picture to Ryan.

"Ever see this man?"

Ryan looked at a large glossy photograph of a sunburned man needing a shave, with glazed eyes.

He handed it back and said, "No, never seen him. He looks sick."

"Yeah. Wandering around in the forest for a week will do that to a fella. Lucky to be alive."

"I think I heard something on the news about him. What's that got to do with my dog?"

"Well, he claims his partner was attacked by a rabid dog."

"Magic isn't rabid, and he sure wouldn't attack anyone."

"I see. You sure about that?"

"I'm sure. Can he describe the dog?"

"That might be hard to do. Seems he's missing. Apparently they came across a bear and the bear attacked his partner."

"I didn't hear that on the news."

"We haven't confirmed it yet. Don't want to get people worried for nothing. The man said when his partner shot the bear with a little .22 pistol, the bear came at them, but his partner couldn't run fast because the dog had ripped his private parts up pretty good."

After a minute, Ryan said, "So you think Magic attacked this guy and he shot him?"

The deputy didn't answer at first. He leaned back in his chair and said, "If we find the remains, which could be a problem if the critters get at him, but I guess we could match the dog bites with your dog."

"You'd be wasting your time."

"Maybe. But we'll see."

Ryan stood and said, "I was hoping to find the bastard who shot my dog. If it's the same guy the bear got, good riddance. Could I talk to this man, the one in the picture?"

"Hard to do," the sheriff said, and waited for a few long seconds before saying, "He left town and we haven't been able to reach him. Seems he gave us a phony address and ID. You have any idea why he might do that, Mr. Quinn?"

Ryan shook his head and said, "No. But if something comes to me, I'll call you."

The deputy stood and offered his hand. "You do that, Mr. Quinn. You do that. Keep in touch."

As Ryan was leaving, the deputy asked, "By the way, what kind'a dog you got?"

"A golden retriever. Gentle, kind, loving dog."

CHAPTER 15

When I awoke from a very long nap with terrible nightmares, I thought I was back in Iran. A few minutes later, a woman came up to my cage and looked in. She acted happy to see that I was awake. She said in English, "Well, hi there. Glad to see you."

The cage was tall enough for me to stand, and I struggled to stand, but that was a big mistake. Pain shot through my shoulder and chest as soon as I put weight on my right paw. Someone had fastened a funny collar around my neck. I couldn't reach down and lick where it hurt. The collar was cone shaped and made of plastic.

The woman said, "Don't try to stand, boy. Let your wounds heal."

I thought, *maybe I am in Iran and they have an English speaking technician.* She acted like she knew I could understand her words.

I looked around and saw other dogs in cages; one barked a greeting to me. I barked back and found my throat was sore. I moved forward carefully and drank out of the water bowl in my cage. It felt good and I laid my head back down and fell asleep.

When I awoke again, I knew I was in America. Both Ryan and Megan were looking in at me. I stood in spite of the pain and tried to reach them through the wire mesh. Ryan unlatched the cage door and reached in to pet me. I licked his hand and tried to move forward, but I was having trouble balancing on three legs. My right front leg was useless.

Ryan said, "Down," and I laid back down. He continued to rub my head while I tried to reach his hand and lick it.

I knew I had been shot, and remembered trying to get back to Ryan. I guess the men didn't get a chance to kill Ryan after I bit one of them. I wondered if they were still trying to find Ryan.

Ryan's next question made me wonder if I had given too much away about my mental powers.

He said, "I wish you could talk."

Megan reached in, patted my back, and said, "I know you didn't attack that man."

Holy cow. What did they know?

It took awhile before I could put all the pieces together, but I am getting ahead of myself. After about ten minutes, a man came in and shook hands with Ryan. It was obvious he was a doctor and Ryan confirmed it by saying, "How is he doing, Dr. Spenser?"

"Much better. You are going to have to limit his movements for a few weeks, but I think he can go home in a few days."

A few days? I was ready to go home then, so I barked. It didn't do any good.

"By the way," Dr. Spenser said, "That metallic object I saw in his stomach. He must have passed it." I wondered if that was the thing I had found under the fender on Ryan's truck.

Ryan came back and reached into my cage. He gave me a hug and whispered in my ear, "Magic, get well. I miss you."

I licked his face and tried to get out of the cage. I wanted to go home. I hate cages, I really hate them, but he pushed me back and said, "Be a good boy. I'll be back to visit tomorrow."

Which he did.

After two days they released me and gave Ryan a long list of things he should do for me and what to do if I had any complications from the surgery. That was the first I knew I had surgery, but I guessed as much.

Once we got home I almost jumped out of the cab, but Ryan stopped me just in time. According to him, I could have pulled a suture out, and that was the first I knew I had sutures. I wanted to get to the computer to find out what a suture was, but it took a while before I was able to handle the keyboard and mouse, left pawed. I am naturally right pawed, so typing and moving the mouse was a learning experience with my left paw.

Ryan carried me into the house, where he had a nice dog bed set up in his bedroom. What a guy. He let me come into the front room and watch television with him. They didn't have a television in the dog hospital. In the evening it was boring with the lights out. Some of the puppies cried and that made me feel bad, because I couldn't get out to comfort them. As far as I could tell, they had never been away from home. With the exception of the lab in Iran, I have never spent much time with other dogs and am not completely comfortable communicating with them. We dogs don't speak, so there is a lot of body language involved, which can lead to serious misunderstandings. Barking has a limited range of communication. It's not as if one bark means one thing and two something else. It's more subtle.

A conversation between Ryan and Megan relieved my concern that the killers were still after Ryan. He told her about the sheriff in Silver Springs, and about one man being attacked and probably killed by a bear. He also told her about the other man who gave the sheriff a phony address and ID before skipping town. I began wondering if the man would come back. There was something strange and dangerous going on.

Ryan had a new job. Apparently, he missed going in to work because of me and forgot to call in. Consequently, he was fired. I felt bad about that, but must admit, having him around was nice even though I couldn't get on the computer until he was asleep.

After a week he got a job as a sales associate—read that as sales person—at the Daytona Mall. He said it didn't pay much but he didn't intend to stay there long. He was going to the FBI academy located on the Marine Corps Base Quantico, Virginia. The only obstacle was some mix-up on his NCIC record, which a lawyer was going to fix.

Once I felt I was getting well enough to help Ryan, I decided to tell him about the men who intended to kill him, plus Megan and me, or is it I? I can never remember that rule.

I wrote him a new e-mail from the mysterious Mr. Kunastros.

> Ryan,
> I have information about the injury to your wonderful dog, Magic, and about two men who were following you with the intent to kill you, your beautiful fiancée Megan, and Magic.

They—the men who appeared to be from a northeastern state—attached a device to your pickup truck. I suspect it had something to do with them following you. They attached it at the Edgewater Park parking lot and Magic removed it at the Divine Springs.

Magic attempted to stop their murderous plan by wounding one of them; unfortunately, the other man was able to shoot Magic.

It is my concern that the man will return again and try to kill you. This was obviously not a random act of homicide but one planned. From that, I conclude that you have an enemy who, for whatever reason, wants you dead. Perhaps the deaths of Megan and Magic would be what the military call collateral damage.

Your previous unpleasant encounter with the men trying to ship a secret power pack to Iran, and Megan's near fatal kidnapping, suggest that both the attempt on your life and the power pack are in fact connected. I would strongly suggest you take a proactive stance and seek out these people before they succeed in taking your life.

For reasons I cannot divulge, I cannot go directly to the FBI with this information; however, you can.

Your friend, Mr. Kunastros.

It took a long time to type with my left paw, but I was getting the hang of it. When I finished, I thought the e-mail was sufficiently verbose to come from a federal employee. I threw in the proactive comment after listening to a local politician talk about what he was going to do about the water problem in Florida. Like it was a new problem. Give me a break.

The next morning I watched Ryan's face as he read my e-mail. He printed it and read it again. Something was bothering him, and I wasn't sure what it was. He finally looked back at me and said, "You never fail to surprise me, Magic. I didn't think you had it in you. Attacked armed men? How did you know?"

He then turned back to the computer screen and I heard him mumble, "They'll lock me up if I keep talking to my dog."

Now that hurt. I don't think he meant it maliciously, but that remark, "I didn't think you had it in you," that got to me. How soon humans forget. I dodged bullets for him in Iraq, risked my life chewing him free. I needed a break, so I limped out to the backyard and sulked the rest of the morning.

***

Special Agent Howard Lowell of the Federal Bureau of Investigation placed a file on his desk after reading it for the second time in as many days. Mr. Ryan Quinn's telephone call didn't sound urgent. He said he had some new information concerning the kidnapping of Megan Alvarez, but Special Agent Howard Lowell heard something in the young man's voice that told him that this was not going to be a routine matter. He would know shortly.

The drive to the FBI office in Daytona Beach took Ryan thirty minutes. Even though he lived only twenty-five miles away, he hadn't been on beachside Daytona Beach in five years. It had changed. More concrete monstrosities blocked the view of the ocean, unless you had a room in one of the many hotels that seemed to grow as far as he could see.

He rode the elevator up to the third floor and entered the outer office, told the receptionist he had an appointment with Special Agent Howard Lowell, and a few minutes later, a tall, lanky man in his fifties came out to greet him.

"Mr. Quinn." He proffered his hand and added, "Good to see you again. Come on in back. Want coffee?"

"No, but thanks."

Ryan shook his hand and followed the congenial agent, who on their last meeting had a completely different demeanor. At that time, Ryan felt he was a suspect in the kidnapping of Megan, or somehow involved in the missing crate from the warehouse in Port Canaveral.

Special Agent Howard Lowell asked Ryan to have a seat in front of his desk and took a moment to throw a few papers into a wastebasket. He sat behind his desk and said, "Well, Mr. Quinn, what can I do for you?"

Ryan exhaled and said, "I don't know where to start."

Special Agent Howard Lowell smiled and said, "The beginning is as good a place as any," and leaned back in his chair.

Ryan did start from the beginning, repeating much of what he had already told the agent about the men at the warehouse and

Megan's kidnapping. He then went on and told him about Magic's wounds and the e-mail from Mr. Kunastros of the CIA.

Now Special Agent Howard Lowell was leaning forward. He didn't interrupt Ryan but seemed anxious to question him.

Ryan finished and then reached into his shirt pocket where he had a folded copy of the e-mail. The agent read it and said, "I would like to show this to someone." He didn't wait for a response before he left his office. A full twenty minutes passed before Special Agent Lowell came back. Ahead of him was a tall woman, dressed in a white blouse and dark slacks. In her early forties, she would have been an attractive woman had she not pulled her hair back and tied it in a large knot. She nodded to Ryan, who started to rise before she motioned him back into his chair.

"Mr. Quinn, I am Assistant Special Agent-in-charge Brenda Louis. Now tell me. Where did you get this e-mail?"

Ryan didn't like her accusatory tone and said, "As I told Agent Lowell, it showed up on my computer. It's e-mail as you can see."

Ryan reached out for his e-mail, which she had pointed at him, but she drew it back and began to read, "Ryan, I have information about the injury to your wonderful dog, Magic, and about two men who were following you with the intent to kill you, your beautiful fiancée Megan, and Magic..." She finished with, "... For reason's I cannot divulge, I cannot go directly to the FBI with this information; however, you can. Your friend, Mr. Kunastros."

Ryan was about to say, *I see you can read, but what's your point*, when she said, "How long have you known this Mr. Kunastros?"

Ryan shook his head. "I don't know him. Never have. Listen, I came here because I thought I should. Someone shot my dog and I think it had something to do with the people I told Mr. Lowell about."

"Special Agent Lowell," she corrected and added, "Mr. Quinn, this," she shook the e-mail, "is... hard to believe."

Ryan shrugged his shoulders and said, "I know, but maybe you could check with the CIA. I don't understand why Mr. Kunastros doesn't contact you himself, but—"

She interrupted, "You want the FBI to contact the CIA and tell them your dog was shot while one of their agents watched? And according to Special Agent Lowell, this CIA agent observed your dog—"

"Look," Ryan said more sharply than he intended, "I don't understand how, but this CIA guy knew about Megan and about the Toyota the kidnapper was driving."

Assistant Special Agent-in-charge Brenda Louis leaned back on Lowell's desk and stared at Ryan. When he stared back, she looked away for a moment and said, "Mr. Quinn, giving false testimony to a federal officer is a crime. Now would you like to tell me why you invented this," she shook the e-mail again, "preposterous story?"

Ryan stood abruptly, said, "Okay, I tried," and walked out. He heard Assistant Special Agent-in-charge Brenda Louis's laughing as he left.

She was still chuckling when Special Agent Howard Lowell said, "You think there is anything to this?"

She frowned and said, "Lowell, how the hell would it sound if I called regional and told him we have an e-mail from a CIA agent who wants us to investigate a dog being shot? Get real."

Agent Lowell shrugged his wide shoulders and said, "Well, he did know about the Toyota and his dog did find the vic. And then there was that missing crate at Port Canaveral."

"Yes, missing. No one ever found the missing crate and they never will, because it is *missing*."

"Well, that Mr. Winn from DHS must have thought it was important or he wouldn't have been poking around."

"Let DHS poke around all they want."

"Allegedly the perp who kidnapped Miss Alvarez was with the DHS guy."

"Allegedly. We don't have diddly on him. Even his name doesn't show up on any of our screens. You said it yourself; the only connection is what this nut Quinn told us. The same guy who wants us to hunt down a dog killer."

"The dog didn't die."

Assistant Special Agent-in-charge Brenda Louis gave Lowell a long, hard look and walked out of his office but paused in the doorway to say, "Is your caseload keeping you busy?"

***

I heard about Ryan's humiliating experience at the Daytona Beach, FBI office before he wrote Mr. Kunastros a scathing e-mail reply. I won't repeat it. Suffice to say he wasn't happy.

Megan sat on the sofa in the front room, her legs curled under her, while Ryan paced back and forth, ranting about the FBI, CIA, and the Justice Department, although I don't know why he was picking on the Justice Department. He even said he had second thoughts about joining the FBI.

Ryan is not a ranter by nature, but he was ranting. After he wound down, Megan said, "Well, your Mr. Kunastros was right about you being followed."

Ryan said, "Yeah... but maybe not. Maybe he made it all up."

She said, "Then why did I get kidnapped by a man in a Toyota?"

This was getting good. I wondered what Ryan would say. It seemed she had made her point but he said, "Maybe he was guessing. Toyotas are big sellers. Lots of rental companies use them."

"How about that thing in the warehouse, that power pack?" Megan asked. She was on the right track.

Ryan said, "I don't know, but then again, I don't really know that there was anything in the missing crate. Only Mr. Kunastros said there was a power pack."

Megan patted my head and said, "Magic is the one who led you to that truck."

It sounded like Ryan was going to give in. Maybe my alter ego, Mr. Kunastros, would be saved, but then he said, "Magic smelled something but that doesn't mean it was a secret power pack."

I heard the men talking about it too, but of course he didn't know that. Then Ryan said something that gained my attention. He said, "Maybe I should take my computer down to their office. Maybe they can find out where these e-mails came from."

Megan said, "That makes sense."

Now she was turning on me too. I think I had covered my tracks as the e-mail was routed by a third party, but I am not a techie and it was possible that the FBI could find out that they came from Ryan's computer. Now I had something else to worry about. I worried that I would become a lab experiment again, but this time somebody would open me up to look inside.

We dogs don't by nature worry. Thinking about yesterday and tomorrow is not our strong suit, but we can worry. And paranoid dogs, particularly those who have been abused, do worry.

So now I have to cover my tracks if possible. I could erase the hard drive, but many good programs can still find what's there. There is a program that writes over everything, but I didn't have it and it might not be perfect. If I had hands I could pull out the hard drive and put it in the trash compactor, but my paws don't do well with a small screwdriver.

After Ryan and Megan stopped talking about the FBI and the e-mail, Ryan asked Megan if she would like to go to a movie. She said she wasn't dressed to go out, but relented and soon they were out the door. I have never been to a movie, but when Ryan's gone, I usually watch the history channel and some news. My first semester college exams were coming due, so I decided to hit the books, e-books of course. After an hour I stopped. I couldn't concentrate. There was still someone out there who wanted Ryan dead. If the FBI wouldn't help, then I would. I went outside and watched the clouds drift over the full moon. That always clears my thoughts. It takes me back to my roots. I howled long and loud.

CHAPTER 16

Preston Winn sat in the front row of the DARPA (Defense Advanced Research Program Agency) sponsored symposium on advanced exoskeletons for military applications, along with other senior civilians and high-ranking military officers. The auditorium was adequate but not elaborate. Located in Arlington, Virginia, it was not a long drive from Preston's office located in the District of Columbia.

Susan Humphrey sat in the sixteenth row, which vexed her, but with so many dignitaries she was lucky to get a seat. Twenty or more civilian and military officers stood in the back of the auditorium.

A three-star Army general walked to the podium and the room fell silent except for a few cleared throats and muffled coughs.

The overhead lights dimmed and a large projection of the Department of Defense logo appeared on a wide screen above and behind him.

"Ladies, gentlemen, distinguished guests, it is with a great deal of personal pride that I announce the Defense Advanced Research Program Agency sponsored symposium on advanced exoskeletons for military applications...." He went on to explain the Army's interest in a machine for footsoldiers who needed to travel long distances with heavy loads. The exoskeleton could also be used by Army medics to carry injured soldiers off a battlefield. He went into the possible civilian uses including an aid to those with disabilities. He then introduced the head of DARPA, Dr. Edward Chu, taking some time to expand on the man's distinguished career and qualifications.

Dr. Chu came to the podium after the applause and talked about the many accomplishments of DARPA, and there were many. He then turned the podium over to the project manager for the exoskeletons project, Dr. Sing.

A DARPA logo appeared on the screen followed by a short video showing a man putting on a pair of boots that were attached to the exoskeleton. Metal legs framed the outside of the man's legs. He then put on the exoskeleton's vest, which was attached to a backpack. A small gasoline engine supplied the power to the hydraulic pumps that provided movement to the exoskeleton. If the engine ran out of fuel, the exoskeleton legs could be easily removed and the backpack dropped.

The man ran up a hill with over a hundred pounds attached to his backpack. He moved quickly back and forth and demonstrated the flexibility of the machine.

Dr. Sing explained that the soldier did not need a joystick or special keyboard to guide the exoskeleton. It was designed so that the wearer becomes an integral part of the exoskeleton. Sensors in his boots and on the backpack send signals to a central processor, which relays signals to the servo motors that move the exoskeleton.

After Dr. Sing talked about future designs that essentially involved a complete body exoskeleton, he ran a short slide show of prototype full body suits. It reminded Preston of movie robots, which in essence they were, but with humans inside to guide them with the help of a powerful onboard computer.

A thought passed through Preston's mind, the battlefield of the future where the nation with the best robots won. My robot can whip your robot. He chuckled and the major general seated next to him glanced over.

The house lights came back up and Dr. Sing introduced a second-generation exoskeleton from a joint effort at the University of California, Berkeley. A man dressed in the exoskeleton came on stage. He moved around and picked up a few heavy weights that had been positioned off the stage. At the conclusion of the demonstration, Dr. Sing asked for questions before the symposium broke up into sub groups concerned with the many issues related to the exoskeleton. The shortcoming of a noisy gas engine was glossed over, but he did say a more powerful and quieter engine was in the works.

Preston didn't intend to stay for any of the working groups, but wanted to talk to the Berkeley people. A newer prototype along with another new power source might bring a lucrative payday. The XSCMES, acronym for the prototype Experimental Self Contained Miniaturized Energy Source, was not discussed as it was still classified Top Secret. Although a few high ranking officials knew about it.

At the coffee break, Preston saw Susan Humphrey corner a man from the private sector company that built the XSCMES. She wore an expensive dress that showed its pedigree and her ample assets. The man was one of the two people Preston wanted Susan to mingle with at the symposium. Background checks revealed recent financial problems, so they might be vulnerable to selling their products or the plans needed to build them. Of course, neither Preston nor Susan would make an offer, that would come from a third party who Susan had cultivated.

There were a number of companies in both Europe and Asia who were working on exoskeletons, but as far as Preston knew, only one American company had a miniaturized power pack, and Preston hoped to ship their prototype along with a few new exoskeletons for thirty million dollars. With customers in China and Iran, Preston wanted to keep his supply of these expensive weapons available. If thirty million was a great payday, sixty million would be his retirement plan.

Preston's musings were interrupted by a short, young bookish woman who introduced herself as Dr. Francis Meadows of the Berkeley group. "Mr. Winn, would you like to try the new exoskeleton suit?" she asked.

"Try? You mean wear one?"

"Yes, Miss Humphrey works for you I believe. She suggested it in a letter to our office just last week."

Preston looked down at his right foot. The support orthosis showed below his trousers. Preston was still very sensitive about his deformed foot and the orthosis he wore. Why had Susan done this, he wondered, to embarrass him? After a long pause, Preston said, "I have an injury to my foot. I don't think I would be a good candidate for the suit."

Dr. Meadows smiled and said, "On the contrary. One of the applications is to aid those with injuries such as yours."

"You knew about my injury?"

She looked at him questionably and said, "Yes. We made a boot inserted to your specifications."

"My specifications?"

Dr. Meadows looked uncomfortable and said, "If you would rather not try the suit—"

Preston interrupted her and said, "Is there a private room where I can try it?"

"Yes, that's what Miss Humphrey suggested. This way please."

Preston followed Dr. Francis Meadows, who he guessed to be in her mid-twenties and young to have her doctorate, to a room off the main auditorium. Inside, three men in blue coveralls with a company logo on the back, stood talking. When they saw Preston, they stopped talking and began taking an exoskeleton out of a storage box.

Dr. Francis Meadows introduced the men whose names Preston immediately forgot. It took only a few minutes for Preston to be strapped in and given a few directions by Dr. Meadows.

"Once we start the engine, which will supply power to the hydraulics and electricity to the computer, you can move about the room."

"How do I get it to move?" Preston asked.

"Simply begin to walk. The sensors will detect the electrical impulses sent to the muscles in your feet, legs, arms, hands and back. They will send a signal to the computer, which will power the legs, arms and hands. It is much easier to do than to explain. We tried to make it simple to use."

Preston moved a bit to adjust to the weight of the suit and then said, "Go ahead."

Dr. Meadows showed Preston the start button and said, "When you are ready, press this once."

A second later, the small engine attached to a frame on the back of the exoskeleton sprang to life. In the small room it was louder than he expected. He moved his arm and the exoskeleton arm moved easily. He took a tentative step and the machine moved. At first he felt like he would fall over, but the machine seemed to sense him trying to balance and adjusted the angle of his back. He took another step and then another. Soon he was moving around the room and even picked up the end of a heavy table with ease. It felt like five pounds, but he was lifting more than a hundred pounds. Preston was starting to enjoy the feeling of power the suit gave him when Dr. Meadows said, "I think we should shut it down now. There isn't adequate ventilation inside."

The small internal combustion engine was pumping dangerous carbon monoxide and other fumes into the room, although in small amounts.

Preston stopped walking and allowed her to shut off the engine. The suit had a small battery, but this particular model was not meant to operate without the engine running. The military was concerned about its lack of stealth, but with the almost silent XSCMES, the suit could be very quiet.

Preston slipped out of the suit and said, "I should like to test this suit with a different power source. My office can arrange for the transportation."

"As long as the power supply is compatible with our units, I see no reason we can't provide a suit for testing."

"Fine. I'll let my office take care of the technical details. Thank you for your time. I enjoyed the... ride, if I can call it that."

Preston was smiling when he walked out of the private conference room where he had worn the new exoskeleton. Susan Humphrey was waiting outside the door. She grinned mischievously and said, "Enjoy the ride?"

Preston lost his smile and said, "Don't do anything like that again without my permission. And I'd like to test the exoskeleton with the XSCMES."

She flipped him off and walked toward a small group of senior military officers who turned as she approached and greeted her by name.

***

My shoulder and leg were feeling much better. Exercise helped, and Ryan's good care did wonders. I had time to get the frustrations out of my system, so I ran around the yard at least twenty times. I settled down and began planning my campaign. The objective was simple: save Ryan's life. To do that somebody had to stop whomever was trying to kill Ryan. By stop I meant, keep them from continuing, disable their ability to kill or have Ryan killed. Obviously, I had to determine who wanted Ryan dead. Thinking ahead, who was going to do the wet work? I got that out of a novel about the CIA. I think it meant to kill someone. I do not intend to take another's life if possible and only after long deliberation. I know I sound wishy washy, but I have seen lots of dead dogs and humans. It is not something to take lightly, killing that is.

Of course, there was that time when I attacked the men who wanted to kill Ryan, and I still carry the scars and have a limp, which should go away in time. I guess I am not as wishy washy as I think I am.

First thing's first. Ryan's attempted death and Megan's kidnapping were both tied to the secret power pack. The name of the man who charged Ryan is Preston Winn, according to Ryan's old boss, Frank Kurns. I found Preston Winn's address after a search for DHS big shots. I also found his home address in Arlington, his apartment in George Town, and his private e-mail address.

The e-mail address was the hardest to find, but I made a new friend on the internet who saw my blog. He is quite troubled and should have professional help, but he did provide a lot of new software that gets me into sites usually off limits. When I can't find something, I ask him and he obliges. In return, I have been helping him with a relationship he is having with a woman. I guess it's not really a relationship, because he hasn't yet spoken to her, but he wants to once he gains the courage. She works in a bookstore and, according to him, she is beautiful. I don't know his real name but he calls himself Zeus. I can only guess what twist of his mind that jewel came from. Maybe I should be Cupid and not Golden One.

Because Preston Winn was high up in the DHS, I couldn't intimidate him easily, but he had one chink in his armor, he was dishonest and potentially a murderer. I guess that's two chinks, but my plan was not yet complete. I intended to shake him up a bit and see what happens. He might make a mistake that would be his undoing.

***

Preston read the official document in disbelief. It could not be happening to him.

"Susan!" he bellowed, not bothering to use the intercom.

His secretary opened the door and stuck her head in. "Is there something you need, Mr. Winn?"

"Get Susan in here *now*."

She closed his office door and pushed the intercom for Susan Humphey's office, and when Susan answered she said, "The boss wants you. He sounds upset. Very upset."

When Susan came through the door without knocking. Preston was standing near the door and held out a two-page document.

"Look at this. What does it mean?"

Susan took the document and began to read aloud, "United States District Court, Middle District of Florida, Subpoena in a criminal case, case number—"

Preston yanked the document back and said, "There," he pointed to a letter V and read, "Preston H. Winn—"

Susan took it back and read in silence. When she was through, she looked at Preston, who was now slumped in the chair behind his desk.

"Something's not right," she said.

"What do you mean?"

"This wasn't served on you. The proof of service section is blank."

"Give me that," Preston said as he held out his hand.

He went over the entire document and said, "Maybe I should have our legal eagles take a look at it."

Susan smiled and said, "Go ahead. Why don't you write a confession while you're at it?"

Preston followed the logic in her snide remark. If the subpoena was a fake, showing it to the DHS legal department was a sure way to bring heat upon himself. Word would reach the director in minutes. If the subpoena was authentic, well, he didn't want to think about that. It was probably a fake, but why? Maybe someone wanted him to go to the legal department and jeopardize his career and lucrative side activities, but who? His contact in Saudi Arabia may have found out about the second power pack and the new exoskeletons going to China, but what did they have to gain?

Preston saw Susan watching his reflection in the large window behind his desk. Maybe it was Susan? Maybe she wanted his job, although she was too far down in the civil service hierarchy to be considered. She had lots of connections; too many for her job description.

Preston looked at the document again. The judge's name was there as well as the courtroom and case number, plus a website where he could get more information about the case. He would check on that later. He reached down and recovered the envelope it came in from his under-desk trash container. It was addressed correctly and was sent from Orlando, Florida, but the envelope itself didn't look like one from a federal court, in his estimation. It was heavy, high quality, similar to those he used for his own personal stationary.

He put the subpoena in the inside pocket of his coat and looked at Susan again. "When will the new XSCMES and exoskeletons arrive?"

"Best guess, three weeks."

"How about our little company?"

While it was Susan's idea, Preston liked the idea and considered it his. With the help of his friend, Cynthia Morgan, he was going to start a business in Florida, called United Services Associates. An innocuous name with the patriotic acronym USA.

She would provide the upfront money, and the papers of incorporation would show her as the owner and principal stockowner, but Susan and he would be in charge of staffing the company, and more importantly, providing the stolen plans to build the XSCMES and advanced exoskeletons. He had already planned on purchasing as many as he could squeeze out of the DHS budget. It was a win/win situation. He would get the credit for increasing the DHS role in fighting terrorism, and would get rich doing it. He almost smiled until he thought about that damn subpoena. Somebody was trying to shake him up, and it had worked.

Finally Susan said, "Your girlfriend already has the building leased and the corporation formed, but there is no reason to staff it until we have the design plans."

"Cynthia is not my girlfriend."

"Whatever."

"We could start interviewing engineers and scientists."

"And tell them what?"

Preston had to think for a minute before he said, "Tell them we will be building robots."

"And about the XSCMES?"

"Hell, I don't even know how it works yet. Better just work on the robot angle for now."

CHAPTER 17

My plan to send a subpoena to Mr. Preston Winn was obvious. I didn't think he would fall for it and show up at the courthouse in Orlando, but I did think it would give him cause to worry, and worried dogs and humans make mistakes. It seemed to have worked. On the subpoena is a website where he can find out the details of the case numbers; however, it took him to a bogus site. When he clicked on the site's menu, it downloaded a little piece of code that gave me a license to steal. A neat little spy program hid on his hard drive and recorded his e-mail keystrokes. It was a new one, and so far anti spyware software hadn't identified it. Every time he sent an e-mail, the e-mail information was sent to me. Don'tcha just love it? I also have to thank the Central Secretarial Service who convert e-mails into typed documents and send them wherever you wish. It didn't cost much, and even my meager bank account didn't suffer. It was all done with computers, so no busybody looked at what I wrote on the downloaded official "Subpoena in a criminal case" form available on the internet.

I only had to wait two days before Mr. Preston Winn started sending love notes to Cynthia Morgan. I found that she lived in Southern Florida. I intended to do a more thorough search on her. Mr. Winn also sent e-mails to a Susan Humphrey. It took me a few days to run her down. Stupid of me, she was his administrative assistant and lived in a townhouse in Centerville, Virginia. I planned on sending her a little surprise too.

Preston had been pressing Susan Humphrey to deliver the XSCMES sooner. He didn't write what sooner meant. Sooner than what, Christmas? I didn't know what "XSCMES" means, but I was working on it. I knew it had something to do with the power pack.

There was something going on in South Florida with the acronym USA. A quick check of the state licensing department showed that the new corporation, named United Services Associates, was owned by the Morgan Trust. Further checking showed that the Morgan Trust was the estate of Howard Morgan, Cynthia Morgan's late husband.

Ryan interrupted my work by coming home unexpectedly with Megan in tow. He found a new job in Daytona Beach with a construction company. As he explained it to Megan, he was a gopher. I looked up gopher on the internet. As he was certainly not a rodent that burrows, I guess he dug holes for the construction company. He didn't seem too happy about the job, but he told Megan it was only temporary.

She must have been in a prickly mood because she asked, "Is our engagement only temporary?"

Then Ryan got in the same mood and said, "It's your call."

Megan stormed out of the house and slammed the front door so hard I thought the glass sidelights were going to shatter. Ryan said something I won't repeat and went to the kitchen and came out with a beer in his hand. He asked me if I understood women. Of course I don't. I'm still struggling with men and humans in general. I barked twice which seemed to satisfy him, then we both watched *Jeopardy* on the television. I got most of the answers right, Ryan did almost as well.

The next day Ryan came home from work and gave me a start. He had a cardboard box and I immediately heard and smelled another dog. My first reaction was that he was going to replace me. He put the box down in the front room and opened the top. I stuck my nose in, and there was a very small puppy. It saw me and tried to lick me but I pulled back. What was going on?

Ryan asked, "What do you think, Magic? Should we keep it?"

Keep it? Why on earth would Ryan want another dog? Wasn't I good enough? Didn't I play with him, protect him, and lay down my life for him? I didn't even bark. I sulked away and went outside.

A few minutes later, Ryan came out holding that little puppy. He put her down in front of me and the darn thing let out a feeble bark and tried to bite at me. I knew it was just puppy play, but I was not feeling playful. I walked off but Ryan said, "Magic, can't you see she wants to play? Come over here."

I came back and nudged the little tike. She looked like a ball of fur with a black button for a nose and two bigger brown buttons for eyes. She kind of wobbled when she walked and her belly almost dragged on the ground. I am no expert on dog breeds, but her coloring was similar to mine, golden but not red, and the tiny head and ears suggested that it might be a golden retriever. Possibly my kin. I must confess, she was a cute little thing. When I walked away again she followed me, trying to bite my tail and barked every few steps.

I had decided I could live with another dog in the house but was still concerned that this little puppy was my replacement. Finally, Ryan eased my fears when he asked, "Do you think Megan will like her?"

Of course, why didn't I think of that? The puppy was a peace offering to Megan. My tail gave him the answer when it went into full speed wag. I barked and jumped around for awhile. I just could not contain myself. The puppy didn't know what to think, so it laid down and took a nap on the back porch.

Ryan telephoned Megan but apparently it didn't go well. When he finished talking to her, his face grew dark, and he looked at the telephone as if it held the answers to his problem. I know better. It wasn't the telephone, it was Ryan and Megan's situation. It was unnatural. They should marry and not try to be so darn logical, like a dog. If a dog wants a mate he doesn't put it off until he owns his own kennel, no, he... well, like all analogies, they break down under scrutiny. There are other considerations.

Ryan sat in the front room and listened to his music CD player. The music matched his mood. Something by Wagner, heavy, with strong undercurrents of impending doom.

After awhile it was getting to me. I suppressed the urge to howl and went outside. The pup was awake again and acted hungry. I pushed open the dog door to the kitchen and she waddled in. My food dish had a few scraps left over and she tried to chew on a bone, but it was bigger than her mouth. By her size, I think she hadn't been weaned away from her mother's milk for very long. She started to whine, which is somewhat like a human's cry. I couldn't get into the refrigerator and pour milk for her, so I nudged her along into the front room. I kept pushing until she was next to Ryan's foot. He had his shoes off but didn't seem to notice the puppy or me. He was lost in the music and his own thoughts. The puppy bit his toe and got his attention.

I thought Ryan might be angry, but he bent down and scooped up the puppy. He laid it on his chest. The puppy laid there quietly with Ryan slowly rubbing its head. She closed her eyes and looked contented. So did Ryan. His face lost its dark expression and a hint of a smile crept across his mouth. It was a nice scene. One that I wished would have been in my puppyhood. I guess I was a little envious, but that's the breaks or as we say, "That's how the dog biscuits crumble."

We kept the puppy that night, but she woke me twice whining. I guess she missed her mother as she tried to snuggle up to me. At first I moved away, but she followed me around, and I didn't want her to wake Ryan, who gets up early for his new job. I finally laid down and let her sleep with me, although she must have been dreaming a lot because she made little noises and even barked once. By morning she was fresh and wanted to play. I wanted to take a nap.

Ryan put her out in the backyard with me, fed us both and poured a big bowl of milk for her. She immediately stepped in it and turned it over. What a mess. Ryan found another bowl, much heavier, and poured a small amount of milk in it, which she lapped up quickly and took a nap.

I waited until Ryan was gone to turn on his computer and read Mr. Winn's e-mail. It was very interesting. The new company, which was going to be located in the Vero Beach Municipal Airport Industrial Park, was going to be staffed with engineers and technicians with robotic experience. He sent a copy of the advertisement he wanted her to place in local newspapers, but told Cynthia Morgan he had other sources if the new ads didn't pan out. He was also interested in computer software and hardware engineers. He would fly down in a commuter jet to interview the applicants after reviewing their resumes. I immediately began to build my own resume or curriculum vitae if I decide to have a doctorate. I love that stuffy word, *curriculum vitae*.

I had no illusions that I would be interviewed, at least not in person, but I was working out the details in my mind of doing work-at-home as a software engineer for the USA Company. With my friend Zeus's help it might work out okay.

***

Preston threw the letter across his desk to Susan, who sat in one of the two comfortable soft leather chairs across from Preston. She didn't bother to pick it up as it fell to the floor.

"Can you believe this? The city of Vero Beach says I'm in violation of its zoning ordinance."

Susan said, "So? Why doesn't your girlfriend find a building someplace else?"

Preston didn't bother denying his relationship with Cynthia Morgan, but he didn't like Susan's impertinence.

"How the hell did the City of Vero Beach learn that the USA Company has anything to do with me?"

Susan hadn't thought of that. She reached down and picked up the letter. She read it and said, "Either she listed you as the owner or co-owner, or this is another attempt to screw with your mind."

Preston frowned and picked up his telephone. He speed dialed Cynthia Morgan, pointed to the door, and said to Susan, "Do you mind?"

Susan shrugged and walked out of his office after dropping the letter in his lap and saying, "Give her my love."

He turned back to the telephone and said, "Cynthia my love. How have you been?"

Cynthia Morgan told him. She hadn't been well at all. He had been ignoring her and she was sick of it. Either he spends more time with her, or he would have to make other arrangements. He was barely able to ask if he was listed on the lease of the building in Vero Beach. She said, "No, I'm not stupid. I know you don't want to be connected with USA, and I have an idea why."

After she hung up, Preston looked up the telephone number of an old contact, a man who could find people discreetly. When he was finished with that conversation, he pushed Susan Humphrey's intercom button and said, "Susan, can you spare a minute? I would like to discuss something with you."

Susan said she would be right there, but she let him wait ten minutes before she came into his office all smiles and sat down in front of his desk.

"What's up?" she asked.

Preston understood her game, but she was too important to his money making plans to let go, and too good looking to be out of his sight for long.

"I guess you got tied up?" he asked.

"Had an important call come in just as I was leaving my office."

"I see." He paused and then said, "I talked to an old contact of mine. He specializes in finding people and keeping his mouth shut. I've asked him to find the author of these little annoyances."

"Sounds like a good person to know. If he finds your nemesis, what will you do?"

Preston formed his fingers into a bridge and thought before he said, "Depends on who it is."

Susan rose and said, "Let me know who he is before you do anything."

As she left, Preston said, "Or she."

***

Ryan was dead tired when he got home from work. Carrying packs of heavy roofing shingles up a ladder all day taxed his legs, even though they were in good shape. He threw off his dirty clothes and stepped into the shower. The hot water washed away the dirt, grime, and some of the fatigue. He shaved quickly and was dressing when his telephone rang. He picked it up in the bedroom and saw from the caller ID it was from the Alvarez home.

"Yes?" he said, hoping it was Megan.

Rose Alvarez said, "Ryan. What have you done to Megan? She won't eat; she doesn't want to tell me what's wrong. What is it?"

Ryan thought, what had *he* done? At most, replied too sharply to Megan.

He said, "I have no idea, except she is mad at me. I tried to talk to her about it yesterday, even bought her a little present, but you'd have thought I was a stranger. I don't get it."

Rose didn't respond for a few seconds. She then said, "I thought maybe you had a new girlfriend. Tell you what. Come to dinner."

Ryan thought about the Alvarez household. Going to dinner with her brothers and father, and maybe Megan starring at him, did not seem like a good idea.

"Mrs. Alvarez—"

She corrected him, "Rose."

"Rose, I planned to have dinner with a few of my new friends from work. Maybe another time."

"Ryan!" she said sharply, "Who is more important, Megan or your new friends?"

"Megan, of course."

"Then it is settled. We eat at eight."

The telephone went dead and Ryan wondered how he was going to get through the evening. He dropped the towel he had around him and began looking in the closet for suitable clothes for an Alvarez dinner. Not a suit and tie, and not jeans and tee shirt. He picked out his best tan dress slacks and found a clean white polo shirt. He laid them on the bed and saw his towel moving. He watched it for a few seconds as it disappeared under his bed. He bent down and looked under the bed. The puppy had one end in her mouth and was wrestling with it.

"What are you doing, you little scamp?" Ryan said as he pulled on his towel. The puppy reluctantly followed with her little legs pushing back against Ryan's pull; however, she held the towel tight in her mouth. Ryan picked both puppy and towel up. He saw Magic watching from the open bedroom door.

"Magic, would you like to visit your friend the cat at Megan's house?"

Ryan thought Magic looked astonished. His eyes seemed larger and his ears popped up before he turned and ran out of the house.

Ryan stroked the puppy's head and said, "I guess that was a no. Well, I think you will like Megan. Now get down while I get dressed."

Ryan put the puppy down and tried to get dressed. He did succeed, but the puppy dragged one of his socks into the front room before Ryan put on his brown loafers. Ryan recovered it and put the puppy out to play with Magic. An hour later, Ryan left the house. He wore a loose fitting sports coat; one with an open pocket large enough for the puppy, even though the puppy's head and front paws hung out. If Megan rejected this little pup, he had a backup plan, the diamond ring sat in a fancy box in the glove compartment. He had never given Megan a ring. Somehow he felt he had to give her a date for their marriage if he gave her a ring. Now, his future did not look bright, but he didn't want to lose her. Megan represented not only the woman he loved and needed, but also the key to a happy future. He had seen the love between his parents as he grew up, but hadn't thought much about it, took it for granted, until he realized that he wanted a life like theirs. Not a perfect life, but one where two people worked together through the road bumps of life.

After Ryan drove off, Magic hurried into the second bedroom and began tapping on the computer keyboard. He moved his paw expertly over the touch pad, moving the cursor with ease. After twenty minutes, he cleared the memory of his searches, deleted the history, cookies and cleaned his tracks. He then went into the front room and watched the history channel.

Rose Alvarez answered the front door, but when she saw the puppy, she told Ryan to wait outside. She went in and told her daughter to answer the door, there was a package for her.

Megan reluctantly went to the door. Obeying her mother was second nature, but she wondered why her mother hadn't simply taken the package. Besides, she wasn't expecting anything. Then she thought, maybe Ryan had sent flowers to apologize for his rudeness. Should she send them back?

She opened the door and a puppy licked her face.

***

Ryan came home happy and smiling. He petted me and said he was sorry that he had to give my little playmate away to Megan, but said we would visit often. Not with that cat there, I hoped.

Then I started to worry about the little tike. What if the cat attacked her? I guess the humans would watch out after her. I was relieved that Ryan wasn't going to keep her, but I must admit, she was kind of cute.

While Ryan was gone, I intercepted a few more e-mails from Preston Winn to various people. Although it was obvious to me what he was doing, he was unusually vague and didn't mention the power pack or exoskeletons. I was not certain how well my tactics were working, but he seemed more guarded in his e-mails.

Ryan let me ride in his pickup when he drove to the New Smyrna Beach Airport. It is a small but active airport for general aviation—not commercial. Ryan learned to fly there after graduating from high school. It was a present from his father, who was a pilot in the Marine Corps. While Ryan didn't want to fly in the service, he did enjoy flying the small civilian aircraft when time allowed. Flight hours are expensive, but Ryan wanted to stay current so he managed to fly the minimum amount of hours needed to maintain his instrument card, meaning he could fly under IFR (Instrument Flight Rules).

I had to wait while he and a friend talked about a flight they planned for the weekend. There is a wooded area near the covered aircraft hangers where Ryan let me run. It was good to stretch my legs. I run around our yard, but I really enjoy a long run and the scenery, lots of old oaks and smooth grass covered ground. Ryan sat on a picnic table and watched me. When I passed him, I usually let out a small bark, just to keep his attention. He walked out near the runway and watched a small airplane take off. It looked more like a big kite with the pilot seated in a lawn chair. Later I found it was a homemade ultra light aircraft, and Ryan had talked to someone on the telephone about buying one.

We went to the beach one night and had a good run. I watched to see if we were being followed; we weren't, or they were very good at concealing themselves. A week later, I did see a suspicious looking man and woman walk by our house while Ryan was at work. I watched from the second bedroom window. They walked by and then came back. The woman walked up to the front door and rang the bell. I didn't bark and didn't go into the front room where she could see me through the door sidelights. After awhile I heard her try the front door handle. I waited and heard her try the back door. I guess she came through the gate on the side of the house.

I was trying to decide what to do. If I barked and ran her off, I would never know what she and her male accomplice wanted. On the other hand, if they got in, I couldn't let them rob Ryan.

I was about to bark when the telephone rang. I always let it go, and it goes to Ryan's voice mailbox. That day I picked it out of the stand where it sat with my mouth and dropped it on the floor. I then panted into it. The telephone went dead and I heard the side gate open and the woman's shoes click on the driveway as she left. I ran to the front door and watched her hurry down the street where a man waited. Neither one of them looked like robbers, but then again, the only robbers I've seen were on television and the movies. Maybe real robbers look like politicians, or undertakers. Who knows? Now I know I should have barked, because two days later, while Ryan took me to visit the puppy at Megan's, somebody broke into Ryan's house and cleaned him out. They took his laptop computer, the PC from the bedroom, television, stereo equipment and a few odds and ends. They also took the shotgun he kept in the house. They tore up the house as if they were looking for something and didn't find it. Ryan's clothes were thrown all over his bedroom and contents of his shelves in his closet were on the floor. Ryan was angry, but acted calm. He telephoned the police and waited on the front porch until they arrived.

I worried about Ryan. He methodically cleaned up the mess and fixed dinner for himself and for me. He found a book to read and sat in his chair in the front room. I, however, didn't take the robbery as well as Ryan. With no televisions or computer, I paced the floor until Ryan got up and brought me into the front room. He told me to sit, and then he opened his book and began to read to me. I had never read or heard the Bible read before. He read for a long time and then we both went to bed, of course I still had to sleep on the floor. I wonder if there is a verse about dogs not sleeping on the floor. The next day Ryan telephoned his insurance agent, but he was told he was only covered for flood and fire.

With Ryan at work, and me alone without a computer or television, I endured some dull days. I guess I missed the excitement and entertainment. I attribute that to my human side.

***

Preston Winn tapped his fingers impatiently while he waited for a man he only knew as Wayne. A woman had telephoned that morning and told Preston that Wayne had something for him, but wanted to meet him at lunch. Preston knew that Wayne wanted to keep a low profile but wondered if he was being paranoid. They planned to meet at a small restaurant in a Holiday Inn near Triangle, Virginia.

Preston got there first and took a table. He told the waitress he would order later. He was waiting for a friend. Preston only knew that the man's name was Wayne. He had never actually talked to Wayne. A young woman had telephoned him. Originally, Preston had talked to another man, but the man never gave his name.

A man walked in and looked at Preston. He walked directly to Preston's table, without a word, and sat down. Wayne didn't look anything like Preston thought he would. He envisioned Wayne to be a James Bond type. Wayne was short, overweight, balding and wore thick glasses. He wore a wrinkled light blue suit with sweat stains under the arms.

Wayne pushed a large envelope across the table to Preston. Preston looked at him for a moment before saying, "I guess you must be Wayne?"

Wayne's voice was also not James Bond's; it was very high and squeaky.

"No, I'm the friggn' tooth fairy. You wanna read what I have or not?"

He was also surly, but Preston took the envelope and slipped out a large photograph of Ryan Quinn. He nodded knowingly and took out a typed report. Preston took several minutes before he looked up at Wayne. "How did you get into his computer?"

Wayne mopped his forehead with a dirty handkerchief and said, "Are you shitting me?"

"Never mind. I don't want to know." Preston read a little more before saying, "Would you like some lunch?"

"How about we can the small talk? Besides, I never eat in joints like this. Now if you're satisfied, how about our money? I'm a busy man."

Preston didn't like Wayne, the person he telephoned was a go-between. Preston doubted that the man before him was really the man who actually found all this information about Ryan Quinn. This nervous little man was not cut out for the spy business. Preston reached into the inside pocket of his suit coat and took out an envelope. He pushed it across to Wayne who stuck it into a coat pocket.

"Aren't you going to count it?"

Wayne gave him a smirk and a condescending look before walking out. Preston shrugged and motioned for a waitress. He was starved.

Preston read the long report while waiting for his meal. So Ryan Quinn was sending him those annoying e-mails. It didn't answer the question of how Mr. Quinn knew so much about Preston and his moneymaking project, but Mr. Quinn was dangerous and had to be neutralized. Preston considered the word neutralized in his mind as something short of murder. He didn't want to think of himself as a murderer, even though he had given in to Susan Humphrey's murderous suggestions. One way or another, Mr. Quinn had to be stopped. He decided to talk to Susan before taking action.

Susan Humphrey didn't come back from her lunch break until three in the afternoon. Preston had left two messages for her, and instructions to his secretary to have her see him the minute she got in.

It was almost four before Susan Humphrey walked into Preston's office and sat in a comfortable chair in front of his desk.

"You called?" she asked.

Preston frowned, pushed the envelope with the report on Ryan Quinn to her, and said, "Read this."

Susan opened the envelope and began to read. She occasionally looked up at Preston without changing her bored expression and then went back to reading. When she was finished she said, "Too bad those goons didn't get to him. We'll have to try again."

"I agree. How?"

Susan crossed her legs, exposing a lot of thigh, and said, "Do you know anyone who will take him out of our hair?"

Preston leaned forward and said, "As in permanently out of our hair?"

Susan said, "Let's not pussyfoot around this. He needs to be killed."

Preston sat back in his chair and said, "There have to be other ways. Hiring someone to, as you say, 'kill him' could come back to haunt us. I was thinking—"

Susan interrupted with, "Thinking is good, but while you are thinking, Mr. Ryan Quinn can screw up our operation. We've got the Vero Beach operation almost started. The new exoskeletons are on their way this week. That little power pack brought us a lot of cash, although it's still sitting in an offshore bank. If our boys in Vero can reverse engineer the new one, it may make us filthy rich, as in billions."

"You think I don't know that, but we must be cautious. One mistake and this could blow up in our faces."

Susan Humphrey stood and looked at Preston. She waited a few seconds before she said, "For the time being, I know how we can get him off the street. What happens to him then will be his problem."

"I don't understand. How will you do that?"

"Do you really want to know?"

Preston thought awhile before he said, "Do whatever needs to be done, but leave me out of it."

Susan shook her head before she turned and left his office.

CHAPTER 18

It took about a week for Ryan to lease a television. Megan had given him an old computer from Ted Lewis's office. It was slow, but I could still go online. I had to build a new set of files and download a few programs, but with limited storage I had to be very selective. My address book went with the stolen computer as well as my favorite places. It would take weeks to get set up again. The files I had for my homework were gone, so I had to redo a lot of schoolwork. I didn't want to get behind on my college courses.

Ryan left me with Megan for the weekend while he and his friend, a local flight instructor named Jeff, flew to Columbia, South Carolina and back in Jeff's Cessna 172. I was glad to see Ryan when he picked me up late Sunday night. To my surprise, the puppy and cat seemed to get along well. The cat still gave me a hard time, but I was big enough to take care of myself. The puppy chased the cat for a long time before she gave up and took a nap. The cat didn't seem to mind. I can't figure out cats.

When we got home that night, I immediately smelled a strange scent. Somebody had been in the house. Their scent was still strong. They must have come in the night before. I sniffed the floor and followed their odor to a place in the hall next to Ryan's bedroom. They must have turned there and left, but I also detected another scent; one that I didn't recognize, and it lingered near where they must have stood for awhile in the hall.

I barked a few times, and Ryan took notice and looked around, but eventually he gave up and we both went to bed.

The next day was worse than terrible. It was happening and I could not stop it. It felt like my heart was being ripped out. That day will always be in my mind. It started like any other day. Ryan fixed my food dish before he left for work.

It was nearly time for Ryan to come home when I heard them outside. Three police cars stopped out front and a van pulled up. Men got out with jackets with large DEA letters on them. Drug Enforcement Agency. What were they here for? Two New Smyrna Beach police officers came to the front door and knocked. I didn't bark and waited in the second bedroom. I heard someone at the back door. They knocked and I heard them say, "Police, open up."

I wasn't about to open up, even if I could. Then they left, but I felt they were not far away. I stayed out of sight not knowing what else to do. An hour later, I heard Ryan's pickup coming. I could hear it a half mile away, maybe further, and recognized its unique sound. I ran to the front door and waited as usual, but I had a bad feeling. Something was not right.

I watched in horror when Ryan pulled in, and a minute later three police cars and a van converged on his pickup truck. Ryan got out of his pickup and said something to them. I couldn't hear clearly because the police were yelling, "On the ground, get on the ground!"

Two police officers grabbed Ryan and forced him onto the ground while another one snapped handcuffs on him. He wasn't fighting them, but they kept shouting. Finally, they pulled him to his feet and told him he was under arrest. The men with DEA on their jackets came to the front door. The police brought Ryan along and took his keys before opening the front door. The DEA men came in and saw me. I had to suppress my feelings and didn't growl. It was very hard not to let myself go and attack them. I kept my eyes on them.

Ryan saw me and said, "Stay."

I stayed where I was but could see the DEA men go to a place in the hall near Ryan's bedroom. One of them carried a small collapsible ladder. He placed it in the hall and climbed up. A small opening led to the attic, although I have never seen Ryan use it. The DEA man shined a flashlight in to the storage space and pulled down a large shopping bag. He handed it down to another agent and then brought down two more. Once he was satisfied there were no more bags, he came down and folded the ladder.

There were drugs and other chemicals in the bags, and both the police and DEA agents appeared happy about the contents. Ryan saw them and said, "I have never been up there. I don't know where that came from."

They read Ryan his rights and told him he was under arrest for possession of more than 10 grams of heroin and possession of a controlled substance.

One agent said, "Are you ready to tell us everything?"

"Of course. I don't know where it came from."

Another agent said, "Save it." He then told the police officer that they would take Ryan in. By in, they meant to arrest him and take him to jail. I felt so helpless, but I stayed where Ryan told me. I felt Ryan would be able to explain, given enough time. After the DEA men took Ryan away, I head the police talking. One of them said that somebody in jail had snitched on Ryan. Another one said that the drugs must have had a street value of a million dollars.

I didn't know what the police were waiting for until I saw two people at the front door. The police let them in. A man and woman came in and looked at me. The man held a long pole with a loop on it and looked like he was going to put it around my neck, but the woman came over to me and touched my head. I usually enjoy humans touching me, but my instincts told me I was in trouble. Maybe I was going to be charged as an accessory to a crime or something like that. In any case, she seemed like a nice human and said, "It's alright, boy. Come with me."

She grabbed my collar and gently pulled me to the door. I didn't resist. Outside I saw a truck with an animal control sign on it. I walked with her to the truck while the man opened a door in the back. They were going to put me in a cage. I looked back and saw the police come out of the house. The woman looked back at them, and I made my move. I pushed at her and she lost her balance. I then pulled away with all my strength. She lost her grip and I was free. I almost ran past the animal control man before he could react, but he must have seen me look around. He dropped the hoop over me and I came to a painful and abrupt stop. I couldn't breathe. I pulled back but the hoop tightened around my neck.

There was no use fighting it. I would have lost consciousness in a few minutes or less.

The man and woman lifted me up and shoved me into the cage. Only then did the man release the hoop around my neck. I took in a deep breath and looked at our house. The police were leaving, and I had no idea where they had taken Ryan. In a few minutes, the truck moved and we were off to the Humane Society. It wasn't too far and I watched the street signs as we drove past them. I tried to remember each turn because I did not intend to stay in a home for orphan pets. I would escape.

The route was simple. The truck drove to Highway 1, then a left on Canal until it merged into Route 44. We drove past Gilley's Pub 44, where Ryan used to go with his buddies before Megan reappeared in his life. We drove on for a few miles and then made a left turn on South Glenco Road. About a mile later we turned by a sign and then into a driveway that took us to the Humane Society building. I could find my way back if given the chance.

As the man and woman were taking me out of the truck, it dawned on me. Nine months ago I was in another prison halfway around the world. Now it was happening again. I couldn't wag my tail if my life depended on it.

***

Preston looked up from his desk as Susan Humphrey walked in without knocking. She wore a revealing low cut blouse that was all but transparent. He wondered whom she had been playing up to today. She sure got around.

"It's done, at least the first part. By next week Mr. Quinn will be history."

Preston said, "I told you I didn't want to know what you were doing."

She shook her head and said, "Then don't listen. But it will cost you."

"Cost me?" How much?"

"These things don't come cheap. I paid for it out of my off-shore account, but I expect you to pick up fifty percent."

Preston nodded and said, "When he is as you say, 'history,' you'll get your money."

Susan stared at him for a very long time before saying, "Preston, you are a real piece of shit."

She turned and walked out before he could form a reply. Her office was down the same hall but was not nearly as large as Preston's. It was nicely furnished and photographs of many famous people lined the walls, some with Susan in the picture and many autographed.

Susan sat at her desk and opened the desk drawer. She took out a pack of cigarettes and a lighter. She lit up and took a deep drag, blowing the smoke out slowly. She ignored the no smoking ban in the federal building and enjoyed her smoke. She didn't expect to live long enough to get lung cancer or heart problems anyway, but she did intend to enjoy her short life. Preston Quinn had made her rich, but now he was a drag. One day she would have to do something about him, but not now. He was too valuable. Ryan Quinn was another matter. He would be dead in a few days, the victim of a fight in jail. Once he was out of the way, Mr. Kurns and that other fellow, she couldn't remember his name, would have to be eliminated, killed. They both knew too much.

***

Ryan found being in jail both humiliating and baffling. He knew he had been set up. Somebody planted three bags of narcotics. He was innocent. Of course, he also knew his denial sounded phony. Why would somebody put dope in his house? The police were not stupid. The DEA agents had read Ryan his rights and then chatted with Ryan, but he soon realized they were digging into his past. Ryan said, "I want to see my lawyer, Ted Lewis," and the questions stopped.

Ryan was processed, which meant fingerprinting, mug shot, a shower to delouse him, his wallet and watch were taken. He was given jail clothing at the Volusia County Branch Jail, and finally put in a cell with four other men. They didn't appear threatening. Ryan was bigger and younger than they were. Only one seemed friendly and started a conversation. Ryan was not in the mood for small talk, but answered a few questions. He did learn that he was in a section for male felons, not yet processed and waiting to see a judge.

***

My expectations of what to expect in the Humane Society building were not met. It was actually not that bad. If I had not been in such a bad mood, because of Ryan's arrest, it could have been fun. The humans were all friendly and nobody hurt me. I was led to a nice large, clean fenced in run. A lady used a scanner to read my chip implant, but I knew they wouldn't be able to raise Ryan because he had gone to jail. I thought that Ryan would be released soon and he would come for me, but that didn't happen, at least not soon enough for me.

A few days passed and I was growing more concerned every day. I had to get out of there and find Ryan. He needed me.

I learned that humans came and took animals away. They called it adoption. While I was a little confused by the term adoption, I figured that if I could get adopted, I would have a chance to find Ryan. It worked out well, but there were some drawbacks. It wasn't free, but the cost included lots of things that most dogs needed, like shots, worming, a checkup by a veterinarian, and neutering if needed. Now that one, the neutering, had my tail down until I realized it wasn't always necessary. There were a few other items, but Ryan had taken good care of me so my vet had a record of my shots.

After awhile they took a picture of me and I learned it would have been on their website, but a man came in looking for a good hunting dog, and while I had only hunted for my own food, my breed is good around water and hunting. The name retriever is a dead giveaway. I heard him talking to the lady who was showing him around, so I took a bird dog pointers stance—I had seen it on television—and he was impressed. When he came up to my cage and said, "Hello, fella," I moved closer and put out my paw to shake his hand. He reached through the wire mesh and shook my paw. I knew I had him. Humans really like to shake hands with dogs. Why? I have no idea.

There was a problem because I did have a microchip, and until they learned what happened to Ryan, they were reluctant to let me go. Finally, after the man signed an agreement, they let him take me. I think the agreement was that he would have to let me go back to Ryan if they ever found him, but I didn't actually read it, just got bits and pieces from the humans' conversations. The man was a little concerned about the scar where the bullet came out, but dismissed it after pushing around near the wound. It hurt when he pushed hard, but I acted as if it was nothing and licked his hand.

The man took me to his home, which was really a ranch with horses, and introduced me to another dog he called Ole Fred. Ole Fred was old. I could almost hear his bones creak. He couldn't see well and sniffed me for awhile before he went back to lie on the porch. I think he was a hound of some kind, possibly a basset. He had long ears and a long body on stubby legs.

The man's name was Willy. He was a big, rawboned man with a nose that reminded me of a hawk. I think it may have been broken at one time. His hair was thinning and he wore bib overalls. A woman came out of his house, which was about three times larger than Ryan's house, and he called her Mamma. I don't think she was his mother because she looked younger than Willy. I am not good at guessing human ages, but she looked about the same age as Megan's mother. He looked older than Ryan's father, who said he was fifty-five.

The lady greeted me and immediately found a bowl for my food and a bowl for my water. She took them out to a big building called a barn and sat them next to two other bowls. I sniffed them and decided they belonged to Ole Fred. The lady then took me on a tour of the ranch. She took me over to a pen where chickens were running around. She watched me as I watched the chickens. I guess I didn't pose a threat so we went on to see the horses. I had never been close to a real live horse. They are much bigger in person. One looked over the door of his stall and put his nose down to me. I sniffed him and he didn't seem to mind and made a funny noise by blowing across his big lips. They have very large teeth, but no sharp canine teeth, which I guess makes sense.

After my tour, the lady took me back to the house. I thought I was going to go inside but she closed the screen door in front of me and said, "Magic, you go visit Ole Fred and keep him company." She knew my name from my ID tag.

I wanted to get inside and use their computer, but I would have to wait until later. I could have simply run off, but I wanted to find out what happened to Ryan. On the drive from the Humane Society, I watched the road signs and kept track of the turns, but we took a few dirt roads without signs, so I would have to rely on my instincts to find my way back to Ryan's house.

The next morning Willy got up before the sun. I heard him inside talking to his wife. Ole Fred didn't move, but I went out to look around. I saw Willy leave the back door open when he came out and went to the barn. The back door didn't shut tight and I used my paw to pull it open. The woman was in the front of the house and I started looking for their computer. I found it off the kitchen in a small room with a few storage cabinets and an old wooden desk. The computer looked like an old one, but I didn't need blinding speed. I turned it on and waited forever for it to boot. Finally it came up with an operating system I had never seen. I didn't see any icons for the Internet Explorer or Netscape. It wasn't an Apple, so I kept looking. It took me longer than it should have for an intelligent dog, but I realized there was no connection to the internet. I look behind the computer and could not find a connection to the telephone, satellite or cable. I looked at a few files and saw the computer was used for recordkeeping. Willy or Mamma kept records of their horses. They bred horses and sold them. I was surprised how much money some of the horses brought and was absorbed in the financials when I heard a board creak and Mamma say, "My word. What are you doing?"

Oh no! She saw me typing. I looked back at her, saw the look on her face, and decided to leave Mamma and Willy's ranch. I didn't wait to say goodbye to Ole Fred and took off for the back door, which I pushed open with my paw. I ran out and headed for the dirt road that led up to the ranch.

***

Ryan had talked to Ted Lewis twice since his arrest. Ted had filed a motion for a bond hearing, but he was still waiting for a judge to rule on it. In the meantime, Ryan languished in jail. Ryan thought he would have been released on bail but the district attorney had swayed the judge and no bail had been set.

Apparently, whoever set Ryan up had done so effectively. Ryan had talked to his father, and once to Megan, who said she would go get Magic. Ryan was not yet allowed visitors.

In the exercise yard other prisoners wandered around the large fenced in area. A double row of fences, with razor sharp concertina wire on the top, surrounded the yard. Ryan stood looking out at the dark clouds that were rolling in and thinking about what he could do to convince a judge that he was not a drug dealer. Maybe a jury trial might be a good idea, but for now, he only wanted out. He had asked Megan to check on Magic and feed him. He had no idea that Magic had also been locked up.

"Hey, Jarhead." Ryan turned to see a thin, middle-aged man with thick, snow-white hair, standing next to him.

Ryan knew that getting into a fight while in jail was very dumb, but he bristled at the comment.

The man's leathery face broke out into a smile and he extended his hand to Ryan and said, "Third Marine Division, '65 to '69. Picked up a heart outside Khe Sanh and they cut me a medical. Still gotta limp."

Ryan relaxed and shook the man's hand.

"How'd you know I was in the Corps?"

The man smiled again and looked around before saying, "Man, I know everything."

Ryan grinned and asked, "You know when I am going to get out of here?"

"Man, that's the point. You ain't gonna get out of here. You understand what I'm saying?"

Ryan's smile faded and he said, "No, I don't understand what you are saying."

The man looked around again and moved closer to Ryan to whisper, "See those guys? Over by the fence. No, don't look now."

Ryan turned back to the man and said, "What about them?"

"The short one with the shaved head. He's gonna stick you first chance he gets."

Ryan said, "Why are you telling me this?"

The man shrugged and said, "Hey, once a Marine." He then ambled away and lit a cigarette.

Now Ryan's senses were on full alert, much like being on a patrol in Iraq or Afghanistan. He felt the hair on the back of his neck stand up. He knelt to tie his shoe and glanced over at the men by the fence. The one with the shaved head had a tattoo on the back of his head, but Ryan couldn't see it clearly from where he stood. If the man intended to stick a knife or some sharp instrument into Ryan, he would have to do it while outside. The metal detectors would have sounded as he entered through the gate. Ryan thought for a moment and decided that the knife had to be hidden outside in the exercise yard. It also occurred to Ryan that the knife might only be a long needle or piece of glass.

Ryan stayed in the same area of the yard, and the man with the shaved head and tattoo didn't come near him. Ryan thought for a moment that the old Marine was bullshitting him, but then he thought, if someone went to the trouble of having him locked up, they must want him out of the way badly enough to pay someone to kill him. The only one Ryan could think of was Babak, but why? Maybe the e-mail had been right on. This had something to do with the Department of Homeland Security. It still wasn't making sense when the buzzer sounded to call the prisoners back into their cells. Ryan watched out of the corner of his eye as the man with the shaved head moved toward the gate that led to the building. He seemed to be falling behind some of the other prisoners, maybe waiting to come up behind Ryan. Ryan thought about waiting until he was the last to go back in, but abandoned that idea. It would only put off the inevitable. Ryan would face his enemy now while he still had the advantage of surprise.

Ryan tried to loosen the thick muscles in his back and shoulders. He had no weapon but his body, but he was trained in martial arts in the Marine Corps and had taken a few sessions with a local Chun Kuk Do master in New Smyrna Beach.

Ryan started walking and soon was in a line of prisoners waiting to go through the narrow gate. He glanced over his shoulder a few times and purposely moved from side to side and let other prisoners pass.

The short man with a shaven head would be hard to see, and Ryan guessed he would have to be moving past other prisoners to reach Ryan before they were at the gate. Ryan moved to one side and knelt, ostensibly to tie his shoe. He saw the man working his way forward. The crowd of men had slowed and bunched up near the single file gate. Ryan could see the man looking for him. He was short and had to jump up occasionally to see over the heads of taller men. Ryan wondered if he would have help from other prisoners. He assumed that he would, so his tactics changed slightly. He would not only attack first in good Marine Corps style, but also separate the man from the crowd.

Ryan slipped up behind the man a few seconds after the man passed him on the other side of the broad line of prisoners. He dropped the man with a hard punch to the kidney. He then spun to face the other prisoners near him, but they were quickly moving away from him.

Now the man with the shaved head lay writhing on the ground. The line of prisoners had swung out to avoid Ryan who bent to search the man, but to his surprise the man rolled over and slashed out with a handmade knife. The knife, made more for puncturing than for cutting, was not sharp on the edges and only cut through Ryan's sleeve and first layer of skin. Ryan drew back and snapped a hard kick to the man's face. The knife dropped from the man's hand and blood erupted from his broken nose. Ryan started to grab the knife and finish the man, but hesitated for a moment. The man was no longer a threat, at least for awhile. He sprawled on the ground, unconscious. Ryan kicked the knife away.

CHAPTER 19

The walk back to Ryan's was much more difficult than I had imagined. It took me most of the day without stopping, and the muscle in my right shoulder was very sore when I got there. Although the direct distance might not have been more than ten miles, maybe fifteen miles, I kept taking the wrong roads. I found out later that I had been close to the town of Samsula, which is west of the big Highway 95. Getting across the highway was dangerous, and I didn't want to become roadkill. Eventually, I found State Highway 44, and from there I knew how to get home.

It was almost dark when I got there, and a great feeling of sadness came over me. Ryan was not there to greet me. His pickup truck was there, but his scent was faint. He hadn't been back since the arrest. To get into the backyard I had to jump the fence. I must have been more tired than I thought, because my first attempt ended in disaster. I slammed into the fence and fell back on the driveway with the wind knocked out of me. I laid there for a while trying to get both my body and mind working. I had to keep my mind on my objective, to get Ryan back.

I walked slowly back to the street, turned and ran hard toward the fence. This time I cleared it and hit hard on the other side. When this is over, I have to work on my jumping and landing skills.

Fortunately, my dog door was not nailed shut. I pushed it open and went into the dark house. It seemed eerily quiet. I walked to each room on the outside chance that Ryan would be there. Of course he wasn't but hope springs eternal. I read that in an Alexander Pope poem, and he was referring to humans, but it works for dogs too.

I went to the computer and booted it. Once I had my e-mail program working, I began composing. I knew who was behind this, Preston Winn, or maybe his sidekick, Susan Humphrey, so I sent them both an e-mail that might save Ryan.

Dear Mr. Winn and Ms. Humphrey:

Your feeble attempts to intimidate Mr. Quinn, while disturbing in their scope and viciousness, have no bearing upon the disclosure of your illegal scheme to sell top-secret power packs and exoskeletons to China and other countries.

Being a reasonable person, and one who understands the potential for good old American profits, I have decided not to contact the authorities. In fact, I have a business proposition for you both. It is one that will allow you both to continue reaping the rewards of your efforts and not spend the rest of your lives in a federal penitentiary. I hope my meaning is clear.

I propose that I become a partner, although a silent one, in your enterprise. Consider the intellectual depth I will provide, along with my influence within the halls of congress and the justice department, the meager one-third of your before tax profits should seem like a bargain and more than generous on my part. I mention the before tax profits only as reminder that your offshore accounts are not as secure as you once thought. The IRS would be ecstatic to see your new wealth; I however, can provide layered security for your funds.

To show good faith, I will destroy the records I have of your activities, and on your front, I think the release of Ryan Quinn will satisfy my need for fair play.

Sincerely,

Well what is in a name?

I reviewed my masterpiece and was about to hit the send key when I heard a noise outside. I looked out a window and saw a police car stopped in front and an officer get out. He went to the front door and rang the bell. He then checked the door. It was locked and he seemed satisfied. I was glad I hadn't turned on the television or a light. I waited for him to leave before going back to the computer.

I sat there and pondered my actions, or what would be my actions by one tap of my nail. What would I be starting? While I knew I had to do something to save Ryan from jail, I also considered that my sense of smell and great hearing were the cause of Ryan's trouble in the first place. Had I never started sending e-mails to Preston Winn, maybe Ryan would not have been arrested, nor would those thugs have tried to kill him. While I was not the initiator of Ryan's troubles, I was the catalyst that began the reaction and possibly escalated the threat until they decided to kill Ryan.

I never thought being a gifted dog would lead to this. I walked into the second bedroom, looked at the display, then the keyboard, and howled.

***

Ryan sat in the isolation cell and thought about Megan, Magic and his parents. He had his first appearance hearing, but the judge had not set a bond. They told him there was no bond allowed. Later, Ted told him that only that same judge could set a bond. Ted had filed for a bond hearing but had not heard back from the court. After Ryan's first hearing, he might have to wait another four to six weeks for a court appearance. Now, with him being isolated, he felt cut off from all help. He had told his story of what happened in the yard to one of the supervisors, but that was two days ago, and he hadn't been outside his cell or talked to anyone since then. The cell was small but there was enough room for Ryan to do setups and pushups. He did them until he was too exhausted to think. He then slept.

***

Susan Humphrey printed her copy of the e-mail from the anonymous person who knew about their scheme to make millions. At first she felt panic, if this person knew so much; his or her power over Susan was frightening. Susan decided it had to be a man. In addition to this new threat, she learned from her source that Ryan Quinn's assassination had been botched. Now, with him away from the inmate community, it would be very hard to eliminate him. Besides, the man who sent the e-mail wanted Ryan to be set free as a gesture of good faith. Good faith, who did he think he was fooling? But Susan was confused. If this person wanted Ryan Quinn free, he obviously did not fear that Ryan Quinn would screw up the deal they had going with the Chinese. She wondered why. The pieces did not fit together.

"Is the boss in?' Susan asked as she passed Preston's secretary and turned the doorknob to his office.

"I think—"

Preston stood next to a small closet that opened into his office. He had his trousers off and was adjusting the orthosis device on his foot.

"Can't you learn to knock?" he shouted.

"Don't get your drawers in a knot. Have you seen this?" She held out the e-mail as Preston hobbled around attempting to pull his trousers over the orthosis.

"What is it?" he said.

"You obviously haven't seen it. Checked your personal e-mail today?"

Preston zipped up his fly and walked barefoot to his desk. He snapped open the enclosed keyboard and pulled up the display. In a few seconds he had his e-mail. He clicked on send/receive mail, sat down and began to read.

Preston, who prided himself on good posture and religiously worked out in an executive health club, appeared to shrink as he read. He stole a glance at Susan, as if she knew more than the e-mail provided. When he was finished he went to the window behind his desk, looked out and said, "We have to find this person."

Susan, who still stood next to Preston's desk, said, "Okay, find him, but what do we do now?"

Preston waited for a while to answer. He turned and looked at his computer before saying, "For now we give him Mr. Quinn, but we are not going to share our hard work with this blackmailer. I will find him." He then asked, "Quinn hasn't been... eliminated yet, has he?"

"No, they have him in isolation. But it won't be easy to spring him."

"Why not?" Preston asked sharply.

"To quote you, it is like a snowball."

Preston blew out a long breath before he said, "Just do it. If this asshole decides to turn us in we'll both be visiting Mr. Quinn, or people like him."

The planting of the drugs at Ryan's house was not done by police or federal law enforcement people, consequently, the charges against Ryan had to run their course unless someone else confessed to planting the drugs in Ryan's house. This problem was going to be very hard to solve. After awhile Susan said, "He didn't say we had to have Quinn's charges dropped, he said release him. Maybe I can get my friend at Justice to whisper in the local judge's ear. Set a low bond. Tell him something about wanting to follow Quinn to get bigger fish."

Preston thought about that for a few seconds and said, "As long as it doesn't come back and bite us in the butt."

"Oh, I meant to tell you. You look cute in those boxer shorts."

She then walked out before Preston could form a reply. Was she being sarcastic or was it a real compliment? He looked back at his reflection in the window and patted his behind. Maybe he would go in for a workout later in the day, but now he had to contact the man who found that Ryan Quinn had been the source of the harassing e-mails. The source of this new e-mail should not be hard for him to find.

Susan went back to her office and began drafting a reply to the anonymous blackmailer.

> From: Preston Quinn:
>
> Whoever you are, you seem to understand the necessity of confidentiality. While I too hope to enjoy the fruits of my endeavors, I am not a greedy man and accept your proposal; however, it will be some time before payment is forthcoming from the parties you alluded to. I will keep you informed about the progress of our project.
>
> Your good faith suggestion will be accomplished shortly. I welcome the opportunity to meet you in person, as there are many issues that do not lend themselves to written correspondence.
>
> Sincerely,
>
> Preston Winn

Susan felt the e-mail was too wordy, but it sounded like one that Preston would write, although he seldom wrote anything himself. He did, however, critically edit his secretary's drafts. She printed the draft, had a smoke and took the draft to Preston.

Preston was looking smug when Susan opened the door to his office. He looked up at her and motioned for her with his fingers. He pointed to the chair in front of his desk, where she intended to sit whether he asked her or not.

She slipped the e-mail draft across his desk and said, "Anything you would like to add?"

Preston looked at the draft and then scribbled on it with his pen.

"I would like to add that we know who you are, but that will take a little longer. His mistake, or hers, was sending an e-mail. My contact said he should be able to run it down."

Susan reached over and picked up the e-mail draft. Preston had added one item. It was now from Susan Humphrey and Preston Winn.

***

I hardly slept that night. I kept hearing sounds. I decided to sleep on Ryan's bed. I could smell his scent on the pillow. He might notice a hair or two when he got home and be angry with me, but it would be worth it. I missed him that much. It was surprising how attached I had become to Ryan. He is like my human father. In the morning I tried to open the new big bag of dry dog food, but the top was closed and I didn't want to destroy it by gnawing through it with my teeth. There was less than a cup full in the old bag, but it filled me for the moment. Ryan always mixed water with it, so it was dry and harder to eat, but I was hungry. The long walk the day before had worn me out.

Twice that morning I thought I heard Megan's car drive by. I even sensed that she was near. If Ryan didn't come home soon, I considered going to Megan's, although I couldn't use her computer because she always put me outside.

I checked my e-mail, which by the way was a new account and one that Zeus set up for me. He said it could not be traced back to me. It would appear as though it came from a Department of Justice computer. That afternoon there was a new e-mail, and it was the mail I had been waiting for. I read it twice. They were giving in too easily. Of course, I didn't trust them. They did indicate that Ryan would be released soon. As far as meeting me in person, well, that was not going to happen.

I hadn't replied to their e-mail, and decided to wait until Ryan was released before doing anything more about Preston Winn. I spent the day working on some of my school assignments but had a hard time concentrating. So far I was pulling straight As, but that could change quickly if I didn't hit the books. Actually, I don't really hit the books, I read them online. I got that phrase from another student. We have a cyber classroom and send e-mails or chat with each other. It is strange, but one girl wants to meet me. She likes the sound of my voice; however, she has never heard it. She was referring to the structure of my sentences, my syntax. What a shock if she ever heard my voice. I wonder if the wolfman was real. Maybe an experiment that went wrong. It is something to think about.

There have been a number of textbooks that have not been available in digital format; consequently, I did independent research to answer some of the quizzes. So far I have been lucky. The classes are very easy, but I am still only a freshman. Ryan graduated with a 3.9 grade point average. So far mine is 4.0.

I finished two assignments, sent them off and then watched a little television. That night I decided that I had waited long enough. I set off to Megan's house. While the trip wasn't long, I forgot to check the weather channel before going out. They warn people, maybe they should warn dogs, too. I wasn't more than a mile from home when the sky opened up and it poured. It came down so hard I could barely see. The streets were flooded and the wind whipped the rain into my face. I was going up the North Causeway Bridge to the beach side when the sky lit up with a tremendous display of cloud to ground lightning. Once in awhile the lightning would crack nearby and the hair on my back would stand up. One strike hit a telephone pole and a transformer blew up in a ball of fire and light. I thought the wind was going to blow me off the bridge, but I managed to make it to the beach side without swimming or becoming a crispy critter. I was getting soaked and chilled even though it was still summer. The wind and rain brought the temperature down and my wet coat added to my discomfort. The five mile trip became a journey in misery. By the time I got to the Alvarez home, I was a mess, shaking and looking like a discarded mop, not a proud golden retriever.

The Alvarez home is on what is referred to as beachside in New Smyrna. It's located in a little group of homes called Inlet Villas. They sit between the river and the ocean, with a short walk to either one. Megan's house is on Villa Way, which is pretty much a circle with houses on both sides of the street. There is a sign that reads "Private Property, Residents Only," but I ignored it and trotted through the puddles to their front door. I was about to scratch at the door when I noticed that the house was dark. The rain was still coming down in sheets that all but blanked out the streetlights. I went around to the side and found the windows were dark and the same on the other side. I couldn't check out the back because of the fence. The neighbors' lights were off, and if it hadn't been for the driving rain, I would have seen that all the houses were dark.

It finally dawned on me. They had gone to bed. What was I thinking? I had watched the late news and then an old movie before going out. I don't usually worry about time, I guess it's the dog in me. I forgot that human's get a little testy if you wake them up. I learned that from Ryan when I first came to live with him. It must have been two or three in the morning and I didn't know what to do. I crawled under the front porch eave and tried to make myself comfortable, but wet, cold and confused, it was hard to do.

***

Ryan heard the corrections officer's footfalls. The cell door slid open and the man said, "Get your belongings and come with me."

He didn't have any belongings, but he followed the corrections officer to the next gate that a turnkey opened electronically. Ten minutes later Ryan stood outside the Volusia County Branch Jail with Ted Lewis.

Ryan hadn't asked any questions. He had been released, and that was good enough for him, but once outside again he was full of questions, most of which Ted could not answer. Ryan thought he would see Megan outside in Ted's car, but Ted's BMW was empty.

"Boy it is good to be out of that place," Ryan said as they walked to the car, "What took so long?"

Ted shook his head and said, "I have no idea why the judge changed his mind. He set the bond so low I made it, knowing of course you are not planning a trip to the Bahamas. The big problem I had was convincing the warden that you would be available to answer questions about an alleged assault on another prisoner. What the hell was that about?"

Ryan waited for Ted to unlock his car before he answered, "Oh, *that* alleged assault. Well this guy tried to stick a knife in me, and I broke his nose. "

"Anybody see it?" Ted asked.

"Most of the yard saw it, but according to the guard who came by my cell, nobody saw a thing. Now tell me, why am I out on bond? Haven't the phony charges been dropped?"

Ted stood with the car door open and said, "You were released on bond, but you will still have to convince a judge that you are not guilty. That might be a big problem."

"So I'm not free?"

"You are free to continue your life with a few restrictions."

Ryan said, "I know. I can't take a vacation to Cancun. And I can't be accepted at the FBI academy, and I can't face Megan and tell her that her future husband to be may go to prison until she is an old lady. And I can't...." Ryan stopped and got into the car.

Ted slipped behind the wheel and started the engine. He put on his seat belt and carefully backed out of the parking lot. Once out on Highway 92, he looked over at Ryan who appeared to be lost in thought, and said, "I've got some bad news for you."

Ryan glanced over at him and then back out the window. "Bad news, you mean worse than being... bad news?"

"Yes. It's about your dog."

"Magic? What happened to Magic?"

Ted merged unto Highway 95 south and accelerated until he was even with the traffic.

"He's in the hospital. Megan took him there."

"What happened? He got out and was hit by a car? He got out once before but I didn't think he would do it again."

"No, that's not it. He has pneumonia."

"Pneumonia? I don't understand."

Ted watched his rear view mirror as he moved into the left lane to pass a tourist. "She found him on her front doorsteps a few days ago. He was in bad shape and having trouble breathing. I guess he had been out in the rain all night."

"Why didn't she take him in when it started to rain? She doesn't have an enclosure outside for him or for her puppy."

"She didn't take him in because she didn't know what happened to him. There was no way to reach you, but your dog has been missing for awhile. It's a long story. The animal control people took him to the Humane Society, and some rancher took him home, but he got away. After that, we don't know. Megan has been looking all over for him. She had been so worried about you, she hadn't thought about your dog until you asked her to take care of him. Then she couldn't reach you."

Ryan said, "Damn," and hit the dashboard with the flat of his hand, which drew a look from Ted.

CHAPTER 20

Preston Winn smiled and pushed the intercom key to Susan Humphrey's office.

She answered, "Yes?"

Preston said, "You'll love this. I'm going to lunch, come with me."

"Give me a minute."

It took fifteen, but when Susan Humphrey opened the door to Preston Winn's office, he knew it was worth the wait. She stood with the light behind her, silhouetted in her cream and red print chiffon dress; he immediately thought they might take a long lunch break, maybe not even come back to the office. Some women seem to grow more attractive when they are pregnant, some when they have a new boyfriend, but Susan grew more attractive when she was making money, big money. In spite of the problems with Ryan Quinn and the anonymous blackmailer, the potential for millions more made her glow.

Susan sat across from Preston at the Army Navy Club. His membership to the private club dated back a few years, and he enjoyed the quiet ambiance and great food. He ordered wine but couldn't wait for the waiter to return before leaning forward and saying, "The new suits are on their way. Four of them and two power packs."

He looked around to see if they were in earshot of the next table before saying, "I have the specs on the power packs. You won't believe it."

Susan slipped her shoe off under the table and rubbed the inside of his left ankle with hers before saying, "Tell me. I can't stand the anticipation."

He looked around once more before saying, "This is classified Top Secret, so keep it quiet. The damn power pack is really a miniaturized nuclear power plant."

Susan sat up in her chair and said, "You are kidding?"

"No, it's a very big breakthrough. Most of the weight is in the shielding. The actual power plant is very small. The latest micro and nanotechnology."

Susan whispered, "Isn't it dangerous. Radiation and all?"

"Without the shielding it is, but the amount of fissionable material is minuscule. It heats some special water just like a big nuclear power plant, and that superheated steam turns a special ceramic turbine wheel that turns a miniaturized generator. It's also has a small, lightweight battery."

The wine steward appeared and Preston stopped for a moment to sample the wine. After it was poured he continued, "Now about the new suits. They are military only prototypes."

Susan said, "I have been having some problems with our pricing. The people in China say they can buy them cheaper from the Japanese and then duplicate them."

"Not these they won't. Our new models are covered with a material that can stop a rifle bullet up to... I forget the velocity and weight, or was it size, anyway, only heavy weapons will pierce the damn stuff. It's not just the exoskeletons, which everybody is working on, but the material that makes them hard to spot on radar and even harder to kill."

A waiter appeared and Preston stopped the description of the militarized exoskeleton and ordered. After the waiter left he continued, "Now, our new suits can also fight, or at least one of them can."

"Fight?" Susan asked after sipping her wine.

"Yes," he leaned forward and said, "It's got this big machinegun built right into the damn suit."

Susan smiled and said, "Sounds like we got ourselves a real bad ass."

***

I guess my immune system needed a tune up. Stress can knock the heck out of it, at least it does to humans, and I feel it has similar affects upon dogs, maybe even cats. A night out in the rain should not have affected me so, but it did, and I ended up in an animal hospital. I must confess, I really felt lousy. I couldn't breathe well and my skin was hot and dry. My chest made a funny noise when I tried to get a lung full of air. The good news, Ryan came home, or at least to the animal hospital. Megan was with him and she kept apologizing about me getting lost.

I was not lost. There were times when I was not certain where I was, but I most certainly was not lost. I am an Alpha Male Golden Retriever, AMGR. I do not get lost.

The vet gave me a shot and then some pills. I learned not to refuse pills during my last stay in an animal hospital. If you refuse, they open your mouth and throw the pill down your throat. It is not a pleasant sensation, so I take pills without drama.

After two more days in the hospital, I was feeling much better and Ryan arrived and took me home. I think he was genuinely glad to see me and to be home, but his overall mood had changed. In the past, his face looked like he had a slight grin on it, as if he knew a funny joke but didn't want to tell anyone. Even when he was sitting reading a newspaper, reading a novel, watching television, or cleaning the house, he looked pleasant. I felt I could approach him, but now, when he wasn't playing with me or talking to Megan, his face showed his new mindset, and it was far from pleasant. At night I heard him tossing restlessly in bed. At first I popped up and looked at him, thinking he was in pain—which he was—but after a few nights, I realize he was wrestling with his own demons, and as much as I wanted to help, I could not. I considered trying my hand at anonymous e-mails again but was hesitant. I didn't know how much they affected the problems that Ryan was having, but I suspected they were a major factor. The moral dilemma: Strive against evil, wrongdoing, and hurt the one you love, or do nothing and let evil survive?

After Ryan woke me last night with his nightmares I couldn't fall back to sleep, so I went back to the computer and looked at the e-mails Mr. Preston Winn and Susan Humphrey were sending. I noticed a new caution in their mail, but the replies from Cynthia Morgan were not as guarded.

She was not happy with Mr. Winn. He had not been down to see her in awhile, and even though I have no experience in such matters of the heart, or loins, I suspect she will soon be seeking a new suitor for her affection.

I was thinking how ineffectual I had been because I couldn't speak, then it dawned on me, I can speak in a fashion. I could use a text-to-voice program to speak. While not perfect, and it would be hard to carry on a real conversation, I might be able to pull it off. I could use the text-to-voice program to convert my typed messages into something that sounded very much like a human voice. I couldn't practice while Ryan was home, so my progress would be slow, and there were a few technical issues I might need help with, but I set out with new fervor to help Ryan. I would have to find the perfect voice for Mr. Kunastros. I sent an e-mail to my internet friend Zeus. If anybody would know about the technology of text-to-voice, it would be Zeus.

Ryan took me over to see Megan tonight and to play in her backyard. The puppy was glad to see me and bit me painfully on the ear. Her puppy teeth were as sharp as needles. The cat jumped up on a picnic table and acted like I wasn't there, but I knew better. I am beginning to understand cats, at least a little bit.

Ryan and Megan were deep in a conversation that I wanted to hear, but the puppy wanted to play and could not be convinced to leave me alone. Consequently, I missed some of it, but I did learn that Ryan would have to go to court. He could even be sent to prison for a long time if whoever planted the drugs in our house did not come forward and confess. Ryan suspected that his problems were all tied to the crate he found and the two men at the warehouse. I wanted to bark and tell him he was right on, but as you know, I couldn't speak, at least not yet.

Megan, who is usually intense and ready to take on the world, also had a mood change. She looked down at her feet as she spoke, as did Ryan. They both needed cheering up. They had so much going for them: health, a wonderful country in which to live, no mad scientist ready to cut them apart to see how they ticked, and they had each other. Nobody, man or dog, knows what tomorrow may bring. They should've been happy, so I ran over and knocked Ryan down and started kissing him. Megan was going to be next, but she piled on and soon we were all rolling on the grass, laughing. They couldn't hear my laughs but they were there inside. Even puppy joined in and let out little barks that sounded like she was saying, "Yipe, yipe." The cat just watched, too sophisticated to have fun.

My antics worked, at least for awhile, and then Mrs. Alvarez came out and sat with us on the back steps. She brought me another big juicy bone. What a sweet and caring human. No wonder Megan turned out so well. Even the cat likes her, for it came over and jumped onto her lap and made this funny purring sound, like a miniature motor boat.

***

Special Agent Howard Lowell of the Federal Bureau of Investigation opened the file on Mr. Ryan William Quinn. He had plenty of work to keep him busy, but the Quinn case kept interrupting his thoughts at the most inopportune times. His wife, Fay, told him at breakfast that he wasn't listening to her. She had gone on about the pool service and how they hadn't kept the pool chemicals balanced. He didn't intentionally turn her off, but her voice fell into the background and Mr. Ryan Quinn's case popped up again. His arrest on drug charges surprised Special Agent Howard Lowell. It didn't fit his profile.

"Well, what are you going to do about it?" his wife had said.

Without thinking he answered, "About what?"

That had been this morning, and he was still feeling the heat from her flare-up. He closed the file, but did not return it. It was available on his monitor, but he was an old-fashioned cop at heart and liked the feel of a paper file and not one in some database in a computer. He had three years to go before he could retire, and his chances for advancement were pretty much zero, but he knew the young man was not lying. Lowell had been an Orlando City policeman before he joined the FBI. He could read body language as well as some of the so-called experts, and he could not let this case go in spite of what his boss told him. He knew he wasn't a team player and maybe that's why he wasn't promoted when others around him were, but something stunk about this case and he was going to do something about it, right after he called the pool maintenance company.

***

Ryan was working again, but this time at a job Ted Louis arranged. It makes sense to have a good friend. I would like one, but so far I haven't met a dog with whom I can communicate nor a human I dare tell about my abilities. Ryan worked at the Municipal Golf Course. Basically, he cut grass and cleaned things.

My text-to-voice project was coming along well. There were many free programs, which I tend to gravitate toward, and some nifty ones that I could buy. Again, Zeus came to my rescue and sent me a program that he had developed. I could develop my own semantic and grammar rules, change the basic male and female voices in pitch, cadence, and tone. I could also borrow a voiceprint of famous people and have my voice sound like them. Maybe John Wayne or James Cagney would work with Mr. Winn. "Okay, pilgrim" or "You dirty rat." Zeus sent the voice of Bart Simpson, but I failed to see humor in that. I was working on a serious problem.

The next step was getting my new voice to talk over the telephone. Zeus said he had a sick (sick as in good) program that used voiceover internet protocol, but I found a simpler method but not one that Zeus liked. Ryan has a speaker telephone sitting next to the computer. By nudging one of his small computer desk speakers over to the telephone, and typing my words into the text-to-voice program, my new voice would carry from Ryan's computer to the telephone.

My first trial ended in frustration. I dialed a dog grooming service to ask about their prices, but I heard a message that they had recently changed their menu and to listen carefully. I did listen, but when they got to the one I wanted, they said, "Press five." I didn't have a five I could press. I can type in five, but that comes out with the word five spoken in my new voice. I tried a few other numbers and finally got one that said, "Press one or say one." That one worked, but I never did get a live person on my first trial run. I also found it strange that everyone had recently changed their menus. It was after I disconnected that it occurred to me. I could have simply used my paw to press the digit five on the speaker telephone. This telephone business was new to me, so I thought I would dial random numbers and talk to humans. I found that some did not have a menu, but many had a recording device or voicemail. As I could not have an intelligent conversation with voicemail, I declined to record my message. I also didn't leave a message because they might have telephoned me while Ryan was at home. Very few humans wanted to talk. I did find that children and teenagers were more likely to chat with me. I did get invited to a birthday party by a female human who was going to be sixteen years of age. It sounded like fun except that they were going to have a blast and I don't like loud noises.

I thought by watching humans on the television using telephones and observing Ryan, I could easily master the fine points. I was wrong. Humans are used to communicating with each other by voice. They've been doing it since they were very young. I have no such experience. Apparently, the spoken word is often a grammatical muddle. Incomplete sentences and fragments are the norm, and phrases that make little sense are sprinkled freely within the communication. As an example: "You know what I mean?" and "Like, you know" or "Like, really." My favorite is, "You're kidding." Is "You're kidding" a question? Equally confusing is the apparent question when they answer the telephone with, "Yeah?" How can I answer that question?

After a few days of intense study, I was beginning to understand the verbal form of American humans in more depth. I also began working on my Spanish vocabulary. One major drawback was my relatively slow typing speed, which made the pause between words unrealistically long. To overcome this problem, I began practicing two paw typing. To be correct I should say two claw typing. My right front leg is almost without pain now, so I can use it freely. Along those lines, I also wrote a few scripts that could be selected by assigned key strokes. Such phrases as, "How are you today? I am fine, thank you," and, "Goodbye" could be typed by hitting the preassigned F keys. I also wrote much longer Microsoft WORD documents that told of the nefarious dealings of Mr. Preston Winn and his accomplice Susan Humphrey. When I telephoned the appropriate law enforcement agency, I would simply let the text-to-voice program speak for me.

I was not completely ready to communicate with humans at the level I believed to be necessary for unconditional acceptance; however, time waits for no one. Unless you can approach the speed of light and then time does slow... but I digress. I intercepted an e-mail from Preston Quinn to Cynthia Morgan. He asked her to have a truck ready for him at their Vero Beach building in a month. He also wanted all personnel to be out of the building on that day and night. He specified that the truck's storage be at least 18 feet long, and the keys were to be left in the truck.

It was obvious that he intended to move something from the Vero Beach site, and I assumed it to be the exoskeletons and power packs, or something else illegal. Earlier, he had responded to an e-mail about the charter of a cargo turboprop aircraft; however, I thought it might be normal business. Then, after seeing the dates, realized that there was a connection between the two. He was going to move something out of the Vero Beach building and fly it somewhere. I decided to try my new voice on Mr. Winn. I had his direct line and prepared some of my speech to him in advance.

This could be the capstone of my career as a dog, and I needed courage to proceed. I tried my text-to-voice to telephone by ordering a pizza with all the trimmings. I told them to leave it on the front porch and paid over the telephone with my VISA. If only I could get doggie treats so easily.

After the pizza was delivered, I worked at opening the front door. As long as Ryan doesn't lock the top dead bolt, I can usually open the door by working the knob around in my mouth and pushing with my front paws.

The pizza was delicious, but it gave me a stomach ache. Too much cheese. I hid the pizza box in the backyard. For a lawn care man, Ryan had recently neglected our backyard. The weeds could hide a small horse. He used to keep it clean and mowed, but since spending time in jail, and the threat of years in a prison, he has changed.

I stared at the computer and even brought up the text-to-voice program. I positioned the computer speaker next to the telephone and stopped. Something wasn't right. What was it? I sat there for another five minutes, thinking. The telephone rang and I looked at the small display. It was Megan's telephone. Then it dawned on me. Caller ID! If I telephoned Mr. Winn, he would know where the call came from. The solution was simple: block my number.

My telephone call to Mr. Winn went fairly well. I made my point, when I said; "Perhaps you misunderstood our agreement. Your part was not complex. Merely have the charges dismissed against Mr. Ryan Quinn."

He attempted to bypass the question by asking to meet in person, saying he didn't want to discuss complex and fragile matters over the telephone. I told him that was impossible for now. Once the charges were dropped against Ryan, I might consider a meeting. Yeah, when pigs flew.

When he finally agreed to my demands he added the caveat, "These things take time."

I remembered that Ryan's court date was in two weeks, so I gave him ten days. After that, I told him that I would feel he had betrayed my trust. The consequences would be severe. I hinted at long jail terms for him and his able assistant, Susan Humphrey. I then hung up, feeling smug. A few minutes later, I started to worry, and my smug feeling vanished. I was becoming too human.

CHAPTER 21

Preston Winn paced behind his desk and alternately stopped to look out the window at the crowded street below. His plans for the future were in shreds. His life's work in jeopardy. The smooth road to wealth had taken an abrupt detour, and he was no longer in the driver's seat. The telephone call had convinced him that he had only ten days in which to act. He was trying to balance the fear inside him with the need to survive. He knew he needed to act and act now. He had talked and talked to Susan about the charges against that bastard, Ryan Quinn, but she was right. Setting the records straight would implicate both of them. There were too many people involved now to simply bribe or threaten. He pressed Susan Humphrey's intercom button, and when she answered, he said weakly, "Susan, can you spare a minute please?"

Susan Humphrey walked into Preston's office with a frown on her face. His voice had unnerved her. It was so unlike Preston to use the word *please*.

"What's wrong?" she asked.

Preston turned around from staring out the window and said, "We have to talk."

Susan sat in a chair and leaned forward. "I asked, what's wrong?"

Preston sat behind his desk but then got back up, too nervous to sit still. He rubbed his hands together and said slowly, "I heard from my friend earlier today. The one who finds people."

When he stopped, Susan said, "Go on."

"He found where the e-mail from the blackmailer came from."

Susan urged him on with, "Well, where?"

"Here in D.C."

"There are a lot of people inside the beltway. Was he more specific?"

Preston nodded and leaned on his desk, as if for support, before saying, "Yes. Our mysterious blackmailer called from his office in the Department of Justice here in town."

Susan sank back in her chair and blew out a breath before saying, "Oh, shit!"

Preston waited for a few seconds before he said, "It gets worse."

Susan stared at him until he continued, "He called me a few minutes ago. You have ten days to get Mr. Quinn cleared of all charges or your ass goes to jail."

Susan stood and thought for a moment before she said, "Too bad I won't be your cellmate, cutie pie, because I don't have a snowball's chance in hell of getting those charges dropped. Believe me; I have tried until my... you don't want to know the details."

Preston shook his head. How had he let this woman ruin his life? He reached into his desk and looked at a spreadsheet he had been developing. He'd started it after the report this morning on the source of the blackmailer's e-mail. He looked down at the figures and said, "If we can deliver the new military exoskeleton suits and the two power packs, we will have enough to live on for the rest of our lives. Anywhere but in the U.S."

Susan's eyebrows arched and she said, "With you?"

Preston didn't want to lose Susan's millions, and if he had to marry her, so be it. Divorcing his wife hadn't yet occurred to him. He seldom saw her and had his own apartment in Georgetown. Once he had his hand on Susan's money, he could live in the manner he had earned.

He answered her with, "You could do worse. Besides, I'll be rich, very rich."

Susan smiled and said, "You know how to sweet talk a lady."

Lady? Preston thought. His wife was a lady. Susan was... Susan.

"We have ten days. I can move up the time schedule for the airplane pickup and the truck. I have a lot to do in ten days."

He stopped and thought about the enormous lifestyle change he was about to embark upon. He could get a new identity easily enough, and he needed to empty his joint bank and broker's accounts with his wife at the last minute.

Susan said, "Your friend, the one who finds people and addresses. Why can't he find this asshole who is screwing with us?"

"Said he needed more time. He also said not to get my hopes up."

"He's narrowed it down to the Justice Department. Do you think you could recognize his voice if you heard it again?"

Preston thought and said with renewed interest, "Maybe. Maybe I could. Do you remember that old actor, Charlton Heston?"

"Before my time, but I've seen him in an old movie and once on TV. Did he sound like Heston?"

"Very much so. He had a distinctive voice, very powerful, like a man who has power."

Susan smiled broadly, "All is not lost. We visit our friends at Justice."

Preston's mood changed as he saw a possible solution to his problem. He went over to his office closet and took out his coat. He then told his secretary to have the motor pool send a car around to get him. He would be at the Department of Justice.

As an afterthought, he said to Susan, "Are you coming?"

Susan shook her head and said, "Don't you think it would be prudent to schedule appointments. Some of those people are actually busy."

"Good point. Give me a list of everyone above the grade of GS 12, plus all ES levels in the building."

Susan asked, "How about the administrative law judges?"

"Why would... very well, even the judges."

Susan turned and left his office and Preston told his secretary to hold off on the motor pool car.

An hour later Susan came back in, threw a pile of papers on Preston's desk, and said, "If you live to be a hundred you won't have time to talk to all these people.

'"What are you talking about? There can't be that many."

Susan began to flip over each paper. "This is just the Antitrust Division." She flipped through half the stack and said, "This is the Civil Division. I haven't even printed the Civil Rights or the Criminal Division, and it goes all the way alphabetically to Tax and then the U.S. Attorneys. In between are more people you and I can never meet before the deadline. I say we pack our bags and get out of town while we can."

Preston looked at his Rolex and said, "Narrow the search to the top four executives in each division and make appointments for me. Try to make them short and come up with something I can use as an excuse to talk to them."

Susan threw the pile of papers into Preston's face and yelled, "Do it yourself! I have bags to pack," and stormed out of his office.

Preston didn't move, even though one piece of paper landed on his head and balanced there. He stared at the open door until his secretary peeked in and said, "Is there anything you need, Mr. Winn?"

Preston brushed the paper off his head and said, "I have some appointments I would like you to make with certain officials over at Justice. I'll give you a list by tomorrow morning." When she stayed in the doorway, he added without emotion, "You may close the door."

Susan was letting the stress get to her. Preston swept the remaining papers off his desk, took out his own directory and found the Department of Justice.

***

After my success with the text-to-voice program and my call to Mr. Winn, I decided it was time to try my luck with Ryan. Just something to keep him alerted to Mr. Winn's plans. I wanted him to believe in me and my pseudonym, Mr. Kunastros. Charlton Heston did not sound Greek, so I started looking for a believable voice and finally selected the Mexican born actor Anthony Quinn. Not that he was Greek, but he played Zorba the Greek and that was the movie I downloaded for the voice soundtrack. I would like to read the book someday, but I have little time now for pleasurable activities. It took me three days to perfect the text-to-voice with an

Anthony Quinn accent and timing. When I was finished, I paused to wonder if somewhere back many years, both Ryan Quinn and Anthony Quinn came for the same Irish bloodline. Interesting and perhaps prophetical.

I blocked my number and tried my first telephone call to Ryan. It lasted only a few seconds. He picked up his cell telephone while at work, I told him I was Mr. Kunastros and he hung up on me, but I don't give up easily. I waited until it was his lunch break and tried again. This time I started with a prepared script, "Don't be rude, my friend. I am trying to save your miserable life and that of your wonderful dog, and lovely future wife Megan Alvarez. Why would I do that? Because I love justice. You are a young and brave man, I respect you. Do not dishonor me by such foolishness. It is unlike you."

I paused there to let Ryan speak, which he did and said, "Bullshit." He then paused before saying, "Don't I know you? You sound familiar."

I accidentally hit one of my preprogrammed F keys and said, "I am fine," but I quickly typed, "I am fine with that, but you have never met me. Now, are you ready to listen?"

There was a delay and some background noise while Ryan spoke to someone at work, but then he said, "Go ahead."

I used another pretyped script and told him about Preston Winn and Susan Humphrey's new company in Vero Beach and about their plan to sell new military prototype exoskeletons and power packs to the Chinese.

At the conclusion Ryan said, "I have to go now. Phone me at home. I get off about six."

My heart sank. How was I going to telephone him while he's in the house?

***

Preston came back from the Department of Justice, ragged and frustrated. His scheduled meetings had not gone well with the busy bureaucrats and even less with the judges. He had loitered in the hallways, listening to the people's voices. One man did have a booming voice, much like the actor Charlton Heston. Preston had followed him for five minutes hoping to hear him speak again. When the man went into the men's room, Preston followed. At the urinals Preston tried to engage him in conversation, but the man finally said while washing his hands, "I don't know what your problem is, but I'm not your type. Now take a walk."

Preston sulked home to his apartment in Georgetown that night both exhausted and discouraged. He knew he needed a good hard workout to clear his mind, but decided to have a drink instead. Two hours later, he fell asleep on a couch in an alcoholic stupor. He awoke during the night and threw up his dinner. He took two aspirins and went into the bedroom but did not undress. He fell across the bed and moaned. His head throbbed and he thought he might be sick again. Thoughts of prison filled his mind. Preston had seen movies and television programs about prisons, and knew he could never survive. People like Ryan Quinn or even Susan Humphrey might do well, but not him. He was meant for the better things in life. Damn that blackmailer. He pledged that he would find him the next day.

Preston arose at eleven the next morning to the ringing of his apartment's telephone. Few people had the number. He picked up the telephone and managed a feeble, "Yes?"

"Nice going. You sound like hell," Susan Humphrey said.

Preston shook his head and then grimaced. He didn't need anyone telling him how he sounded.

"What do you want?" he asked.

"Have you found our Charlton Heston, or have you been partying all night?"

"No, and never mind the sarcasm. Have you gotten to anyone who can drop the charges on Quinn?"

"I'm working on it, and I have packed. I hope your airplane has plenty of room."

"This is not a vacation cruise we're taking. Buy what you need when we get there. I have someone working on our new passports and other identification."

"Tell me. What is my new name?"

"I have no idea. It is up to the people who do that sort of thing."

Susan didn't reply immediately; when she did she said, "I've closed out most of my accounts. How about you?"

"I'm holding off on the joint accounts. Don't want my wife screwing this up."

"Why bother? You'll have plenty of money."

Preston decided not to tell her that almost all of his wife's money was in joint accounts. It was a considerable amount. Their total portfolio was in the millions, but much of it was in stocks and some bonds. She had her own credit cards and checking account, but after five years of marriage, Preston had most of her money in joint accounts with him. He considered the money his and had no qualms about taking it with him. He did regret the loss of his government pension, but unless he found the mysterious blackmailer, that would be left behind.

"I'll work on it," he said.

After Susan's telephone call, he showered, shaved and dressed. He looked at his appointment book and saw that he'd already missed three, but if he hurried he could make it to the Department of Justice headquarters on Pennsylvania Ave. The thought of food nauseated Preston but he prepared a bowl of oatmeal and ate a few bites before leaving.

At the end of the day, he had made no progress and still had a headache, but he managed to keep down a light dinner. The next morning he tried again. Sober and feeling better, his mood changed. He felt confident that he would find the blackmailer and then kill him. He had never thought of himself as a person who would kill, but that had changed. He wouldn't have someone else do it. He looked forward to the grizzly process himself. He even began fantasizing about how he would do it. That afternoon he went back to his office at the Department of Homeland Security. His voicemail was full, as was his incoming e-mails and in-basket, which his secretary usually kept out of sight. Preston looked at the work ahead and thought, *why bother*. Then again, if he succeeded in finding the blackmailer, who he now thought of as Charlton

Heston, he needed to maintain at least the appearance of carrying out his duties.

His personal telephone rang and a stranger said, "Hello, Mr. Winn. Time is getting short."

***

The time limit I gave Preston Winn was almost up, and I decided to telephone him and see if Ryan was going to be a free man. I prepared a few new scripts and typed a new word document to save me from typing a long passage without a mistake. Sometimes typos sound really weird on the text-to-voice output.

I started off with "Hello, Mr. Winn. Time is getting short."

As soon as I heard the words spoken by my text-to-voice program, I realized I had the wrong voice. I was Anthony Quinn again, but I thought fast and typed, "I have many voices. Now tell me, when will Mr. Quinn's charges will be dropped?"

Mr. Winn hemmed and hawed, but never gave me a specific date. I let him talk, because I was still not fast at typing. I finally used the prepared WORD documents that said, "It appears that you are not taking my kind suggestions to heart; consequently, I have prepared a media release which will read as follows: Preston Winn, senior official in the DHS and his assistant have been caught with their greedy little hands in the top secret military cookie jar. A senior military official said, under the cloak of anonymity, that the results of Mr. Winn and Miss Humphrey's theft of military secrets could threaten the security of our nation and vital interests abroad. Both FBI agents and Army Intelligence operatives are at this moment arresting the couple..." It went on a bit longer to tell the public about how they managed to hide narcotics in Ryan's home to take pressure off of them.

Mr. Winn's reply to my news release was silence. He finally shouted, "I'm doing the best I can! Leave me alone! For God's sake, leave me alone," and hung up.

I didn't know he believed in God. Strange?

***

Preston Winn gave up the search for the anonymous blackmailer, and regained some of his composure once he realized he had no choice but to run. But running with millions of dollars was not too bad. He had always liked the south of France and parts of Italy. Susan favored the Caribbean, but it was crowded with American expatriates and the long arm of the CIA might reach them there. He had the plans for the new power pack, and that was his ace in the hole, potentially a billion dollar hand.

He didn't want to leave easy to follow tracks when he left Washington, so the plan was to fly to Miami, take a limo to West Palm Beach, see Cynthia Morgan and borrow one of her vehicles for a ride up to Vero Beach. Once at Vero Beach they would load the newest exoskeletons and the power packs into the rental truck and take them next door to the airport. The charter Beechcraft 1900D turboprop would fly them to Cancun, Mexico. From there they would wait for the Chinese contact to take the suits and power packs. Payment would be to his new offshore account. They would send their personal effects and clothing on a commercial carrier to a storage facility in Bahrain. Once they settled on a permanent site, they would arrange for the shipment to be sent to them.

He tried to cover his tracks and gave Susan cash for their commercial flight to Miami. One more day before they left, and Preston was on pins and needles. Susan Humphrey walked into his office, took one look at him and said, "You look like an old man."

Preston felt like an old man. He always considered himself a man of steel nerves. All through the initial set up with the Arab connection and the first power pack, he had felt reasonably calm, but this time his nerves were cracking. He wanted it over with. He considered leaving a day early, but moving the flight date out of Vero Beach would be a problem.

Susan took a seat in front of his desk, crossed her long legs and said, "I know what you need," and smiled.

She was wrong. He needed to be a million miles away, sipping a gin and tonic and listening to waves gently coming ashore; however, Susan might be right. She often was. His thoughts were lost when his secretary called on his intercom and said, "There is a Mr. Mancini to see you, sir."

Preston pressed down his talk button and said, "I don't have any appointments this afternoon and I don't know a Mancini."

She replied, "Mr. Mancini is an FBI agent."

Preston grew visibly pale and even Susan stiffened in her chair. He looked at Susan and mimicked the words, "What should I do?"

She said, "Stall him while I leave."

"No you don't." Preston keyed the intercom and said, Please send Agent Mancini in."

He swallowed and tried to clear the cotton out of his mouth. The door opened and an enormous man in his late fifties came in. He was nicely dressed, not in the expensive suit that Preston wore, but one that fit well on his offensive lineman's frame. His large features were a bit on the fleshy side, and he spoke with a graveled voice that echoed from somewhere inside.

Preston stood, came around his desk and proffered his hand. "And how can I help you, Agent Mancini, or is it Special Agent?"

Special Agent Mancini didn't correct Preston, he merely showed his open ID and badge briefly and then, almost as a contradiction, said, "Just wanted to run something by you. Nothing official." His hand engulfed Preston's hand as he shook it and looked over at Susan Humphrey.

Preston said, "This is my administrative assistant, Susan Humphrey."

Susan nodded and smiled, but didn't rise or offer her hand.

Preston said, "Please have a seat. Would you like something to drink, water, coffee, tea, soft drink, we have...?"

Susan gave him a glance. He was beginning to run on. Special Agent Mancini nodded to Susan and said, "Nice to meet you, Miss Humphrey, and negative on the drink. This won't take long."

Susan immediately wondered how he knew she was a miss and not missus.

As the big agent settled into one of the two soft leather chairs in front of his desk, Preston sat in his chair and repeated, "Now, how can I help you?"

The big agent adjusted his body in the chair and it squeaked before he said abruptly, "You know a Mr. Ryan Quinn?"

Preston said too quickly, "No, never heard of him."

The agent wrinkled his mouth as if trying to wet his lips and said, "A personal friend of mine, works out of Daytona Beach, Florida, called me this morning. Are you sure you never heard of him?"

Susan broke in and said, "Pardon me, sir, but wasn't one of those men in Port Canaveral named Quinn? It might be the same man."

Preston realized that Susan was saving him from incriminating himself. He was on record in that town when Ryan Quinn assaulted him, and unfortunately, that information was on a police record and the FBI could easily find it if they hadn't already.

"I believe you are correct, Susan. Thank you. It was an unfortunate incident, a mix up really, but I am sure it has been—"

Preston was at a loss for words and Susan stepped in with a question to Special Agent Mancini: "Why do you ask, sir?"

"Just checking for a friend of mine. Nothing official."

"I guess he wants to close an old case or whatever you call them."

The FBI agent nodded as if he understood and stood up. "Something like that. Well, that's about it. Thanks for your time," he said, and walked to the door. Preston had hurried to open it for him but was too late. Preston watched the big man leave and then closed the door to his office.

He smiled weakly at Susan and said, "That went well. I must say, I was a little concerned for a moment."

Susan shook her head and said, "Went well? I thought you were going to say, 'Sure I know him. I tried to have him killed and then put away.' He was on a fishing expedition, Preston, and you took the bait."

Preston looked angry and said, "If he would have known anything we would be in jail. Now let's get out of here. I want to stop off at my home and say goodbye to my wife."

"Should I laugh or cry?"

Outside the building, Special Agent Michael Mancini used his cell phone to call his old friend and drinking buddy, Special Agent Howard Lowell in Daytona Beach, Florida.

When Special Agent Howard Lowell answered his cell phone Mike said, "Howard you old bastard, how are you?"

"Not as old as you, my friend. Turn up anything?"

Special Agent Michael Mancini worked, if worked could be the right term, out of the FBI headquarters in Washington DC. He no longer was a field agent and he did little but wait for two months and his retirement. He, like his buddy Howard Lowell, was at his terminal pay grade. He hadn't lied to Preston, he was checking unofficially for an old friend, who could not go through channels or his boss would have his head.

"Saw Winn and that knockout assistant of his. She's pretty cool, but Winn almost shit his pants when I asked him about your Mr. Quinn. He's covering something. Want me to dig around, unofficial of course?"

"No, but thanks. Something's going on, but I can't get time to run it down. I'll think of something. How's the wife?"

"Lucy's fine. Mean as ever. Out in California watching the grandkids. And Fay?"

"She's fine. Gets a little pissed at me once in a while but that's life. I told her I was going to call you. She said not to, but she sends her love."

"Gotta go now, amigo, before someone notices I am not sleeping at my desk."

"Take care."

CHAPTER 22

I read the latest e-mail from Preston Winn and realized it might be too late to save Ryan from a long prison term. As I read the e-mail, Mr. Winn was on his way to West Palm Beach and then to Vero Beach. In fact, he and his assistant, Miss Susan Humphrey, might already have been driving up to Vero Beach from West Palm Beach. I could not waste a minute. I hurried and set up my text-to-voice program and typed the following WORD document: "My dear Mr. Quinn," I stopped and backspaced over "My dear Mr. Quinn." I didn't have time to try sounding Greek. I wrote, "Quinn, this is urgent. You must act at once to save your future and the future of your lovely Megan and Magic. Mr. Preston Winn and Miss Susan Humphrey are at this moment about to steal the latest version of a military exoskeleton and I believe two top secret power packs. Not only will our nation's security be greatly compromised, but you will never be cleared of the bogus drug trafficking charges against you. They plan to leave the country. They have a chartered Beechcraft 1900D waiting at the Vero Beach airport. It will fly them to Cancun, Mexico. From there they will make other arrangements, unfortunately, I do not know how they will precede from Cancun.

"Quinn, you were a Marine, correction, you are a Marine, so get off your butt and take that objective. Good luck and Godspeed."

I dialed Ryan's cell telephone and heard it ring in the next room. At first I could not believe it. Ryan had left his cell telephone on his nightstand. It was close to lunchtime, but he stopped coming home since he took the job at the golf course. I almost panicked but said to myself, calm down, think calm thoughts, but I couldn't think of any so I dialed Megan. I thought maybe I could persuade her to get Ryan to come home and listen to his cell telephone.

As I was dialing, it occurred to me, If Ryan came home, I wouldn't be able to send my voice to his telephone.

It was then I decided, if I absolutely had to, I would show him that I could understand him, communicate with him and with other humans, and hope that secret never got out. I also hoped I wouldn't have to tell him and risk my life.

Megan didn't answer her telephone; Ted Lewis answered. I typed quickly and asked to talk to Miss Alvarez. He said she was out but he would take a message. He then asked if he could be of assistance. I had to think before typing my reply. I finally typed, "It is urgent that I contact her. It is a matter of life and death."

He asked, "Who is this?"

I lied. "I am her father, Eduardo Alvarez. Now where is my daughter?"

I guess my Greek accent and urgent appeal worked, because he said, "She's at the Municipal Golf Course with Ryan Quinn. She said she was taking lunch out to him. Maybe you can reach her there?"

I wrote, "Thank you," and hung up. I am not used to conversations with humans, or with any creature for that matter. I should have written, "Do you have the telephone number?"

I dialed information and asked for the telephone number of the New Smyrna Beach golf course. The answer was a question, there are two. Which one did I want? I picked the municipal course and an electronic voice, inferior to mine, gave me the number. I dialed it and waited and waited. Finally a lady came on and asked if I could hold. I was going to type no, but she put me on hold anyway. I waited and waited. She finally came back on, and I asked if I could talk to Ryan Quinn. She said she had no idea where he might be on the course but would give him a message. I asked if she could run out and find him. She must have thought I was nuts by the tone of her voice, but she did say she would asked Fred; whomever he was, to look for Ryan and have him call back. I gave her Ryan's home telephone number and hung up. It then occurred to me that he would be confused by a call from his own home telephone, and I couldn't answer Ryan when he called his own number.

Time was running out and I didn't know what to do. I ran outside to empty my bladder and then hurried back to listen for the telephone. In a moment of clarity, I came up with an answer. I would block the home telephone number, and call Ryan's cell telephone, where I would leave a message; the same message I had typed earlier telling him about the urgency to get to Vero Beach and stop Preston Winn. After that, I would take Ryan's cell telephone to him. I knew the route; I had come by it on my way back from the horse ranch. As an insurance policy, I also wrote a quick speech to FBI Special Agent Howard Lowell, who Ryan had mentioned. Ryan had his number on his telephone directory. I worked fast and soon had both calls completely typed. It turned out that I had to leave a message for Special Agent Howard Lowell, which worked out okay. If he would have asked who I was, I didn't want to lie. It's wrong and against the law, I think. I blocked the number and made the call to Ryan's cell telephone. It began to ring in the next room. It went to his voice mail and I ran my text-to-speech program and left a message. I then hung up.

I shut down the computer, went in to Ryan's bedroom and picked up his cell telephone carefully between my teeth and headed out the back door. The jump over the back fence was still difficult, but I did it without swallowing Ryan's little cell telephone. I took off at a full run and burned out too soon. I had to drop back to a fast trot before I got there. The golf course is about five miles from Ryan's house, and I may have set an Olympic record; however, I didn't expect a gold medal. Actually, I don't know if there is a record for a five-mile dog run, but I digress.

Somehow, I expected to see and smell Ryan as soon as I got there, but no, I found his scent and started following it until some man came running out of a small shack and tried to chase me away. I took off running again and he followed in a little car. I had seen golf on the televisions, but never one of these little cars. It was fast but no contest for me. I cut through the woods and found

Ryan's scent again. Some humans were hitting golf balls but stopped to yell at me. It was not like I was going to leave big brown ones on their lawn, but I ignored them and kept looking for Ryan. He must have been all over that golf course. They have numbers at each hole, just like on the televisions, and I had seen most of them by the time I picked up another familiar scent, Megan's. I followed it like a road map and found them by a sign that read, "Driving Range." They sat in one of those little cars and were eating turkey sandwiches. I love turkey but it puts me to sleep.

I ran up to a startled Ryan and dropped his cell telephone in his lap. He picked it up and said, "Magic! What are you doing out?" and then added, "And slobbering all over my phone?"

Megan got out of the little car and rubbed my head as she looked me over. "Are you all right, boy?"

No, I was not all right. I was exhausted and I wanted Ryan to check his messages, but he put the cell telephone in the pocket of his work shirt. I pulled away from Megan and barked at Ryan in frustration. He didn't understand and said sharply, "Magic, stop that. Come here."

I obeyed, and he motioned for me to jump up onto a little space behind the seats. I jumped up there and then back down again. I was not going to simply be the good dog that let his master die. I jumped up in front with Ryan and pawed at his shirt pocket, but he pushed me away and said, "What is wrong with you? Stop that," but I didn't. I ripped the shirt pocket off with my teeth and the cell telephone fell onto Ryan's lap. I picked it up before he could react and ran a few feet away. Megan came near me and I dropped the cell telephone at her feet. She picked it up, and I mean no disrespect for Ryan's intelligence, but she seemed to understand. She handed it back to Ryan and said, "He brought this all the way from your house. It has something to do with how he's acting."

Ryan held the few shreds of his pocket in his other hand and said, "Okay. He sure isn't acting normal."

I couldn't stand still. My tail began to wag on its own and I licked Megan's hand. Come on, Ryan, listen to your message.

Ryan took out a rag from the little car and wiped the cell telephone off before opening it up and looking at the display. He was going to listen and I couldn't help myself, I barked; however, the man who had been chasing me came up in his little car and said gruffly, "Ryan, Is that your dog?"

Ryan said, "Yes sir. I'll take him home."

The man frowned but drove off after saying, "You know better. Don't bring him again."

The jerk, Ryan didn't bring me. I ran all the way. Ryan asked Megan to get in the little car and told me to get back in the space behind the seat. He drove the little car, which made a funny whirling sound, back to a building where other little cars were parked. From there we walked to his pickup truck, which was parked outside a fence that runs parallel to Wayne Ave.

I was trying to be patient, but time was critical. Once we got to his truck he opened the passenger door and said, "Magic, get in." But I did not obey. It was time for a confrontation. I have been a good dog who always obeyed his master, but not this time. I was not going anywhere until he listened to his message. I looked him right in the eye and barked loudly. When he came toward me, I backed up and kept barking. I was not going to give in, not this time.

"Magic, hush. Get in the truck, now."

I shook my head and my ears flopped back and forth. I kept that up until Megan said, "Ryan, look, he is saying no."

I stopped shaking my head and Ryan knelt down on one knee. He motioned for me to come to him. Now I had to decide if I trusted him or not. With some trepidation, I eased forward until I was close enough for him to touch me. He reached out, patted my head, and said, "Take it easy. Magic. Good boy." He then stood up and opened his cell telephone. He pressed a few keys and I could hear his messages playing. One was from his old boss, Frank Kurns, who wanted Ryan to call him back, and then my message came on. He listened and frowned, but when it was finished, he played it again and handed it to Megan. She listened and when it was over she looked at me and said, "Magic, are you really a magician? How did you know?"

Of course I couldn't answer, so I just stood there. Ryan said, "Dogs have a sixth sense. Somehow he knew it was important."

It wasn't my sixth sense, but let him think that. Megan inflated my ego when she said, "I think your dog actually understands what we say. In any case, let's get a move on."

Ryan said, "I'm going to Vero Beach, but I want you and Magic to stay here."

I barked and ran around in a circle. I had to go with him. He would need me.

They both looked at me strangely for a few seconds before Ryan said, "What the hell, let's go." We all piled into the pickup and Ryan took off throwing gravel into the air as his tires spun. Megan had his cell telephone and listened to my message again. She then said, "Ryan, that man sounds familiar. If he's telling the truth, we don't have enough time to get there before they leave."

***

Cynthia Morgan had already met Susan Humphrey, but she let Preston sweat through the introduction. He had forgotten that Susan had been to Cynthia's lavish home when he was in the hospital, while she was looking for the first power pack. He had sent Cynthia an e-mail, which she answered, asking her to have a truck available at the Vero Beach complex. He told her to get one at least 18 feet long, but he didn't tell her why.

Cynthia led them from the entry hall to the sundeck by her pool. A servant appeared and brought iced drinks. He hovered in the background awaiting Cynthia's orders. She slipped off the dressing gown that covered the skimpy bikini she wore and laid on a chaise lounge. She motioned to two other lounges and said, "My tan is fading. Too much time in the Alps."

She studied Susan, who wore a simple green skirt and a white blouse, and said, "If you would like, there are bathing suits in the cabana. I think Phillip could find you one. Size 12?"

Susan smiled and replied, "A six will fit, thank you, but not today. We do have business. Do we not, Preston?" She glanced down at the briefcase he carried.

She laid her hand on Preston's neck as he tried to take his eyes off Cynthia before saying, "Yes, we do have business, but I always have time for you, Cynthia. Unfortunately, I can't stay long. The first shipment of our new product will fly out in a few hours, but only if I'm there."

Cynthia sipped on her ice tea and then said, "Why don't you let your secretary take care of those mundane chores? You don't mind, do you, Susana?"

Susan corrected her by saying, "It's Susan, and we left our secretary at the office. I am Preston's administrative assistant."

Cynthia waved her hand dismissively and said, "Whatever. I can never understand all those titles. I assume you can supervise a shipment of those things you make."

Preston answered, "There are a few details that I must take care of myself, but it shouldn't take long."

They sat on the lounges and drank their ice tea while Cynthia told them about her latest adventures in both Europe and Africa. Cynthia motioned for Phillip to refill the glasses but then said, "What a terrible host I am. Would you like something stronger?" She looked at Preston and said, "Single malt scotch?"

He shook his head and said, "No, I will be driving up to Vero soon. Ice tea is fine."

Cynthia glanced at Susan, who sat on one of the lounge chairs, and asked, "A beer for you? I'm sure we have one somewhere."

Susan rose and said, "Thank you, but you can have it after we've gone. Now, Preston, we really should be on our way. Our customer might not wait."

Preston sat his ice tea down on the marble tile deck and rose from the other chaise lounge. "Yes, we must be on our way. Do you mind waiting outside for me? I'll be right along."

Susan's expression denied her reply, "Of course not. Don't be long. And don't forget your briefcase."

Susan didn't wait outside; she waited in the front courtyard. Preston came out five minutes later with a key in his hand. He dangled it in front of Susan. Susan shrugged her shoulders and said, "Not another sports car?"

Preston answered, "No, she was a little hesitant since the last time. She let me use the Hummer. Said it was safer."

"How sweet. She gave you a truck to drive."

***

Vero Beach is approximately 125 miles by road from Ryan's house. Getting to the Vero Beach complex in under an hour seemed impossible until Ryan turned his pickup around and headed for the New Smyrna Beach Airport. Once there, he jumped out of the pickup. Megan and Magic ran with him to the aircraft parking area where his friend's Cessna C172 sat. He found the key hidden under the map case. He held it up and said to Megan, "Jeff won't mind, but I'll call him once we're airborne and let him know what's going on."

He got out of the airplane and quickly checked the fuel levels in both tanks, untied the tie-downs, pulled the wheel chocks and opened the cockpit door. He motioned for Magic to get in and then directed him to the back seat.

"Megan, you can get in on the right side," he said, which she did. Once inside, Ryan checked the brakes, movement of the yoke and rudders, and started going through the check sheet; calling off each item and answering himself with, "Check." He looked outside to see if the propeller was clear of any obstacles and started the engine. His eyes scanned the instrument panel gauges. Once he was satisfied the aircraft was ready to fly, he used the radio and contacted the tower. He then taxied out and held short of the runway after checking the flaps and elevator settings. Once the tower cleared him for takeoff, Ryan said, "Everybody strapped in? Okay, folks, here we go." He pulled out the throttle and swung the little Cessna onto the runway. He glanced around to see if he was clear and then watched the airspeed indicator as it began to climb. Once it reached 60 knots, he eased back on the yoke and the little airplane lifted off the runway.

Magic seemed fascinated with the myriad gauges and indicators on the instrument panel. He poked his head between Megan and Ryan. He turned to look out the side windscreen and watched the runway drop away and the tall pine trees begin to shrink. He looked over at Ryan as if to say, "What is happening?"

Megan, who had flown with Ryan, said, "Magic, don't be scared. Ryan is a good pilot."

Magic studied Ryan for a few seconds before turning back to look at the scenery below.

The straight line distance from New Smyrna Beach Airport to the Vero Beach Airport is 88 nautical miles. Ryan turned onto the heading that would take him there and watched the airspeed climb. When he reached 126 knots per hour, he trimmed it for level flight and reached back to rub Magic's head. Magic barked and looked out of the side windscreen.

CHAPTER 23

Ryan landed the Cessna, quickly taxied to the transit aircraft line, and set the parking brake. After talking to ground control, he shut off the engine, replaced Jeff's key, and said, "Megan, I don't want you to go in with us. Would you wait with the airplane?"

She didn't honor him with a reply; instead, she got out and said, "Come on, Magic. Let's go find them."

The building in the Vero Beach Airport industrial complex was nondescript from the outside, flat concrete block walls without paint. Inside a striking transformation took place. Numerous small office spaces and larger laboratories filled the spacious interior. While the equipment inside was very high-tech, the security system was old style. Hardwired single connectors on the entry and exit doors and a central alarm bell above the door, a single digital control box completed the configuration.

Ryan thought about breaking a window to enter when he noticed a dim light reflecting off the window. He said to Megan, "Let's go around back and see what we can see."

Magic immediately trotted ahead of them and around the building, which was much larger than it appeared from the front. In the rear, Ryan saw a loading ramp and three large doors where trucks could enter. A black Hummer parked next to a large U-Haul truck. Ryan walked up to the truck, pulled out his Glock .45, and shined his flashlight inside. He did the same with the Hummer. Both were empty.

Magic sniffed the car and then the truck before moving up the loading ramp, stopped at one door and waited for Ryan.

"You think he's in here, Magic?"

Magic looked up at Ryan and barked softly. Ryan petted his head and tried the door while holding his pistol's muzzle pointing up. The door was unlocked. He turned to Megan and said, "Wait here and yell if anybody shows up.

"I'm going with you."

"If you watch my six, I'll have a better chance."

Megan crossed her arms in front of her and said, "Alright, but if you need help, just whistle."

Ryan turned the door handle and stepped into the building, now holding his pistol in both hands while scanning quickly for movement. The door opened into a storage area where boxes were stacked in neat rows near the larger doors. A wide hall led between two sets of glass enclosed offices. Magic moved around Ryan and sniffed the floor before walking slowly down the hall. Ryan followed with his weapon ready. Thirty feet down the hall, Magic stopped and looked back at Ryan.

Ryan whispered, "What is it, boy? Do you think someone's in there?"

Magic sniffed the base of a metal door and looked up at Ryan. Ryan tried the door but it wouldn't budge. He then noticed the electronic keypad next to the door.

"Looks like we'll have to find another way in."

Magic immediately started walking down the hall, stopping occasionally to sniff. Ryan followed with his pistol held at the ready.

The long hallway ended at a T intersection with wide hallways leading off in two directions. Magic hesitated before taking the left one. The hallway was similar to the first one with doors on both sides. Magic picked up the pace until he came to another metal door with an electronic keypad.

Ryan tried the door, but, like the first one, it would not budge. He patted Magic's head and said, "I guess breaking it down might alert them."

Magic scratched at the metal door with his nails and then walked away, stopping after a few yards and looking back at Ryan.

"You've got a better plan?" Ryan asked.

Magic barked softly and continued down the hall, stopping occasionally to sniff and look around. His ears perked up and he looked back at Ryan. Ryan heard it too. A door slammed. Someone had either come in and closed a door, or left the building. Ryan looked for a place to hide and found a small storage closet. He motioned for Magic to enter, which he did. Ryan closed the door, leaving an inch opening to view out. He waited as the sound of high heels clicking on the concrete floor came toward him and then stopped. He opened the door a bit more and saw an attractive woman punching a code into a keypad. A door opened and she stepped inside.

Ryan moved back into the hall, hesitated, and went back into the closet again. He shined his flashlight up at a large grating. The grating covered an air-conditioner's air inlet with a filter.

He mumbled to himself, "That's how I'm going to get in," and went out to find an air-conditioning outlet large enough to crawl through. He found one at the end of the hall where empty crates were stacked.

Magic watched Ryan pile empty crates under a large grating in the ceiling. Magic cocked his head to one side and whined. Ryan, who was using his knife to loosen screws, looked down and said, "Magic, you go play hide. I'm going in through the a/c vent."

The grate swung down and Ryan used his arms to pull himself up and into the air-conditioning duct. It gave him little room, but he did fit and reached down to pull the grate up, but having no way to secure it from the inside, he let it fall back open. He looked down before moving through the air duct and saw Magic round a corner and disappear from view. Magic was good at playing the hide and seek game at home, and Ryan hoped he would stay unseen until he could confront Mr. Winn with the evidence to clear himself.

Ryan crawled on hands and knees with his flashlight illuminating a spot a few feet ahead of him. After a few yards, he shut it off and looked for light shining up from below. About twenty feet ahead the duct turned left and Ryan followed it. A light shone up from below and Ryan slowed his crawl and tried to avoid making noise. Once he got to the vent, he looked down and saw he was over an open area. Maybe storage for the exoskeletons, he thought. Fortunately, the vent was another large one and he used the blade of his knife to break the tabs that held the screws in place. Once the last one popped out, the grate swung down, making more noise than Ryan wanted. He pulled his pistol and waited; when nobody appeared below, he returned this pistol to its holster and leaned forward to look into a room filled with computer workstations. He shined his flashlight around the vacant room before lowering himself carefully through the opening. He dropped the last six feet to the floor below and landed on his feet, but rolled to absorb the impact and quickly sprung to his feet. He pulled his pistol and replaced the flashlight on his belt.

Ryan found a door out of the computer station room and heard voices as he entered a large storage area. Large pipe racks held various models of exoskeletons. Some Ryan had seen on the internet, which reminded him of metal frameworks in which a person could fit and control the walking skeleton; however, a few were more elaborate. A woman appeared to be talking to one of the suits that completely enclosed the person in it, or it was a robot.

When the suit began to talk to the woman, Ryan realized it was an exoskeleton he had never seen on the internet. It had a helmet covering the person's face and dull metal or plastic covered both the upper and lower body. The feet were enclosed in boots covered in the same material as the rest of its body. It carried a backpack and an antenna sprung out of its helmet. Four large mechanical fingers protruded out of gloves on both hands and an open pipe extended out of the right hand glove. It moved around freely and even gestured with its hands while talking.

Ryan slipped behind a large crate and listened.

"How do I look?" the suit asked with an electrically amplified voice, with a slight reverberation.

The woman answered, "Like a big robot nightmare. Preston, will you stop playing and help load the damn truck?"

"Stand aside, mortal. I will load it myself."

"Alright, but hurry. This makes me nervous."

"It should," Ryan said as he came out from behind the crate and leveled his pistol at Preston Winn in the new exoskeleton.

The woman swung around to look at Ryan and said, "What?"

"You heard me. Now turn around and place your hands on that wall." Ryan motioned with his weapon toward the wall nearest them.

She started toward the wall, which was not more than ten feet away, and said, "Who are you?"

"I think you know. I'm the man whose life has been ruined by you two greedy assholes. You must be Susan Humphrey, and that," he motioned toward the exoskeleton, "must be Preston Winn."

Susan didn't answer and was now at the wall, but Preston, still in the suit had not moved. "You too, ugly. Get over by the lad... woman."

Preston said, "I think not. Now put down that peashooter before you get hurt. Susan, take his gun."

Susan Humphrey started toward Ryan who swung his pistol toward her and said, "I'm in no mood to screw around." He then turned the weapon on Preston and said, "I'm not going to fire a warning shot. Now move to that wall, and then get out of your plaything."

Preston, in his exoskeleton, started toward Ryan, who took aim and fired hitting the exoskeleton in the chest. It staggered slightly but kept coming, but now it brought its right arm up and aimed the built-in machinegun's muzzle at Ryan.

Ryan fired two more rounds but it had no effect on the exoskeleton. Susan Humphrey covered her ears against the tremendous noise in the confined space.

"Damn," Ryan said, aimed for the facemask, and fired two more rounds with the same tremendous sound. The helmet moved back with each impact of the heavy .45 caliber bullets but the exoskeleton kept coming.

The machinegun was now aimed at Ryan, but he fired first hitting the exoskeleton in the right knee, which swung the suit around before Preston fired a short burst from the machinegun, blowing plaster out of the wall and hitting Susan Humphrey, who collapsed to the floor. The blast covered both Susan's scream and the growl from a lightning blur of golden fur as Magic hit the exoskeleton in the back.

The exoskeleton staggered but didn't fall as Magic held onto the backpack. Preston reached back and grabbed at Magic, who moved away from the powerful mechanical fingers, all the while growling and biting at the backpack. Ryan, unable to shoot now without hitting Magic, came rushing forward and hit the exoskeleton with a hard low block. The exoskeleton toppled forward landing on its face. Magic stayed on its back, and with a snap of his head, pulled loose the power pack's connecting plug. Preston yelled, "Get me out of here!"

"Be so good as to drop your weapon, Mr. Quinn."

Ryan turned to see a familiar figure dressed in a floral sports shirt and black trousers. Babak Shirazi stood fifteen feet away with a revolver, his arm wrapped around Megan's neck and the revolver's barrel pressed against her head.

"And tell your animal to stay or I will shoot it."

Ryan glanced at Magic and said, "Magic, hide."

Magic, who was standing next to Ryan, sprang to one side and disappeared down a hallway. Ryan considered the risk of a head shot at Babak, but he hadn't spent any significant time on the pistol range since leaving the Marine Corps and decided the risk was too great. He might hit Megan.

Babak pulled Megan closer; she winced, and he said, "Do not trifle with me."

Ryan hesitated a moment and then slowly lowered his pistol. Once it was on the floor he kicked it a few feet away and said, "Okay. Now what?"

"Now, you will load these suits," he motioned to the exoskeletons, "into the truck outside."

Ryan didn't argue. He went about loading the suits off the pipe rack into the back of a U-Haul truck parked at the rear of the building. They were heavy and Ryan was covered in perspiration in a few minutes. Babak followed him but kept his pistol pointed at Megan, who he pulled along. He had already picked up Ryan's .45 caliber Glock pistol and stuck it in his waistband. Once Ryan had the military exoskeletons in the truck, Babak said, "Now we go back and get the last one and poor Mr. Winn."

Preston had not moved. With the power pack unhooked, he couldn't reach around and reconnect it, and the armored military suit was too heavy to move without power to the hydraulics and electric motors. He lay helpless on the floor. Susan lay still where she had dropped in a growing pool of blood.

Babak said, "Mr. Quinn, leave the power pack disconnected and help poor Mr. Winn out."

Ryan bent over, pulled the backpack and power pack off before unlatching the back of the suit, which fell open. Preston struggled to get out, and Ryan grabbed the back of his belt, yanked him clear of the exoskeleton and was about to hit Preston when he looked at Megan and relented. Babak still had his pistol pointed at her head. Instead, Ryan shoved Preston roughly toward Babak. Preston tripped and fell to his knees before standing and looking back at Ryan.

"You will regret that, Mr. Quinn. You and your girlfriend."

Preston walked back to Babak and said, "Good to see you, my friend. How did you know—"

Babak interrupted by saying, "I know many things. Now where is the second power pack?"

Preston's smirk faded and he said, "In the Hummer outside. In a large briefcase."

Ryan asked, "Which one of you is the boss of this little scheme?"

As if to answer Ryan's question, Babak moved the pistol from Megan's neck and shot Preston in the side of his head.

Megan let out an involuntary scream and tried to move away from Babak, who pulled her to him and said, "Do not misunderstand me. I may let you live, but one move, one attempt and I will kill you both. Now come with me."

Babak glanced at the body of Preston Winn, showed no emotions, and led Ryan and Megan to the front of the building. He looked outside, scanned the parking area, and said, "This way. You go first to the car."

A Toyota sedan sat in front of the building. Ryan walked to the car, stopped, and looked back at Babak. A man sat unmoving in the front seat of the Toyota.

Babak reached into the pocket of his trousers and pulled out a key. He threw it to Ryan and said, "Open the trunk."

"The trunk?"

"Yes. Enough questions. Do as I say."

Ryan looked at the man who sat in the driver's seat. The man glanced back once and then looked forward again. He resembled Babak, but was much younger. Ryan opened the trunk and said, "Why? What the hell did we ever do to you?"

"Get in and shut up. Throw the key back." He dug the barrel of the revolver cruelly into the side of Megan's neck, and Ryan threw him the key before climbing into the trunk of the Toyota. Babak pulled Megan to the car and said, "Now your turn."

To Ryan's surprise, Megan didn't resist, even after her previous encounter in a hot car trunk. She climbed in and moved around to get clear of the trunk lid before it came down. She said to Ryan, "Watch your head."

Babak backed away from the car and reached under his shirt to pull out Ryan's weapon. He expertly checked the chamber and then took the rounds out of his own revolver. He aimed Ryan's .45 at Ryan and walked back to the trunk. "Take this," he said and handed the revolver to Ryan, who took it, puzzled at the turn of events.

"Now what am I going to do with this empty revolver? Throw it at someone?"

Babak barely grinned and held out his hand, in which he now held a handkerchief.

"You are going to give it back."

Ryan nodded knowingly and handed the revolver back to Babak.

"I see. Now with my finger prints, I'll be charged with murder."

Babak slammed down the trunk lid. He yelled at the closed trunk, "They won't bother charging a dead man!"

Inside the trunk, Ryan rubbed his head where the trunk lid hit him and said to Megan. "Don't worry. I'll get us out."

Megan found his mouth with her hand and placed a finger over his lips. She whispered, "I remember how I got out before. Now be quiet."

Outside, Babak walked to the driver's window and knocked on it softly. The door opened and he handed the key to the man inside.

"You know what to do."

The man nodded and started the engine. Babak hurried back through the building and then to the truck at the loading ramp.

***

The ride down to Vero Beach was exciting. I flew from Saudi Arabia to America, but from the inside of a huge cargo airplane and I could not see out. Flying in the little Cessna was a new and invigorating experience. I thought I might be fearful, but I quickly learned to enjoy it. I was also fascinated by the flight instruments and by Ryan's skill as a pilot. Maybe it's a genetic thing. His father is a pilot. The fun ended when we landed at the Vero Beach Airport.

When Ryan left me outside of the locked area and went in through an a/c duct, I hid for awhile, but then I decided to try my luck at opening the locked doors. The keypad was at the right height for me to stand up on my hind legs and look at the small display. I thought for a few minutes and made my first try. Bingo, the lock clicked open and I pushed the door with my paws. The code word was simple. Preston Winn's ego overcame his intelligence. The code was W I N N, Winn. Everybody knew he was the boss and not Cynthia Morgan.

I heard a ruckus and slipped behind some boxes. They were small boxes so I had to crawl so as not to be seen. The noise from Ryan's pistol was deafening. I tried to cover my ears with my paws but it didn't help much, and I wanted to get closer so my paws had to be free. I could see Ryan shooting and then I saw the big Robo Monster, actually a military exoskeleton, fire his machinegun. Talk about noise. I don't know why they don't put silencers on them, on second thought, I do know. It was a heavy caliber weapon and blew a hole in the wall. It also hit the woman, but later I checked on her and found she wasn't mortally wounded. Most of her injuries came from the debris that flew off the wall and maybe a ricochet. If the machinegun had hit her directly, she would have looked like... well you get the picture.

I hit the exoskeleton from behind, and with Ryan's help, we knocked it on its face and I was able to pull its power pack loose. We are a pretty good team.

When Ryan told me to hide. I took off so fast it even surprised me. I was really pumped up after taking that monster down and saving Ryan's life, but then that human I bit at Port Canaveral showed up again. His name is Babak. I don't think I ever heard his family name. After I hid and I listened, I heard him tell Ryan to move the military exoskeleton suits and the power packs to the truck outside. I checked on the woman while they were busy outside, and when they came back in, I snuck out and hid in the back of the truck. I thought Ryan and Megan would be put in the truck too, but that didn't happen. Instead, Babak came back alone and closed the back door of the truck. He didn't see me because I was hidden under one of the exoskeleton suits, which lay on the bed of the truck. I felt someone, probably Babak, get into the cabin of the truck, start the engine and drive off.

The truck didn't drive far before it parked. I heard the driver get out and walk away. I moved from the front where I was hidden and found I couldn't get out, so I went back and hid under an exoskeleton again.

CHAPTER 24

Inside the trunk of the Toyota, Ryan and Megan heard the engine start and then the car move. Megan whispered to Ryan, "There's an emergency trunk release. It should be right over here." She guided his hand to a little plastic knob.

"If you pull it, the trunk will pop open."

Ryan whispered, "How long have you known that?"

He could not see her shrug, but he did hear her say, "It just came to me when I looked in the trunk. It must have been in the back of my mind. But now, what do we do?"

"When he stops the car, I'll pop the trunk and you jump out and run like hell. I'll get out and see if I can take out the driver."

Megan didn't have time to argue because the car came to a stop.

"Now!" Ryan yelled as the trunk swung up. He shoved it harder and Megan crawled over him, stepping on his chest as she got out. Ryan threw himself out, hit the pavement and jumped up. He looked up at the surprised driver in the Ford sedan behind him but didn't hesitate. He ran to the Toyota's driver's door, pulled it open, and hit the driver in the side of the face, knocking him senseless. The driver, who didn't have his seatbelt on, fell over onto the passenger's seat. Ryan reached in, pulled the drive selector into neutral, and yanked the man out in one motion, dropping him on to the pavement. Ryan looked around and saw Megan a few feet away on the other side of the car.

"Get in!" he yelled, and she did.

Ryan looked around at the traffic, slammed the car into drive, made a tire burning U-turn through an intersection, and passed surprised motorists who honked their horns in anger.

Ryan mashed the accelerator to the floor and headed back to the Vero Beach industrial park. As he headed back, a truck going in the opposite direction caught his eye. It turned into the airport entrance and Ryan made another U-turn, but this time he held back. He wanted to see where Babak and the truck were going.

Megan recognized the truck and said, "What are you going to do?"

Ryan glanced over at her and then back at the truck ahead. "I am going to save our future together. With Winn and that woman dead, Babak may be the only one who can clear me. I need to take him alive."

Megan sat back and wondered how Ryan was going to do that without a weapon, but she had new found confidence in him after seeing him fight that exoskeleton and manhandle the driver of the car like he was a child. It was a side of Ryan she had never seen before.

Ryan watched the truck make a turn and stayed far enough behind so Babak wouldn't be able to recognize him in the rear view mirror. The truck stopped at an airport building's parking lot and Babak got out. Ryan drove by and said, "Watch him in your mirror. See where he goes."

After a few seconds, Megan said, "He went inside that building. Now what?"

Ryan circled back and parked a few spaces away from the truck, putting two cars between them.

"I need to even the odds."

As he got out Megan said, "Where are you going?"

"To get on one of those suits. You stay here."

Ryan made his way to the back of Babak's truck. Megan, who had followed Ryan, touched his back and said, "You forgot me."

Ryan jumped and said, "Damn it! Don't do that. I almost busted you."

Megan ignored him and looked at the long one story building where Babak had entered.

"I'll watch for him while you get the suit."

"Yell if he comes out," Ryan said, and opened the handle that held the rear cargo door closed. The door slid up and he jumped up into the truck. He was reaching for an exoskeleton when Magic ran from the back of the truck, jumped on him, and almost sent Ryan back out the open door. Ryan was dumbfounded but managed to say, "Down, boy. Megan, look, it's Magic."

Megan took her eyes off of the building door and looked into the dark truck.

"Magic, how did you get in there?"

Magic barked and started for her, but stopped when Megan looked back at the building and said, "He's coming."

Ryan said, "Quick, close the door and hide."

Megan hopped into the truck and pulled the door down. She held her foot against the bottom of the door and said, "You can't get rid of me that easily."

Ryan said sharply, "Megan, one of us has to be in charge. No more democracy. If you want to live, listen to me, got it?"

In the dark he couldn't see her salute, but he did hear a sarcastic, "Yes, sir."

After a few seconds, Ryan whispered, "If he opens the door, I am going to kick his teeth out, so stay away from the door."

Megan moved around in the dark and found Magic, who didn't lick her hand. The hair on the back of his neck stood out and she felt his muscles quiver. The truck moved slightly and then the engine started. Ryan whispered, "He's going to move the truck. My guess is he will take it to an airplane, probably close by."

"What now?" Megan whispered. The truck jerked and began moving.

Ryan said, "Most of these rentals have a light in the cargo area, I just needed to find it." A dim light came on and Ryan said, "Now help me put on one of the suits."

Megan quickly helped Ryan select a suit. Only one had a machinegun installed and Ryan checked the ammunition before pulling it on. Once it was on he said, "Can you put that backpack on with the power pack?"

Megan helped him but then said, "There is only one power pack. What am I going to do?"

Ryan hadn't lowered the visor down on the helmet and talked to Megan without his voice being amplified. "It must be in the cab of the truck. Just get inside one of the suits to hide, and put Magic in another one. If shooting starts, they should shield you and Magic."

She reminded Ryan. "If you shoot him, who will clear you?"

"Nevermind. Get you and Magic in a suit and out of sight."

Less than a minute later the truck's rear door rolled open. Ryan, who stood with the machinegun barrel pointing out, didn't move. He wasn't sure how to fire the machinegun if needed, and Megan hadn't had time to connect the power pack's receptacle.

Two men in workman's clothes looked into the truck. One said, "I'll hand them down to you." He climbed up in to the truck and moved toward Ryan. Babak stood off to one side and watched as the freight handlers prepared to move the exoskeletons to a low flatbed truck with a small tow tractor attached.

When the man in the truck tried to lift Ryan in the suit, he stopped and said, "This thing weighs a ton. Gimme'a hand." The other man jumped up into the truck and they both struggled to lift it down to the flatbed.

Babak said sharply, "Careful with that."

"Sure, but you said they weren't heavy. Damn thing must weigh three hundred pounds."

"This one's got a pack on its back. Can I take it off?"

Babak said, "Yes, but be careful. Hand it to me."

The man unhooked the power pack, slipped off the backpack harness, and handed the whole assembly to Babak.

Babak, thinking the weight was caused by the heavy machinegun, said, "The others are lighter, but you two are weaklings. One man loaded all of those."

After more struggling, the men got Ryan and the suit on the flatbed, not suspecting Ryan was inside. The next suit was the one Megan put Magic inside.

"This one's lighter," one man said and then added, "What's in these things?"

Babak scowled and said, "Enough complaining. Hurry, the airplane is waiting."

Megan and her suit was next, but the men didn't complain although it was slightly heavier than the one before it. The last ones were much lighter, but still heavy. By the time they had the flatbed loaded they were both soaked in perspiration. Babak took the power pack from the cab of the truck, and along with the power pack from the cargo area, sat next to the driver of the tow tractor and said, "You know the way to the flight line?"

The man said, "Been workin' here five years. Think I'll find it. What's the tail number of your ride?"

Babak didn't know the aircraft tail number and said, "Jamaican Tours Beechcraft 1900. It's the only one there."

The ride to the flight line was short and they had no trouble finding the two engine turboprop aircraft. Babak jumped off the tractor as it pulled up next to the Beechcraft, which had its cargo door open. He walked over to the pilot, a tall, thin black man wearing a crisp blue short sleeve shirt with golden applets. The pilot, who was completing an aircraft preflight, smiled and said, "You must be Mr. Rubin. I am Captain Rashard," and offered his hand.

Babak shook his hand but said, "He will be here shortly. I am his assistant."

Babak knew that Preston had used an alias to book his flight out of the United States, but Babak hadn't had time to have new forged identification papers made with the name Rubin. Babak said, "I would like to be ready to go when he gets here. Can we load the cargo now?"

The pilot said, "My copilot will supervise the loading. I'll get him," and hurried into the aircraft. A few seconds later a short Hispanic man, dressed in the same uniform as the captain, came out of the aircraft carrying a clipboard, and walked to the men on the tow tractor.

He looked at the exoskeletons and said with a thick Hispanic accent, "What are these?"

Babak intervened and said, "Deep sea diving suits."

The copilot looked at the freight manifest and said, "The freight bill say they are biochemical hazard something..." He stumbled over the words "containment envelopes" and said, "How much they weigh? Say here six hundred thirty-five pounds."

The man on the tow tractor seat said, "More like a thousand, maybe more."

The copilot looked confused and said, "I better talk to Rashard."

Babak stopped him by putting his hand on the copilot's arm and saying, "If there is any extra charge I would be happy to pay you now," and shoved five hundred-dollar bills into the copilot's hand.

The copilot glanced down at the fresh bills and said, "A few pounds will not matter."

Babak motioned to the two freight handlers on the tow tractor and said, "Load them carefully." The men got off the tow tractor and began the job of carrying the exoskeletons with Ryan, Megan and Magic inside them. The copilot showed them where he wanted them in the aircraft's cargo area. He looked at one of the freight handlers and said, "God bless you."

The man said, "Pardon?"

"God bless you. Did you not sneeze?"

The man said, "I don't think so," and continued placing the heavy suits on the deck of the aircraft. When they were finished, Babak gave them a small tip and waited until they were out of sight before entering the aircraft.

The Beechcraft 1900D is a 19-passenger, pressurized twin-engine turboprop aircraft. While designed for use as a regional airliner; it is also used commercially as a freight aircraft and corporate transport. Without the passenger seats, there is a long and relatively high cargo area. Babak saw that four seats, two on each side, had been installed forward, close to the cabin. He worked his way up to the flight cabin and looked over the shoulder of the pilot who was checking instruments and setting frequencies in the radios. He looked back at Babak and said, "Has Mr. and Mrs. Ruben arrived yet?"

"Not yet, but if they don't, my instructions are to fly with the cargo to Cancun."

The pilot turned and said, "If they don't arrive soon I will have to cancel my flight plan."

"Don't do that. They can always catch another flight, but it is most important that the cargo arrive on time. If you are ready, we can leave now."

"Very well. Please take a seat and write your name on the passenger manifest." He handed Babak a clipboard with custom declaration forms and a passenger manifest on top.

Babak walked back and took a seat. The copilot slipped past him and took the right seat in the cockpit. A few minutes later, Babak heard the turboprop engines starting and watched the long, thin propellers begin to turn. Soon they were a blur and the whirring sound of them cutting through the air rose but not uncomfortably.

Babak had ridden in many aircraft in his forty-five years. He had a few years to go before he could retire from the United States Central Intelligence Agency's Clandestine Service. His retirement plans with the Iranian Ministry of Intelligence and National Security were not finalized. He couldn't safely accept both. The chances of him being discovered as a double agent were too high. Perhaps he wouldn't apply for either one. The sale of the power packs and exoskeleton suits would give him the freedom he wanted.

The aircraft moved with a shudder and began to taxi smoothly to the runway. Babak watched the small aircraft parked on the tarmac slip by and soon felt the brakes bring the Beechcraft to a halt. The engine's sounds changed and rose in level. Shortly after that the pilot swung the aircraft onto the runway and applied takeoff power. The aircraft seemed to spring forward and push Babak back in his seat. Aircraft parked near the runway whizzed by, and then they were airborne. The wheels came up and locked with a loud clunk and Babak watched Vero Beach drop away.

The aircraft kept climbing and finally leveled off at their cruise altitude of 19,500 feet above sea level. With the pressurized cabin and cargo area, Babak felt as comfortable as being at ground level. Their flight plan would take them across the southern end of Florida and across the Gulf of Mexico to Cancun, Mexico. The large Lake Okeechobee passed below and Babak unfastened his seat belt, took his .38 caliber snub-nosed revolver out, checked the weapon and put it back under his loose floral print shirt, and went forward.

He looked out between the pilot and copilot at large thunderheads in the in the distance. Lightning danced across the clouds; sending strobes of white light through the windscreens. The copilot glanced back at Babak and slipped off his earphones.

"Can I help you, sir?"

Babak asked, "How are we doing?"

The pilot pointed to the towering clouds and said, "We are asking for clearance to take a route around them. It may add a little time, but we have plenty of fuel."

Babak nodded knowingly and returned to his seat. He still had time to take control and decide the fate of the copilot. He would keep the pilot alive as long as he needed him.

The detour around what was now being called a tropical storm took an additional hour, but as the pilot had said, they had plenty of fuel. Two hours later the pilot made a textbook landing at Cancun and rolled to a stop at the end of the runway. As he began taxiing to the flight line for smaller commercial aircraft, Babak came forward and said to the pilot, "Could your copilot help me for a minute?"

The pilot looked over at his copilot and nodded. "Sure. Raymund, will you give our passenger a hand?"

Raymund followed Babak into the cargo area after closing the cockpit door and said, "What is it?"

Babak pointed to the exoskeleton suits and said, "What is that?"

Raymund leaned over to see where Babak had pointed, and Babak brought the heel of his pistol down on the back of Raymund's head. The blow was vicious and Raymund collapsed in a heap on top of a suit. Babak used adhesive tape he carried in his pocket, and bound Raymund's hands behind him. He then gagged him with a rag and ran the tape across Raymund's head.

The Beechcraft slowed to a stop and Babak walked back to the cockpit, opened the door and sat in the copilot's seat. He pointed his pistol at the pilot and said, "Do nothing stupid and I will not have to kill you."

"Where is Raymund? What have you done to him?"

"Raymund will be fine. Now listen to me and listen carefully. I will not repeat myself."

***

Flying in the little Cessna was one thing, but flying inside a heavy exoskeleton was another. I am not claustrophobic, but I was on the verge of panic when Megan closed me inside that suit. It was hot inside and grew hotter as time went by. We dogs cool ourselves by panting, but that would have given my hiding place away. Once they found me, Megan and Ryan would have been next. I felt myself being lifted out of the truck and heard the men talking, I wondered when Ryan would spring up like a super action hero and take over, but he didn't. I guess he had his own idea about taking Babak to the authorities alive. I used the term authorities because I am a little confused about who will help us.

There must have been some kind of packing material, maybe powder inside the suit, because I sneezed and then had to hold my nose with both paws before I gave away my hiding place. I worried that Megan would be hurt when the men lifted her, and I listened, but she was quiet.

It seemed like a very long time before I heard men talking, but inside the suit the sound of the engines made hearing the men difficult. Then I felt a heavy load fall on my suit. It didn't crush me because of the suit's outside skeleton structure. Nevertheless, I couldn't move at all. Prior to that, I was able to move around in the suit to a limited degree. I smelled the odor of blood but it's wasn't Ryan's or Megan's.

CHAPTER 25

Susan Humphrey was trying to reach a telephone, but the loss of blood had made it a Herculean effort. She used the wall of the storage room to lean on as she worked her way toward the door. Her purse and cell phone were in the Hummer. She alternately held one hand over the bloody wound in her side and the other on the wall to keep from falling. She hadn't made much headway and had to rest every other minute. Her trail of progress was visible as a blood smeared road map along the wall. Preston Winn's body was now out of her sight. She winced at each movement and wondered if she was going to die. The thought of dying in some God forsaken building made the thought even more degrading. She took a deep breath and the lights grew dim. She slipped down the wall until two strong hands grabbed her under her arms.

Special Agent Howard Lowell held her upright for a few seconds and then slowly lowered her to the floor. He knelt beside her and checked her pulse, which was fast and shallow. Her lips were purple and her eyes unfocused. Her lips moved but she didn't speak. He said, "You'll be alright," knowing he might be lying. He opened his cell phone and speed dialed 911, identified himself as an FBI agent, and called for an ambulance. He laid her head on his jacket and pulled up her bloody blouse. A ragged wound seeped blood. He rose and looked around. He had a first aid kit in his car, which he had parked in the rear of the building next to an open warehouse door.

When he first came in the open door from the loading dock, he had walked the length of one hall checking for inhabitants. He didn't have a search warrant or permission from his boss to be there, but when he saw the body of Preston Winn, he was quick to draw his pistol and continue looking for the killer. He didn't have to examine the body to know Preston Winn was dead. The pool of blood and gray matter was enough. However, when he checked the body for identification, he was surprised to see an identification card of a Mr. Fredrick Ruben of South Africa. He followed a blood-smeared trail on a wall and found Susan Humphrey.

The strange message in his voicemail gave the names of Preston Winn and Susan Humphrey as the perpetrators of a serious national security crime and their location in Vero Beach. Considering what he had already discovered about the case, he now wondered if Ryan Quinn might have taken matters in to his own hands and tried to kill them both, but left before he finished the job.

This was no longer a case he was following off duty. He knew the backlash from his superiors would be severe, but he dialed his own office to tell his boss before notifying the local FBI regional office. The 911 call would bring the local police. He was coming back from his car with the first aid kit when he heard the siren of the paramedics.

***

Babak kept the barrel of his revolver pointed at the pilot as he said, "We are going to take a little ride. If you do as I say, you will live to fly again. How much fuel do you have?"

The pilot looked at the fuel gauges and said, "One hundred fifty-three gallons in both tanks."

Babak thought for a minute and said, "Not enough. Order fuel."

"Why? Where are we going?"

"I will tell you once we are airborne."

"What will I file?"

"Local VOR flight. Whatever you need to ensure we are not stopped or have to leave the aircraft. By the way, I am familiar with the emergency procedures for skyjacked flights. Don't be stupid.

"Now order the fuel service and do not make a false move or your friend will die."

The pilot did as he was told, and after a lengthy wait for fuel, he contacted the tower and asked for a local visual flight rules flight. Once granted, he taxied out and waited in the long line of

aircraft filled with vacationers trying to leave before tropical storm
Brenda came roaring through.

***

Ryan worked his arm inside the exoskeleton, and finally felt
the inside latch on the right side of the suit. It had taken him hours
of painful manipulations to free his arm, but now he had more
room to work. He made a mental note to tell the designers about
that problem, assuming he lived long enough. With the power pack
disconnected, he hadn't been able to use the suit as intended. He
had heard Babak and the copilot talking and the thud before the
man had collapsed. Fortunately, the copilot was not lying on top of
Ryan's suit.

Ryan felt the aircraft accelerate as it took off again. He waited
a little longer and unsnapped the suit's side release. He felt it give
but the weight of the heavy machinegun made opening it difficult.
He took a deep breath, hoping Babak wasn't watching, and pushed
the suit's upper torso open. He quickly opened the visor and looked
around. Instead of disconnecting and removing the helmet, which
was probably the normal method for entry and egress, he slipped
down inside and pulled his body out the side of the suit.

Ryan had never been in a Beechcraft 1900D, but recognized it
for what it was, a medium sized turboprop aircraft. He saw that
there were four empty seats close to the cabin door, which was
closed. Thanks for small favors. He started to free Megan and
Magic when he saw the copilot, bound and gagged. He felt the
man's neck for a pulse. He had one, but it was uneven and faint.
Ryan moved the man's head, which flopped from side to side. He
was obviously unconscious and badly hurt. Ryan pulled him off
one exoskeleton and rolled it over so he could open it from the
back. A few seconds later, Magic sprang out, knocked Ryan on his
back, and covered him with kisses. Ryan fell but grabbed Magic's
snout and clamped his hands around it. He bent close to Magic and
said in a whisper, "Quiet, Magic. Quiet." He then let go and Magic
shook his head sending his ears out to flap from side to side.

It took a little longer to extract Megan, as she fit within the
suit. Once out, she looked around and grabbed Ryan. He held her

tightly for a few moments and then pushed her back slowly and said, "Megan, I need your help. I'm going to put on the suit. Babak is in the cabin with the pilot. The copilot is behind you on the deck."

Megan looked back and saw the copilot. "Is he hurt?" she asked.

"Yes, but I don't want him making noise yet. Once I take care of Babak, we'll see what we can do for him."

Megan began to help Ryan put the suit on again and asked, "How do you know his name?"

"He's the same creep that pulled a gun on me at Port Canaveral and the same one who kidnapped you."

Megan, who remembered very little of her ordeal with Babak, said, "Yes, that is him. Now I remember. What are you going to do?"

"Throw him out."

Megan opened the faceplate and looked at Ryan. "Are you serious?"

"No, I need that scumbag alive. Now hurry and attach the power pack and let me see how this thing works."

While Megan finished putting on Ryan's backpack, Magic went forward and sniffed the door to the cockpit. He came back and began sniffing the copilot and then looked up at Ryan and whined softly.

"It's okay, Magic. We'll help him in a minute. Now stay back here and be quiet."

"All set," Megan announced and tapped Ryan on the top of his helmet.

With the faceplate still open Ryan said, "I saw what looks like a switch on the power pack. Turn it on and let's see what happens."

Megan found the switch and pushed it. A hum began coming from the power pack and Ryan was surprised to feel the suit move. He had been pushing upright to support its weight, but now the suit moved from his waist back. He stopped pushing and the suit stopped. He started to move his hand and the suit moved. He moved his other arm and the suit moved so quickly that it seemed to anticipate his moves. He tried moving his fingers and the four mechanical fingers moved. Ryan spent a few minutes trying various moves, closing and opening the fingers and finally took a step and then another. The aircraft dropped and then rose again abruptly. Ryan put out his arm to balance himself but the suit reacted first and centered his weight.

"Not bad," he said. "Now I've got to figure out how to fire the machinegun."

"Be careful," Megan warned.

After a bit Ryan said, "I think I've found the trigger, but there must be a safety somewhere."

Megan said, "If you fire that thing, won't it blow up the airplane?"

Ryan gingerly touched a few switched inside the suit before saying, "It depends on what it hits. I don't intend to use it. Just don't want to accidentally fire it."

The door from the cabin opened and Babak walked into the cargo area. When he looked up, he stopped abruptly and rushed back into the cockpit, pulling the door closed behind him.

Ryan flipped the visor down on the suit and walked to the closed cabin door. He grabbed the knob and pulled. The doorknob broke off and came away in his mechanical fingers. He then shoved his hand through the thin door and pulled it away from its hinges.

Babak held the barrel of his revolver against the head of the pilot and looked at Ryan. Ryan dropped the torn door and said, "Give it up, Babak. You shoot him and you'll die too."

Babak pushed the revolver painfully into the pilot's ear and shouted, "As will you and your girlfriend. I'm not afraid to die. It is your choice."

Ryan glanced back at Megan before saying to the pilot, "Where are we going?"

The pilot kept his face forward but said, "Vera Cruz."

Babak dug the barrel into his ear and said, "Shut up."

He used his free hand to pull out Ryan's .45 caliber pistol from his waistband and aimed it at Ryan. "Get back."

Ryan said, "Not a good idea, Babak." When Ryan moved, Babak fired the .45 at him. The sound inside the small confines of the aircraft was deafening. Magic let out a sharp bark and Megan clamped her hands over her ears. The aircraft's nose rose abruptly and then suddenly dropped. The pilot slumped foreword and pushed the yoke over. The Beechcraft picked up speed as it hurtled toward the ground.

***

When Ryan saved me from that crazy suit, I must have overdone it a bit, because he grabbed my snout and held my mouth closed. It hurt a bit and it was hard to breathe, but I understood when he cautioned me to be silent. It was sure good to see him. All that time in that hot suit seemed worth it. Megan hadn't complained and I felt a little ashamed of myself. Of course, neither of them knew how I felt, so that was a plus. Didn't want them to think they had a cowardly dog.

The copilot had been hurt. I wanted Ryan to untie him but he had other priorities at the time. I guess it was a smart move because that Babak guy came in when Ryan was finishing with the suit. After that, pandemonium broke loose. Babak must have panicked and fired a pistol. The sound was unbelievably loud and I think I might have barked, or worse, yelped. The airplane started to go up and then down like a ride in the carnival, not that I have ever been to a carnival, but I saw one on television. My stomach felt like it was going to come out my mouth, but after awhile, and I might add, a very scary while, the airplane leveled off. My body felt heavy and my legs would barely hold me up. I believe it is called G force, which stands for gravity. We were defying gravity, and I don't think it is wise to defy any natural laws.

The bullet Babak meant for Ryan had hit the pilot. It must have hit Ryan's armor and bounced back. At first I didn't understand why Ryan didn't just knock the you-know-what out of Babak, but then true to form, Babak was using others to save himself. I doubt if he really wasn't afraid to die as he said. It's unnatural not to be uneasy about the unknown, unless you already know, but then it's not unknown. Am I making sense?

The pilot, although wounded, was able to pull the airplane out of the dive. I know Ryan is a good pilot, but with that suit on, he couldn't fit inside the cockpit. He came back to us and said, "Babak told the pilot to set us down. We are near the airport at Campeche, Mexico. The pilot's arm might be broken and he is bleeding. I told Babak that I would let him go but not if the pilot dies. My guess is Babak will make a run for it, but you two stay out of the line of fire. I wouldn't put it past him to try to kill just for spite."

So there we were; in a skyjacked plane with a homicidal maniac who Ryan needed to clear his own name, but who he had to let escape to save the life of the pilot. That's my Ryan, always thinking of the other guy. But Ryan's no dumbbell. He had an ace up his artificial sleeve.

Megan began taking the tape off the poor copilot. I would have helped, and have some experience with doing that, but she seemed to be doing okay. The man was still unconscious but he could breathe better without that dirty rag Babak stuck in his mouth.

Ryan went forward, and I heard him tell Babak that he wanted an ambulance to meet them. Babak hesitated but finally relented and told the pilot to use his radio and request an ambulance. He also threatened to shoot the pilot in the knee if he tried anything. The pilot radioed and spoke in Spanish to the air controller. My Spanish is weak, but I could follow some of it. I thought the pilot would tell the controller about Babak, but he didn't. I guess he didn't know if Babak knew Spanish or not.

The landing was bumpy, but what can you expect with a bleeding pilot with a broken arm and a gun pointed at his head? Made me nervous.

The airplane slowed at the end of the runway, turned off onto a taxiway, and stopped. A bunch of emergency vehicles with their lights flashing came at us. Ryan watched closely as Babak pushed open the door from the cockpit to the outside. It swung down and he hurried down the steps and ran to one of the ambulances. A few seconds later the driver of the ambulance jumped out, and the ambulance sped off. Ryan used the cargo door to exit the aircraft, and before I could get out to help him, he took off on foot chasing the ambulance. Maybe on foot is misleading. The exoskeleton suit ran after the ambulance. Ryan was inside it. While I felt I should go with Ryan and help him capture Babak, I knew he would want me to protect Megan, so I stayed with her.

Medics came aboard and checked on the wounded pilot and copilot. They asked Megan questions in Spanish and she answered. I forgot her father is Mexican. I guess they must speak Spanish at home, although I don't recall hearing them when I stayed there. Maybe they spoke English for me to be polite. I caught a few words and I heard the word police twice. It's pretty much a no brainier: "Policia." With the police on the way, I wondered what would happen to Ryan. If the pilot could talk he might clear Ryan, but that was iffy. It looked like he passed out over the yoke after he got us safely down. I hope they give him a medal.

***

Ryan was surprised how easily he learned to run and run fast. While he wasn't gaining on the ambulance that Babak commandeered, he kept it in sight. He cut across a field and closed the distance between them. The ambulance came to a stop before a closed chain link gate. It backed up and then drove head-on into the gate. The gate sprung loose but became tangled under the ambulance's wheels. The ambulance came to a stop, and Ryan reached for the rear door, caught the door handle, and yanked it open. Babak turned with panic-filled eyes and fired the remaining rounds from his revolver at the exoskeleton. He was reaching for Ryan's .45 Glock when strong mechanical fingers closed around his shoulder and ripped him out of the driver's seat. The Glock fell to the floor.

Ryan pulled Babak out of the ambulance and threw him over his shoulder. Babak yelled and kicked, trying to get loose, but Ryan held him tight and jogged back to the Beechcraft.

Megan and Magic stood next to the aircraft as Ryan approached. All the emergency vehicles had left but a service truck was pulling up with tow bars, prepared to move the aircraft off the taxiway. When Ryan reached the aircraft, the men were out of their truck, but stopped at the sight of a strange looking robot carrying a man. Ryan had grown tired of Babak's yelling and hit him on the head, knocking him unconscious, or at least groggy enough to stop trying to get loose.

Ryan saw them and said through his amplified voice, "Stay back. I will move the airplane shortly. Do not interfere."

The men jumped back into their truck and sped off. Ryan dropped Babak on the taxiway and said, "Megan, find something to tie him up and then help me out of this suit."

Megan rushed back into the aircraft and soon came back with a first aid kit. She took out the adhesive tape and bound Babak's hands and feet. Ryan then lifted him off the taxiway and threw him into the cargo area of the aircraft. Magic jumped up into the aircraft and stood looking at Babak. A low growl came from his throat.

Megan quickly unplugged the power pack and took off the backpack. She helped Ryan out and he let the suit fall to the pavement. "Let's get out of here," he said to her and rushed to the cockpit.

Megan followed him and said, "What are you doing? The pilot will tell the police what happened."

Ryan kept his eyes on the myriad gauges and instruments while saying, "I'm not going to take a chance that the scumbag will get away. The pilot's badly hurt. I hope he makes it, but he's lost a lot of blood. I'm not supposed to leave Florida, let alone the U.S."

Megan looked at the complex cockpit, waved her hand across the instrument panel and asked, "You fly this?"

Ryan kept scanning the gauges and switches before he said, "Yes, but I need a little time. Look behind the copilot's seat. There should be a manual there."

Megan found a pilot's manual for the Beechcraft 1900D model and handed it to Ryan. He said, "Take this kneepad and read off the takeoff section."

Megan said, "Are you going to leave that suit out there?"

"Damn. I might need it as evidence. I'll be right back. Open the pilot's manual and find the performance section."

Ryan slipped past her and out of the aircraft. He hefted the heavy suit, shoved it into the cargo area, and closed the cargo door. He saw Magic standing over Babak and smiled. He didn't have time to say, "Good boy."

***

I was trying to listen to Ryan and still keep an eye on Babak, although Megan had him tied up like a thanksgiving turkey. That reminded me, I was hungry, and I didn't smell any in-flight snacks. After a short conversation with both ground control and then air traffic control, Ryan taxied the Beechcraft down the taxiway and behind other aircraft waiting to taxi onto the runway. Once they were clear, he was told over the radio that he was cleared for takeoff. Ryan spoke in English but the controller had no problem and replied quickly. He was instructed to maintain a heading and report once he got at a certain altitude. I missed some of it, but knew Ryan was in control of events. I began to relax for the first time since we found Mr. Winn in the suit.

Megan asked Ryan about the tropical storm and he said they were going around it. She asked if they had enough fuel and he didn't answer as quickly as I would have liked. Ryan taxied onto the runway, checked some instruments and had Megan read off the airspeed. She did a good job and soon I felt the nose rise, and soon after that, the ground dropped away.

We were flying back home with Babak tied up and all was well.

***

Megan watched the land pass under the wing and saw the white caps break the constant blue green of the Gulf of Mexico. Ryan had the Beechcraft in a gentle climb. She watched Ryan as he adjusted the navigation display and talked on the radio. She had on the copilot's headset and could hear Ryan listening to other aircraft. The tropical storm had grown in to a level one hurricane and had changed course catching the weather guessers by surprise.

Ryan glanced at Megan and saw the concern on her face. He reached over and patted her hand. "Don't worry. I'm going to head farther north. It should pass to the south."

He pointed out of the windshield and said, "Those are feeder bands. We will have some rough weather but nothing she can't handle."

Megan said, "You've never flown one of these before. How do you know?"

Ryan listened to another report from an airliner before he said, "The aircraft has a good reputation. Lots of them in service. If it gets too bad, we can still go back. He pointed to the fuel gauges.

"Can we climb over them?" Megan asked and pointed to the towering cloud formation in front of them.

"No, they must be fifty, maybe sixty thousand feet or more."

They flew on in relative silence for another hour before the clear blue sky had all but disappeared. The visibility was dropping fast, and although there were a few hours of daylight left, it grew dark. Megan watched the lights on the wingtips flashing. Occasional rough air bounced the Beechcraft around but not severely. Magic came up into the cabin and looked at the gauges and out the windshield. Megan patted his head and said, "It's okay. We'll be home in an hour or so."

He looked at Ryan and whined. Ryan didn't notice. He was studying the aircraft's weather radar. He adjusted the range and looked at Megan before saying, "It looks like that monster is following us. I'm going to try going farther north."

Megan didn't reply as Ryan contacted air traffic control and requested a change in his flight. He was given a new vector and a new altitude. Ryan made a slight turn to the north and applied power to the two turboprop engines. The altimeter began to climb and Megan asked, "Can we go back?"

Ryan looked at the fuel gauges and said, "Not a good idea. We are closer to Florida than to Mexico." After a few minutes he said, "If I don't change course, we will end up over Texas."

"Texas?"

"We can refuel there and fly southeast to Florida. We are indicating about 260 knots, but with the headwinds we are only making about 195 over the ground."

"We're over the ground?"

"Okay, over the water. It means we will take longer to get home and use more fuel."

A few minutes later he said, "The storm has turned to the west. We should be able to turn back toward Florida soon."

Megan said, "How much longer? I have to use the potty."

"I think there is a head in the rear of the cargo area. Go back and check it out."

Megan unstrapped and started back. The headset pulled her up abruptly. She slipped it off and worked her way between the two cockpit seats.

While Ryan had used the naval term "head" for a bathroom, Megan found a small toilet behind a door at the rear of the aircraft. She had to walk past Babak, who was now conscious and watching her closely, which made her feel uneasy. Magic moved close to Babak and snarled, which made her feel better. When she came out of the head she walked past him, and he spoke to her. She went back to the cockpit and said to Ryan, "That man is awake."

Ryan said, "I should have hit him harder. Did he say anything?"

"Yes, but I don't want to repeat it. He is filthy."

Ryan set the autopilot and said, "She'll fly herself okay. I have to go back to the head."

"Do I need to do anything?"

"Just sit there and don't touch a thing. I won't be long."

When Ryan came back to the cockpit, he checked the instruments and talked on the radio. After a few minutes he acknowledged the new route and turned the Beechcraft before saying, "We've been cleared to Tampa. About an hour if the winds don't change again."

Megan asked, "Do you have enough gas?"

Ryan, who had been calculating his remaining fuel and estimated consumption for the flight to Tampa, said, "It's not gas, it's jet fuel, but we have enough. It is a little close, but we should lose this headwind soon."

Outer bands from the hurricane began to pummel the Beechcraft and Magic came up to the cockpit and looked at Ryan;

however, Ryan didn't see him. He was watching his instruments, specifically fuel consumption and remaining fuel in the tanks. Megan reached down and patted Magic's head. He worked his way in closer, and put his head on her lap.

Ryan placed his hands over the headset's earphones. Megan heard the crackling radio and wondered how Ryan was able to understand the garbled communications. He looked at Megan and said, "We've been ordered to return to Mexican airspace and land as soon as possible."

"Are you? Megan asked.

"No way. Sitting in a Mexican jail while this gets straightened out is not an option. I'm trying to get clearance for an instrument approach to Tampa, Florida."

Megan looked at the instruments. While she didn't understand many of them, the fuel gauges were simple, showing both gallons and pounds of fuel. They were much lower than the last time she looked. A severe gust hit the airplane and shook it violently. Magic looked up and whined. Megan patted his head again, but he whined until Ryan said, "That's his I-gotta-go whine. He'll have to hold it."

"How long before we land?" Megan asked.

Ryan waited until he finished doing the calculations and said, "The good news, my calculations are the same as the computer."

"And the bad?"

"We need a tail wind to make it to Tampa."

Magic pulled his head back and moved to the rear of the aircraft. Megan was looking back at him when the lightning struck.

CHAPTER 26

I guess my "All was well," comment was ill timed. I could see by the fuel consumption and distance to Tampa that we weren't going to make it. Ryan had been listening to the weather guys, or girls, who said the hurricane was going to swing further south. They were wrong, and now we were in serious trouble.

Ryan came back after Babak cursed Megan and gagged him. He used an old rag and tape from the first aid kit. Babak didn't like it, but saw Ryan's angry face and didn't resist. Then Ryan went back to the cockpit and I joined him and Megan. He told Megan that we were going swimming unless we had a tail wind. Those are my words; he said it much nicer. He didn't want to worry her and didn't actually use the word swimming.

I didn't think this airplane floated and I didn't want to swim home. Speaking of floating, I really had to empty my bladder. I could not open the handle on the small toilet at the rear of the airplane, and didn't want to soil the exoskeletons, so I peed on Babak. It seemed the right thing to do. He was the source of our problems. He didn't like that at all and tried to kick me, but I'm no dummy. His feet were bound together and he had to flip around to get to me. I stayed out of range after I hit my target.

Then a white light filled the cabin and my hair stood on end. I heard a sound that sounded like a train came by outside, of course we were thousands of feet in the air and no trains were at that altitude. The airplane shuddered and started to drop. I guess Ryan got it under control quickly, but I heard him trying to talk on the radio and I went back to the cockpit.

The instruments looked different. Many of the gauges were not indicating and some of the heads-up displays were gone. The big GPS display was gone and the weather radar was not showing anything. How could it miss a hurricane?

I figured it out and Ryan corroborated my theory. We had been hit by lightning. It fried many of the instruments; mainly the radios, and Ryan said the automatic pilot bought it. By bought it, he meant it was dead. He told Megan we were blind, but I could see well enough. Plenty of black clouds outside that were lit by lightning flashing from cloud to cloud.

Ryan said we were lucky because the engine computers were still functioning. Big deal. We could fly into a mountain and not know it. Well, I guess we would know it, and there aren't any mountains in the Gulf of Mexico, but you get my meaning.

Megan did not panic. I did, but I couldn't talk and tell anyone how I felt so they thought I was brave. Sometimes I am brave, but I wasn't brave then. I went back into the cargo area because I didn't want them to see me shivering and it wasn't cold. It did get cold after awhile and then it got hot. My ears hurt and I felt pressure on them. They were okay for awhile. I guess Ryan was doing something with the cabin pressurization or maybe it broke too. The airplane bounced around in the rough air, and shuddered as if to shake off the water that came at us like it was out of a fire hose.

After my heart stopped trying to beat its way out of my chest, I went back to the cockpit and watched Ryan fly. I got there in time to hear him say, "We can't make it to Tampa."

Megan asked, "What are you going to do?"

"If I turn north again we won't have the headwind. Might even pick up a little wind on our tail."

"Where will that take us?"

Ryan had an aeronautical chart on his lap and was using a pencil to measure mileage, I think. It took him a long time but he finally looked at Megan and said, "Pensacola, Florida."

Megan looked confused and said, "But that's almost in Alabama."

He nodded and folded the map. "I know. Now please go back and check on the flotation devices."

Oh boy! Floatation devices such as life vests. I didn't think they would have one for a dog. I was right, but they did have an inflatable boat, according to Megan. She stopped and looked at Babak. I guess she didn't know about the gag.

I could tell that Ryan had turned the airplane again because we weren't jumping up and down so much. Maybe we could make it to land. I kept my paws crossed.

***

Special Agent Howard Lowell stood outside Susan Humphrey's hospital room. A Vero Beach Police Department detective stood a few feet away. They had been talking for a few minutes before a doctor came out and said, "You may talk to her, but make it brief. She has lost a lot of blood and is still sedated from the surgery."

Susan Humphrey's wounds, while appearing fatal, were not. A bullet fragment had cut across her stomach but hadn't entered a vital organ before exiting. Pieces of plaster from the wall had complicated the wound by embedding themselves. Her loss of blood was the doctor's primary concern.

Jurisdiction in the case of Preston Winn, AKA Mr. Fredrick Ruben of South Africa, was not an issue, yet. After Lowell told his boss about the killing, she chewed on him for being there before she said she would check with regional and get back to him. For now, let the local yokels do their thing.

The building had been cordoned off as a crime scene and a local television station was already there asking questions. The local police chief said he would issue a statement later, but only said there appeared to be a homicide.

Susan Humphrey would not have liked anyone, certainly not a man, seeing her with her hair a mess of tangles and her makeup off. She still had an attractive face, but her pale complexion and dull eyes did little to foster the attention of the two officers who stood next to her bed.

Detective Rice Mullen identified himself, as did Special Agent Howard Lowell. Detective Rice Mullen said, "Mrs. Ruben. I won't keep you long, but could you tell us what happened to your husband?"

"Rubin?" she asked.

"You are Mrs. Rubin?" he asked.

Susan was too confused from the anesthesia to lie. She said slowly, "I'm Susan Humphrey. What happened to me?"

Both officers looked at each other, but Special Agent Howard Lowell said, "Do you know Preston Winn?"

"He's my boss."

A moment later she said, "He was shot. I saw him lying there, but I couldn't help him." She then thought for a moment and added, "But he shot me?"

"Who shot you, Miss Humphrey?"

"Preston shot me, I think. I can't remember clearly. It happened so fast."

"Take your time. Did you see anyone shoot him?"

"Who?" she asked.

"Preston Winn?"

Detective Mullen asked, "Who is Preston Winn?"

Special Agent Howard Lowell answered, "The man in your morgue. Let's step outside for a minute."

***

Ryan reduced power to the engines and had Megan call off the prelanding checklist. Some of the items were not going to work, but thankfully the flaps worked, and when they got slower he would drop the landing gear, assuming some servo or motor was not burned out by the lightning strike. Ryan could not reach any controlling agency and was dropping down into controlled airspace. Hopefully, radar had him sighted and would keep other aircraft clear. Navigating by wet compass alone was scary at night. Without visual clues, estimating drift would be a wild guess. He wanted to land at the Pensacola Regional Airport, but could be miles off, maybe even a hundred. It was hard to know. The feeder bands from the hurricane reached out with its deadly fingers hundreds of miles from the storm center. If one was over Pensacola, Ryan could only hope for the best and prepare for the worst.

He looked at Megan and said, "If we have to ditch in the water, you and Magic get in the inflatable raft first. I'll follow."

"What about him?" she motioned to the rear of the aircraft.

Ryan didn't answer and Megan prodded, "You can't let him drown."

"Yeah, who would clear me?"

Megan let his comment go. She knew, or at least thought she knew, he wouldn't let Babak drown even if he wasn't vital to Ryan's defense. She did say, "Are you going to untie him?"

Ryan sighed and said, "Only if I have to."

A dim light shown through the dark clouds below. It was off to their right.

"Did you see that?" Ryan said.

Megan looked out for a few seconds and said, "There is a light down there."

Thin clouds obscured the light for a few moments before it began to pulsate. Now other lights began to appear. Ryan reduced power again and the Beechcraft lost altitude. He found the switch for his landing lights and checked the landing checklist again. When he looked at his fuel gauges he said, "I'm only going to have one chance at this so hold on." He had been ignoring the flashing fuel warning light for some time.

"Is that Pensacola?" Megan asked.

"I hope so. Tell Magic to hold on."

Megan looked back, saw Magic standing guard over Babak, and yelled back at him, "Magic, come boy." He immediately ran to her. Megan unbuckled and pulled Magic into one of the seats behind the cockpit. She tugged the seat belt over him, pulled it tight and said, "Stay."

She had to steady herself as Ryan made an abrupt turn and she felt the aircraft slow as he dropped the flaps further. The gear clunked down seconds before he said, "I'm going to have to take it around."

One engine began to wind down and lost power. The prop feathered automatically and Ryan yelled, "I guess not! Hold on, we can't go around."

A few seconds later, the tires screeched and the nose dropped. Megan watched the runway lights flash by at an astonishing speed.

She unconsciously pressed her feet against the floor as if there were brakes there. The end of the runway was coming up fast.

Ryan pressed down on the brakes and tried not to lose control or blow out a tire. Many of the safety features were destroyed by the lightning strike. They passed the last turnoff to the taxiways and came to a jarring stop a few feet from the runway's end.

Ryan sat there for a few seconds and watched the remaining engine rundown. It too had run out of fuel. He looked at Megan, who was still praying and reached over to pat her shoulder. She looked over and said, "We made it," and smiled.

From the back cabin, they heard Magic bark his approval.

***

I never doubted Ryan's ability to get us back safely. I won't lie and say it wasn't a little touch and go at times, but we were down and not swimming in the Gulf of Mexico.

It would have been nice if we had landed at the Pensacola Regional Airport, but we hadn't. We landed at the Pensacola Naval Air Station without permission, and that tends to make the military a bit cranky. In no time we were surrounded by trucks with flashing lights. Megan came back and unbuckled me and I went forward to look outside. Men with automatic rifles surrounded the airplane and two Humvees had machineguns on top of them. It was hard to see because of the lights that were focused on our airplane. An amplified voice from outside told us to come out with our hands in the air, one at a time. That would be difficult for me but not impossible.

Ryan went out first. I watched four men in blue utilities approach. Ryan knelt down and then laid on the runway. The men put handcuffs on him and led him away. Megan came out and they did the same with her. I followed her and waited to be handcuffed, but they stayed back, so I went to Megan and gave her a big lick. She needed my encouragement. She had tears in her pretty eyes and it broke my heart. I decided to bite anyone who came near her, but she talked me out of it by saying, "It's okay, Magic. They're on our side."

Well, it turned out they were on the side of the United States government, which is understandable, but that didn't help us at the time. Megan was led to another Humvee, and some more men and a woman entered the aircraft. A few minutes later, Babak came walking out. His gag was gone and his hands and feet were free of the tape. They led him to a sedan with Navy markings and it drove off.

I waited for my ride but none came. An emergency truck came out and a tow tractor. It looked like they were going to tow the airplane away. I thought about Ryan and the problem he might have to prove any of his stories. I had this feeling that Babak was going to get away and not be arrested for killing Mr. Winn, injuring the pilot and copilot, or stealing the airplane. Then I remembered the exoskeletons and power packs. I couldn't carry a heavy military exoskeleton, but I could carry one of the power packs. I ran back to the airplane, ran up the cargo door stairs and found the power pack. There was another one, but I couldn't carry two of them very far. One was heavy enough. I grabbed the straps and lifted it off the deck. It was heavier than I thought, but I managed to lift it and walk down the stairs.

A man saw me and yelled, but I trotted off past the lighted area and across the grass beside the runway. By the time I got clear of the taxiway, my neck muscles were already beginning to ache. I slowed to a walk and after awhile I dropped the power pack and rested. I had passed through low scrubs and tall weeds but I could still see the lights around the airplane. It was too far away to make out any details. I hoped to find where the police, or whoever they were, took Ryan and Megan. I started out again but came to a chain link fence. It was too tall to jump over and too tall to climb. This wasn't going to work very well. After a few minutes, I dug a hole in the soft sandy soil and buried the power pack.

I made my way back to the airplane, or where it had been and looked around. It was gone and I was alone. The runway lights were on and I watched another airplane land. It was a small, sleek jet painted blue. It taxied away under its own power. It began to rain and I looked for shelter, but found none. I hunkered down in the weeds near the runway and waited for Ryan to return.

CHAPTER 27

Ryan sat on a wooden bench inside the NAS Pensacola Police Station. Megan sat near him on a separate bench. They were still handcuffed and a policeman stood nearby. Megan asked, "Why are we being treated like criminals?"

Ryan answered when the policeman ignored her. "It might have been because of the illegal landing, or maybe that aircraft may have been reported skyjacked, or maybe they believed Babak and we are being held for the murder of Preston Winn and his girlfriend, or—"

Megan interrupted, "Don't worry, Ted will get us out of this."

"I would like to make a phone call," Megan said to the policeman.

"You will have time for that, but there are a few people who want to talk to you first."

"I don't intend to talk to anyone until I talk to my lawyer."

"That's your business, lady."

Ryan said, "What did you people do with my dog?"

The policeman looked puzzled and said, "What dog?"

"My dog, Magic. He was on the airplane."

Megan added, "He's a golden retriever. He got off with us. Somebody must have seen him."

"Nobody told me about a dog, but I'll check with operations. Maybe the crash crew has him."

The policeman made a telephone call and then said to Ryan, "Yeah, someone saw a dog come out of that airplane but it ran off. I asked them to look around for it. I'll contact the roving patrol."

Ryan said, "Thanks. His name is Magic."

Two men, dressed in suits, came into the police office and looked over at Ryan and Megan. They walked past and went through a door into the interior of the NAS Pensacola Police

Station. A few minutes later, a policeman came out of the door and said, "Come with me, Mr. Quinn."

Ryan looked over at Megan and said, "Call Ted if they give you a chance."

Ryan followed the policeman into a small room with a table and three chairs. The two men he had seen a few minutes before stood near the table, both neatly dressed in lightweight suits with ties and white shirts.

One said, "Have a seat, Mr. Quinn." Ryan sat at the table and the two men took out their identification cards. "I'm Edward Stillson and this is Henry Cline. We're with the NCIS, Naval Criminal Investigative Service."

Both men were in their late thirties and about the same size and height. Ryan guessed them to be a little under six feet and less than 180 pounds. Stillson might have been the older of the two and sported a trimmed black mustache and short wavy hair. Cline had a lighter complexion, clean shaven with neat brown hair

Ryan glanced at their IDs and said, "Okay. You want to know why I landed here?"

Edward Stillson, said, "I think we know, but why don't you tell us.? Do you mind if we record your statement?"

Ryan said, "Go ahead. I have nothing to hide."

The NCIS agent clicked on a small recorder and sat it on the table. He recorded a brief message citing the date, time, his name, Cline's name, and Ryan's name. He then said, "Go ahead, Mr. Quinn."

Ryan took a deep breath and began reciting the events starting with his arrest for possession of illegal substances. He finished with, "I managed to land here instead of Regional, and that's about it. Oh, and my dog, Magic, ran off and I need to find him."

The agents had been silent while Ryan spoke. Now Stillson said, "Has your dog had his rabies shots?"

"Yes, why?"

"Mr. Noparast said he was almost bitten by your dog. He also said your dog was dangerous and should be destroyed."

"Who is this Noparast guy?"

"The man you kidnapped, gagged, and bound in the airplane."

"What?" Ryan shouted. "His name isn't Noparast. It's Babak something or other. You believe that scumbag? I told you what he did."

Agent Cline said, "Mr. Quinn, you admittedly left Florida while under bond, awaiting trial for a felony. You admittedly took an airplane owned by Jamaican Tours. You want us to believe you and not a federal agent of the United States government?"

Ryan shook his head in disbelief and said, "Did you bother to check on his identification. Is he really with our government?'

"Yes. He definitely is with our government. Now would you like to tell us the truth?"

Ryan said, "I want to talk to my lawyer."

The NCIS agents stood and said, "As you wish." Agent Stillson went to the door and said to a policeman, "We are finished with Mr. Quinn. You can take him for now, and would you bring in Miss Alvarez?"

Ryan was led out by a policeman, and while the NCIS agents waited, Stillson said to Agent Cline, "You did check?"

Cline answered, "Yes, he's Allen Noparast of the CIA. He was taking those exo suits back to Washington when this happened. The Navy is arranging transportation for him and the suits."

***

I was dozing off when I heard a pickup truck go by on the taxiway. Inside were two sailors dressed in blue utilities. One was shining a light out over the weeds where I was laying. I heard him call my name and I jumped up. If they knew my name, Ryan or Megan must have told them. If that was the case, it was probably safe to let them see me. I barked loudly and ran to the pick-up truck. They must have heard me, because the truck stopped and a young sailor got out.

I ran up to him, and being polite, sat and offered my paw. He backed up but then eased forward and said, "Hi there."

He looked nervous so I stood on my hind legs and begged with my front paws. It must have settled his nerves because he said to the man in the truck, "Hey, look at this. He's doing tricks. He doesn't look dangerous to me."

Now that bothered me. Who told him I was dangerous? This was not good, but I trusted my instincts, the young sailor was not going to hurt me. He put out his hand and I put my paw in it. He smiled and patted my head. I jumped up, put my paws on his shoulders, and gave him a big kiss. He didn't seem to mind but took my paws and lowered me to the pavement. He shined a flashlight on my nametag and yelled to the sailor in the truck, "Call in and tell them we found the guy's dog. Come on, Magic. We'll find somewhere dry."

He opened the door to the pickup and I jumped in and sat in the middle. The driver, who was also a young man, said, "Smells like wet dog. Put him in the back."

The other sailor said, "He might jump out. Now let's go."

I rode with the two young sailors to a brightly lit building with large glass windows. The sailor who found me got out, and a few minutes later an older sailor dressed in khakis came out. He had a shiny billed hat and wore chevrons on his sleeve. He looked in at me and I tried my best smiley face. His droll expression softened a bit and he said, "Take him to animal control in the morning. I'll check with the OOD and see what she wants us to do until then."

The first sailor said, "Okay, Master Chief," and got back in the pickup truck. He rubbed my head and said to the driver, "Swing by the chow hall. Maybe Chief Benford's got something for the pooch."

Chief Benford, a very large black man, came out to see me. He told the young sailor to take me out of the truck. He then studied me for a moment, as if deciding if I was worthy of the red meat he held behind his back. I could smell it and started salivating but was careful not to drip on his polished shoes. He finally placed a large piece of butcher's paper on the ground, and in its center was the biggest piece of meat I had ever seen not walking. I looked up at him, waiting for permission to tear into it. I sat there and waited and waited. Come on, I thought. Enough is enough. Was this torture allowed by the Geneva Convention?

He finally said to the young sailors, "This dog has been trained and trained well. You say he was out near the runway?"

One sailor said, "Yeah. We were told he was dangerous, and we might have to shoot him."

"Be a waste," the chief said. Then he said to me, "Okay," and I dug in. That had to be one of the best meals I ever had, at least in America. Sometimes after not eating for days in Iraq, even garbage tasted good and the beef patties the Marines gave me were delicious.

The big chief chuckled as I tried to get my mouth around the huge streak. The driver said to the chief, "When are you gonna feed us like that?"

The chief gave him a hard look and said, "When you are as disciplined as this animal. Now find his owner and don't shoot him unless he shoots first."

The chief went back inside the mess hall and I gulped down the last piece of the steak.

***

Allen Noparast watched as the Navy working party loaded the exoskeletons into the back of a rented Ford van. One of the power packs was missing, but he couldn't take a chance staying longer to find it. His section chief at Langley knew he was working on the possible theft of secret Army exoskeletons and power packs by Preston Winn and Susan Humphrey, and their sale to Iran, but he didn't want him to start asking too many questions. Allen Noparast, aka Babak Shirazi, needed to leave with his treasure now. His Chinese connection expected the suits and power packs, and his superiors in the Iranian Ministry of Intelligence and National Security had a new assignment for him.

A Navy sedan and driver had been assigned to him by the station duty officer, and once the van was loaded, Noparast told the van's driver to follow him in the sedan. A few minutes later, a Navy pickup truck drove by in the opposite direction and Noparast yelled to his driver, "Stop. Turn around and follow that truck."

The driver did as he was told and soon pulled close to the blue pickup truck. Through the back window, Noparast could see Magic sitting up between two sailors. He said to the driver, "Stop that truck ahead of us."

The driver, also a young sailor, said, "Pardon me?"

Noparast didn't bother to explain. He reached over and pressed on the horn. The driver of the pickup looked back and Noparast said, "Pull up alongside that truck."

Once the sedan was next to the pickup, which had slowed, Noparast leaned out of the window and yelled, "Stop!"

The pickup pulled over and the Navy sedan stopped behind it. Noparast hurried out and ran to the driver's window. He held out his badge and ID before saying, "I want that dog destroyed *now*."

Magic saw him and snarled. The driver rolled down the window and looked at the CIA identification before saying, "Why? He's not mean."

Noparast said, "Do as I tell you."

The other sailor held on to Magic and said, "We're not armed and even if we were, we're not dog killers."

Noparast said, "Who's your commanding officer? Get him on the phone."

"Lieutenant Simpson, but she's probably sleeping."

"Then wake her. This is an urgent matter."

"Can't do that, sir. You wanna talk to the chief?"

"Yes, and hurry up."

The young sailor pressed the transmit button on the portable radio he carried, and once his chief answered, he held out the radio to Noparast, who yanked it from him.

"Who is this?" Noparast demanded.

"Master Chief Sanchez," the chief said flatly.

"Chief, I am Allen Noparast of the Central Intelligence Agency. I want the dog who came in on the aircraft destroyed, and *now*. Do I make myself clear?"

"Clear enough, but you'll have to take that up with the animal control people. We don't destroy animals."

"Get them out here. You think you can do that, Chief?"

"It's Master Chief, and they don't open until about oh eight hundred hours."

Noparast felt his anger getting away from him. He took a deep breath and looked at Magic, who was watching him carefully.

"Very well. For now, tell your men to put the dog in my truck." He didn't wait for an answer and handed the radio back to the sailor.

The sailor talked to the master chief for a few minutes before he said, "Yes, Master Chief," and got out of the pickup.

The rental van holding the exoskeletons and the power pack had stopped behind the Navy sedan. Noparast walked back to it and opened the rear door. The young sailor reluctantly pulled Magic toward the van. Magic didn't bite at him, but he did his best to pull away. Noparast stood clear as the sailor lifted Magic into the rear of the van and closed the door.

***

Master Chief Sanchez was not a man to accept being berated by some dumbass civilian cop, even if he worked for the Central Intelligence Agency. He walked into the office of the air station police department and looked for his friend, a retired Navy master-at-arms, who was now a federal police officer. He wanted to know more about that asshole who wanted to kill a dog. Didn't seem right to him. He looked around and saw someone who might be even more helpful. Ed Stillson, whose son played on the same little league team as the chief's son, came out of the inner offices and said, "Hi, John. What's got you up this late?"

"That civilian bird that landed earlier. What's with the CIA guy? Something bothering him about dogs?"

"Why do you ask?"

"Got a call from one of my roving patrols. They found the dog that was missing, but this CIA nut wanted me to check out a sidearm and kill the mutt."

"Did you?"

"Hell no. You know why his shorts are in a bind about a dog?"

Agent Stillson thought for a moment before he said, "Apparently he thinks the dog is dangerous."

Master Chief Sanchez said, "Yeah, that big friendly mutt tired to lick Seaman Swartz to death. They took him over to the chow hall and Chief Benford fed him. You know Benford. He doesn't like anybody, but he liked that dog."

"Where's the dog now?"

"I let him take the dog, but I'm having second thoughts."

Agent Stillson said to a policeman, "Would you call the gate and tell them to stop a Mr. Allen Noparast? He's a federal officer. Tell him I would like to talk to him before he leaves the base. Have him escorted back to the naval air station police station."

The policeman asked, "What's he driving?"

Stillson looked at Master Chief Sanchez, who said, "Navy sedan. Should be a rental van with him too."

Ten minutes later, Allen Noparast banged through the doors of the police station; Agents Stillson and Cline were waiting.

"What is this?" Noparast demanded. "I have urgent government business and you interfere? Who is your superior?"

Stillson's jaw tightened and he said softly, "We too are working on government business, but this won't take long. Now please come in back with us."

Agent Cline handed Noparast a business card with the name and number of their superior without comment and followed Stillson and Noparast to an inner office. Both Ryan Quinn and Megan Alvarez were in holding cells nearby, awaiting their lawyer, Ted Lewis, who was trying to find a flight to Pensacola, Florida. If he couldn't find one soon he would drive the 463 miles to the Florida panhandle.

Driving by the police station, Seaman Swartz saw the van he had put the dog in. It was parked next to a blue Navy sedan. The drivers of the van and sedan were nowhere in sight.

"Pull over and let me out," he said to the driver.

The sailor stopped the pickup and said, "Now what are you gonna do?"

"Be right back."

Seaman Swartz had grown up with a golden retriever as his best friend until the dog was hit by a car when Swartz was ten years old. He still carried a picture in his wallet. He looked around and went quickly to the rear of the van. It was a large one-ton cargo van but the rear door was not locked with a padlock. He pulled the hasp open and released the door, which hit him in the face.

Magic sprang out and ran fifty feet before he looked back and saw the dazed sailor getting up. He then ran back and jumped on him, licking his face. The sailor fell back again, but laughed as Magic jumped around happy to be free again.

The driver of the van came out of the police station and saw Magic and Seaman Swartz. "Hey, what are you doing?" he called out.

Swartz grabbed Magic by the ears and said, "Run, my friend. Don't let that man catch you. Now go." He let Magic go, and Magic exploded in a blur of golden fur, disappearing into the night.

CHAPTER 28

I ran fast, but I didn't go very far. Ryan was near. I could feel it. The police station was a nondescript concrete block structure with patrol vehicles parked in the rear. Civilian and Navy policemen came in and out of both the front and the rear doors. There were a few windows along the sides of the building and I saw a human who looked like Babak through one of them. Lights illuminated the front but not the sides of the building. I decided to have a closer look.

Babak, or whoever he was calling himself now, was waving his hands. If I can read body language, and I can, he was trying to sell his version of some lie. I snuck closer and could hear them.

A man dressed in a short-sleeved white shirt with tie was talking on the telephone, his coat was hung over the back of a chair. Babak was talking to the other man.

The man on the telephone put it down and said, "I am sorry to inconvenience you, but my orders are clear. Until we can iron out a few wrinkles, we will have to hold onto the items found in the airplane."

Babak said, "You are going to regret this. I am taking the evidence with me. Now get out of my way."

Babak started for the door, but the man in the short sleeve white shirt put his hand on Babak's shoulder and said, "You may leave, but the things in the van outside are now under my jurisdiction."

I could tell that Babak was about to explode, but he didn't. He said, "How long do you intend to keep my evidence?"

The other man said, "No longer than necessary. I have a call in to your CIA section head at NCS. It seems that we may have to wait until tomorrow morning to get this cleared up. In the meantime, I am also notifying the DARPA, the Defense Advanced Research Program Agency, that their stolen property is here."

Babak seemed to change tactics. He acted like everything was fine and said, "I am sorry about all of this. Perhaps it is best if you, as you say, 'sort out a few wrinkles.' I need to find the driver of the van and tell him he will not be needed until, shall we say nine o'clock?"

The agent with the short sleeve shirt said, "Hopefully, but it depends on how quickly your section head replies. If you need to change clothes, the chief at the front desk can make arrangements."

Babak looked down at the leg I had peed on and said, "I could use a shower and clean clothes."

Babak was up to no good, of course, he was always up to no good, but I could almost hear his devious mind working out a new angle. He walked out of the room and then came back in. He said, "I need to make a few telephone calls. Could I use one of the offices? It's classified."

One agent said, "There's a secure line to this room. Do you want to have it encrypted?"

"No, just some privacy."

"We'll step out for awhile. The phone's on the desk."

Both men left and Babak quickly dialed a number without looking at a directory. I guess he has a good memory or only phones a few people. When someone answered, he started talking in Farsi, which I understand. I should, it was my first language.

I would not try to tell you the complete conversation, because they always spend a lot of time asking about each other's family and being polite. Once they were through that, Babak said there was going to be a delay. He then hung up the telephone and quickly dialed another number. This time he greeted someone in Chinese, using the mandarin dialect. He then switched to English. I think his Chinese may be poor, mine is. He told whomever he was talking to that there had been an unfortunate delay, but he hoped to have the product soon. He talked some more about holding the transportation in Mexico. After he hung up, he walked out of the office, and I ran around to the front and hid behind a hedge. In a few minutes, he came out with the two men from the room. They walked to the van and looked inside.

They opened the rear door and one man said, "We can't lock the dog in so we will put him in a cell until morning when the animal control people open."

After a few seconds he looked at Babak and said, "Where's the dog?"

Babak looked into the van and then around outside. For a moment I thought he might see me under the hedge. I wanted to see the expression on Babak's face, but I would have to move out of my hiding place. I did hear Babak say, "He didn't get out by himself."

One of the men put a padlock on the rear door of the van, and Babak got into the blue sedan and left.

I was very thankful that I wasn't inside the van, locked up. Speaking of locked up, I wondered what happened to Ryan and Megan. Maybe they were locked up somewhere.

***

Ted Lewis arrived at the Pensacola Regional Airport in a private jet. He was tired and red eyed. The telephone call from Megan had reached him at 1:30 in the morning. He had been in bed for twenty minutes and his mouth still tasted like the scotch he had shared with his girlfriend. One of his wealthy clients owned a Bombardier Learjet 45 and told him to ask if he ever needed it, and at 2 in the morning Ted called him and asked.

It took a few hours to get hold of a pilot, and it was almost 6 a.m. before the sleek jet left New Smyrna Beach and headed for Pensacola, Florida. It landed at 7:10 that morning and by 8, Ted Lewis was escorted into the holding cell of Megan Alvarez.

The policeman left them alone and Megan flew into Ted's arms and hugged him.

"Ted, I have never been so happy to see you." She wiped away a tear and stepped back.

He said, "Even the time I gave you a raise?"

She nodded and sat on the cot. She motioned for him to sit next to her and said, "Even then. Now can I go?"

"No formal complaints have been filed against you. I talked to one of the NCIS agents, Ed Stillson. He is checking. But we should be able to get you released soon."

"And Ryan?"

Ted shook his head and said, "Doesn't look good. Even if the feds don't charge him with air piracy, or kidnapping a federal officer, he left Florida without the court's permission."

"He captured a killer, the man stealing those suits and things. And he is being held?"

"I have some phone calls to make, but I expect the court will order a sheriff to pick him up here and take him back to jail."

Megan sighed and looked at Ted. "Do your best." She reached over, took his hand in hers, and said, "How can I thank you enough?"

Ted stood and knocked on the cell door. He smiled at Megan and said, "Try showing up at the office on time."

As the policeman opened the cell, she said to Ted, "I'm always on time. You just come in early."

Ted Lewis then went to Ryan Quinn's cell. Ryan was lying on the cot and rose when Ted came to the cell door. Once inside the two shook hands and Ryan said, "So what's the verdict?"

For a second Ted misunderstood and said, "There has been no verdict... I mean I don't know what the court is going to do about your little escapade, and I am not sure if the federal government is going to bring charges against you. It will look better if I can take you back and you turn yourself in, but I don't know if I can pull that off. I've never worked around the military or other federal types. This CIA agent, the one who says you kidnapped him, pulls a lot of weight. We'll have to see how this washes."

Ryan sat on the cot and said, "And while the wheels of justice turn, Babak will fly away with those exoskeletons and power packs."

"Maybe, but I got the feeling that those NCIS guys don't like him. Maybe they can derail his caboose."

"Hope so. Have you seen Megan?"

"Yes. Chances are she can leave with me, but I'm not certain. I haven't talked to this person you call Babak. He calls himself Noparast. That's where I'm going now. So don't go away."

Ryan gave him a weak smile and said, "Wouldn't think of it. By the way. Would you check on Magic? He ran off but they were going to look for him."

"You brought Magic along on this?"

"Good thing I did. He saved me from being shot by Preston Winn."

Ted Lewis had too much information to digest. He simply knocked for the policeman and said, "I'll check."

He stopped to talk to the NCIS agent once again, and then asked where he could find Mr. Noparast. He was told that the Navy driver took him to the Comfort Inn, which is close to the air station. Ted asked directions to the Comfort Inn and decided to take a room there to freshen up and to use it as a base of operations until he was able to get Megan released. He would also try to find the CIA agent, the man Ryan and Megan said was a killer and talk to him. He wanted to meet him soon and get back to Megan and Ryan.

Outside, he walked to the rental car and saw a large golden retriever sitting next to the driver's side door. The dog barked once and ran up to Ted.

"Is that you, Magic?" Ted asked and examined Magic's collar. Magic licked his hand.

"I guess you're not lost anymore."

Ted started to go back into the police station and tell Ryan he had found Magic, but hesitated. The NCIS agent told him that Mr. Noparast said the dog was dangerous, and that he wanted Magic destroyed. Ted petted Magic's head and got a few more gratuitous licks. He thought about Magic for a few more seconds and then opened the door of the rental car and said, "Get in, boy. Let's take a ride."

Magic bounced up into the car and Ted said, "Move over, unless you'd like to drive?"

Magic looked back at Ted, cocked his head to one side, but then moved to the passenger seat.

As Ted got in, a flight of six blue Boeing F/A 18 Hornet jets streaked overhead. He looked out and saw the famous Navy Blue Angels flying by in perfect formation. Magic was trying to see them from the passenger's side.

***

I was sure happy to see Ryan's friend, Mr. Ted Lewis. Ryan thought a lot of him and so did Megan. I don't know enough about law to know if he was a good lawyer, but I suspected he was a good human. He drove to a nice hotel called the Comfort Inn; however, he made me stay in the car. He rolled the windows down a bit to let air in, but I worried. I had seen what happens when stupid humans left their children and dogs in closed cars. I didn't even want to think of it. Florida gets hot, and the inside of a car can be an oven. Baked golden retriever is not a dish that will catch on, I hope.

Mr. Lewis came out in a few minutes and got back in the car. He then drove to another hotel a few miles away. Apparently, the Comfort Inn was full. The second hotel was not as nice, but he checked in quickly, drove around the building, and parked again. He looked around like he was a teenager sneaking a smoke, reached over, and grabbed my collar.

He led me out of the car and said, "Magic, don't bark."

As he led me to the side door, I heard him mumble, "I hope I don't regret this."

"I had never been in a hotel, or in this case, an inn. It was comfortable and looked clean. The room had two beds. I guessed mistakenly that one was for me and I hopped up on it and checked out the soft pillows. Mr. Lewis didn't yell but his voice told me he didn't appreciate my jubilation about being in my first hotel. I got down and hid under the bed, a little embarrassed. They don't have signs about dog protocol, you know. Mr. Lewis went back out to the car and came back in a few minutes. He had a suitcase with him that must have been in the trunk of the car. He hung up his clothes and used the telephone. I couldn't hear both ends of the conversation, but he was talking to, of all people, our nemesis, Babak, except he called him Mr. Noparast. Apparently, they planned to meet here shortly, because Mr. Lewis gave Babak our room number. I began to wonder if Ryan's friend was working for the dark side. Maybe he worked with Babak? I dismissed that thought. Was I getting paranoid? A paranoid golden retriever is not a dog you want to be around. Of course, maybe I wasn't paranoid and they were all after me? I told myself to snap out of it and smacked my snout with my paw a bit too hard. It made my eyes water.

Mr. Lewis proceeded to take a shower. I have seen lots of military men and a few women without their clothes on. I've seen Ryan hundreds of times, but I had never seen any human with so few muscles on their frame. His arms were thin and his legs even thinner, but he had a little pot belly. He didn't look that way with clothes on.

Ted Lewis paraded around the room naked, completely oblivious to my scrutiny, and I began to feel like a voyeur. The television was on, so I watched the weather channel. The hurricane was headed into south Texas as a category two storm. Once I heard the shower running, I looked into Mr. Lewis's suitcase. I wasn't being nosey, I wanted to see if there was anything there I might use in my fight for Ryan's freedom. Besides underwear and socks, he had a thin laptop computer and a pistol. The pistol looked smaller than Ryan's and maybe the same make, a Glock. It looked like a semi automatic and was in a black holster. I wanted to use the computer, but I would not be able to close it soon enough if he came out of the bathroom. Or would I? I thought about it for a few seconds and made my mind up when I heard Mr. Lewis singing. He wasn't bad for a skinny guy. Of course, Frank Sinatra was skinny, and I love to hear Ryan's old recordings of him.

The laptop was easy enough to use. I pulled the top up with my paw and it sprang to life, as if it had been sleeping. It must have had Wi-Fi, because I was able to get online quickly. I guess the hotel had the internet connection and wireless router, or I was riding on someone else's connection, but I didn't stop to worry. I typed in the location of my e-mail and entered my password. I addressed it to the FBI in Daytona Beach; fortunately, I remembered their e-mail address.

I wanted them to know what happened to Ryan. I had sent one to them before I left to find Ryan at the golf course. Now maybe they would believe. I told them where I buried the power pack near the runway, and was wondering if I needed to add more when my nose told me someone was behind me, and I knew who it was. I smashed down the send key and lunged for Babak, who stood in the doorway watching me. He pulled the door shut before I could reach him, and I hit it with a bang. I didn't realize I was barking, but Mr. Lewis came out of the shower dripping wet and yelled, "Magic, stop. What's wrong?"

What was wrong? He had to be kidding. The only human outside of the lab people in Iran who knew I had unusual mental powers, and who was also my worst enemy, and had just seen me writing an e-mail letter. I was devastated. Absolutely whacked. I ran in circles until Mr. Lewis grabbed my collar, which was also about the time hotel security knocked on the door and we got evicted.

CHAPTER 29

Special Agent Howard Lowell looked at his e-mail and printed a copy. Whoever had been sending him information about Preston Winn and Susan Humphrey had been very helpful. He now had a good idea about what had transpired based on Susan Humphrey's statement and the anonymous e-mail. While her statement, made while under the influence of the anesthesia, might not stand up in a court of law, it did satisfy his own feelings about Ryan Quinn. Now he had the break he was hoping for. The missing exoskeleton suits and power packs were on the Naval Air Station at Pensacola, Florida, along with Ryan Quinn, and Megan Alvarez, who had been reported missing by her father.

He took the e-mail with him and knocked on Assistant Special Agent in-Charge Brenda Louis's door. Her attitude about the Ryan Quinn case had changed dramatically after Lowell found Susan Humphrey in Vero Beach. Preston Winn's body was in a morgue, and a partially disassembled exoskeleton was found to be part of a military contract with a California company. It was turning out to be an interesting case, one that would make the national news soon. She had already talked extensively with her regional division head in Jacksonville, Florida.

Special Agent Howard Lowell came out of her office after ten minutes with what he wanted. He would fly to Pensacola after he confirmed that Ryan Quinn and Megan Alvarez were there in the custody of the air station police.

***

Ted Lewis placed his hurriedly packed suitcase in the trunk of his rented car and looked at Magic, who sat next to the door with his head down, looking forlorn. Now Ted would have to find a place for Ryan's dog to stay before he could meet with the CIA agent. He telephoned him again but it went to his voicemail. Ted left a message telling him he would drive to the Comfort Inn once he found a place for his client's dog. The hotel manager was still upset with Ted Lewis, but did give him the telephone number of an animal friendly motel. Ted opened the car door and told Magic to get in, which he did with some reluctance. Ted then called and made a reservation. He drove out of the parking lot but didn't notice a blue navy sedan following at a discreet distance Ten minutes later he parked at the Rest Stop Motel. He went in and came out with the key to his room and a lock for a small kennel, which sat next to the one story motel building.

The Rest Stop Motel was not one that Ted Lewis would usually pick, but it was close to the base and not far from the Comfort Inn where he hoped to meet the evil Mr. Noparast, aka Babak something or other. He took Magic to the small kennel and locked him in. It looked clean and there was room for Magic to run back and forth or to sleep out of the sun in a small covered enclosure. There was water for him, and Ted intended to shop for dog food later that day.

His cell telephone buzzed, and he looked at the caller's number.

"Yes?"

"Mr. Lewis, I am returning your call?"

Ted recognized Noparast's voice and said, "Thank you. Unfortunately, I had to make other lodging arrangements. I hope it hasn't caused you any inconvenience."

Noparast answered, "None at all. I think meeting at my hotel is an excellent idea. Why don't you come over in, let us say, thirty minutes. I'll meet you in the lobby."

Ted agreed. He knew how to get there. It was the hotel that was full when he first tried to check in.

He went to his room and opened his suitcase, took out his 9 millimeter Glock, and checked the magazine. He had a permit to carry a concealed weapon, but not on a federal reservation. Based on Megan and Ryan's comments, he did not trust the so-called CIA agent Allen Noparast. Ted slipped the pistol behind his belt in the back, and let his shirt fall over it. He had quickly dressed in sports clothes after the last hotel had asked him to leave and, "Take your dog with you." He sat on the bed and wondered where this would take him. His objective was clear; get Megan and Ryan released, but the alleged stolen military equipment, skyjacking, and kidnapping charges were beyond his expertise. A retired federal judge who lived in New Smyrna Beach came to mind. Ted knew him well. He didn't have his telephone number but would look it up later. He telephoned the NCIS Agent Stillson and asked if there were any charges yet, and if he would release Megan Alvarez into his custody. Agent Stillson asked him to come to their main office and gave him the address and directions. Ted wrote the address down and left his hotel room. He walked around the building and found Magic with his nose at the gate of his kennel. He looked at Ted with big sad eyes that said, "Take me with you," but Ted didn't unlock the gate. He reached in and patted Magic's head and said, "Sorry, boy. Maybe we can take you and Megan home later. Be a good boy and don't bark."

Magic waited quietly until Ted was out of sight, but a few minutes later he began barking. He didn't bark out of spite, he barked because a blue Navy sedan pulled up and Babak got out. He walked up to the kennel gate and looked in at Magic, who snarled and bared his teeth.

Babak also showed his teeth, but with a sinister smile and said, "I have read about a dog like you in Iran. It was a classified document. Could it be you are the missing experiment from our Ministry of Health? If you are, you may understand my words and you will suffer greatly for desecrating my trousers."

He examined the lock, went back to the Navy sedan, and spoke to the driver. He got in and the sedan left to take him to a car rental agency with a short stop at a hardware store, where he bought a large lock cutter. He told the Navy sedan driver he was no longer needed and signed for the big Lincoln he rented. He would certainly be late for his appointment with Ted Lewis, but now he didn't care. This magical dog was probably worth more to Iran than the exoskeletons or power pack. His best course of action was to grab the valuable dog and leave before his house of cards collapsed on him. Mr. Noparast was a survivor, but he was also greedy.

Perhaps he could have both the dog and the military version of the exoskeletons and power pack, which he would sell to China. His chief at the CIA would verify that he was an agent and not mention the National Covert Service, but what troubled Noparast was the possibility that his CIA chief might not demand that the exoskeleton and power pack be returned to him. He decided that for now, he would grab the dog and then try to convince the NCIS to release the suits and power pack. Ryan's lawyer would have to wait. He had only agreed to meet him to play the part of the victim and see what the lawyer had up his sleeve. Seeing the dog typing on a laptop computer was providential.

Mr. Noparast stopped to buy a large dog carrier before he drove back to the Rest Stop Motel. On the way he bought a canister of pepper spray and a roll of adhesive medical tape. If the dog gave him any trouble the spray would take the fight out of him, and the tape around his snout would keep those sharp teeth where they belonged.

He backed the rented Lincoln up to the kennel and left the engine running. It had a huge trunk and the dog carrier fit in it nicely. The dog was already watching him as he approached the gate to his kennel. Noparast looked around quickly before he brought the lock cutters up and snipped though the lock. It hung loose and he stepped back as the dog lunged against the gate, shaking it. He waited until the dog tried to push through the gate before spraying him in the eyes with the pepper spray. The dog jumped back and pawed at his eyes and nose. Temporally blinded and unable to smell, Noparast had no trouble grabbing him and wrapping tape around his snout. The dog lunged and tried to break loose, but blind and without its sharp teeth, Noparast was able to pull him to the car and shove him into the dog carrier. The dog; however, was able to use his nails to dig painful groves in Noparast's forearm, which began to bleed.

Noparast slammed the trunk on the Lincoln Town Car and grabbed his bleeding forearm. He could not leave the dog in the trunk for long. He was much too valuable, but he was tempted to let it die there. Greed overcame revenge and he used the medical tape to stop the flow of blood before driving back to the Comfort Inn.

Noparast parked the Lincoln and glanced at his wristwatch. The hotel was animal friendly, but his room on the second floor was not one reserved for pet owners. He opened the trunk and lifted the heavy dog carrier out. Noparast was strong and had trained in Iran as a teenage weight lifter, but the carrier was heavy. He looked in at the red-eyed dog and said, "You need to be put on a diet," and smirked. It might be awhile before the dog had another meal.

He carried the dog carrier to the elevator and received a few odd looks, but no one said a thing as he got on. By the time he reached his room, he was breathing hard and perspiring. He opened the door, took the carrier in and sat it on the floor by the window. The dog was watching him but didn't move. Noparast used the bathroom and left, stopping only to put a do-not-disturb sign over the doorknob. He had arrangements to make.

***

Getting kicked out of a crummy hotel, even if it was the first one I had ever been in, was embarrassing. I know Mr. Lewis was upset with me, but I had just seen my worst nightmare and knew he was out there. I had this feeling of impending doom, and as usual, I was right.

Mr. Lewis locked me in a dog kennel that was connected to the motel, which wasn't too bad, but then Babak came along, as I knew he would. Do not think pepper spray is like smelling a little pepper on your hamburger. It is not. It burns and stings and you can't breathe and you can't see because your eyes are on fire and... well, I could go on and on. To make matters worse, while I was trying to breathe, that bum snuck up on me and wrapped tape around my snout. I had to breathe through my nose, which was also on fire. He then hauled me off in a little cage. After a short ride, he took me to another hotel. I felt like a seasoned traveler, except they won't be doing a commercial where I say, "I slept in a Holiday Inn last night."

I had been trying to pull the tape off my snout for an hour. I was able to move it a few centimeters but it also pulled the hair off with each tug of my nails. I didn't give up, but I feared that Babak would come back before I could free myself.

***

Ted Lewis waited in the Comfort Inn lobby for forty-five minutes before he went to the desk and asked the clerk to call Mr. Noparast's room. The phone rang but Mr. Noparast didn't answer. Ted waited another fifteen minutes and then left.

He started to drive to the naval air station but remembered the gun in his waistband. He couldn't take it on government reservation. He drove back to the Rest Stop Motel and took the weapon to his room, and then went to see Magic.

Ted examined the cut lock and looked inside the enclosure for Magic. He stood there for a minute before going to the motel office, where he told the manager about the cut lock and missing dog. The manager, a short overweight man in his early fifties, acted as if he didn't believe Ted and went to see for himself. This had never happened before, but he said, "We've got a surveillance camera. You want me to call the cops and see if they can find who stole your dog? Is he a show dog or something? Maybe some kids did this just for fun."

"Good idea," Ted said, "He's not a show dog. He's a big golden retriever. I think he's about a year and a half old. I'll be back as soon as possible." Ted left the office but came back a minute later and handed the manager his card. "Call my cell phone if you hear anything."

Ted went back to the NAS Pensacola police station and asked if he could talk to his clients, Ryan Quinn and Megan Alvarez. The chief master at arms at the desk asked for identification and then said, "Sir, I've been told Miss Alvarez can be released to you. Here's a form you need to fill out."

Ted asked, "How about Ryan Quinn?"

The chief looked at a listing and said, "Nope. But there is a note. You need to talk to Mr. Stillson. Here's his number."

"Chief, do you know why my client, Mr. Quinn, is still being held?"

The chief said, "I guess because he skyjacked an airplane, kidnapped a federal officer, stole government property, landed illegally on a military installation, but other than that I can't see why he can't be released."

The chief kept a straight face and Ted didn't know if he was being facetious or not, decided he was but let it go. No use knocking heads with the law.

Ted said, "Has he actually been charged with those crimes. Brought before a federal judge?"

The chief said, "Look, why don't you check with Mr. Stillson, but you can see them if you like." He pressed a buzzer, which opened a door to the inner offices and holding cells. A policeman came out and escorted Ted Lewis back to Megan's cell.

She looked better than the last time he saw her and apparently had been given breakfast. "Ted," she said as he appeared at the door of her cell. He walked in and she hugged him.

Ted said, "A little paperwork and you're free to go with me." He got another hug before he said, "I don't know what is going on with Ryan. Once we get you out of here, I have to see some Navy investigator."

Megan asked a few questions about Ryan, which Ted was unable to answer. He told Megan to relax, and then Ted went to visit Ryan. Once he was in Ryan's cell he said, "I've got some good news and some bad news."

Ryan, who sat on his cot looked up at Ted and said, "I am not in the mood for silly ass games."

"Okay. I found Magic."

"You did?" Ryan said and his face brightened.

"Well, he actually found me in the parking lot, right here at the police station. But then someone cut the lock on his kennel gate. He's gone again."

Ryan shook his head and said into his hands, "Am I having a nightmare while I'm awake? What the hell is going to happen next? What crime am I being charged with?"

Ted didn't want to repeat the chief's remarks so he said, "Megan is being released into my custody."

Ryan brought his hand down from his face and said, "Good, she didn't have anything to do with this. Can she go home now?"

"I don't know the conditions. I think they will simply want her back to testify if they charge you. I can take her home in the jet."

"Jet?"

"Yeah. It helps to have rich clients. He lent me the jet. I have to pay for fuel and the pilot, which reminds me. I need to phone him."

Ryan said, "How the hell am I ever going to pay you?"

Ted smiled and said, "I'll think of something."

Ryan looked at his old friend. Something in his eyes caused Ted to say, "What?"

Ryan looked away and said, "'Nothing, let it pass. I'm getting paranoid."

Ted left and filled out the release form, which Megan also signed. Megan wanted to see Ryan but the chief said, "No, only his lawyer."

Once outside the station, Ted told Megan about Magic. She immediately said, "It was that Babak guy. I know it was."

Ted didn't comment. He drove to the NCIS central field office at 341 Saufley Street. Megan followed him in, and soon they were seated in a small conference room with Agent Stillson.

It took a few minutes before Ted stopped talking and demanding, in his quiet southern way, that Ryan Quinn be released because there was no evidence that he—

Agent Stillson waited patiently before he finally interrupted and said, "Your client is not being charged."

All Ted could think to say was, "Come again?"

"The pilot has regained consciousness and made a statement. Looks like your boy was telling the truth and Jamaican Tours is sending a flight crew to take their airplane back."

Megan said, "Of course he was telling the truth."

"Miss Alvarez, you must admit that under the circumstances —"

Megan cut him off with, "I understand, but it still makes me mad."

Ted said, "Then I can take him home?"

"No, not yet. The FBI is interested in talking to him, and there is the matter of him leaving the state, but that doesn't fall under our jurisdiction."

Megan asked, "Are you going to arrest Babak or whatever he's calling himself?"

Agent Stillson cringed but said, "That has to be handled by other people, not the Navy."

Megan said, "He kidnapped Magic."

"I don't think I follow?"

Ted said, "Megan thinks Mr. Noparast stole Ryan Quinn's dog, Magic."

Agent Stillson smiled before he said, "Excuse my candor, but this is the nuttiest case I have ever been on or heard of. You're saying that the CIA agent not only stole the airplane, kidnapped Mr. Quinn and Miss Alvarez, shot the pilot, injured the copilot, but then came back and stole Mr. Quinn's dog?"

Megan chimed in and said, "He also killed that man in Vero Beach."

Ted's cell phone rang. He looked at it and said, "Sorry, but I should take this."

Ted listened and said, "I'll be right here. Ask them not to leave."

Ted stood and said, "The motel manager has a surveillance tape of the person who stole Magic. He showed it to the police. I think we should look at it. Megan can identify this Mr. Noparast if it is him."

Agent Stillson said, "Let me know how that turns out."

Ted said, "You want to come with us?"

Agent Stillson shook his head and said, "No. Dog-napping in the city is not part of our mission, but I am interested to know if Mr. Noparast is on the tape."

***

Noparast left the NAS Pensacola police station more frustrated than ever. Nobody seemed to know who had the authority to release the exoskeletons and power pack to him. His telephone call and message to Agent Stillson went unanswered and time was Noparast's enemy. Earlier he had purchased a small .32 caliber semi automatic pistol, which he carried in a quick release holster under his loose fitting sports shirt. Both trousers and shirt were new. His old ones went into the trash. He still held the keys to the rental van that was parked in the police station parking lot, although the rear door was padlocked, and he didn't have the key to the padlock.

Noparast used a new cell telephone to call and confirm the cargo plane that would fly him and his cargo to Vera Cruz, Mexico, where he would meet with the Chinese. He had two hours. Not much time, but too long to wait around. A message left at his hotel from the FBI made him nervous. They wanted to talk to him. He weighed his options. If he tried to take the van and was stopped, he would have no way to get away without killing whoever stopped him. If he took it too soon, there would be time for the navy or FBI to find him before his flight. If he simply left the suits and power pack and took the dog back to Iran, he would be a hero, but not filthy rich.

Noparast decided to wait, kill time, and then move at the last minute. It would cut down on his chances of being stopped after he took the van and collected the dog.

CHAPTER 30

"That's him," Megan said as they watched the somewhat grainy surveillance tape. "I would know him anywhere."

The Pensacola policewoman asked, "And you know his name?"

"Yes. He use to call himself Babak. I don't recall his last name. Now he calls himself Noparast. Allen Noparast. He's says he's a CIA agent and has identification to prove it, but they must be fakes. He killed a man in Vero Beach and stole an airplane, which my fiancé took over and flew here from Mexico."

The policewoman, who had been looking bored while she wrote a report, said, "You say he is a CIA agent? He killed a man and then stole an airplane and your boyfriend—"

"Fiancé."

"Your fiancé took the airplane away from him?" She stopped and put her pen back into the device that held her report papers and said, "Is this some kind of sick joke? If so, I—"

Ted intervened and said, "I'm Ted Lewis, an attorney from New Smyrna Beach. I flew up here to represent Miss Alvarez and Ryan Quinn. Strange as it sounds, Megan is telling you the truth."

The policewoman looked back at Megan, who was nodding her head, and then to Ted Lewis, who held out his card. She took Ted's card and said, "I've got to call my sergeant. Don't leave. I'll be right back."

***

I was able to get that tape off my snout, finally. Wow, that took forever and really hurt. If I ever got a chance, it was going to be payback time. I was wasting time thinking about things to do to Babak when he came flying in the door. His face was red and he was wet with perspiration, which did not make him smell any better. He started for my dog carrier cage and stopped. He must have noticed the tape had come off.

"I see you have been busy my little friend. Now be a good dog and hold still while I tape your mouth closed. Don't want you barking, do we?"

What a dumb question. Of course, I wanted to bark. Maybe I should have started sooner, but I was so busy plotting revenge, I missed the opportunity. So much for revenge.

I did start barking and loud. I even howled a bit, but then he said, "So you liked the pepper spray?"

That got my attention and it was a little weird. I had only had one human ever talk to me while knowing I understood completely, but that was at the lab in Iran. Babak knew I understood, and I knew he knew. I stopped howling and didn't bark. I was brave but that pepper spray would make me a useless doggy. It was better if I used my mind and not my canine vocal cords.

He said, "That is better. Now I am going to open your cage. Stick your nose out. If you try to bite me, I will use this." He pulled out a small pistol and aimed it right at my face. I didn't want to be shot again, once is enough. He unlatched the cage door and I tentatively stuck my nose out. He wound that darn tape around my snout again right where it was sore and tender. He pulled it tight, but this time I had my wits about me and opened my mouth ever so slightly. After he was satisfied that I could not bark or bite, he closed the cage again and secured the latch.

He went into the bathroom and closed the door. While he was in there, I tried moving my jaws and found I could close them tight and the tape became loose. When he came out, I opened my jaws until the tape stopped my movement. He couldn't see the gap, and I could get a little air into my mouth. That nose breathing was getting old.

The telephone rang and Babak ignored it. He grabbed my cage and lifted it. I heard him grunt and offer an Iranian curse at me. Maybe he forgot I could understand Farsi.

He finally got me down to the first floor and out into the parking lot. He was red faced and perspiring again, but the big car he put me in before was not there. In its place was the small van he had on the naval base. He didn't take me to the rear; he opened the passenger door to the van and lifted me up onto the seat. I was going to ride in style, how nice I thought. What was he up to now? Then I noticed the large tool he had used to cut the lock off on my kennel cage. He was going to cut another lock, but I didn't figure out which lock for awhile. He drove too fast for conditions and traffic, and kept looking in the rear view mirror until we got to the Pensacola Regional Airport. He didn't park in the short-term or long-term parking; he went around to a side entrance and pulled up to a small hanger. He jumped out and actually ran into a hanger. He came out shortly and got back into the van. He drove slowly now, around to the front of the hanger where there was a big airplane. Well it wasn't big like an airliner, but it wasn't small like the single engine Cessna. It was more like the airplane Ryan took away from Babak. It had two engines and a sign painted on it that read, Texas Air Freight.

He backed the van near it and got out with the lock cutter, leaving the door ajar with the engine running. I thought, now is my chance if I didn't want a ride with that maniac back to the lab in Iran. I closed my mouth as tight as I could and used my paws to dig at the tape. The loose tape moved but not as fast as I had hoped. I could hear him back there. He had the lock cutting tool with him and was trying to cut something. The tape popped off and I started working my teeth around the cage's wire mesh door. It was strong but my life was at stake. I pulled so hard I thought my teeth would break off. The wire mesh tore lose at one end, and I pushed my head through the opening and nudged the hasp open. I pulled back and was temporally caught by the wire mesh, but I pulled harder and finally broke loose. I pushed through the cage door, and was almost out of the van door when Babak blocked my way. He seemed startled but reacted quickly. He pulled his pistol and aimed at me. I pushed the drive lever into reverse with my paw and jumped down onto the accelerator peddle.

***

Special Agent Benjamin Whitehurst from the Pensacola FBI resident agency met Special Agent Howard Lowell at the

Pensacola Regional Airport. Ben, as he told Lowell to call him, was nearly as old as Lowell was and had the same KMA attitude but was glad to be doing something interesting. An hour before Lowell's airplane landed, a commuter airplane had burst into flames and the fire trucks had roared to the site of the conflagration. Apparently, a vehicle ran into the airplane and started the fire that destroyed both the vehicle and airplane before the fire could be contained. Ben had been on the way when it happened, and he hurried to the airport when there was speculation that the explosion was caused by terrorists. It appeared that the van driver was at fault, but the site was still too hot to recover any bodies.

Ben led Lowell to the bureau car and drove to the Navy base while Lowell briefed him on the case. Lowell had an arrest warrant for Babak Shirazi in connection with stolen military secret equipment and the murder of Preston Winn. Babak Shirazi was also wanted in connection to the skyjacking of a Jamaican Tour aircraft.

Ben asked, "How'd you get a lead on Babak Shirazi?"

"It's been a case in my too-hard box for awhile, but what broke it open was a civilian in Port Canaveral named Kurns, Frank Kurns. I ran him down after Preston Winn was murdered. I showed him a picture of Susan Humphrey, who according to an anonymous source was involved with Winn. Looked like they were both stealing secret military equipment and selling them to the highest bidder. Kurns told me that he gave a device to this Susan Humphrey of the DHS and was told by her not to tell the FBI. That was bothering him and he opened up and told me enough to put the screws to sweet Susan. I presented the information and she told me where the plans to the secret power pack were located. She also volunteered to turn federal witness, you get my meaning, and identify Babak Shirazi, and put the blame on Preston Winn. According to her, she was just following orders from her boss."

"Sounds familiar."

"We have enough to put it to her, but life will be much simpler if we grab Babak and return the secret equipment. DHS will have egg on its face, so I don't know what Justice will do with this. The Army is not happy about this stuff getting out and I don't blame them. If my tip is right, I know where the power pack is buried."

"Buried?"

"I can't go into that confidential source."

Lowell told Ben as much as he could about the exoskeleton and power pack, but even Lowell did not know the full potential of the power pack or its design.

Special Agent Benjamin Whitehurst drove Special Agent Lowell to the Naval Air Station police station and parked in front. A key player in the case was Ryan Quinn, who according to the Navy Criminal Investigative Service, was being held pending formal charges. Lowell wanted to talk to him. They went inside and found there was a crowd. A policewoman from the city of Pensacola was talking to a naval station policeman and to a Navy chief master-at-arms. An Army intelligence agent was talking to two NCIS agents and a woman and another civilian were trying to talk to anyone who would listen. Lowell recognized Megan Alvarez and approached her.

"Miss Alvarez?"

She turned, and for a moment didn't look like she recognized him. Then her face changed and she smiled. He had visited her in the hospital and came by her house while she was recuperating. She said, "Yes, you are the FBI man from Daytona Beach. Are you here because of Ryan and to arrest Babak?"

He smiled and said, "Something like that. This is Special Agent Whitehurst."

Ted Lewis heard their conversation and introduced himself. They began discussing the events that started in Vero Beach, Florida and terminated at the Naval Air Station Pensacola, Florida. The NCIS men and the local policewoman also heard the conversation, introduced themselves, and joined in. Finally, when the noise grew too loud, the chief master-at-arms at the front desk yelled, "Keep it down in here!"

It took some time to get to Ryan Quinn, but both FBI agents spoke to him. Unfortunately, while they believed his story as he retold it, they could not release him because he was awaiting trial in Volusia County on drug related charges, and a Volusia County sheriff was coming to take him back to jail. The Navy was in the process of turning him over to the local Escambia County sheriff.

The hunt for Babak Shirazi or Allen Noparast began in earnest by the FBI and local law enforcement offices, including the Army Criminal Investigative Service. Unbeknown to those agencies, the Department of Homeland Security and the Central Intelligence Agency were conducting their own search. Roads leaving Pensacola and all airports were being watched.

The search went on. They traced Babak to the Comfort Inn, and then to the Rest Stop Motel. He had made many purchases: an animal carrier, a gun, clothes, and a lock cutter. His rental of a Ford van finally took them to the airport and the remains of a burned out van. Inside the rear cargo area, the FBI agents found what they believed to be exoskeletons and a power pack. The army confirmed their find. No bodies were found in the burned van or airplane, and they believed he had escaped. They also thought he might be badly burned, and set out to check local hospitals and emergency clinics.

Ryan Quinn was taken to the Escambia County jail, where Megan and Ted Lewis visited him. The next day, a Volusia County sheriff arrived and took Ryan away. Megan would return to New Smyrna Beach, Florida with Ted Lewis.

Megan was upset and tried hard not to cry when she learned that there had been the melted remains of an animal carrier in the burned out van, although no bones were found. Ryan had repeatedly asked anyone who would listen, to search for Magic. The FBI agents said they would pass the word and watch for his dog. Megan contacted the local Humane Society, but no new golden retrievers had been found.

Ted assured him that it was only a matter of time before Ryan would be cleared of all charges and that Magic would turn up.

As they left the terminal and walked out to the private jet, Ted said, "I talked to the FBI agent. He said he would pursue finding out if there was a connection between Ryan's drug arrest and the theft of Army property."

"Isn't it obvious?" Megan asked, but before Ted answered, something caught her eye. A blur of golden fur came from behind a nearby hanger and ran toward her at an amazing speed.

"Magic!" she shouted a second before he slowed slightly and then his front paws were on her shoulders. He kissed her as she hugged him, and she began to sob. Ted thought the big dog was crying too.

CHAPTER 31

It has been four months since I was almost a crispy critter in the Pensacola Regional Airport. I would like to tell you that everything turned out well, the bad guys went to jail and justice prevailed. It didn't happen exactly that way.

When I dove down and hit the accelerator pedal on the van, it took off backwards and Babak was thrown out, but I was still in it when it hit the airplane. For a moment, I didn't know what happened. I was stunned, but very soon I heard this big whoosh and flames were everywhere. The open door was crushed up against the burning airplane and I couldn't get out. I fought to get the passenger door open but it was jammed. Then someone yanked it open from outside. I was ready to thank whoever it was with one exception, and wouldn't you know it, it was that one exception, Babak. His arm must have been injured when the van jumped backwards, because it hung at his side. He reached for me with his good hand, which was a big tactical error on his part. I sunk my teeth into his hand, and when he pulled it back, I hung on. Once I was out of the van, I let go and dropped to the pavement. About that time, the jet fuel must have reached its flash point. The explosion blew me away from the van and airplane. By the time I regained my feet, Babak was gone. The thick smoke and flames made following his scent beyond my capabilities, at least at that point. I ran away from the heat, which was already singeing my fur. I hid at the airport, knowing that eventually Ryan would come through there to go home. Again, I was mistaken, but it worked out okay.

I never saw Babak again. Maybe he gave up his evil ways and became a missionary; on the other hand, if I were a betting dog, I would put my money on him sneaking through the roadblocks and police nets that I heard about on the airplane ride back to New Smyrna Beach. He was not only evil and greedy, but also smart.

Not at my level, but smart. He probably had a backup plan and connections with terrorist cells. But that is speculation.

I enjoyed the ride in the comfortable private jet. Megan treated me like royalty, and I had a great in-flight meal, but I missed Ryan. Mr. Lewis told Megan that Ryan would soon be free, but it took almost a month. He was released on bond again after his father took out a second mortgage on his house in Tampa Bay, but it turned out well. The charges were finally dropped, and then it took another month to get his record cleaned. Now Ryan is waiting to be accepted to the FBI academy. I would think he would be sick of the law by now, but Ryan does not discourage easily. I heard him tell his father he has new insight in how complex the law can be. His mother wants Ryan to be a lawyer.

During my wait for Ryan to be released from jail, I stayed with the Alvarez family. The puppy was growing fast but they still called her puppy. The cat grudgingly accepted me, but never wanted to play with me. She did play with the puppy.

By the time I got back to Ryan's home and his computer, I had a ton of unanswered e-mails. Zeus had all but given up on me, and my blog was too dated. I had missed so much school that I received an incomplete on two classes. So much for my grade point average.

Ryan and Megan have been talking a lot about their future. They plan to marry after Ryan graduates and get his first assignment, wherever that may be. Me, I live from day to day. Out there somewhere is a man who knows my secret. I keep alert.

The other day after visiting the puppy and Megan, while Ryan flew up to Quantico for some type of an interview, I decided on a name for puppy.

On Ryan's computer, I typed an e-mail to Megan that read:
Dear Miss Alvarez:

You don't know me, but I have your best interest at heart as well as your wonderful family and charming puppy.

I am a close friend of both Ryan Quinn, a wonderful human, and his magical dog. It seems only proper, considering your plans for matrimony, that your puppy should be given a suitable name; consequently, I believe you should name her *Charm*.

Yours truly,
Mr. Kunastros

END

If you would like your pet's picture shown next to Magic, please send one to me at Publishyour@aim.com, or go to my web site at: http://www.magicadventurenovels.com/

If you enjoyed *Magic*, please take time to write a review.

The sequel to *Magic* is my new novel, *Charm*, (The search for), which is due to be out shortly. If you enjoyed *Magic*, I think you will find Magic's next adventure equally enjoyable.

My young adult novel *Strange Magic* is not a sequel to *Magic*, but you may like it. It features the same wonderful dog and Ryan, but the protagonist is a teenager named Beth.

This review is from: *Golden Goose* (Paperback)

I read the *Golden Goose* and found it a page-turner that I could not put down; it belongs up there with the best thrillers of the day. It has everything one wants in a thrill-packed, action-packed suspense novel along with mystery and intrigue. It's as good, if not better than, most I've read from the bestseller list. Jean Harris is an amazing character and for Ed Humm to create such a believable character in a gender not his own is another testament to the author's ability along with setting the scene, dialogue that moves, and an amazing, twisting plot. For a first novel debut, this is a winner of the first order.

Robert W. Walker, author of City for Ransom, City of the Absent, and DEAD ON

About the Author

Edmond Humm is a retired Marine Corps officer who has not only studied war but has fought in two wars. The combination of his formal military schools, firsthand combat experience, and a lifetime love of history and creative writing provided both the desire and substance to create a novel based on a true story.

Made in the USA
Lexington, KY
09 December 2012